Between Heaven
and Texas

Between Heaven and Texas

MARIE BOSTWICK

KENSINGTON BOOKS
www.kensingtonbooks.com

KENSINGTON BOOKS are published by

Kensington Publishing Corp.
119 West 40th Street
New York, NY 10018

All Kensington titles, imprints, and distributed lines are available at special quantity discounts for bulk purchases for sales promotion, premiums, fund-raising, and educational or institutional use. Special book excerpts or customized printings can also be created to fit specific needs. For details, write or phone the office of the Kensington Special Sales Manager: Kensington Publishing Corp., 119 West 40th Street, New York, NY 10018. Attn. Special Sales Department. Phone: 1-800-221-2647.

ISBN-13: 978-1-4967-0727-7
ISBN-10: 1-4967-0727-3
First Kensington Trade Edition: May 2013
First Kensington Mass Market Edition: February 2016

eISBN-13: 978-0-7582-9265-0
eISBN-10: 0-7582-9265-1
First Kensington Electronic Printing: May 2013

10 9 8 7 6 5 4 3 2 1

Printed in the United States of America

With Thanks

I've said it before, but it bears repeating: Writing a book is a team sport. This being the case, I extend my sincere and heartfelt thanks to . . .

The Virginia Center for the Creative Arts (www.vcca. com), a very special place that fuels the creative flame of artists in every medium and where a large portion of this book was written.

Joyce Ely and Sarah Ely, of JEllen's House of Fabric in Lyndhurst, Ohio, for inviting me into your lives and helping me to more accurately and meaningfully articulate the experience of people with Down syndrome and their parents. You are heroes to me and so many other people. God bless you both.

My darling and wise big sister, Donna Gomer, as well as Michael Keity, the most interesting farmer I know, for their insight and enlightenment on matters of agriculture and animal husbandry. You were both an enormous help to me.

Another darling and wise big sister, Betty Walsh, who has raised nagging with love to an art form and without whom I'd probably never even have finished writing a letter, let alone eleven books. This is not an exaggeration.

My editor, Audrey LaFehr . . . whatever would have become of me if you hadn't seen something in my work that others had overlooked all those years ago? I don't even want to imagine. Thank you for that and for all the cheerleading, championing, and wise counsel you've offered in the years since. And most especially for your keen insights, which helped make this a book we can both be proud of.

Liza Dawson, a shining beacon in the firmament of literary agents, and, on so many occasions, my north star.

You keep me calm and on course, you push me forward, and guide me home, and always with kindness, humor, integrity, and exactly the right amount of grit. You are the author whisperer, Missus D. You truly are.

And speaking of teams, to the incredible people at Kensington Publishing: Laurie Parkin, Lesleigh Irish-Underwood, Karen Auerbach, Vida Engstrand, Alexandra Nicolajsen, Meryl Earl, Paula Reedy, Kristine Mills-Noble, Martin Biro, and the entire sales division, as well as everyone involved in production, marketing, administration, accounting . . . thank you so much for all you do to help turn an idea and some loose sheets of paper into that most precious of objects, a book.

The writers—Dorothea Benton Frank, Robyn Carr, Kristan Higgins, and Lauren Lipton—for taking time to read the early manuscript and being so generous with your feedback. I took your observations to heart, and it has made all the difference.

And, of course . . .

The readers. In choosing this book, you have honored me with the most finite and valuable asset in your possession: your time. Please know how grateful I am for your ongoing support and encouragement. My very best wishes and humble thanks to each and every one of you.

Marie

Gentle Reader,

Greetings! And welcome to Too Much, Texas, my new favorite spot in the landscape of imagination.

Embarking on a new series of books is something like vacationing in a foreign country. The anticipation of a new adventure is thrilling, but also a little nerve-racking. What if you don't like the people? The food? The tour guide? Maybe you should have gone to the beach instead. After all, you already *know* you like the beach. Can this new journey possibly measure up to those you've taken and enjoyed in the past?

The answer, I have discovered, is yes. Yes, it can.

Some of you have accompanied me on one, or two, or even five trips to the fictional village of New Bern, Connecticut, the setting for my Cobbled Court Quilts novels, and have fallen in love with that town and those characters. Some of you are reading one of my books for the first time. Whichever category you fall into, longtime reader or rookie, I can assure you that a trip to Too Much, Texas, is absolutely worth taking—just as good as the beach, but different.

After writing five well-received Cobbled Court Quilts novels, some might wonder what made me take this sudden detour to Texas (don't worry, Gentle Reader, it *is* a detour. I'm already working on my next Cobbled Court Quilts novel). The answer is easy: Mary Dell made me do it.

From the first moment Mary Dell Templeton—Evelyn Dixon's best friend from her old life in Texas—walked onto the stage of my first Cobbled Court Quilts novel, *A Single Thread* (actually, make that barreled onto the stage: Mary Dell knows how to make an entrance!), I knew I wanted to write more about her. She is my absolutely favorite character—funny, unflappable, optimistic, loyal, industrious, creative, and confident, with a style all her own and a heart as big as all Texas. And if you've ever been to Texas, you know just how big that is!

If you've ever lived in Texas, as I have at various times in my life, you know that list of adjectives could just as easily be applied to the Lone Star State itself. I guess that's what makes Mary Dell so compelling a character: She really is a microcosm of the state that gave her birth. Just as there's no state in the Union quite like Texas, there's no character in my books quite like Mary Dell Templeton.

And when you bring all that personality to the page, then add a supporting cast of characters, cowboys, and quilters—well, all I can tell you is that Mary Dell got herself involved in adventures that surprised even me.

I could tell you more, but I don't want to be a spoiler. Instead, why not kick off your spurs, find a Dr Pepper and a comfy chair, turn the page, and join me and Mary Dell on a journey to Too Much, Texas. You'll be glad you made the trip.

Blessings,

Marie Bostwick

P.S. As has been the case with many of the Cobbled Court Quilts novels, my dear friend and partner in crime and fabric collecting, Deb Tucker, has designed some companion patterns for this book. By the time you are reading this, my *registered* Reading Friends will be able to download one (and possibly two) new, free patterns at www.mariebostwick.com, not to mention the four free patterns from previous books, designed by Deb Tucker and another friend and fabulous quilter, Chris Boersma Smith.

Also, Deb Tucker has designed a simply beautiful version of the Lone Star project that Mary Dell speaks of near the end of the book. (I saw it come together in my quilting studio just last weekend, and it is amazing!) That pattern and several other companion patterns for my books are available on her website, www.studio 180design.net.

P.P.S. I always enjoy connecting with readers, and computers make this easier than ever. You can find me on Facebook and Twitter almost every day of the week (but don't tell my family—I've convinced them that every time I am on the computer, I'm writing. Every single time). You can also write to me via my website, www.mariebostwick.com, or by taking pen in hand and sending a letter to:

Marie Bostwick
P.O. Box 488
Thomaston, CT 06778

CHAPTER 1

Too Much, Texas
1970

Nineteen-year-old Mary Dell Templeton pushed her white lace veil away from her face, knelt down in front of the toilet, and seriously considered vomiting.

She could hear the staccato tapping of her mother's high heels coming down the hallway and reached up to click over the lock only a moment before Taffy tried the knob and then started hammering on the door.

"Mary Dell? Open the door. I will not put up with any of your nonsense today, young lady. Cousin Organza only knows three songs on the piano, and she's played them through four times already. People are starting to notice. Do not embarrass me in front of half the town, young lady!"

Taffy Templeton paused, then rattled the knob again.

"Mary Dell? Do you hear me? You unlock that door and come out here right now!"

Mary Dell closed her eyes and leaned down, resting her forehead on the cool curve of the porcelain seat. "I can't. I feel sick."

Taffy made an exasperated sound. "Well, of course you feel sick. It's your wedding day. What did you expect?"

It was a fair question.

What in the world was she doing, marrying Donny Bebee? When he'd proposed, she'd immediately said yes, relieved that her problems had been so easily solved by uttering that one little word. But what if marrying Donny wasn't the solution it seemed to be? What if she was just exchanging one set of problems for another? She barely knew Donny. Four months ago, she'd never even heard his name.

Another wave of nausea hit her as she realized that even now, she didn't know his middle name. Or if he even had a middle name! How could she possibly promise to love, honor, and cherish until death did them part a man whose middle name was a mystery to her?

Before she'd met Donny, she was unattached and content to remain that way for the foreseeable future. Now she was engaged, nauseous, and crouched in front of the commode in a wedding dress, minutes away from either becoming Mrs. Donald Middle-Name-Unknown Bebee or busting through the bathroom door, knocking down her mother, and making a run for the nearest pickup truck and the Mexican border.

How had she gotten herself into this mess?

CHAPTER 2

As Mary Dell's maternal aunt, Miss Velvet Tudmore, the executive director of the Too Much Historical Society, would tell you, it is impossible to separate the present and future from the history that precedes it. So to understand how Mary Dell Templeton came to lock herself in the bathroom on her wedding day, you have to take a look back through her personal and family history and, more importantly, the history of the town.

Like a lot of towns in that part of the state, there appears to be no geographic or economic reason to explain the existence of Too Much, Texas. Ninety-five miles slightly southeast of Dallas, it simply rises out of the scrubby brown landscape as though someone of great stubbornness, fortitude, or both simply woke up one day and decided to build a town, like Moses striking a rock and summoning forth water in the desert. According to legend and Miss Velvet, that's pretty much how it happened.

In October of 1962, Mary Dell Templeton and her twin sister, Lydia Dale, along with the rest of the fifth graders of Sam Houston Elementary, took a field trip to the historical society to learn about the origins of Too Much. It was an important rite of passage, one that the town's youngest citizens had taken part in for many years.

The day began with a tour of the society's collection of artifacts, housed in the basement of the courthouse, a mishmash of memorabilia that included a rusty hand plow; a menu from the Blue Bonnet Café signed by Bonnie Parker and Clyde Barrow, who stopped in for banana cream pie before robbing the First Reliable Bank; the journal of Justine Tudmore Plank, Too Much's most famous citizen, who wrote a series of children's books in the 1920s; a pine pulpit that emerged unscathed from the flames when the First Baptist Church burned to the ground in 1912; a wheel and axle from a pioneer wagon; and the black leather bag filled with rusty surgical instruments and glass bottles bearing labels for sterile catgut and chloroform that once belonged to the town's first licensed physician.

After the tour, Miss Velvet shepherded the children into the town square, ordering them to form a half circle in front of a bronze statue of a slightly scowling woman dressed in pioneer garb with her arms crossed defiantly over her chest. Then she related the tale of Too Much's founding mother, Flagadine Tudmore, just as she had learned it from her mother, who had heard it from her mother, and so on.

"When Texas was still a republic, George and Flagadine Tudmore and their four children set out from Arkansas to Austin with the intention of claiming the six hundred and forty acres of land that was being offered to new settlers. The journey was hard and long, and George, who never was much of a planner, didn't start off until high summer. By the time the Tudmores reached the Texas border, the temperatures had been above one hundred for twenty-two days running, and the family's water supply was dangerously low.

"On the seventeenth night of August, 1840, George picketed his two tired, lame horses out next to a little patch of scrub near Puny Wallow—"

Without raising his hand, Jack Benny Benton interrupted. "Don't you mean Puny Pond?"

Miss Velvet's flinty features became even sharper as she scowled at the boy. "No. If I'd meant Puny Pond, I'd have said so. Back then it was a wallow, little more than a mud pit with a couple of inches of brown water at the bottom. Flagadine sieved out the mud and boiled it to use for drinking, bathing, and doing laundry.

"When George was hitching up the horses the next morning, Flagadine, whose thinking had been cleared mightily by rehydration and clean undergarments, grabbed the reins of the bay horse and said, 'It's just too much, George. Too much sun. Too much wind. Too much heat. Besides, there's something about this place, don't you agree? But whether you do or you don't, this is as far as I go.'

"And George," the old woman went on with a proud tilt to her chin, "knowing the kind of woman she was—and being the kind of man he was—figured there wasn't any point in fighting her. He unhitched the horses while Flagadine unpacked the wagon. And that, boys and girls, is how Too Much, Texas, got its start: on the conviction of a strong-willed woman and the indolence of a handsome but shiftless man. Which," she concluded with a sorry shake of her head, "pretty well describes the makeup of our population to this day."

Elbowing the boy next to him, Jack Benny Benton,

whose father spent his days sitting on the porch at the Ice House, nursing a bottle of Lone Star and tying knots in a length of rope, asked the plain-featured old lady, "Is that why you never got married, Miss Velvet? Because the men in Too Much are too lazy?"

"Yes," the old spinster said without a trace of irony. "Yes, it is, Jack Benny."

When the children lined up for the walk back to school, Jack Benny Benton jockeyed for a spot behind Mary Dell and Lydia Dale. He was about to give one of Lydia Dale's blond braids a tug when Miss Velvet's voice rang out from behind.

"Lydia Dale! Mary Dell! Come back here for a minute."

The two girls ran up to the old woman. "What is it, Aunt Velvet?"

Miss Velvet crouched down low and whispered urgently, "You steer clear of that Jack Benny Benton."

"Why?" Lydia Dale asked. "He's all right."

"And Momma says the Bentons are richer than Midas," Mary Dell added.

Mary Dell didn't have a clear understanding of who Midas was, but she did understand that the Bentons, the largest and, aside from the Tudmores, oldest family in town, were rich—at least in comparison to everyone else. It wasn't that the Bentons owned everything in Too Much, just everything that was worth owning: the Ice House, which sold more beer and whiskey than ice, the Tidee-Mart, the Texaco station, the Feed and Grain, and pretty nearly every commercial building in downtown Too Much, which gave them influence and garnered them a good income without engaging in much actual work.

It was a strange thing that in a town full of lazy men, it was the laziest line of them all that had accumulated the most wealth, but the key to the Benton fortune lay with the Benton women, who were shrewder and tougher than any of the menfolk, and not just the women who were born Bentons, but even the ones who'd married into the family. Jack Benny's mother, Marlena, born a Pickens, was a case in point. It seemed to be part of their makeup, a trait that ran through their bloodlines. Every family has them. As a student of history, genealogy, and human relations, Velvet knew this for a fact.

Her studies had helped her to identify a Tudmore family trait, actually more of a weakness, that ran all the way back to Flagadine, and it was this: At some point, and sometimes at many points, nearly every woman in the Tudmore lineage, herself a notable exception, allowed lust and biology to trump morality and reason. Miss Velvet had dubbed this weakness the Fatal Flaw.

But at age nine, Mary Dell and Lydia Dale were too young to understand such things, so Miss Velvet just said, "You just stay away from Jack Benny. Stay away from any of the boys from Too Much. You hear me?"

Though impossible to prove scientifically, Miss Velvet's theory of the Tudmore Fatal Flaw cannot be dismissed entirely. But even more than this, it was an unusual codicil in the will of Flagadine Tudmore that most profoundly influenced the history, character, and fortunes of her descendants.

Flagadine Tudmore outlived her husband by three decades. She spent those years raising children and buying more land, eventually accumulating twelve hundred acres. In that part of the country, depending on weather, the ratio of cattle to grazing acres may be eight, ten, even fifteen to one, so the F-Bar-T was not a huge spread by Texas standards. But it was some of the best grazing land in the county and enough to provide a modest but independent living for the Tudmore clan. Figuring her sons could fend for themselves, Flagadine willed the ranch in its entirety to her daughter, Calico, stipulating that Calico should pass it on to her daughter in turn.

And so the tradition began. Each succeeding generation of Tudmore women signed the title of the ranch over to her daughter upon the younger woman's marriage, yielding the house and land to the newlyweds, with the understanding that the older woman's financial needs would be met in her lifetime. It was an unusual arrangement for the times, and if challenged in a court of law, it's doubtful that the wills of the Tudmore women would have been allowed to stand. However, no one ever did challenge those wills, perhaps because they had too much sense to try to separate a Tudmore from her land.

Most of the Tudmore women lived their entire lives within a tight radius of the ranch without a desire to roam farther. It was their Eden, their context, the lens through which they saw the world and themselves. A few did travel across the country and even the world, and enjoyed the scenes, scents, and sights of exotic lands, but in the end, the daughters of Flagadine never found a scene to match the beauty of the sun setting over the small ridge of hills on the western edge of the ranch, or a perfume as intoxicating as the scent that rose from the thirsty soil of the pasture and the leaves of the velvet mesquite trees after a rare hard rain, or a deeper sense of satisfaction than came from being granted temporary stewardship over the land that had nurtured and nourished them and eventually passing it intact to the next generation.

Mary Dell was not born with a complete appreciation of her inheritance or a full understanding of the honor and solemn responsibility that was her birthright, but it would come to her in time. There was no avoiding it. Like the Fatal Flaw, it was all part of being born a Tudmore and female.

Still, Mary Dell was her own brand of Tudmore. For one thing, she was the first of the line who, teetering on the brink of matrimony, actually stopped to ask herself if this was a good idea. There had never been a Tudmore quite like Mary Dell, though it took some time for people, her mother especially, to realize it.

CHAPTER 3

When the twins were born, Taffy intended to carry on with the family custom of naming female children after fabric, in homage to the Tudmore tradition of producing women who were experts with a needle, even though she personally had no talent for sewing. But her husband, Dutch, objected.

"Hell, no!" he exclaimed. "You're not doing it, Taffy. All the good names are gone. Your cousin got the last one—though I'm not crazy about Organza. But it's sure better than Corduroy. Or Hopsack. Or Flannel! That's about all that's left."

"I was thinking of naming them after Momma and Aunt Velvet," Taffy countered.

"Silky and Velvet Templeton?" Dutch spread his boot-shod feet and crossed his arms over his chest, aping the bronze resolve of Flagadine Tudmore. "Do that and these will be the last babies you have a chance of getting off me. I mean it."

Dutch was not a man inclined to making proclamations and even less inclined to follow through with them, but Taffy sensed that he was serious. Only hours before, in the agony of childbirth, she had sworn never to allow Dutch to touch her again. But now, as her eyes traveled from his handsome head, his sandy hair streaked with sunlight streaming through the hospital room window, to his wide shoulders, to his trim waist encircled by a dark leather belt and the largest of silver belt buckles, then down his long, lean legs, clad in jeans so tight they might have been denim skin, her resolve melted like ice on a hot skillet.

"All right, Dutch. You pick the names," she said as she passed the pink bundles into her husband's arms.

"I was thinking about Mary Dell and Lydia Dale. Should sound real good together, you know? Dell and Dale? But," he said with a frown, "which name for which baby?"

Taffy shrugged. "Does it matter? They're just as alike as two peas in a pod."

Taffy's observation was accurate, at least regarding the twins' appearance. Though they were fraternal twins, knit together in the same womb but from two separate eggs, at birth Mary Dell and Lydia Dale were almost identical in appearance, sharing their mother's bluebonnet eyes and their father's full lips and blond hair. They were undeniably pretty, even a little bit beautiful. Taffy had been pretty too, once, prettier even than her daughters.

Taffy was one of the most popular girls in her high school—at least as popularity was measured among the boys. She was not loose, but she was a tremendous flirt, able to keep any number of boys angling for her attentions without them ever realizing that she was the one who had set the hook and held the line. It was all a game to her, one she relished and played recklessly, honing her skills through multiple readings of her favorite book, *Gone with the Wind,* as well as assiduous study and emulation of the heroine. In the process, she ended up repeating many of Scarlett's mistakes. It was not until after her marriage that she realized that no one man, however handsome and doting he may be, can take the place of a brace of admirers. A married woman needs friends, and Taffy had none. Her careless antics had earned her the enmity of nearly every woman in town. And though she tried her best to make amends, it was too late. The ladies of Too Much, especially Marlena Benton, had long memories.

Marlena Benton, née Pickens, could not forget the humiliation of spending the night of the senior prom sobbing in her room because her date, Noodie Benton, canceled on her, enticed by a last-minute promise to serve as Taffy's escort. Noodie was miffed when he got to the dance and realized that he was one of three young men who had been offered this privilege. But when Taffy chose him as her partner for the first slow dance, he forgave her. Marlena never would.

And though Noodie proposed to her not long after Dutch and Taffy's wedding, Marlena never entirely forgave him either. Some in town posited (but never within Marlena's hearing) that she married Noodie just so she could spend the rest of her life punishing him. That wasn't wholly true, but the seed of resentment Marlena carried within her, coupled with an unhealthy devotion to their only child, Jack Benny, did nothing to help their marriage. And what *is* certain is that Marlena, who, by virtue of being a Benton as well as president of the Too Much Women's Club *and* the Episcopal Church Altar

Guild, was the most influential woman in town, and she was more than willing to use that influence to make sure Taffy Tudmore Templeton would live her life on the lower rungs of the town's social ladder.

After years of trying and failing to work her way back into the good graces of the women of Too Much, Taffy started searching for satisfaction in other areas. She tried to join the Women's Club but received no response to her application. And though she found the rite too formal and dry for her Methodist sensibilities, she visited the Episcopal church, thinking that if she transferred her membership, then Marlena would have to accept her, if only out of Christian duty. But though Father Winston greeted her warmly after the service, the ladies of the church were decidedly cool, and Marlena actually turned her back when Taffy approached, embarrassing her in front of everyone.

Deciding that if she could not achieve social success she would try to distinguish herself personally, she attempted to pick up the family mantle and take up needlecraft, but had little talent for it and less patience. She took up the culinary arts next, becoming a good cook and an outstanding baker, but became discouraged when, year after year, her entries in the county fair failed to earn ribbons. Taffy was a natural competitor, but it's no fun competing when there's no possibility of winning. As long as the game was being played in Too Much, Taffy knew she didn't stand a chance.

But one day, when the twins were about ten, Taffy saw an advertisement for the Miss Goody Gumdrops Beauty Pageant to be held at a Holiday Inn outside of Waco. She filled out two forms, one for Mary Dell and another for Lydia Dale, sent in the entry fee, and got Silky to whip up some fancy dresses for the girls.

Lydia Dale placed first in her age group and was

awarded a crown and a twenty-five-dollar savings bond. Mary Dell was named Miss Photogenic and placed third in the talent division for her energetic and mostly on-key rendition of "I Want to Be a Cowboy's Sweetheart."

The thrill that ran through Taffy when she saw that rhinestone tiara placed on Lydia Dale's head was electric. When she returned to Too Much, she bought an enormous glass display case and made Dutch move the television cabinet into a corner to make room for it.

"Don't you think it's sort of big to hold one little crown?" he asked after Taffy placed Lydia Dale's tiara on one of the empty shelves. "It looks lonely sitting there all by itself."

"It won't be lonely for long," Taffy said, her eyes glittering with conviction.

Thanks to Lydia Dale, Taffy's prophecy came true. More malleable than Mary Dell and blessed with poise her sibling lacked, Lydia Dale filled the display cabinet with tiaras, sashes, and scepters. The pageant costumes and gowns were stored in a closet lined with cedar paneling that Taffy had made especially for the purpose. It stretched the length of the girls' bedroom wall and was stuffed to bursting with glittery, satiny, silky gowns, most belonging to Lydia Dale. Mary Dell's pageant career was over before her thirteenth birthday.

Puberty hit Mary Dell early and hard. Almost overnight she grew up and out, towering over her sister by six inches and developing a figure that had, as they say in Texas, "more curves than a Coke bottle." Mary Dell was as pretty as ever, but pageant judges preferred petite, perky little Lydia Dale. That, and Mary Dell's unfortunate tendency to speak her mind in the question-and-answer portion of the competition, spelled her doom. She just wasn't pageant material.

Mary Dell was not entirely sorry when her pageant days came to an end. Aside from the fancy costumes, she'd never cared for them and hated being away from home so much. However, she did miss her sister when Lydia Dale was off with Taffy at competitions, and she felt the lack of her mother's attention, which was now focused like a laser beam on Lydia Dale and her future (Taffy would have said her destiny) as a beauty queen. Every other concern and responsibility, even those Taffy owed to her other child, came a distant second to her desire to see Lydia Dale win.

Another girl in similar circumstances might have resented her sister, but Mary Dell loved Lydia Dale too much for that. And another girl, desperate for her mother's attention, might easily have turned rebellious and wild. But fortunately for Mary Dell, Taffy was not the only sun in her orbit.

When Taffy and Lydia Dale were off at pageants and Dutch was busy on the ranch, Mary Dell spent her weekends at the little house Silky and Velvet shared in town, adored but never coddled by those two worthy old women, especially Silky, who became her mother in all but biology. Silky was the one to whom Mary Dell turned for advice, encouragement, comfort, and womanly example. Mary Dell even adopted her grandmother's colorful, countrified form of speech, replete with the old-time Texas sayings and exclamations that Taffy, who so wanted to be elegant, had expunged from her vocabulary. Silky loved Mary Dell with all her heart, and the feeling was mutual. That didn't mean that Mary Dell, at some level, didn't miss her mother's affection and regard, but her grandmother's love filled most of the gaps.

And anyway, Mary Dell was never one to moan about things that couldn't be helped. That was another thing she'd learned from her grandmother.

Mary Dell loved watching as Silky sat hunched over an ancient Singer Featherweight machine as she worked making dresses or doing alterations. Silky was a master seamstress. Taking in sewing kept her busy and was a supplement to the income she received from the ranch, which had shrunk since Dutch took over the running of the F-Bar-T.

In time, Mary Dell progressed from watching her grandmother to helping her. At the age of fifteen, she was designing and sewing her own clothes. At sixteen, her school guidance counselor asked if she'd given any thought to what she wanted to do after high school. Without a moment's hesitation, Mary Dell answered.

"Oh, yes, ma'am. I'm going to open a dress boutique on the square. I'll design and make everything myself. And I'm going to call it Mary Dell's Too Cute Creations," she said, lifting her hands and spreading them wide, as if she could already visualize the painted sign of her some-day dress shop.

The counselor glanced at the girl's transcript with its long list of Cs, the monotony broken by one B in algebra and one A in geometry. Mary Dell was a sweet girl but, the guidance counselor concluded, clearly not college material.

"Ambition is a fine thing to have. But it's always good to leave yourself open to the possibilities. Why don't you take a look at this?" She smiled and handed Mary Dell a brochure for a trade school that offered bookkeeping courses.

The counselor underestimated Mary Dell, but that's understandable. Mary Dell had not yet bloomed into the

full flower of her personality and grit. It would take another fifteen years for that to occur. Back then, Mary
Dell was still just a girl, consumed by dreams, as easily
distracted by fancies and flirtations as any other, perhaps
more so. After all, other girls were not Tudmores. Other
girls were not subject to the ungovernable influences of
the Fatal Flaw.

CHAPTER 4

Mary Dell met Donny Bebee at the county fair in August of 1970.

The fair was always an exciting time for the residents of Too Much, a week of leisure and entertainment for folks who could afford little of either. And for the Templetons, this year's fair held special promise. Lydia Dale was competing for the title of Miss Limestone County. If she won, she would earn the right to go to Fort Worth and compete for the title of Miss Texas.

For the previous eight years, all of Taffy's maternal energies had been focused on bringing Lydia Dale to this moment. Taffy was in a tizzy, and who could blame her? On the long list of things that Texans revere—the Alamo, quarterbacks, good barbecue, and the Lone Star flag—beauty queens figure right near the top. And the girl who wins the Miss Texas crown is more than a conqueror, more than a beauty queen, for though her claim to the title lasts only a year, from the moment that tiara touches her head, the woman christened Miss Texas is transformed for life, a monarch for the ages, Rio Grande royalty.

Mary Dell was excited for her twin, as well, and proud that Lydia Dale had asked her to sew her dress for the evening gown competition. The full-skirted, starlight-white-satin gown, with a scoop neckline and 150 turquoise bugle beads hand-stitched to the smooth bodice, was made up according to her sister's exact instructions.

Mary Dell worried that the gown was too sedate to catch the judge's eye, but she was certain that no other contestant's dress would be better made, just as she was sure that no dress in the Homemade Fashions competition could possibly outshine her entry. Mary Dell had labored over every detail of the design and construction of her entry and couldn't wait to model her creation at the 4-H fashion show later that afternoon.

Mary Dell had been praying about this day for weeks— that His Will Be Done, of course, but humbly pointing out to the Almighty how perfectly perfect it would be if His plans meshed with hers. There was no harm in making a *suggestion,* was there? And if everything went the way Mary Dell prayed, she and Lydia Dale would haul home the top honors from the fair—honors that could launch them into enchanted futures. Lydia Dale might end up in Fort Worth at the Miss Texas pageant and then on to real foreign realms like Atlantic City, New Jersey, and the Miss America Pageant. And for Mary Dell, a place she could visualize more clearly than ever—a shop on Main Street with a big picture window. And around the block she could see the line of women who had traveled hundreds of miles, from all over Texas, and were willing to stand patiently for hours for the chance to buy a Mary Dell original. It could happen, couldn't it? Good things had to happen to somebody, after all. Why not her?

* * *

Taffy and Lydia Dale hauled four suitcases filled with clothes, high heels, every sort of undergarment known to womankind, makeup, tweezers, eyelash curlers, blow-dryers, curling irons, hairbrushes, teasing combs, and six cans of Aqua Net hair spray into the auditorium. Dutch was off to the midway in search of deep-fried food and a shooting range. Mary Dell, with the garment bag containing her dress held high so it wouldn't wrinkle, headed to the 4-H pavilion.

As she passed the rodeo ring, a voice coming through a crackling loudspeaker was announcing the preliminary rounds of the bull riding competition. In a hurry and with her vision partially blocked by the garment bag, she didn't see the stray horseshoe on the path. She tripped, accidentally knocking the hat off a cowboy who was walking by, and landed in a heap in the dirt. Before she could get to her feet, a big, calloused hand reached down to help her.

Mary Dell's eyes traveled from the hand, down to a pair of black Justin boots, well-worn but polished, and up again to a pair of long legs in denim, past a shiny silver belt buckle as big as a pack of cards, to a slim torso clad in a clean white Western shirt, to a pair of broad shoulders and a handsome head topped with thick dark hair.

In truth, she couldn't tell if the cowboy was handsome, not at first. When she looked up, the sun was so bright in her eyes that she couldn't make out his features. Sunbeams radiated out from his dark halo of hair, leaving his face in silhouette, but from the sound of his voice and the way her heart was pounding in her chest, she figured he must be handsome. And when he reached down to pick up his black Stetson from where it had fallen, then put it back on his head, blocking out the sunlight, she saw it was true.

"Oh, my . . ." she said weakly.

The cowboy frowned, his dark eyes concerned. "Are you all right?"

"I'm fine." Mary Dell blushed. "Clumsy but fine."

"One of the farriers must have dropped that horseshoe. They should be more careful."

He picked up the garment bag, smiled, and handed it to her. His teeth were as straight as pickets in a new fence. And so white! She'd never seen a grown man with teeth so white.

The voice of the rodeo announcer came crackling through the loudspeaker. "Oh, my! That one hurt! But it was a good try by J. D. Hooper from Corpus Christi. Let's give him a hand, folks. Up next, we'll have young Graydon Bebee from Lubbock . . ."

The cowboy's head jerked up as he heard his name. He touched his hat. "Nice to meet you, ma'am."

"Lubbock," she sighed to herself as she watched him run off toward the rodeo ring. "I knew he was too handsome to be from around here. Too bad."

But it was just as well, she decided as she resumed her date with destiny, the first stop on the journey being the 4-H pavilion and a blue ribbon with a rosette. She couldn't afford to be waylaid by distractions or detours today. And a man as good-looking as Graydon Bebee could be very distracting indeed.

Taffy was too busy fixing Lydia Dale's hair for the pageant to attend the 4-H fashion show, but Dutch sat in the third row, eating a deep-fried Twinkie on a stick and waiting for his daughter's name to be announced.

When it was, Mary Dell, wearing her red satin dress with a bow at the back and three rows of rhinestones at the neck, sleeves, and hem, walked across the platform. The skirt hit Mary Dell just below the knee, or would have, but for the six layers of netting underneath. She had used two yards of every color of netting available at Waterson's Dry Goods Emporium to make the underskirting, which lifted the red satin and made it stick out at an angle from the waist, giving everyone a generous peep at the petticoat rainbow beneath. It was, in effect, a square-dance dress modeled after one she'd found in Grandma Silky's closet, but Mary Dell had decided to make her version "more elegant."

As Mary Dell moved to the front of the stage, Dutch bolted down the last of the Twinkie and sprang to his feet, clapping and hooting for all he was worth. Dutch wasn't the most capable provider on earth, but he loved his wife and children with his whole heart. He stuck his fingers into the sides of his mouth and let out an ear-splitting whistle, so loud that Mary Dell didn't hear the snickers from the rest of the crowd.

As she executed a graceful pirouette in front of the judges, Mary Dell was positively beaming. Passing in front of her father, she blew him a kiss from the tips of her fingers. Dutch wiped a tear from his eye. The dress was awful, he knew that, but his daughter was beautiful, and he was proud of her.

When Dutch reached into the back pocket of his jeans, searching for a handkerchief, he noticed another man a couple of rows away who was also on his feet, whistling and clapping as Mary Dell made her turn, a tall fellow with a black Stetson covering his dark hair and wearing a rhinestone-studded shirt in a shade of peacock blue he'd never seen on a cowboy. For a moment, Dutch thought the man was making fun of Mary Dell, but when he gave the fellow a second look, Dutch could see his admiration was sincere. That cowboy was applauding for all he was worth.

After the contestants had changed into their regular clothes, their creations were hung back up in the display booths, and the judges pulled out their clipboards and gave the entries a closer look. When they got to Mary Dell's dress, one of them commented that she'd never seen a better-constructed garment. The inset of the sleeves was perfect, the fit and tailoring flawless, the hand stitches on the hem as tiny and even as possible, and every single seam had been "frenched," encased within an envelope of fabric so not a single raw edge was visible. The overall visual image was a nightmare, they agreed, but the work-manship was impeccable. After a lengthy discussion, they pinned a ribbon on Mary Dell's gown and moved on.

Mary Dell tried to look nonchalant as the judges made their rounds. But when they moved away from her gown, she rushed to the booth, eager to see her ribbon, sure that she had won the prize, that her real life was fi-nally about to begin. But instead of the first-place blue or even a second-place red ribbon Mary Dell had ex-pected, the judges had awarded her gown only a green ribbon—an honorable mention.

Her shoulders drooped. She rubbed the green slip be-tween her fingers. The fabric was a cheap nylon blend, not satin, not silk. It didn't even have a rosette.

A deep voice rumbled behind her, catching her so by surprise that she jumped. "Pardon me, ma'am. Hope you don't mind my saying so, but you were robbed. That's about the prettiest dress I ever saw."

Mary Dell quickly swiped her nose with the back of her hand and turned around. She nearly gasped when she saw the black Stetson, dark hair, and dark brown eyes, thinking the handsome bull rider had tracked her down, but a second look told her that this was not the same man. His build was the same, his hands just as capable looking, his teeth picket-fence straight, and he too was handsome. But his nose was a little longer, his eyes a little wider-set, his frame a little shorter, just an inch, and this cowboy's shirt was peacock blue and studded with rhinestones instead of plain white. An improvement, Mary Dell thought.

The cowboy touched his fingers to the brim of his hat and gave a slight nod. "I'm Donny Bebee, from Lubbock, and I was wondering—can I take you out dancing? You and that beautiful dress?"

CHAPTER 5

1970

The nausea had passed, but Mary Dell was still locked in the bathroom, kneeling on the floor in her wedding gown. Her head was still pounding and so were Taffy's fists, demanding that Mary Dell open the door that instant or so help her . . .

"I just don't know if marrying Donny is the right thing," Mary Dell wailed.

"Well, you should have thought about that before!" Taffy barked.

I should have thought about a lot of things before.

She should have been more forceful when she told Donny that she couldn't leave the fairgrounds and go out with someone she barely knew. If she hadn't been so disappointed by the judges' response to her dress and her wounded pride so buoyed by Donny's, she would have. Even though she was just a few months from reaching the then-legal drinking age of nineteen and the bartender hadn't asked to see her license, she should never have ordered that bottle of beer, the first liquor she'd ever had in her life, and two more after that. And she should have left the honky-tonk at six and gone to the pageant, like she'd promised herself she would when they arrived. And she shouldn't have let Donny hold her so close during the slow songs, crushing the red satin bodice of her dress against his peacock-blue shirt. And she definitely shouldn't have driven to Puny Pond with him to look at the moon. And she shouldn't . . . Well . . . All the stuff that had happened after that, most of which she couldn't even remember clearly.

But she did recall how the moonlight had shone so bright in her eyes and how her heart was pounding again, just like it had when Graydon picked her up out of the dirt, and the ringing of bells in her ears. Or was it violins?

It didn't matter. Whatever it was, she shouldn't have given in to it.

The morning after her date with Donny was a Sunday. The family drove to the Methodist church like they did every week and sat where they always sat, fourth pew back on the left. Mary Dell bowed her head and promised herself and the Good Lord she'd never let herself get in that kind of situation again. And she didn't. Not even when Donny came around later, begging her to go out with him again—not that she could have accepted his invitation even if she'd been so inclined. Taffy had grounded her for coming in late and for skipping Lydia Dale's pageant.

She felt bad about that. She should have been there to support her sister especially since, to everyone's shock, Lydia Dale had *not* won the county crown. She'd blown the question-and-answer portion of the competition and finished as first runner-up.

Taffy was, by turns, furious, brokenhearted, and confused over the outcome. She couldn't understand why Lydia Dale had drawn a blank when asked what sights and attractions she would recommend to someone who was visiting the county for the first time. They'd gone over the question at least three times in rehearsals.

But Mary Dell thought she knew what had gone wrong. Donny's brother, Graydon, had been in the pageant audience that night. Mary Dell figured that when Lydia Dale had spotted that tall, handsome cowboy sitting right up front, everything she'd practiced and all her good sense flew clean out of her head. Mary Dell understood how that kind of thing could happen to a girl.

After the pageant, Graydon asked Lydia Dale if she'd like to go for a ride on the Ferris wheel. He'd been coming around ever since. He and Donny took temporary jobs at the Baker ranch—temporary because Graydon would be shipping out for Vietnam soon.

For a girl who'd blown her shot at immortality and being crowned the Queen of all Texas, Lydia Dale was awfully chipper—in fact, she was downright giddy. Lydia Dale and Graydon went out almost every night, and she urged her sister to come along, to make it a double date with Donny, but Mary Dell declined. She didn't trust herself. Or Donny.

It wasn't that she thought he was a masher or anything. They'd lost their heads, both of them. But she didn't want to take the risk of it ever happening again. She resolved to put Donny Bebee out of her mind completely. For a month or so, she did. Until she started feeling sick in the mornings.

She knew from the first that she was going to go ahead and have the baby. Mary Dell's theology was as straightforward as she was. She figured if God had decided to make a baby, there must be some good reason for it, and far be it from her to thwart the plans of the Almighty. But that was about the only thing she knew for sure. She felt so alone.

After a couple of weeks, she confided in Lydia Dale, but swore her to secrecy.

But Lydia Dale wasn't very good at keeping secrets. She told Graydon and he, in turn, told his brother. Upon hearing the news, Donny drove to the nearest Sears department store, bought a little ring with a diamond chip from the jewelry counter, drove to the ranch, and asked Mary Dell to be his wife. At the time, she'd felt relieved, but now she was afraid she'd made a terrible mistake.

"Momma, just tell Organza to play the songs one more time. Please? I need to think this through!"

She sat down cross-legged on the bathroom floor, hearing the sound of more footsteps and more female voices as her sister, grandmother, and great-aunt joined Taffy in the narrow hallway.

"Where's Mary Dell?" Lydia Dale asked in an urgent half whisper. "Everybody's getting restless. Uncle Dwayne opened the bar. He's standing in the back drinking bourbon. Looks like a lot of the men are thinking about joining him."

"Not that," Taffy groaned. "Remember what happened the last time?"

Taffy, sounding almost hysterical, yelled through the keyhole. "Mary Dell, did you hear that? If Uncle Dwayne gets drunk and tries to rope one of the bridesmaids, I will never forgive you! If Marlena Benton were to hear about something like that, I'd never hear the end of it. You have *got* to come out here and get married right this second!"

"Oh, for heaven's sake," Grandma Silky said in an exasperated voice. "No, she doesn't. What do you care about Marlena Benton anyway? She sure doesn't care about you."

Silky moved next to the door and shouted, as if trying to make herself heard across a mile-wide canyon rather than two inches of a hollow-core door.

"Mary Dell? It's Granny. Now you listen to me, honey. Baby or no baby, you do *not* have to marry Donny Bebee. Not unless you want to. Do you want to?"

Silky pressed her ear to the door, listening for her granddaughter's answer. After a long moment of silence, she heard sounds of rustling silk and the toilet lid being closed and, finally, a metallic click as Mary Dell unlocked and opened the door.

"I don't know what I want," she said, looking into her grandmother's eyes. "I really don't. I'm sorry. Guess I got the whole family into this mess, haven't I?"

Mary Dell spread out her skirts and sat down on the commode with her shoulders slumped. Silky hurried into the bathroom followed by Taffy, Lydia Dale, and Velvet—five women in one room, packed so close that the scent of their perfumes melded into a sickly-sweet smell, like leftover funeral flowers, so overpowering that Mary Dell's nausea returned.

Aunt Velvet, who was nearsighted from so many hours spent poring over books, slid her glasses to the end of her nose and clucked her tongue.

"There, there," she said as she patted Mary Dell's shoulder. "Don't be so hard on yourself. It's the Fatal Flaw, that's all. All the Tudmore women have suffered from it."

Taffy made a face. "That's ridiculous. I wore white on my wedding day." She sniffed. "Because I deserved to."

"More like because I nailed your bedroom window shut once Dutch came back from Korea looking so good in his uniform," Silky muttered. "Don't think everybody doesn't know how it is between you and that husband of yours, Taffy. Every time Dutch looks at you sideways, you just about fall over backward."

Taffy colored a bit, lifted her chin, and continued without acknowledging the comment. "Well, Aunt Velvet doesn't suffer from any 'fatal flaw,' " she said. "She's always saying how, if she had to choose between the worst hound dog on earth and the best man in Too Much, she'd take the hound any day of the week."

"But that's because a careful study of our family history helped me identify and overcome the Fatal Flaw," the older lady explained. "And that's why I have stayed away from face powder, lipstick, and hair dye, and only wear black or gray dresses. No darts, no belts, no hemlines above my calves. By rigorously following this formula, I've successfully kept lust and suitors at bay. And," she said with a self-satisfied nod, "I've been a happier woman for it."

Taffy rolled her eyes. "Fine. Then how do you explain Momma?" she asked, gesturing to Silky. "Momma and Daddy never . . ."

Silky cleared her throat, looked at the floor, and gave her head a quick shake. Taffy stopped in mid-sentence, turning suddenly pale.

"Momma! Are you telling me that . . ."

Silky sighed, as if disappointed by her daughter's density.

"Taffy, your daddy and I got married in May. You were born in November. Didn't you ever stop to do the math? Oh, don't look at me that way," she said irritably. "I was young and stupid once too. Anyway, that's all ancient history. What matters now is Mary Dell."

Silky crouched down on her haunches and took Mary Dell's smooth, pretty hands into her rough and wrinkled ones. "Honey, do you want to marry Donny?"

"Maybe. I don't know. Grandma, how long did you know Grandpa before you married him?"

"Not long. We got married pretty quick."

"Did you love him?"

"Hooty fell out the back of a pickup and broke his neck before your momma's first birthday. But, for as long as it lasted, we were as happy as most folks.

"Listen, baby girl, I've made mistakes, plenty of them. Everybody does. But I'm not sorry I married your grandpa. And I'm not sorry I had your momma."

She squeezed Mary Dell's hands and glanced up and winked at Lydia Dale, who had been listening to all this with an anxious expression.

"I like my life. And no matter what you decide to do today, when you're my age, you'll like your life too, if you just make up your mind to do it. See if I'm not right. You've got good instincts, honey. You just need to follow them."

Mary Dell sighed heavily and chewed on her bottom lip. "I just wish I knew him better. Donny *seems* nice. . . ."

"Oh, he is!" Lydia Dale exclaimed, squatting down next to Silky so she could be at eye level with her sister. "He must be! He's Graydon's brother, isn't he?"

Taffy crossed her arms over her chest. "I don't see that as much of a recommendation. If Graydon Bebee hadn't gotten you all distracted at the pageant, you might be Miss Texas by now!"

"Momma," Lydia Dale answered evenly, "I love Graydon. And the second he gets back from Vietnam, I'm going to marry him. We've made up our minds, so you'd just better get used to the idea. As far as what happened at the pageant . . ." Lydia Dale looked at her mother and swallowed hard, as if trying to decide whether to speak her mind or hold her tongue. "That wasn't Graydon's fault. I answered that question exactly the way I planned to."

Taffy's eyes bulged. For a moment, she almost looked as if she might faint.

"I don't understand. What are you saying? You can't mean . . ."

Lydia Dale took a deep breath, rose to her feet, squared her shoulders, and turned to face her mother.

"I blew the question on purpose, Momma. I *wanted* to lose."

Taffy sputtered and clutched at her heart, but Lydia Dale refused to be interrupted.

"Hear me out, Momma. I know how hard you worked to make me Miss Texas, but that was your dream. Not mine. It was fun at first, but I'm tired of pageants! I'm tired of false eyelashes and lip gloss and getting my hair teased. I'm tired of walking down a runway in four-inch heels and a swimsuit I had to get glued into. I'm tired of tiaras and sashes and smiling and answering stupid questions about how I'll bring about world peace when everybody knows I'm just going to ride in parades or cut ribbons at the grand openings of supermarkets and car dealerships. And I'm tired of being so far from home all the time. . . ."

Taffy turned pale. Looking dazed, she sank slowly down, as if her knees wouldn't support her, until she was seated on the edge of the bathtub.

"And so far from my sister," Lydia Dale continued. "Things haven't been the same since I started doing the pageants. I've missed you, Mary Dell. But if you marry Donny and I marry Graydon, we'll never have to be apart again!"

Lydia Dale crouched down again so she was at eye level with her twin.

"Graydon is a good man. And I'm sure Donny is too. He must be! If he wasn't, would he have been so quick to propose after he heard about the baby? Maybe he didn't do right, not when you two went out that night, but he's trying to make it right. That tells you something about him, doesn't it?

"And think!" she said urgently. "Think how it will be for us to be married to brothers and live right here in Too Much! We'll get to see each other every day—just like Grandma and Aunt Velvet. We'll spend holidays and birthdays together. Our children will grow up together and be very best friends. Doesn't that sound wonderful?"

Lydia Dale's question hung in the air, but before Mary Dell could answer her, there was a knock on the door. Dutch stepped into the crowded bathroom.

"Well, this is cozy. Kinda late for a bachelorette party, don't you think?" He looked at Mary Dell and grinned. "You look beautiful, baby girl. You truly do. Now, what do you say? You ready to get married?"

Mary Dell hesitated for a moment, then stood up, picked an open tube of lipstick up off the counter, and applied a coat of ruby red to her lips. When she was finished, she took her father's arm.

"Yes, Daddy. I'm ready."

CHAPTER 6

The Belmont Motel, a cluster of low-slung stucco cottages perched on a hillside on the west side of the Trinity River, was not an elegant establishment, but it had a nice view of the Dallas skyline. Of course, by the time Donny and Mary Dell, still dressed in their wedding finery, checked in at the motel, it was too dark to see it. Even if it had been otherwise, the newlyweds were too weary to appreciate the scenery.

The day had been long and taxing. After the ceremony Donny joined Uncle Dwayne at the bar, matching the old man's toast to their happiness drink for drink. Mary Dell took the wheel for the drive from Too Much to Dallas and was relieved when, after unloading the suitcases and carrying her over the threshold of the motel room, her groom collapsed on the bed and immediately fell asleep.

Early the next morning, as the first fingers of sunlight

slipped through the cracks of the venetian blinds, Mary Dell slipped out of bed and into the bathroom.

A few minutes later the sound of muffled sobbing roused Donny from sleep. He opened his eyes slowly and blinked, confused by the strange surroundings, wondering how he had gotten out of his clothes and who had folded them so neatly on the seat of the orange Naugahyde armchair that sat next to the window.

After a moment, Donny remembered the where and why of his circumstances. He was married now and on his honeymoon; that he understood. What he didn't understand was why his wife was crying in the bathroom.

Groaning as he lifted his hurting head from the pillow, silently cursing his new uncle-in-law and promising himself that his first taste of bourbon would also be his last, Donny got up and slipped a clean T-shirt over his head. He pressed his ear to the door of the bathroom for a moment before knocking tentatively.

"Mary Dell? Honey? It's Donny. Your husband?"

He cleared his throat awkwardly, feeling ridiculous. Of course she knew he was her husband. She could hardly have forgotten. If anything, the sound of her distress led him to believe she remembered only too well.

"Mary Dell, are you all right?"

He heard the sound of bathroom tissue being pulled from the roller, a nose being blown, and sniffling.

"Yes. I'm fine."

Donny didn't believe her. He tried the door handle, rattling the knob. "Mary Dell? Open up. Please."

There was no response. He tried another tack.

"Open the door, honey. I need to use the bathroom."

"All right. Just give me a second." He heard the sound of movement and more sniffling, the toilet flushing and, finally, a metallic click as she unlocked the door.

"Are you all right?" he asked, taking in her red-rimmed eyes and the gray-black half-moons under them, stains from tear-smeared mascara. "Tell me what's wrong."

"I'm fine," she insisted. "I just . . . I mean . . . I might need to see a doctor."

Her composure crumpled like a tossed-away tissue, and her eyes filled with tears.

"Oh, Donny! I think I lost the baby!"

She was weeping again, and loudly, sobs pouring out like water from a bucket. Mary Dell was big and tall, but Donny was bigger and taller, and much stronger. He scooped her up in his arms and carried her to the orange armchair, kicking aside his carefully folded clothing before sitting down with Mary Dell in his lap, cradling her in his arms, smoothing her blond hair with his hand, murmuring soothing sounds into her ear, using the same tone and vocabulary he used when calming a nervous colt—"hush now" and "all right then"—adding a few endearments to the mix.

Mary Dell leaned close, wrapped her arms around his neck, buried her tear-streaked face into his muscular chest. "I'm sorry. I'm so sorry."

"For what, darlin'?"

"For getting you into this mess. For making it so you had to marry me. And all for no reason!"

Donny frowned and pressed on Mary Dell's shoulders, pushing her face away from his chest so he could see her eyes.

"For no reason? Is that why you think I married you? Just because of the baby?"

Mary Dell sniffled and wiped her eyes on the sleeve of her nightgown.

"Isn't it?"

"I married you because I love you. The minute I laid

eyes on you, walking across that stage in the beautiful red dress, I said to myself, 'Donny Bebee, you're either going to get that girl to marry you or die trying.' Of course, I got kind of carried away on that first date. I'm sorry about that. That wasn't fair to you."

Donny smiled and looked her straight in the eye.

"I promised myself I wouldn't let it happen again, not until the wedding. My plan was to marry you by November, December at the latest, so Graydon could be best man before he shipped out. And when you wouldn't go out with me again or even speak to me, it just about broke my heart."

"Really?" Mary Dell asked, blinking away her tears.

"Ask Graydon, if you don't believe me. He'll tell you." Donny shook his head sorrowfully. "Yes, ma'am. I thought I'd blown my chance with you. Happiest day of my life—well, up until yesterday—was when Graydon told me you were pregnant. Boy, I couldn't get myself to that jewelry counter fast enough! Almost drove the truck into a ditch, I was going so fast.

"I knew it wasn't right, what I'd let happen on our date. But I figured that maybe you having a baby was God's way of giving me another chance."

Mary Dell sighed and dropped her head onto his shoulder, as if the weight of keeping it upright took more energy than she could muster.

"Except now there is no baby," she said quietly.

He kissed the top of her head. "But there will be. We're going to have lots of babies, Mary Dell. You'll see."

"Do you think so?"

"Sure do." He kissed her again, squeezing his arm tight around her shoulders. "I think we ought to take you to a doctor, just to make sure you're fine. Then I think we ought to spend some time making plans, thinking

about where we're going to live after we go back to Too
Much . . ."

Mary Dell's eyes went wide. "But . . . aren't we going
to live on the ranch?"

"Of course we are," Donny assured her. "It's nice of
your folks to let us live with them, but I'd like us to have
a place of our own as soon as we can afford it. What if
we got a trailer, a double-wide? It'd be the quickest way
to get a house of our own. There's some nice ones out
now, and those double-wides are roomier than they
look."

"I don't care where we live as long as it's on the ranch
and we're together."

"That's what I thought too," Donny said. "We don't
need anything fancy. Just someplace close to the big
house, but not too close, where we can have some privacy but still be close to the barns."

He stroked her hair with his big, broad hand and said
wistfully, "The F-Bar-T might not be the biggest spread
in Texas, but I never saw such good grazing land. I think
we can really make something of it, honey. I've got
some ideas."

"You do?"

He looked at her and nodded, coming back to himself. "All kinds of ideas. And you're part of them all.
And you know something else? After we see that doctor
and whenever he says it's all right, whether that's today
or tomorrow or next month, I think we ought to spend a
whole lot of time trying to make a whole lot of babies.
What would you say to that, Mrs. Bebee?"

Mary Dell turned her face toward his shoulder so he
wouldn't see her embarrassing eagerness and smiled.
"I'd say that sounds like a real good plan. And I'd say I
love you, Donny. I'd say I love you something terrible."

CHAPTER 7

July 1983

Dr. Eloisa Brownback pulled off her latex gloves and tossed them into the wastebasket before snapping off the goosenecked exam light.

"All right, Mary Dell. You can sit up now."

Mary Dell took her feet from the stirrups and pushed herself into a sitting position at the end of the table. She didn't ask the doctor if the baby was all right. Eloisa's solemn expression told her everything.

"I'm so sorry." Dr. Brownback sat down on a rolling stool and sighed as she took Mary Dell's hand. "Did you tell Donny you were pregnant?"

"I didn't want to talk to him until after the first trimester. Didn't want to get his hopes up again."

"I think you *should* talk to him—about adoption. It's time."

Mary Dell shook her head. "I've tried. Donny is dead set on us having a child of our own. He says it's up to him to carry on the family name."

The doctor sniffed. "Look, Mary Dell. Maybe it's not my place to meddle in family affairs, but it's not like the entire future of the Bebee clan rests solely on Donny's shoulders, does it? He does have a brother, after all. Can't *he* be the one to carry on the line?"

Eloisa raised her eyebrows to underscore the question, then turned her back and started scribbling notes on Mary Dell's chart. Mary Dell slid off the exam table, wrapping the white sheet around herself like a sarong.

"Doesn't seem likely," Mary Dell answered as she stepped behind a privacy screen and started to dress. "Graydon's up in Kansas now, works as a hired man and lives like a hermit. He lives in one room, doesn't have a telephone of his own, doesn't keep company with anybody, never even goes to town unless he has to. I can't see him getting married and making babies anytime soon."

Mary Dell sighed as she reached around back to hook up her bra. She felt sorry for Graydon. Life in that POW camp must have been unimaginably difficult, but that wasn't what had driven him to his hermitic lifestyle. No, it was coming home to discover the woman he'd pinned his dreams on had married someone else that had done it. Of course, it had to have been a terrible and heartbreaking shock. But it was so sad. Having lived through the misery and isolation of one prison, Graydon had returned home and entered another, but this time he'd done it by choice.

Lydia Dale, on the other hand, was stuck. Mary Dell had tried to talk her out of marrying Jack Benny, but she'd accused Mary Dell of trying to "spoil her last chance at happiness," unable to see that if anything was going to spoil her chance for happiness, it was marrying Jack Benny. She knew that now, of course.

Mary Dell did up the green rhinestone buttons on her bright blue blouse, thinking back on the vision of happiness that Lydia Dale had conjured all those years ago, the one that had propelled Mary Dell out of the bathroom and down the aisle, a picture of them living next door to each other with passels of towheaded children running back and forth between the houses, stealing cookies and causing havoc, of holidays and birthdays celebrated with a crowd of relatives, of being best friends again and for always.

It hadn't happened.

The sisters lived close, but they weren't close—not like they had been. They talked all the time, and Mary Dell saw the children, nine-year-old Jeb and six-year-old Brocade, known as Cady, at least twice a week. The kids were sweet, and Lydia Dale and Jack Benny's little house was just six miles from the ranch. But Jack Benny was a wedge between the sisters. Lydia Dale refused to discuss her marriage, and because they couldn't talk about that, they couldn't talk about a lot of things.

So many fine plans, but none of it had worked out.

The only thing that had turned out better than she could have hoped was the one thing she'd never planned on at all. She'd never figured on falling in love with her husband on her honeymoon, but that's what had happened.

Donny was not only a handsome man but a good one, and a loving husband, a little incommunicative and hard to unglue from the television during football season, but that was all right. Mary Dell loved football, like any true Texan. She'd grown up going to the high school home games every Friday night during the season and still did, along with everybody else in town. Friday night football was the social highlight of the week in Too Much. And, of course, they watched televised college games on Saturday and professional teams on Sunday after church, especially if the Cowboys were playing. Mary Dell couldn't wait for the start of the new season. Sitting snuggled up next to her husband on the sofa while they watched a game together was just one more pleasure of being married to Donny. But for their inability to have children, Mary Dell would have described her marriage as perfectly happy. Who'd ever have figured that the man she'd "had" to marry thirteen years before would be the ideal man for her? How did she get so lucky?

And Donny wasn't just good to her; he was good to her folks too. She didn't know how the family would have survived without him.

After Dutch developed diabetes and lost part of his left foot to the disease, he wasn't capable of doing as much on the ranch—not that he'd ever been much of a go-getter to start with. When Dutch was running things, the ranch barely broke even. But things changed when Donny joined the family.

Donny worked sunup to sundown, adding a new breed of beef cattle to the mix of livestock, sheep too, putting those ideas he'd talked about on their honeymoon into practice and making the ranch profitable enough to support the whole family—the *whole* family, not just himself and Mary Dell but Dutch and Taffy, Grandma Silky, even Jack Benny and Lydia Dale.

Jack Benny was a Benton, which, in theory, should have made him a wealthy man, at least by Too Much standards. But he and his daddy didn't get on. Noodie kept a tight grip on the family finances, swearing that his worthless son wouldn't get a dime of his money until he was dead and buried. Since Noodie looked to be in pretty good health, that might take some time. Until then, Jack Benny was supposed to be working at the ranch to help support his family. Mary Dell couldn't remember the last time he put in a full week's work, but he had no compunction about taking a full share of the profits.

That was something else they couldn't talk about. Mary Dell knew Lydia Dale was embarrassed by her husband's shiftless ways and hated accepting money that he'd done so little to earn, but what else could she do? She had two little children to support. Mary Dell didn't blame her or resent her. Lydia Dale deserved more from life than she'd been given.

After sucking in her breath and zipping up her jeans, Mary Dell came out from behind the screen and sat down on a metal side chair. The doctor scribbled something on a pad of paper.

"I don't think you're going to need it," she said, tearing the top sheet off the pad and handing it to Mary Dell, "but here's a prescription just in case. If the pain is severe or the bleeding gets worse, call me. Take it easy for a week or so, and no driving today. Is somebody coming to pick you up?"

"Lydia Dale will be here as soon as her meeting lets out."

"Good. And tell Donny to keep his hands off you for a few days. Or maybe I should be saying that to you instead?" the doctor asked with a wink. "Your aunt recently gave me a very informative lecture about the Tudmore clan's Fatal Flaw. Velvet is quite a character."

Mary Dell grinned at the mention of her aunt. "Well, she's got a lot of theories, but I think she's right about the Fatal Flaw. I don't know why, but every now and then, Donny starts looking like Robert Redford and Paul Newman all rolled into one."

The doctor laughed. "That's no fatal flaw; that's biology, nature's way of making sure the human race goes on. And thank heaven for it, or I'd be out of business."

She got up from her chair and slipped Mary Dell's file into a rack near the door. "Speaking of business, how is Lydia Dale feeling? She should be over the nausea soon, but if not, tell her to call the office."

Mary Dell's eyes went wide. "Nausea? You mean Lydia Dale is . . ."

Dr. Brownback covered her mouth with her hand. When she removed it, her smile was replaced by a stricken expression. "She's your sister, so I—I assumed she'd told you by now. I shouldn't have said anything. I'm so sorry."

"It's all right," Mary Dell said. "She was probably trying to spare my feelings." She attempted a smile.

Mary Dell wanted a baby so badly, but three doctors and five miscarriages after her first, no one seemed to be able to explain or solve the problem.

Lydia Dale, on the other hand, could use her husband's toothbrush and get pregnant—at least that's how it seemed. Mary Dell was certain that this baby was a surprise, perhaps even an accident. It was so unfair. Why should Lydia Dale so easily be granted the thing Mary Dell wanted most? But then again, maybe Lydia Dale had the same sort of questions. Maybe she wondered why Mary Dell should have so easily and unexpectedly found what Lydia Dale wanted most: the love of a good man.

Mary Dell got to her feet and slipped the strap of her purse over her shoulder. She would not be jealous of her sister.

Dr. Brownback opened the door for Mary Dell. "I'm really very sorry," she repeated. "It was a stupid mistake. Please tell Lydia Dale that I'm going to call her later. If she wants to find another doctor, I completely understand. And if she wants to file a complaint with the medical board . . ."

Mary Dell rolled her eyes. "Oh, for pity's sake. Stop it. She's not going to file any complaint. Lydia Dale's not the complaining kind. And anyway," Mary Dell said with a shrug, "I was bound to find out before long. Last time Lydia Dale was pregnant she blew up like a bloated fish. But don't tell her I said so."

"Your secret is safe with me," Dr. Brownback said, holding up her hand and then letting it drop on Mary Dell's shoulder. "Are you sure you're all right?"

"Why wouldn't I be? I'm going to be an aunt again. I get a new baby to snuggle and I don't even have to get morning sickness or stretch marks to do it."

"That's kind of how adoption works too." Eloisa squeezed her shoulder. "You're going to talk to Donny?"

Mary Dell bobbed her head. "I will. Just as soon as the time is right."

CHAPTER 8

Mary Dell paced up and down in front of the clinic, waiting for Lydia Dale. She was late. Mary Dell supposed she must have been held up at the meeting. Taffy was always going on breathlessly about this "crisis" or that involving the Women's Club.

Honestly, Mary Dell didn't see what could be so difficult about putting on a Christmas ball or organizing a charity turkey shoot, but to listen to Taffy, these activities were as complicated to stage as the Normandy invasion and just as critical to the continuance of truth, justice, and the American way of life.

Now that Lydia Dale's pageant career was finished, the Women's Club was the main focus of Taffy's life. She poured all her energy into it, thrilled that she'd finally been accepted as a member. Mary Dell didn't understand how Taffy could be so blind. Those women still treated her like a redheaded stepchild. They only let her into their cursed club because they had to; there was no way on earth they could blackball the mother of Marlena Benton's daughter-in-law.

Marlena hadn't been any happier about admitting Taffy to the club than she'd been about seeing her son marry a Tudmore. But she could never refuse her baby boy anything he truly wanted, and Jack Benny had wanted Lydia Dale in the worst way. As far as Mary Dell was concerned, he'd courted her in the worst way too, when she was vulnerable and grieving. Her sister would never have married him if she'd been in her right mind.

Where *was* Lydia Dale? She was just about to go back into the doctor's office to call the house when Lydia Dale's blue pickup came speeding around the corner. Mary Dell opened the door and climbed into the passenger seat.

"I am *so* sorry." Lydia Dale clapped her hand over her heart, looking genuinely distressed. Her eyes were red.

"It's all right," Mary Dell replied. "Are you coming down with a cold?"

Lydia Dale gave her head a quick shake and pressed her lips together. "No. I'm fine. It's just that . . . It doesn't matter. How are you? What did the doctor say?"

Mary Dell swallowed hard. "It was like I thought. I lost the baby."

Lydia Dale's eyes filled. She laid her head on the steering wheel and started to sob for all she was worth, her shoulders convulsing.

Mary Dell was stunned. Lydia Dale was never much of a crier. Maybe the pregnancy was making her emotional. Mary Dell twisted sideways in the seat, leaned closer to her sister, moved her hand in slow circles over Lydia Dale's back.

"It's all right, sis. I know you're pregnant, and I'm happy for you. Really, I am. I'll have a baby of my own someday," she said. "I'm going to talk to Donny about adopting. Don't cry. It's not your fault I lost the baby."

Lydia Dale lifted her head. Her face was red, and her nose was running. She tried to say something but couldn't, tried again, closing her eyes and taking in three big, ragged breaths before finding her voice.

"I'm sorry, Mary Dell. I'm so sorry about the baby. But that's not why . . ."

She covered her mouth with her hand, pressing so hard that when she removed her hand, her lips were almost white.

"I didn't go to the meeting. After I dropped you off, I realized I'd forgotten my notes about caterers for the Christmas Ball at home, so I swung back by the house to get them. Jack Benny's truck was idling in the driveway. He didn't go to work."

What else is new?

"Somebody was sitting in the truck waiting for him. A woman. Carla Jean Nesbitt."

Mary Dell gasped. "That two-bit tart who tends bar at the Ice House? Are you kidding? She's as loose as ashes in the wind, and everybody knows it. I can't believe Jack Benny's stupid enough to be seen with that sorry piece of goods."

Lydia Dale let out a short, sharp laugh. "Oh, he's doing more than being seen with her; he's moving in with her. And divorcing me."

Mary Dell's jaw went slack. How could Jack Benny consider leaving his children and beautiful former beauty queen bride for a cheap tramp like Carla Jean Nesbitt? Why, Carla Jean wasn't even a natural blonde!

"He's leaving you for *her?* Has he lost his mind? He must have. Either that or he was blind and stupid drunk!"

"No," Lydia Dale replied with a quick shake of her head, "he wasn't drunk. Not today. He's been seeing her for months now."

"And you knew?"

Lydia Dale nodded. Mary Dell was speechless, but not for long.

"I can't . . . I just can't believe you'd let him treat you this way. Why did you? Why aren't *you* the one who's leaving him?"

Lydia Dale snapped her head around.

"Because it isn't just about me! I have two children to think of, Mary Dell. Jeb loves his daddy. I don't know why; Jack Benny hardly gives him the time of day, but he does. He's just a little boy, and he wants his daddy. Cady isn't so attached to him, maybe because she's a girl and she has me. I don't know . . . but I'm just trying to hold my family together. Children need a daddy."

Mary Dell felt terrible. Her sister had been carrying this burden for months, and she'd been too wrapped up in herself to notice.

"I'm sorry. Don't listen to me. What do I know about raising kids? I guess any daddy is better than none. Did you tell Jack Benny about the baby?"

Lydia Dale frowned. "How did you know about that?"

"Dr. Brownback accidentally let it slip. You could have told me, you know. I'd never be jealous of your happiness."

"Oh, Mary Dell . . ." Lydia Dale's voice quavered. "That's not why I kept it from you. I just . . . I felt stupid. Because I am. How stupid do you have to be to let yourself get pregnant when you know your husband is sleeping with another woman? It was right after I figured out what was going on. I confronted Jack Benny, and he told me I was imagining things.

"You know, he can be very convincing when he wants to. It helps that I wanted to believe him. Anyway, he got me drunk, and I left my diaphragm in the drawer, and now . . ."

Mary Dell leaned across the gearshift to fold her sister into an awkward embrace. "Hush now," she ordered. "No more of that."

"I didn't tell you because to tell you the truth, I wasn't happy about the baby. I know how terrible that must sound to you." Lydia Dale closed her eyes and rubbed her forehead. "I am such a fool. You warned me about him. But would I listen? No. I just got mad and told you to mind your own business. What am I going to do, Mary Dell? What am I going to do?"

"Quit beating yourself up, for a start," Mary Dell said. "You're going to figure this out. And I'm going to help you. Donny will too. And Daddy and Momma. And Grandma and Aunt Velvet. Jack Benny might be leaving you, but we never will. We're your family and we're not going anywhere."

She squeezed her as tight as she could.

Lydia Dale buried her head in her sister's shoulder, muffling the sound of her voice. "You don't understand. Jack Benny isn't just going to go away, not without a fight. He wants everything."

"The house?" Mary Dell puffed. "Let him have it. It's a shack anyway. You and the children can move back to the ranch. It'll be a little tight, but Momma and Daddy will be thrilled to have you back. We'll make do."

"No, it's not that. I mean . . . he *does* want the house, but that's not all he wants."

Mary Dell frowned. "You mean the kids? He's going to fight for custody?"

"No. He's not interested enough in the children to sue for custody. I almost wish he would."

Lydia Dale lifted her head and looked at her sister, her blue eyes streaming tears and regret. "He doesn't want the kids, Mary Dell. He wants the ranch, the F-Bar-T. Part of it, anyway. And he's willing to go to court to get it."

CHAPTER 9

Mary Dell stood with her feet resting on the bottom rung of the gate, watching her husband stride across the paddock with a bucket of oats for Georgeann, the Appaloosa mare he'd ridden back in his rodeo days. Georgeann nickered when he approached, greeting him. She was still a handsome horse, sleek of coat and straight-legged, but starting to show her age.

Glad I'm not the only one, Mary Dell thought as she watched Donny stroke the mare's neck while Georgeann lowered her head and munched contentedly.

Other than a slight paunch around his middle, evidence of his fondness for Tex-Mex and pork rinds, and a few lines around his eyes that made him look rugged and experienced, Donny didn't look a day older than he had on their honeymoon, at least in Mary Dell's estimation. All these years later, the sight of him on horseback, sitting tall in the saddle and scanning the horizon for signs of danger or rain, or bent over the engine of their old Ford pickup, his Wranglers stretched as tight as a second skin, or hefting a bale of hay up onto his shoulder as easily as if it were a bale of feathers, still melted her butter, made her feel fortunate and breathless, even a little faint.

But this was no time to let herself get distracted. They had serious matters to discuss, though Donny didn't seem to agree.

"Donny? Did you hear what I said?"

"I heard."

"Well. Aren't you worried?"

"Nope."

"Why in heaven's name not?"

"Because he doesn't own one square inch of this ranch. Taffy signed the deed over to you and your sister—"

"When we got married," Mary Dell interrupted. "I know. Just like Grandma Velvet signed it over to Momma when she married Daddy. The ranch has always passed from daughter to daughter."

"Well, that's my point," Donny said. "I don't own the land; I just get to work it and live off what we make from it. And," he said under his breath, addressing himself to the horse, "support the entire extended family while I'm at it. Heckuva deal."

"What was that?"

"Nothing. I'm just sayin' that the land doesn't belong to me or to Jack Benny. We don't figure into it. It goes from daughter to daughter, like you said."

"But that's just our tradition. Nobody's ever questioned it before. We've never had a divorce in the family. It could change everything. A judge might say we have to split the ranch up or buy Jack Benny out or I don't know what all. Jack Benny went to Waco last week and hired himself some fancy lawyer. Doesn't handle a blessed thing but divorces."

Donny tipped the bucket forward, then shook it so Georgeann could get at the last of the oats.

"Don't go getting your bloomers in a twist. Jack Benny's just trying to get your sister riled up. Divorce makes men mean-spirited, even when it was their idea in the first place. Maybe he just needs to pick a fight so he'll feel like the whole thing was Lydia Dale's fault.

"Anyway, I think he's bluffing. Why would he want this place? Jack Benny's too lazy for ranch work. He's too lazy for any work, if you ask me."

The oats finished, Georgeann jerked her head out of the bucket and nudged Donny with her nose, hoping for more. "Sorry, girl. That's all for now. How about I bring you a fresh bale of hay, huh? Be back in a minute."

Donny walked across the paddock carrying the empty bucket. When he got closer he gave the gate a good shove with his boot, making it swing wide. Mary Dell, still perched on the bottom rung, went along for the ride like a little girl swinging on a garden gate, smiling in spite of herself. Donny smiled too. He liked seeing his wife happy.

Mary Dell held on as Donny closed and relatched the gate, then hopped down and followed him toward the barn.

"Good riddance is what I say. Don't know why she ever married him in the first place. If she'd have just waited a little longer . . ."

"Now, don't start in," Mary Dell said. "You can't go laying all the blame at Lydia Dale's feet. Graydon owns some of this too, you know. He's not the first person who's had his heart broken. Nobody forced him to go hide out like a hermit, cutting himself off from the family. That was his doing."

"Nobody is saying it wasn't," Donny groused. "I just wish Lydia Dale had waited a little longer, that's all."

"But how was she to know? The war department said he was dead, and she believed it. We all did. And she did wait, Donny. She waited a whole year."

"Let's talk about something else. It's too hot to fight."

Donny stepped up to the water trough by the barn, took off his hat, doused his head with two ladles full of cool water, then shook off the excess moisture from his head before lowering the dipper back into the water and offering Mary Dell a drink.

"I'm not fighting," she said, wiping her lips with the back of her hand. "I'm just saying I wish you'd let the past be past. Lydia Dale needs us now. She's got nobody."

"Suppose so," he said with a shrug and dipped out a drink for himself.

Donny didn't resent his sister-in-law, not exactly. Any mistakes Lydia Dale made, she'd surely paid for ten times over being married to Jack Benny. But he felt bad for Graydon. Life had not treated him fairly, but ten years had passed since the war department had declared Graydon dead, nine since he'd come home.

About three years before, Donny drove up to Kansas and told Graydon it was time he got on with his life. His advice had not been well received. In fact, they'd come to blows, just like they had when they were boys, except this time their mother wasn't there to douse them with a bucket of cold water and pull them apart. He and Graydon didn't speak for more than a year. They were both stubborn. But to Donny's mind, Graydon was worse.

"Anyway," Mary Dell continued, handing him his hat from the fence post where he'd hung it, "maybe we can figure out some way to wind back the clock now that Jack Benny is going to be out of the picture."

"What do you mean?"

"Maybe we can get them together, like they were always meant to be."

Donny frowned deeply and shoved his hat low onto his brow. "Mary Dell, you're not to go messing with those two, you hear me? Every time you go poking your beak into other people's love lives, it turns out bad."

"It does not!"

"No?" Donny raised his hand and started counting off couples, digit by digit. "Cathy Mae Carradine and Randy Smith, Grace and Gordon Williams, Lila Tyrell and that traveling salesman . . ."

"Now that's not fair! Grace and Gordon were very happy together. Until the gunfight. And how was I supposed to know that salesman was already married?"

"To three different women in two different states." Donny shook his head and grinned. "You're no matchmaker, honey. Even if you were, my brother hates your sister now, almost as much as he loved her before. Let's you just leave bad enough alone."

Mary Dell shifted her shoulders with a grudging resignation. "Doesn't matter anyway. Lydia Dale has no more use for Graydon than he has for her."

Donny frowned, the complicated hackles of brotherly loyalty raised again. "What do you mean? She has no right to—"

Mary Dell raised her hands. "Calm down. I don't mean that she hates him or anything like that. It's just that when I brought up the idea of her maybe getting back in contact with Graydon, Lydia Dale said she's got no interest in him or anyone else. She is through with men forever."

Donny rolled his eyes. Lydia Dale was always so dramatic. He walked into the barn with Mary Dell still dogging his heels. She climbed onto the grain bin and sat with her legs dangling over the edge, watching him silently as he hefted a few fallen hay bales and put them back on top of the stack.

She looked pretty sitting up there, like a redbird on a perch, bright and perky in the scarlet sateen blouse she'd made herself, studded with purple buttons rimmed in gold and fitted as tight as could be over all God gave her.

After a few minutes he stopped to wipe the sweat from his brow and said, "Something on your mind?"

The sound of his voice brought her back to herself. "Well, yes. I wanted to talk to you about something. Something besides Lydia Dale. I went to see Dr. Brownback last week . . ."

Donny grinned and pushed his Stetson to the back of his head. "You did? Honey, does that mean you're . . ."

Mary Dell shook her head. She didn't have the heart to tell him that she had been pregnant, briefly. His face had already fallen like an undercooked cake.

"I just went in for a checkup. The doctor said . . . that is, I'd been thinking and she agreed, that it's time we look into adopting."

"We've been over this before. I want us to have a child of our own. A son. A Bebee."

"I know," Mary Dell said, trying to keep her tone understanding even though she really didn't understand, "but we've been trying for so long. I'm already thirty-one."

"So what? That's not so old. My momma had me when she was thirty-five."

"But she'd already had Graydon. If I haven't had a baby by now, after we've tried so hard . . ." Recognizing that stubborn glint in her husband's eye, Mary Dell tried another tack.

"You know, if we adopted, there's no reason we still couldn't keep trying for a baby of our own. If that didn't work, we'd still have our adopted baby. And it would be a Bebee, honey. It would still carry your name. And you could teach him everything you know—how to ride a horse, and rope a steer, and run a ranch."

"Wouldn't be the same," Donny replied, grunting as he pressed a bale over his shoulders and onto the top of the stack. "And how do you know what kind of child you'd be getting? How do you know he'd be healthy? That the mother or father weren't drug addicts, or criminals, or carried some kind of disease?"

"Those adoption agencies check on that kind of thing," she reasoned, though she didn't know this for a fact. "They'd tell you if the baby was likely to have any problems."

"Maybe. But you'd never know for sure, and by the time you found out, it'd be too late. You couldn't just send it back, you know."

"No, of course not. But there's no guarantees with any child, is there? You take what you get and love them just the same. I mean, if we were to have a baby of our own . . ."

"He'd come out perfect—with your blue eyes, I hope. And my horse sense. The best of the Bebee line, because he'd have the best of both of us in him.

"The way I figure it," Donny said philosophically, taking a seat on a nearby bale of hay, "breeding a baby is a lot like breeding livestock. If you put good lines together, you're bound to come up with a good result, an even stronger bloodline than the two you started with. If it works with cattle, it oughta work with people. Just stands to reason."

Mary Dell wasn't about to argue with Donny when it came to livestock. He'd bred some of the best cattle in the county. But she couldn't help but feel that it was a mistake to apply those principles to people.

And anyway, Mary Dell didn't want a bull, she wanted a baby. Her baby. Whether born of her body or not. A child to love just because it was in her to do so, because babies were not created for what they gave to their families but because of what their families could give to them.

Mary Dell had never been very good at putting her feelings into words. Donny didn't have much patience for speeches or long explanations anyway, and as he'd said, it was too hot to fight. So she said, "Momma is planning a baby shower for Lydia Dale. I was thinking I'd give her that layette I made a while back. No point in letting it sit in a drawer and collect dust."

Donny reached out for her and buried his face in her hair, breathed in the scent of it, like strawberries and peaches, then moved his head lower, tracing a line of kisses from her ear to the soft flesh just above her collarbone.

"You smell so good."

"It's the shampoo. It's new."

He moved her knees apart and she wrapped her legs around the small of his back, locked her ankles one over the other, pulling him close. "What are you doing?" she teased. "I thought you said it was too hot."

"It is. Too hot to fight," he said, unbuttoning the top button of her red sateen blouse with one hand. "I've got a better plan."

She laughed. "I can tell."

He lifted his head, paused a moment, stared into her blue eyes. "Uh-huh. A much better plan. I say we try one more time to have a baby of our own, just one more. And if it doesn't work this time . . . we'll adopt. How does that sound?"

A slow smile spread across Mary Dell's face. "Like the best plan you've had in a real long time."

"Thought you'd say that."

He shifted her weight forward onto his hips, reached low with his hands to intertwine his fingers to create a cradle beneath her backside, and carried her toward the rickety wooden staircase that led to the haymow. Mary Dell squealed and wrapped her legs tighter around him to keep from falling.

"Donny! What are you doing?"

He grinned. "Well, now that we've got ourselves a plan, we might as well put it into action."

"Here?" She laughed. "Now? In the barn?"

"Sure, honey. Don't you know what haylofts are for? What kind of farmer's daughter are you?"

CHAPTER 10

November 1983

"Good riddance," Dutch mumbled through a mouthful of turkey and cranberries. "It's worth giving up child support just to be done with him. And to keep his hands off the ranch. Who needs him? We take care of ourselves and our own." He used his fork to point toward a serving bowl. "Lydia Dale, pass me some more of those potatoes, will you?"

Lydia Dale quickly complied with her father's request, then turned to nine-year-old Jeb, who was sitting slumped in his chair, kicking the leg of the dining room table with the toe of his shoe.

"Jeb, why don't you take your sister into the TV room? Go watch the parade. You don't want to miss seeing Santa Claus."

"The parade's already over," Jeb grumbled, giving the table leg another thump. "And there is no Santa Claus."

Cady dropped the fork she had been using to carve a crisscross design into her mound of uneaten mashed potatoes. "There is too! And he's going to bring me a Cabbage Patch Kid for Christmas. Isn't he, Momma?"

Lydia Dale arched her eyebrows. "Not if you keep shouting at the dinner table, he won't. Go on, you two. Jeb, see if you can find out what channel the game is on."

Dutch grinned at his grandson and scooped up another forkful of potatoes. "Cowboys versus Cardinals. We wouldn't want to miss that, would we, Jeb?"

The boy didn't answer. Instead, he got up from his chair and whispered a question in his mother's ear.

Lydia Dale frowned as she listened, then said, "I won't. You go on now. And take your sister with you, you hear?"

"Yes, ma'am." Jeb rolled his eyes and grabbed his sister's hand. "C'mon, shrimp."

"But we didn't have any pie yet," Cady protested.

Mary Dell, worried about the dark circles under Lydia Dale's eyes and the fact that she'd barely touched a bite of the Thanksgiving feast, stepped in.

"I'll bring your pie into the TV room. We can all have dessert while we watch the game. You save a good spot on the sofa for me and Grandma Silky. I heard the cheerleaders are trying out some new uniforms today. If we pay real close attention at halftime, I bet we can figure out how to copy the pattern. But you've got to help us, all right?"

Cady, whose stated goal in life was to be a Dallas Cowboys cheerleader and who had asked her aunt and great-grandmother to sew her a pint-sized cheerleader's uniform for Christmas, nodded and ran from the room. Jeb trailed behind her, slowly.

Dutch frowned. "What's the matter with that boy? Doesn't he like football?"

"He doesn't like people talking mean about Jack

Benny," Lydia Dale said. "Neither do I, Daddy. Not in front of the kids."

Dutch squirmed in his chair. "I'm sorry, honey. I'll mind my tongue in front of the children. But don't forget that you're my little girl too. You can't expect me to just sit back and say nothing when I see Jack Benny treating you so bad."

Dutch scowled, reached for the cut-crystal bowl of cranberry sauce, and plopped a big spoonful on his already heaping plate. Taffy had scolded him about watching his blood sugar earlier, but Dutch didn't think he ought to have to worry about his blood sugar on Thanksgiving. Besides, he always ate more when he was upset, and this divorce had him wolfing down his food so fast he hardly had time to taste it.

"I don't know how he could desert his wife and children, not to mention his unborn child," Dutch said, nodding at the seven-month mound that swelled under Lydia Dale's red plaid maternity smock, "to take up with that slut Carla Jean . . ."

Taffy gasped. "Dutch!"

Silky looked up from her plate. "Oh, for pity's sake, Taffy. Now that they kicked you out of the Women's Club, you can stop putting on airs. It's not like we've never heard the word before. Besides, I think Dutch has it about right.

"Lydia Dale, I think you're crazy to let Jack Benny get away with paying no child support, but," Silky said, "maybe your daddy is right. Maybe it's worth it just to see the back of him. And to get him to give up this crazy idea that he could lay claim to half our ranch! I'd rather drop dead of dysentery than see one acre of land pass out of the Tudmore line. I don't know what Jack Benny was thinking, supposing we'd lie down for that."

"He was thinking it would play out exactly how it

did," Donny said, pausing to pick a shred of turkey out of his teeth. "He never cared about the ranch. He just wanted to get out of paying child support. He was bluffing all along."

"I disagree," Aunt Velvet said, raising her fork and pointing it at her nephew-in-law. "Now, Donny, if you knew the history of the town the way you ought to, you'd know that every Benton born shares two qualities: a hunger for real estate and a willingness to do just about anything to get hold of it. How do you think they came to own so much of Too Much? But I don't think Jack Benny came up with this plan himself; he's not bright enough for that. This has Marlena's fingerprints all over it."

Velvet, much more interested in the conversation now that it had turned to matters historic, cleared her throat.

"This didn't start with Taffy and Marlena, you know. The enmity between the Tudmores and Bentons stretches all the way back to 1845 and the early days of Texas statehood, when the Bentons made an unsuccessful grab for this very piece of land," she said, pointing her fork to the green carpeting and, presumably, the brown earth that lay hidden under the floorboards of the house. "The Bentons have an insatiable desire for property, especially if they can come to it by underhanded means. It's in their blood."

"If that's so," Donny countered, "then why did Jack Benny give in so quick when Lydia Dale said she'd give up her right to child support if he gave up his claim on the ranch?"

"Because," Silky said, "Jack Benny is greedy and broke. His daddy won't give him a dime. Marlena Benton carries a lot of influence with the women of this town, but none at all with her husband—or her son. Try as she might, she never could control that boy. If she had, he might have turned out to be a halfway decent man instead of still *being* a boy—or at least still acting like one. She spoiled that child."

Velvet clucked her tongue. "Well, if you ask me . . ."

Lydia Dale, who had been quietly sawing her turkey into smaller and smaller bites, looked up from her plate. "Could we talk about something else?"

"Lydia Dale is right," Taffy said, raising her napkin daintily to her lips. "We shouldn't be talking about Jack Benny that way. He's still Jeb and Cady's father, and with the baby coming in just a couple more months . . ."

She turned toward Lydia Dale with an expression of motherly concern.

"Honey, are you sure you want to go through with the divorce? This . . . infatuation of Jack Benny's is bound to burn itself out. Marriage is a two-way street, you know. Maybe if you could just try a little harder."

Mary Dell could see her sister's jaw tighten at Taffy's suggestion, but she didn't say anything, just sat silently staring down at her bulging stomach.

"Momma!" Mary Dell shouted. "How can you say such a thing? Lydia Dale did everything she could to keep her marriage together. Nobody could have done more!"

"I'm not saying she didn't, Mary Dell. I'm just suggesting that she could give it a little more time, try to see things from Jack Benny's perspective, figure out where and why things started to go wrong or what more she could have done to make things work."

"Like what?" Mary Dell scoffed.

Taffy cast her glance upward, her eyes drifting to and fro as if some new insight regarding her daughter's failed marriage might be written on the popcorn ceiling. "Well. For instance, like trying harder to get along with her in-laws."

Mary Dell's face flushed. She was used to Taffy's

thoughtless comments, her self-absorption, her obsession with being accepted into the town's social circles, but this was too much. She was about to lay into her mother and rise to her sister's defense, but was interrupted by the sound of silverware being dropped on Taffy's best china with a clatter and Grandma Silky's raspy bark.

"Oh, for heaven's sake, Taffy! Your own daughter is seven months pregnant by a cheating husband who deserted her for some round-heeled barmaid, and you're *still* going on about Marlena and getting tossed out of the Women's Club?" Silky shook her head, her expression a mixture of fury and hopelessness.

"I'm not going *on* about it," Taffy said in a defensive tone. "Of course I care that Lydia Dale is suffering. But I'm suffering too, you know. This is the first time in ages that I won't be able to go to the Christmas Ball. And I've lost all my friends . . ."

Silky sat up a bit taller, locking eyes with her daughter over the top of the wicker cornucopia stuffed with orange and yellow chrysanthemums.

"Taffeta Tudmore Templeton, you listen to me. Those women are not your friends. If they were, they'd have stood up for you against Marlena, voted down her motion to vote you out. But they didn't. They went along in lockstep with Marlena because that's what they do. They are never going to change.

"Frankly, I'm glad you're out of that silly club. Now maybe you'll start acting sensible. Maybe you'll finally see who and what really matters. Your children, your grandchildren, your husband, your family. Because these are the people who care about you, Taffy. We are the ones who love you."

Taffy wiped her nose with her napkin. "I know, Momma," she said. "But it's not just that. I'm worried about my daughter too." She looked at Lydia Dale. "I don't want you to end up all alone and with no friends, like me. Face it, with three little children, you'll be hard-pressed to find another husband. That's why I think you ought to give Jack Benny a little more time to come to his senses. Maybe go see one of those marriage counselors."

Lydia Dale lifted her head. Her eyes were dry, but her voice was choked. "It's Thanksgiving. There must be better things to talk about. Something we're thankful for. Anything but Jack Benny. Please?"

Mary Dell glanced toward Donny, a question in her eyes. He gave his head a quick jerk, a smile twitching at the corner of his lip, giving Mary Dell tacit permission to go ahead and say what she had to say.

"As a matter of fact, we do have something to be thankful for. We weren't going to say anything until after supper, but . . ." Mary Dell grinned. Her eyes lit up like blue beacons.

"We're pregnant! Donny and I are going to have a baby!"

Mary Dell, who had mentally rehearsed this moment for weeks, had expected a response of whoops and hollers, hugs and handshakes. Instead, her declaration was met with an awkward silence. Donny realized what was going on.

"It's different this time," he assured them. "Mary Dell is already five months along. We waited to tell you until we knew for sure. The doctor says everything is just fine." Donny put his arm around Mary Dell's shoulders, beaming with pride.

"In another four months, our son, Howard Hobart Bebee, will be born. We're going to name him after my daddy. If he turns out to be anything like the old man, the world had just better watch out!"

Donny gave his wife a smacking kiss, and the room

erupted into exclamations and applause. Taffy jumped out of her chair to give her daughter a kiss and her son-in-law a hug, then collapsed into another chair, so overcome with hiccups and happy tears that Dutch had to pour her a glass of water.

Aunt Velvet, who hated emotional displays, said, "Well, that's just wonderful news! Howard Hobart Bebee. There was a Hobart family who settled in Too Much back in the 1890s. They didn't stay. The parents passed on, the son was killed in the Great War, and the daughter married an oilman and moved to Houston. I wonder if your daddy was any relation? I'll have to look it up," then pressed her fist against her mouth for a moment before whisking away Mary Dell's empty wineglass and scurrying into the kitchen to fill it with milk.

Grandma Silky, who, over the years, had spent hours on her knees praying for this, squealed, lifted her hands high, and shouted, "Thank you, dear Lord!"

After seeing to his wife, Dutch squeezed Mary Dell in a big bear hug and lifted her off the ground. "If that don't beat all! And here I just thought you was getting fat like your old man!" He punched Donny in the shoulder and declared him a prime bull before pouring himself and his son-in-law two fingers of good bourbon.

Donny, who had never before broken his post-nuptial vow to steer clear of the hard stuff, clinked his glass against his father-in-law's before toasting his unborn child and tossing the bourbon back in one gulp.

While Taffy was sitting in the chair, one hand resting against her heart to check for palpitations, and Aunt Velvet was in the kitchen pouring the milk, and Grandma Silky was walking around praising Jesus, and Dutch was pounding Donny on the back to keep him from choking to death, Lydia Dale gave her sister a hug.

"I'm so happy for you!"

"Me too!" Mary Dell laughed, hugging her sister back, but when she pulled away, Mary Dell could see that something was bothering her.

"Are you all right?"

"Yes. I'm fine. I mean . . . it's not anything I should bother you about, not right now anyway. It's just that . . . you and Donny sent me another check. Now that Jack Benny isn't helping out on the ranch, I don't feel right about taking the money."

Mary Dell waved her hand. "Don't worry about it. Jack Benny was never that much help anyway. And you've got to live on something, don't you?"

"I was thinking I might get a job."

Mary Dell rolled her eyes. "With two children and a baby on the way? Don't be crazy. Besides, you're part owner of the ranch. You're entitled to a share of the profits."

"But Donny is doing all the work. I just don't feel right about it, Mary Dell."

"Oh, stop it. You'd do the same for me. We're the only sisters we've got. Like Daddy said, 'We take care of ourselves and our own.' And, anyway, you and I have to stick together. If only to keep Momma from riding roughshod over all of us."

Mary Dell laughed, trying to keep things light, but Lydia Dale's face was serious.

"I would do the same for you, Mary Dell. If you needed it, I'd do anything I could to help you. I hope you know that."

"I know."

Lydia Dale smiled, looked her sister up and down. "I don't know how you were able to keep it a secret so long. Five months along! You can hardly tell."

Mary Dell looked down. "Well, these ta-tas of mine

make it easier to hide. Kind of balances everything else out."

"I'm so excited for you! Howard Hobart Bebee. How do you know it's a boy? Did you have one of those new ultrasound things?"

Mary Dell made a face. "We had one, but the picture was fuzzy and the baby was turned the wrong way, so we couldn't see anything. The doctor said we could get an amniocentesis test if we wanted; that would have told us the sex for sure, but we didn't want to risk it. The heart looked fine, so that's all I was worried about. I'm calling it Howard because Donny is sure it's a boy. I don't care one way or the other. I just want it to be happy, and healthy, and kindhearted."

Lydia Dale moved close to give her sister another hug. The two sisters' bellies were pressed so close that, but for the separation of skin, tissue, and amniotic fluid, the unborn cousins could have had a hug of their own.

"That's all any mother wants," Lydia Dale said. "And he will be, Mary Dell. Howard Hobart Bebee will be all that and more. I'm sure of it."

CHAPTER 11

December 1983

Very early on Christmas morning, Mary Dell woke to the sight of Donny coming through the bedroom door wearing a Santa suit and carrying her breakfast on a tray.

"Merry Christmas, little momma!"

Mary Dell rubbed her eyes and took a look out the window. It was still dark. She groaned and propped herself up on pillows.

"What time is it?"

"Five o'clock. I was up half the night putting Howard's Christmas presents together, so I figured I might as well make breakfast. Look here," he said as he set the tray down next to Mary Dell on the bed, her stomach now too prominent to allow him to place it over her lap. "We've got eggs and orange juice and bacon and grits. The bacon is a little burnt, and the grits are a little runny, but I think they'll taste all right."

Mary Dell kissed him on the cheek. "Bacon is good a little burnt. Thank you, honey. That's quite an outfit you're wearing."

Donny held out his arms so she could get the full effect. "Saw it on sale at the Woolworth's in Waco. It came with a sack to put the presents in too, but it wasn't big enough to hold everything so I didn't fool with it."

Mary Dell sipped her orange juice, wishing Donny had thought to make coffee too. "We've got too many presents to fit in Santa's sack?" She yawned.

"Not us. Howard. Let me tell you something, those people who print 'some assembly required' on toy boxes are the biggest liars on God's green earth. I about needed an engineering degree to put the fire engine together. Still have three washers left over. Can't figure out where they go."

Mary Dell blinked several times, willing herself into wakefulness. "Fire engine? You bought our unborn child a fire engine?"

Donny grinned. "Yep. Big enough to ride in. Has a siren, a battery-powered engine, and a hose that squirts real water. Finish up your breakfast and come out to the tree. You can see for yourself."

Donny shared his wife's love of all things big, gaudy, and shiny. Together they had picked out the biggest, gaudiest, shiniest tree they could find—a nine-foot-tall fir with a circumference as wide as a fat woman in a hoopskirt, coated in a thick spray of white flocking flecked with gold glitter—and decorated the branches with fourteen strings of blue bubble lights before hanging them with purple, gold, scarlet, and lime-green glass ornaments and five boxes of silver tinsel.

The living room of the two-bedroom, two-bath double-wide Donny and Mary Dell bought when they married and installed on its own electric and sewer system about a half mile from Dutch and Taffy's place wasn't large. The Christmas tree by itself took up about half the floor space; the toys took up most of the rest.

Besides the fire engine—which truly was big enough for a child, and not just a toddler but a child of seven or eight, to ride in—the gifts Donny purchased included a football, a basketball, a baseball and bat, a four-foot-tall stuffed giraffe, a replica of the space shuttle made from chunky plastic and suitable for toddlers, a red toy lawn mower that spat out soap bubbles, two tiny green bicycles with training wheels already attached, as well as a larger purple one with a white banana seat and matching wicker basket, and an even bigger blue bike with a horn on the handle and orange flames painted on the chain guard, a fishing pole and tackle box, a toy six-shooter and holster, a teeny-tiny Western shirt of blue gingham with rhinestone snaps instead of buttons and white fringe on the yoke, a tiny white Stetson, shiny black cowboy boots with silver stitching, a prancing plastic palomino horse suspended on springs hung from a metal frame, a set of wooden ABC blocks, a jack-in-the-box, a toy doctor's kit, a chemistry set, and an entire set of the Encyclopedia Britannica.

Mary Dell's eyes bulged when she saw the evidence of her husband's generosity.

"Donny! Have you lost your mind? Where did you get all this?"

Donny's smile faded. He scratched his left ear.

"Mostly at Toys'R'Us in Waco," he said. "But I found the boots, shirt, and hat in the Sears catalog, and I bought the encyclopedia from a man who knocked on the door one day while you were over at your sister's. What's the matter? Don't you like it?"

Mary Dell spread out her hands helplessly, searching for words. "Well, it's . . . it's just . . . you've got four bicycles here, honey. How many do you think we need?"

"I bought those other three for your sister's kids. Jeb's been moping around so much. Thought it might cheer him up, and of course, I had to get something for Cady and the new baby too."

"That was real nice of you, Donny."

"We can afford it, if that's what you're worried about," he said defensively.

"I'm not worried," Mary Dell said gently, aware that she'd wounded his pride. "It's just that this is an awful lot of Christmas. What's there left to give him next year?"

"Have you been to that Toys'R'Us store?" Donny asked. When Mary Dell shook her head, he said, "Well, it's about as big as Texas Stadium, no kidding, stocked floor to ceiling with toys, sports equipment, remote-control cars, games, bicycles—even playhouses and swing sets. I didn't buy but a tenth of what I could have. Didn't want to overwhelm the little guy, not right off."

Mary Dell tried to suppress a smile. "That was good thinking, honey."

Donny narrowed his eyes. "Fine. Make fun of me if you want," he said, "but this is my first and probably my only son we're talking about. He's going to have the best of everything and all the opportunities I never did.

"If Howard wants to be a rancher, then fine. He can be a rancher. And if he wants to be a doctor, a lawyer, a fireman, an astronaut, or a quarterback, or president of the United States, then he can do that. I don't want anything to hold him back. I don't know what our boy is going to do, but I do know it's going to be something great. Something you and I could never have imagined. He's going to surprise us, darlin'."

Donny crossed the room, stepping over the bubble

mower to reach his wife's side, knelt down in front of her chair, and rested his head against Mary Dell's stomach.

"You wait and see if I'm not right. This boy is going to be something special. One of a kind. Aren't you, Howard?"

The baby kicked. Donny looked up at Mary Dell with a broad grin.

"Did you see that? He heard me!"

Mary Dell bent forward and kissed the top of her husband's head.

CHAPTER 12

February 1984

Donny was a good provider, and that was fortunate because he had very definite ideas about who should and shouldn't play the role of family breadwinner.

Not long after they married, Mary Dell had put out the idea of her getting a job in town, but Donny was absolutely against it. Since Mary Dell figured she'd soon be too busy raising children to work outside the home, she had not fought him on it. However, when a third miscarriage made it apparent that motherhood was not going to be her full-time career anytime soon, she decided it was time to think about resurrecting her childhood dream of becoming a dress designer.

Though his position on the roles of men and women hadn't altered, Donny could see that Mary Dell was unhappy, so he withdrew his earlier objections to the idea of her working, *if* she could figure out a way to work from home and *if* it didn't interfere with her taking care of him and their home. At the end of a long day of work, he wanted to see his wife's pretty face. That was the best part of his day.

Mary Dell agreed to this. Using the $350 seed money he gave her, she purchased fabric, notions, a not-too-used used sewing machine, and booth space at the annual Methodist Women's Christmas Craft Show. This, Mary Dell decided, would be the perfect venue to launch her new clothing business.

She stitched up twenty dresses, all beautifully constructed and sewn from a collection of fabrics in colors, patterns, and textures that only Mary Dell could love, hung them up on a rack at the craft show, and waited for customers. None came. She didn't sell a single dress.

Mary Dell was heartbroken. But she was never one to wallow in self-pity, or waste expensive fabric, so she ripped out the seams (which she'd sewn in sizes that fit a more standard figure, in other words, one smaller and less voluptuous than her own), trimmed off the raveled edges, salvaged the yards of rickrack, lace, buttons, and froufrou trimmings, and spent the whole winter, spring, and summer turning the unwanted dresses into scrap quilts, with surprising results.

Those garish, gaudy, overtrimmed creations that no one besides Mary Dell would consider wearing didn't work as dresses, but when patched into crazy quilts and decorated with bits of beading, and ribbons, and lace, then further embellished with all the fancy hand embroidery Mary Dell had learned at Grandma Silky's knee— blanket stitches, bird tracks, back stitches, French knots, and whatnot—the results were charming and feminine, the kind of quilts a Victorian lady might lay at the foot of her brass bed or drape over the back of her red velvet sofa.

When the holidays rolled around, she carted her pile of quilts back to the craft fair, hoping to sell at least one or two. By lunchtime, every quilt was gone. Mary Dell was surprised and delighted by her success. Several ladies who arrived too late to buy a quilt tried to commission her to stitch up more in time for Christmas gift-giving, offering to pay in advance. She was flattered by the offers, but considering the pittance she earned per hour of effort and the tight schedule, Mary Dell declined.

But when two ladies, sisters, begged Mary Dell to give them a class in quilt making, Mary Dell agreed to give it a try. She'd been teaching quilting ever since.

Because it was impossible to accommodate more than three students at a time in the living room of Mary Dell and Donny's trailer and she only taught classes on Monday, Wednesday, and Friday, Mary Dell never made much from her classes. However, she did earn enough to support her fabric habit, make payments on a fancy made-in-Switzerland sewing machine, and take Donny out for a round of beers and an evening of line dancing at the Ice House every other Saturday. Teaching quilting was more of a hobby than a business, but Mary Dell enjoyed it.

Of course, she had her fits and starts. It took time for her to appreciate that what seemed obvious to her was not always obvious to others and to understand how to explain things in clear and simple language. The most important quality in a good teacher, she realized, was the ability to instill confidence in her students, to give them permission to experiment and help them realize that mistakes aren't really "mistakes" as such, but an opportunity to learn something new or rethink your original idea and come up with a different one, sometimes a better one. Her biggest and best tools for communicating that were her sense of humor, her ability to laugh at herself, and her insistence that quilting was supposed to be *fun*. If it wasn't fun, Mary Dell often told her students, then it was time to take a break.

When students saw that even the teacher had her "uh-oh" moments and could chuckle about them, they didn't feel so self-conscious about their failures. As the years passed and Mary Dell honed her communication skills and added to her own knowledge about the history, art, and techniques of quilting, she became a very good teacher.

About five years after she began teaching quilting, Mary Dell was flipping through the glossy pages of *Quilt Treasures,* her favorite quilting magazine, when she came upon a set of instructions explaining how readers could submit designs to the magazine. Mary Dell was excited right down to the tips of her pink cowboy boots. Until then, she'd never stopped to consider that the quilts shown in magazines might come from the imaginations of ordinary people—people like her!

Without telling anyone what she was doing, Mary Dell took and printed several photos of a quilt she'd designed using a Churn Dash block, wrote a pattern and cover letter, and sent everything off to C. J. Evard, editor-in-chief of *Quilt Treasures* magazine, Dallas, Texas.

Then she waited.

While she waited, she conjured up mental images of what C. J. Evard, who she'd decided must be named Claudia Jean but went by her initials because it sounded more genteel, was like. Mary Dell spent a lot of time thinking about C. J. Evard, coloring in the outline she'd created in her own imagination, until the name C. J. Evard summoned up a three-dimensional image in Mary Dell's mind, an independent and glamorous woman who lived the sort of life others could only dream of.

She was, Mary Dell decided, a tall and willowy natural blonde with hazel-green eyes. Being a businesswoman, C. J. Evard dressed in suits with big shoulder pads made of satin or shantung, maybe even silk brocade. She read a lot, being an editor and all, so Mary Dell figured she wore glasses, but very elegant ones that made her look wise and serious but stylish. She owned a pair of diamond earrings the size of dimes and always kept a thin gold pen tucked behind her ear. She was, of course, a brilliant quilter. She could join the points of an eight-pointed star in her sleep and could hand-quilt fourteen stitches to the inch. She was a master of every technique—piecing, appliqué, reverse appliqué, trapunto, foundation piecing, English paper piecing, and a bunch of other styles and techniques that Mary Dell had probably never even heard of.

Miss Evard (Mary Dell had decided that she must be single. How would a married woman have had time to develop all these accomplishments and run a whole magazine?) was well traveled. She had gone to college. And Paris and Rome. She had a big office with an enormous white French Provincial desk and a secretary who hung on her every word, following her down the hall taking notes on everything Miss Evard said.

Mary Dell was sure that Miss Evard was always on the lookout for new talent. And that when she saw the photos of Mary Dell's quilt and read the pattern, she would be so overcome that her knees would actually go weak. She would have to sit down for a moment to collect herself, her heart palpitating beneath the lapels of her silk brocade suit. Then she would press a button that would sound a buzzer to bring her secretary, who Mary Dell had decided was named Mrs. Frost, to her desk, pen and pad in hand.

C. J. Evard would look up at Mrs. Frost with tears of joy in her eyes and say, "Mrs. Frost, take a letter. . . ."

A letter. *The* letter! The letter that would change Mary Dell's life! But not more than she wanted it to. Not in any way that might upset Donny or mean she had to leave Too Much. Well, not very often. Maybe just once or twice a year. Maybe to Houston? Or Paris? No. That would be too far. Houston, then.

After three months, a letter in a creamy envelope with a *Quilt Treasures* logo bearing a Dallas postmark did arrive. Mary Dell took a deep breath, opened the envelope, and pulled out a letter that said:

Dear Quilter,

Thank you very much for your recent submission to *Quilt Treasures* magazine. While your work is interesting, it does not meet our needs at this time.

Cordially,

C. J. Evard
Editor-in-Chief

It would be the first of many such letters she would receive. Mary Dell refused to give up.

Her Wednesday class was her favorite because it was composed of her three original students, women who had signed up for her very first class and become friends. Pearl and Pauline Dingus were the eldest and youngest of the six daughters of Marvel Anne Dingus and the Reverend Charles Dingus, retired former minister of the First Baptist Church. Susan Satterfield, known as Sweetums, was their cousin.

After so many years together, the Wednesday classes were more like open sewing sessions than formal quilting lessons. She felt funny about taking money from the Wednesday group, but the ladies insisted on continuing to pay the five-dollar-a-week class fee, so Mary Dell worked hard to make sure they got their money's worth, continually searching out new techniques and projects to challenge them.

This week, because Valentine's Day would soon be upon them, the ladies were working on wall hangings with a hearts-and-flowers motif. The design was Mary Dell's own, but her students had realized long ago that Mary Dell's success in fabric selection was limited to crazy quilts. Pearl, Pauline, and Sweetums always picked out their own fabric. While the three women worked on their wall hangings, Mary Dell hand-stitched the binding on a crib quilt for Lydia Dale's baby.

"I thought you already made a baby quilt for Lydia Dale," Pearl commented when Mary Dell explained what she was working on.

"Lydia Dale didn't like it. She didn't come right out and say so, but she said that she wasn't sure that orange, pomegranate, and lime would go in a nursery with yellow-striped wallpaper. Momma said it looked more like a fruit salad than a baby quilt."

Pearl chuckled. "Orange, pomegranate, and lime? That sounds like how one of my migraines looks."

Mary Dell tied off a stitch and shrugged. She was used to their teasing and tried not to take it personally. She liked what she liked and didn't care, not much anyway, that the rest of the world preferred to wear a different shade of rose-colored glasses.

"Well, *I* thought it was nice, so I kept it for Howard and made another quilt for Lydia Dale's baby. Good thing she's overdue, or I never would have finished in time. The doctor says if the baby doesn't come on its own by tomorrow, they're going to have to induce."

She snipped off the tail of the thread, flipped the now-finished quilt to the front, and asked, "What do you think?"

The women gasped.

"Gosh-all hemlock! Will you look at that?"

"Isn't it just the sweetest thing you ever saw?"

"Well, I never did! It's beautiful!"

The baby quilt, composed of six-inch Grandmother's Fan blocks, was intricately and precisely stitched with a skill few quilters could hope to match. Knowing Mary Dell, the perfection of the stitching didn't surprise the women, but the color composition did.

The "slats" of the fan, radiating like pointy-edged flower petals surrounding a center circle of deep yellow the color of egg yolks laid in winter, were made up of small-scale prints of jade, emerald, sapphire, cobalt, azure, and amethyst, rich colors, exotic colors, radiant colors, like gemstones lying at the bottom of a tropical lagoon or orchids growing wild behind crumbling walls of a secret garden, colors that none of the women would have thought to put into a baby quilt but, especially when set against a background of egg yolk yellow that matched the block centers, which looked exactly right together, surprising but not jarring, harmonious but not dull. It was a stunning quilt.

Pauline, who was a little bit nearsighted, which probably explained why the points of her quilts never quite matched, put her hand against her cheek and leaned down to get a closer look at the quilt.

"Mary Dell, you've made some awful nice quilts in

your time, but this is the best ever. So pretty! Honey, if I didn't know you were the only woman in three counties who could stitch six-inch Grandmother's Fan blocks and have every one of them come out perfect, I'd have said somebody else made this quilt. Or at least chose the colors."

Mary Dell's skin was thick but not impermeable, and she frowned, annoyed by the backhanded nature of Pauline's compliment.

"Lydia Dale picked out the fabric," she admitted.

The women exchanged knowing glances. It all made sense now. Lydia Dale didn't quilt but she had beautiful taste. When Sweetums decided to redecorate her family room, she'd asked Lydia Dale to help her pick out wallpaper and paint.

Pauline didn't want to hurt Mary Dell's feelings, but felt compelled to point out what she was sure everybody else was thinking. "Mary Dell, honey, have you ever thought about asking your sister to help pick out your quilt fabric? Because I'll tell you . . ." She sighed and clasped her hands to her breast, seemingly enraptured as she gazed at the beautiful baby quilt. "If she did, I think the fair judges would have awarded your quilts a pile of blue ribbons by now, instead of all those honorable mentions."

"They weren't *all* honorable mentions," Mary Dell mumbled as she heaved her pregnant body out of the chair she'd been sitting in. "I got a third place once."

"I know," Pauline replied. "I'm just saying you deserve better. If your sister were helping you, maybe you'd finally get the credit you deserve. Who knows? You might even get a design accepted by that quilting magazine you're always writing to."

Two months previously, Mary Dell had received yet another "thanks but no thanks" form letter from C. J.

Evard. Disappointed again but still undaunted, she had submitted still another design and sent it to Dallas via registered mail earlier that week.

She was certain that this quilt, utilizing an original block she called Tricky Tumblers, would be the one that would finally get C. J. Evard's attention. The "trick" of Mary Dell's design was that the central block, which was based on the classic Tumbling Block pattern, required none of the Y-seams that even accomplished quilters dreaded. All modesty aside, it was a clever, even ingenious design, and she was certain Miss Evard would agree. However, Mary Dell didn't mention this to her students. They'd see soon enough that her quilt designs could stand on their own without anyone's help—even her sister's.

Mary Dell turned her back to the women and started folding up the baby quilt.

Sweetums, who came by her nickname honestly, said in a gentle but hesitant voice, "Nobody is trying to hurt your feelings, Mary Dell. Everybody in this room knows you're the best quilter in this whole part of the state, maybe in all of Texas. But . . ."

Pearl, the oldest and bossiest of the Dingus sisters, a preacher's child and a big proponent of "speaking the truth in love," became impatient with all this pussyfooting.

"Mary Dell, it's time you faced facts. When it comes to quilting, you've got all the talent in the world but no more taste than a hothouse tomato. However, Providence has paired you with a loving sister who can't sew a stitch but is amply supplied with the color sense you so sorely lack.

"Don't you see? You and Lydia Dale are like biscuits and gravy; one is too dry and the other too wet, but put them together and you've got yourself a meal! And if you'd just put aside your stubborn, sinful pride and admit that, you might finally be able to make use of the gifts and talents the good Lord has granted you!"

Mary Dell was still standing with her back to the others, trying to toss their comments into the trash can of her mind, the same way she tossed all those cheap rayon honorable mention ribbons into the actual trash every August after fair week. But when she heard Pearl accuse her of pride, she winced.

Mary Dell could never be jealous of her sister personally, but Pearl's blunt assessment forced her to admit that she was still jealous of her sister's accomplishments—specifically of the glass display case filled with pageant sashes and tiaras that still held center stage in her parents' living room. Actually, not that the pageant memorabilia itself made her jealous, but the fact that, after all this time, Taffy still insisted on showing these relics off to every person who visited the house, from the minister's wife to the man who delivered their propane.

How silly.

Silly of Taffy to still try to bask in her daughter's glow and silly of Mary Dell to still be trying so hard to secure a spot in Taffy's display cabinet, believing that winning a blue ribbon would also win her mother's approval. What an idea.

It wasn't wrong for a child to desire her mother's admiration, but Mary Dell wasn't a child anymore. Nor was it wrong for her now, as a woman, to have dreams and ambition, or to desire a little recognition for her talents. That was natural enough, wasn't it? Where would the world be if people hadn't been created with the longing to lean into life, to push the boundaries inch by inch, to do things that were hard simply because they *were* hard?

As a girl, in Sunday school, Mary Dell had been taught that work, the absolute necessity to scratch out a living, was part of the curse of original sin, and she believed it. But wasn't it also a kind of salvation? No one had told her so, but Mary Dell thought it must be true.

As a true daughter of Texas and a Tudmore to boot, Mary Dell knew in her bones that her town, her state, her world, the harsh, hot, dry, and vast land she sprang from, stark and starkly beautiful, could never have been peopled or planted without the stubborn ambition of her ancestors, those women of strong conviction from whom she had inherited her desire to leave an imprint on the world, some mark, however small, even if she had to patch it together from imagination and scraps of cloth.

To dream was not wrong. And ambition was no sin.

But to be so desperate to gain a toehold in the trophy case of a mother's heart, to be hobbled by childish envies, desiring prizes awarded only for solo performance, so unwilling to share the spotlight and credit that it thwarted the ambitions you were born, equipped, and uniquely placed to fulfill, *was* wrong. And proud. And pride, they'd told her in Sunday school, wasn't just wrong; it was a sin. She believed that too.

Mary Dell turned around. Pearl stared at her with arched eyebrows and an expression that dared Mary Dell to refute the facts as she'd laid them out.

"I heard you," Mary Dell said.

"And?"

"And," Mary Dell said in an exasperated voice, "although Lydia Dale is due to deliver any second, and I'm about five weeks behind her, and neither of us will be doing anything besides breast-feeding and changing diapers anytime soon, the next time I start a new quilt, I'll ask her to help me pick out the fabric."

Pearl smiled and sat back down at her sewing machine.

"How is Lydia Dale anyway?" Sweetums asked. "I haven't seen her in an age."

"Better now that the divorce is final."

Mary Dell squatted down to pick up some stray pins off the carpet and a pair of scissors she'd accidentally knocked off the counter, no easy feat in her swollen condition.

"Sometimes I wish Jack Benny would just leave town and never come back," she said, grunting as she got to the floor. "That man is so low you can't put a rug under him."

"His momma is just as bad," Pauline said, squinting as she tried to poke a piece of thread through the needle of her machine. "Marlena's been going around town dropping hints that your sister's baby isn't a Benton, that Lydia Dale had been stepping out on Jack Benny and that's the reason for the divorce."

"What!" Mary Dell's face flushed red. "Who's she been saying that to? That's a lie! Jack Benny was the one who was cheating, and Marlena knows it! How could she say something so terrible about her own grandchild?"

Looking furious enough to disembowel Marlena with the scissors she held clenched in her fist, Mary Dell tried to push herself up from the carpet, but was impeded by her big belly. Pearl jumped up from her sewing machine to help.

"Pauline," she scolded, "stop your gossiping. Nobody in town is going to believe that story. Everybody knows what Jack Benny is. Marlena is just mean and bitter. Everybody knows that too. Best thing to do is ignore her."

"But that's the problem!" Mary Dell exclaimed. "Everybody does ignore Marlena. It's about time somebody stood up to her!"

Pearl reached out her hand. Mary Dell grabbed it and tried to get to her feet, unsuccessfully.

"She's not worth it. You know what they say, 'Lie down with a dog, and you'll get up with a flea.' And Marlena Benton is definitely a dog. Of the female variety. If you take my meaning."

Pearl smiled momentarily, pleased with her little joke, and then frowned again as she looked down at Mary Dell, who was still struggling to get up.

"Here, honey. Let's try this."

Pearl grabbed both of Mary Dell's hands, braced her feet against the floor, counted off one-two-three, and pulled as hard as she could.

Mary Dell got to her feet with a grunt but immediately doubled over, groaning in pain. Sweetums and Pauline leapt up and scurried to her side.

"Oh, honey! Oh, my!"

"Does it hurt?"

"Is it time? Is it the baby?"

"No!" Mary Dell protested, gripping her stomach. "It can't be. It's too soon!"

But another groan, another wave of pain, and a flush of fluid proved her wrong.

Pearl, herself a mother of five, stroked Mary Dell's back, spoke in a calm and even voice, assured her that it wasn't so very early, asked her if she'd packed a hospital bag, then looked up and started issuing orders.

"Here, honey. Come sit down in this chair for a minute while I go pack your toothbrush and robe. Sweetums, take my keys out of my purse and pull my car up to the door. Pauline, get on the phone. Call the doctor, Miss Silky and Miss Velvet, Taffy and Dutch, and go find Donny. Tell him the baby is coming."

CHAPTER 13

Pauline phoned Dr. Brownback but was unable to reach Silky, Velvet, Taffy, or Dutch because only a few minutes before, Lydia Dale had come into the TV room and announced that her own labor pains were ten minutes apart. They were already on their way to the hospital, so flustered they hadn't thought to call Mary Dell, not knowing she was following close behind.

Pauline hadn't been able to find Donny either. She drove to the barn to look for him. His truck was parked outside, but when she called his name, he didn't answer. Just that morning he'd decided to saddle up Georgeann and ride the fences, making note of any sections that needed repair. In another couple of weeks, he figured he'd have to start sticking closer to home, in case the baby came during the day.

Lydia Dale's baby came quickly. Four hours after she'd arrived at the hospital, a nurse entered the maternity waiting room and told the assembled relatives that

Rob Lee Benton, a healthy, eight-pound, twelve-ounce boy with long eyelashes and a perfectly formed head as round and bald as a cue ball, had been born and would be available for viewing through the window of the newborn nursery in about half an hour.

When asked, the nurse told them that Mary Dell was doing just fine, that there was nothing to worry about, that first children always took longer to be born.

"But isn't it too soon?" Dutch asked, his weathered face creased with anxiety.

"We're taking good care of your daughter, Mr. Templeton. And your grandchild. The neonatologist has been called. As soon as the baby is born, it will be taken to the NICU. They have all the right equipment and staff to care for preemies," she said, then patted him on the arm and left the room with rubber-soled efficiency.

Dutch dug three quarters out from the pocket of his jeans and dropped them into the vending machines. He bought two candy bars for Jeb and Cady and a cup of bad coffee for himself.

The nurse had spoken with authority, using words that Dutch didn't understand—"neonatologist" and "NICU"—but she hadn't answered his question.

Was it too soon?

After all the years of waiting, the pain of watching his daughter's hopes of motherhood be raised and dashed over and over again, was this baby, too, coming too soon? Was another of his grandchildren going to die before it had even lived?

Dutch went to church every week of his life and served as an usher every third Sunday of the month. Even so, he'd never been much of a praying man, but he prayed now, as hard as he could. Staring into the black lake of a cardboard coffee cup, he prayed to the God he'd always believed in but had spent precious little time talking with.

CHAPTER 14

Donny got home later than he'd planned. Georgeann had picked up a stone in her shoe. Donny was able to dig it out, but the horse kept favoring one leg and so he decided to come home on foot, leading her by the reins.

He removed Georgeann's saddle and bridle, washed her down, curried her, fed her, and checked her leg again to make sure it wasn't swelling. Then he hopped into his pickup and drove home, where he found Pauline's note taped to the front door.

He didn't even go into the house, didn't take time to change his dirty boots or shower off the smell of human and horse sweat, just jumped back into the truck and drove to the hospital in Waco as fast as he could, which was pretty fast. The drive normally took forty-five minutes. Donny made it in thirty-four.

He spent the whole of the trip worrying about what was happening to his wife and son right at that moment, cursing himself for deciding to check the fences today, cursing Georgeann for picking up a stone, cursing. It was only the twelfth of February. The baby wasn't due until the twentieth of March. Five weeks too soon. But was it *too* soon? Too soon to survive?

In the months since he had learned of Mary Dell's pregnancy, he had spent endless hours imagining all the fine things his son would be and do.

Dr. Bebee. Astronaut Bebee. H. H. Bebee, Attorney for the Defense. Professor Bebee. Howard "Hard Hands" Bebee, the best wide receiver in the history of the Dallas Cowboys. Senator Bebee. President Bebee.

No title would be out of his reach, no honor beyond his grasp. His son would be able to do anything he dreamed of doing—go to college, travel the world, reach for the stars. That was what Donny had wanted for his boy—everything. A world without limits.

Now he would trade it all, the titles, the honors, the fantasy son Donny had created in his own mind, for something simpler but more wonderful, something concrete: a heart that could beat, lungs that could breathe, a living child.

Hurtling down the empty highway through the dark of night, Donny said aloud, "Just let him live, Lord. That's the only thing that matters. Let him live. Do that, and I'll never ask you for another blessed thing."

CHAPTER 15

Because Mary Dell had not stopped bleeding on her own after the delivery and the doctor had ordered the administration of a Pitocin drip, essentially putting her back into a mild labor to force the uterus to clamp down, she was pale and still in some pain. But when Donny entered the hospital room, she beamed.

"About time you showed up," she teased.

He walked to the side of the bed and kissed the top of her head, leaving his face buried in her hair because he was afraid if he looked at her, he might start to cry. After a moment, he collected himself and kissed her again, on the lips.

"I was here," he said. "Came as soon as I heard. I've been out in the waiting room with your folks all night, pacing and listening to your mother tell the story of how she almost died having you and your sister."

"How many hours was she in labor with us this time?"

Mary Dell asked. "Last time I heard that story, it was thirty."

"She's up to thirty-six now."

"Why didn't you come back here and sit with me instead? You could even have come into the delivery room if you wanted to. Didn't the nurses tell you?"

"They told me," he said gruffly. "But a man doesn't want to see his wife in that kind of condition."

Mary Dell shook her head. "Donald Bebee, that is about the silliest thing I've ever heard. If I had a nickel for every time I've come into the barn to find you with your arm stuck up a ewe's hoo-ha, I'd be a rich woman. If you can do that, why can't you watch your own child being born?"

"Because it's different, that's why."

She didn't ask him to explain because she knew he was done talking. And he didn't say more because he didn't want to tell her the truth—that he'd been afraid to come into the delivery room because he was worried that something was going to go wrong, and he couldn't bear the idea of not being able to do anything to stop it.

He'd seen it happen plenty of times. Animals sometimes died in labor, especially when the births came on early. Sometimes you could help, sometimes you couldn't. That was nature's way, but there was nothing in the world Donny hated more than feeling helpless. Hard enough to endure when he was dealing with cows and sheep, but the thought of being helpless to aid his wife and son was beyond imagining, beyond endurance. It was different.

But that was all over now. Donny took hold of Mary Dell's hand as he pulled a chair up next to the bed and sat down.

"You look beautiful."

"Do I?" She smoothed her hair with her hand. "Because I feel like somebody pulled me through a knot-hole backward."

"No," he protested. "You look beautiful. How's the baby?"

"He's fine," Mary Dell said, beaming again. "A little bit scrawny but fine. You should see the head of hair he's got on him—thick, brown hair, just like yours. His eyes are blue. I guess we'll have to wait and see if they stay blue, but they sure are pretty. Like big blue almonds. Don't know where he got those, not from my side. Does anybody in your family have eyes like that?"

Donny shook his head. "No."

"Well," Mary Dell said philosophically, "maybe he just looks like himself."

Mary Dell's happiness helped ease the knot of anxiety Donny had been carrying with him for the last twelve hours. But he knew the knot wouldn't untie itself completely until he could see his boy for himself. Until then, he wanted more information about his son, measurements more meaningful than how thick his hair was or how blue his eyes were, something concrete.

"What did he weigh?"

"Five pounds, four ounces," Mary Dell reported. "They say that's real good considering he came so early. One of the nurses told me they don't let babies go home until they're over five pounds. He started crying as soon as the doctor spanked his little hiney. His Apgar score was seven."

"Apgar score?"

"It's some kind of test they give babies right when they're born. They look at things like heart rate, breathing, color—things like that—and then add them up. Ten is a perfect score. Howard got seven."

Seven. If you translated that into grades, a seven was about a C. His son had taken his first test. And gotten a C.

It wasn't bad. But it wasn't great. It was average. Only a few hours ago, all he wanted in the world was for his boy to be allowed to live. And it had happened. He was lucky. His son was alive. He weighed five pounds, had brown hair, blue almond eyes, and scored a C on his Apgar test. A C wasn't bad, especially considering he'd come so early.

Still.

"When can I see him?" Donny asked.

"Soon, I think. I asked the nurse, but she didn't know for sure. Said the pediatrician was checking him out. I was only able to see him for a second myself. They whisked him out of here and off to the preemie nursery so quick, but he was squalling so I know his lungs were fine, and he was pink as a rose, so his heart must be pumping just fine too. Hope they bring him back soon, though," Mary Dell said and then closed her eyes.

She was quiet and Donny thought she might have dropped off. He couldn't blame her. He was tired too, and he hadn't been doing anything nearly as strenuous as having a baby. Donny closed his eyes too and dropped his head forward, but before he could doze off, Mary Dell opened her eyes and started talking again.

"How is Lydia Dale? They told me it was a boy. Rob Lee?" Donny nodded in confirmation. "That's a good, strong name. Have you seen them?"

"Not yet. Your momma and daddy are over in Lydia Dale's room now, down at the other end of the hall. The nurse was going to bring the baby in, so they could hold him," Donny said, wondering when he'd be able to do the same with his son. "I saw him through the nursery window. He's big, all right. Near nine pounds."

Mary Dell's eyes went wide. "Nine pounds?" she repeated, then shook her head. "That's darned near two of Howard. Must be some baby."

"Of course your sister's baby's bigger. He was two weeks late and Howard was more than a month early. It just stands to reason."

Mary Dell, picking up on the defensive tone in his voice, squeezed Donny's hand reassuringly. "I know. I was just thinking about Lydia Dale. She must feel more worn out than a flour-sack dress after pushing out nine pounds of baby. Poor thing."

"Suppose so," Donny said. "Rob Lee got a head start, but Howard will catch up to him."

Mary Dell was about to say something about it not being a race, but stopped herself. It was natural, she figured, for Donny to already be standing up for Howard. Men were so competitive, especially about their sons. Howard was less than two hours old, and already, Donny was a daddy. If you thought about it that way, it was sweet, him being so protective.

Mary Dell smiled to herself, imagining how protective Donny would be after he actually got to hold his son. How long were they going to have to wait for that anyway?

There was a knock on the door. Mary Dell pushed herself up higher on the pillows, and Donny sat up straight in his chair, supposing it was a nurse bringing Howard to them.

Instead, the door opened to reveal the face of a very short, pale, sandy-haired man wearing a white lab coat and a pair of wire-rimmed glasses. He seemed very young to be a doctor, and the glasses, which had enormous lenses, made him look a little goofy. The blue plastic tag pinned to the coat said "Dr. Tibbets."

"I'm a neonatologist on staff here at the hospital," he said. "That's a pediatrician who specializes in the care of newborns, especially infants who are born prematurely or have conditions that require special medical care."

Donny, whose eyes had been fixed on Dr. Tibbets's

face as he was speaking, interrupted as soon as the man paused to take a breath.

"How is my son?"

The doctor flipped a couple of pages on the clipboard he was carrying and looked down as he glanced over his notes.

"Considering his prematurity, Howard is doing quite well," the doctor said, in a voice that sounded just slightly surprised. "Five pounds, four ounces is just about what we'd expect to see in an infant of thirty-five weeks' gestation, the heart rate is good and sounds strong, respiration is good, response to stimulus is normal. His one-minute Apgar score was seven. And his five-minute score was eight."

Donny glanced at Mary Dell and grinned. Eight! Eight was a B. On the second test of his life, Howard had gotten a B. That was above average.

"However," the doctor went on, drawing out the word and squinting as he continued to study the chart, "your baby does have low muscle tone, unusually shaped ears, and his eyes are somewhat slanted. We'll have to do some tests to make absolutely sure, but the signs point strongly to trisomy 21."

Mary Dell glanced at Donny, who wasn't smiling anymore. The doctor removed his glasses, which made him appear older and more serious.

"Mr. and Mrs. Bebee, I know this is hard to hear, but I am almost certain your son has Down syndrome."

CHAPTER 16

People with Down syndrome have an extra chromosome in some or all of their cells, forty-seven instead of forty-six, possessing three copies of the twenty-first chromosome rather than the usual two. That is why physicians often refer to it as trisomy 21.

A syndrome, as Dr. Tibbets explained, refers to a collection of signs and symptoms that point to the presence of a particular disorder. Low muscle tone, a slanted set of the eyes, the almond shape that Mary Dell had noticed, and an unusual shape to the ears, symptoms which Howard possessed, are typical signs of Down syndrome. Other common signs of the disorder include a protruding tongue, a single crease across the center of the palms, and a wide space between the big toe and the one next to it. Howard didn't have any of those symptoms.

There are more than fifty characteristic features of Down syndrome, but the number, nature, and consequences of those characteristics vary greatly. Dr. Tibbets explained that it was too soon to know exactly how Down syndrome would affect Howard's health and quality of life, but babies with trisomy 21 often had difficulty suckling, so being patient and allowing plenty of time at feedings was important, especially since Howard was premature. He would probably be shorter than average, stocky, with a thick neck, short arms and legs, a wide face, and pushed-in nasal bridge.

Also, the doctor informed them, children with Down syndrome often suffer from respiratory ailments, and digestive problems, a slower walk due to the sort of low muscle tone Howard presented, as well as vision problems, hearing issues . . .

Dr. Tibbets kept talking. Mary Dell's eyes were focused on his face, but she couldn't take in all that he was saying; his words blurred into noise, the meaning of them muffled, pushed aside by the deluge of questions that flooded her mind.

Why had this happened? Was it something she had done? Or not done? Was it because of the miscarriages or her age? Was it because, before she'd realized she was pregnant, she'd gone line dancing at the Ice House with Donny and had a beer?

What would life be like for Howard? Would he ever be able to walk? Talk? Read a book? Ride a bicycle? Hold a job? A conversation? Fall in love? The doctor had said that Howard would probably be short, stocky and have a wide face, but what was he going to look like when he grew up? If he grew up. Would he?

When Mary Dell was in the third grade, Nancy Gayle's mother had given birth to a baby boy with Down syndrome, except they hadn't called it that back then. She'd overheard the school librarian and one of the teachers talking about it one day. They were whispering together about how Mrs. Gayle's baby had turned out to be a mongoloid and wasn't that a shame, bless her heart, and wondering how it could have happened. Nancy seemed so normal, at least that must be a consolation to her parents, bless them, what a shame, and how terrible Mrs. Guyle looked, saw her in the frozen food section of the Tidee-Mart holding a bag of peas and crying, poor thing, must have been so hard to send the baby off to that institution, but it was really for the best, wasn't it, a child like that would be such a burden, and they never lived long anyway, those mongoloid babies, so it must be for the best, mustn't it, and think how terrible it would be to have to mourn that child yet again, once when it was born and then again when it died, as it surely would soon, consider how much harder it would be on the family if they took that baby home and fell in love with it? Oh, it must be better this way, surely it must be. Mustn't it? Bless her. Poor thing.

Mary Dell hadn't thought about that baby boy with Down syndrome for years. Why would she? She'd never even seen him. She wasn't sure Nancy Gayle had either.

When they were in the fourth grade, Nancy missed a week of school. The day before she returned, the teacher told the class that they must be very kind to Nancy when she got back because her little brother had died, but they mustn't talk about it because it might make Nancy feel bad. And so they didn't, ever again. Since that day, she had never heard anyone mention that little boy. Mary Dell didn't even know the baby's name, or if he had one. She'd never heard him called anything but "that poor Gayle baby, the mongoloid."

Mary Dell wasn't going to let that happen to her baby, no matter how many extra chromosomes he had. She grabbed the metal railing of the hospital bed.

"We're not sending Howard to an institution!"

Dr. Tibbets jerked, startled by the interruption. "Of

course not, Mrs. Bebee. No one is suggesting that. For many, many years, and even into the seventies, it was standard procedure to institutionalize Down syndrome babies almost as soon as they were born. The feeling was that parents were not equipped to handle the medical needs of the children and that because the mortality rates were so high, it was better to separate the children from their parents before they could form a bond. In 1929, the average life expectancy for someone with Down syndrome was nine years."

Mary Dell let out a short, choked cry, and Donny turned his face to the wall. Dr. Tibbets held up his hand.

"Please, you misunderstand. Everything is different now. In the 1960s, two scientists conducted a study showing that the practice of institutionalizing children with Down syndrome had a negative impact on the patients. Depriving the children of the kind of emotional support and stimulation they would have received in a family was actually adding to the problem, causing lower life expectancy and cognitive ability."

"Cognitive ability?"

"Intelligence," the doctor explained, "as measured by IQ. People with Down syndrome generally have a lower-than-normal IQ."

Donny, who had been looking at the wall all this time, turned toward the doctor. "How low?"

The doctor spread his hands and gave a half shrug. "As is the case with just about every aspect of Down syndrome, cognitive ability varies from person to person. Most people with Down syndrome score in the mild to moderate range of intellectual disability, meaning their IQs fall anywhere between 40 and 70. However, some may suffer from more severe disabilities, while others may possess intelligence in the near-average or even completely average range. It's really too soon to tell. But you need to remember that IQ isn't the only measure of intelligence or ability. Howard is going to have strengths and weaknesses, just like any other child. The best thing you can do to help Howard reach his full potential is to build on his strengths and provide him with a loving home, filled with lots of intellectual stimulation.

"You," the doctor said, looking first at Mary Dell and then at Donny, "will be Howard's first, best, and most important teachers. There aren't many books written about Down syndrome, not for lay people, but I'll make copies of some articles from medical journals that might help you better understand what you're dealing with. And I'm going to get you two books written by people who *have* Down syndrome, so you'll know what your son might be capable of. The first, *The World of Nigel Hunt,* was written by a teenage boy from England back in 1967, when most people, even medical professionals, didn't believe people with Down syndrome could read books, let alone write them. The second, *My Friend David,* just came out recently. The coauthor, David Dawson, is a forty-seven-year-old man with Down syndrome."

Mary Dell, who was now taking in every single word the young physician uttered, said, "Forty-seven? So . . . people with Down syndrome can live into their forties? What about Howard?" she asked. "Will he . . . Can he . . ."

The doctor smiled benignly and stood up. He was only four years past his residency, but he already knew that there was only so much information a family could take in immediately after hearing a diagnosis of Down syndrome. Much of what he had said today, he would have to repeat again in the coming days. The father still looked shell-shocked. The mother, though, seemed to be handling it pretty well so far. That was encouraging.

"Again, when it comes to Down syndrome and life

expectancy, there is a wide range of outcomes. The numbers are rising all the time, however, and there is every reason to hope that your son will live a close-to-normal life span—forty, fifty, even sixty years or more is possible. Something your baby has going in his favor is his heart. About fifty percent of Down syndrome babies are born with heart defects. Obviously that is a worrisome and dangerous condition. But so far at least, Howard's heart appears to be completely normal. You're very lucky."

Donny, who was looking at the wall again, let out a sound halfway between a laugh and a grunt. Mary Dell shot him a look.

Dr. Tibbets took a business card out of the pocket of his lab coat. "I'll be back to go over the test results. If you have any questions before then, feel free to call me."

"I will."

"The biggest hurdle that people with Down syndrome face isn't the syndrome itself but the ignorance of others. The minute you leave here and for the rest of his life, Howard is going to run into people who will tell you what he can't do. Don't you believe it," he said earnestly, looking Mary Dell squarely in the eye. "And don't you accept it, not for a second. When people tell your son he can't, it's your job to tell him he can and to show him how. You've got to lead by example. You're his mother, Mrs. Bebee. He'll believe you."

CHAPTER 17

Visiting hours were over. Donny had gone home; the whole family had. Everyone except her and Lydia Dale, of course, who was asleep in her room at the far end of the hall. Rob Lee slept in a clear plastic bassinet placed next to her, waking every three hours and bleating like a hungry lamb, demanding to be put to the breast.

Earlier that day, one of the younger nurses, Mandy, brought a wheelchair into Mary Dell's room and took her to visit Lydia Dale and Rob Lee. Donny trailed along behind. Mary Dell held her new nephew in her arms and smiled at her sister, said he looked just like her and not a bit like Jack Benny and thank heaven for that. They both laughed and Donny smirked a little.

Next, Mandy wheeled Mary Dell to the NICU, past two scrawny babies in clear plastic boxes with bluish skin so thin you could see their veins. Howard was not closed up inside a plastic box. He was sleeping in a regular bassinet, just like the one Rob Lee was in, though, unlike his cousin, he had heart monitor wires taped to his chest and an IV tube taped to his ankle. It was a little jarring to see him hooked up to tubes and wires, but he was sleeping peacefully, his tiny hands tucked up under his chin. Compared to those other, scrawnier babies in the plastic boxes, Howard looked plump and healthy.

Mary Dell felt bad for those other babies and their parents, but the nurse told her not to worry. They were fine, just a little small, having come even earlier than Howard. After a few weeks, Mandy assured her, those babies would fill out, go home, and be just fine. By the time they went to kindergarten, nobody would ever guess they'd been premature or be able to tell the difference between them and other children.

Mandy scooped Howard out of the bassinet and settled him in Mary Dell's arms. Donny stood looking on, frowning, as Mary Dell, at Mandy's urging, unbuttoned the front of her nightgown, exposed her breast, and tried to get Howard to nurse, but the baby wasn't interested and kept turning his head away. When he yawned, Mary Dell tried to shove her nipple into his open mouth, hoping he'd take the hint, but that didn't work either. After ten minutes, Mandy said she had to go check on some other patients.

"It can take a while for the preemies to get the hang of it," she said as she took the baby from Mary Dell's arms and laid him in the bassinet, wrapping the receiving blanket around him so tight he looked like a tiny blue bean. "Don't worry, Momma. We'll try again tomorrow."

Now Mary Dell lay in her bed, too tired for sleep, staring out a crack of her partially opened door into the twilight half-light that is common in hospital corridors, places that simmer down after dark but are never completely at rest, the maternity ward the most restless of all.

There was a shift change at ten. Near midnight, another nurse, a heavyset black woman with short-cropped hair, smiling brown eyes that radiated confidence, and a name tag reading "Roberta," came in to take Mary Dell's temperature and blood pressure.

When she was through, Roberta stood by the side of the bed and said, "You been crying, honey? Baby blues?" She patted Mary Dell's hand. "You wait right here. I'll be back in a minute with something to help you sleep."

She returned ten minutes later, carrying Howard.

"Can't leave him here all night," Roberta said. "But he's good-sized. It won't hurt to pull him off the monitor for an hour. No need for Dr. Tibbets to know, though. He's a good doctor. Nice too, not like some of them. But he's young. Doesn't know everything there is to know about babies and mommas, not by a long shot. So, this has got to be our secret, all right?"

Mary Dell nodded and rolled slowly onto her side. Roberta tucked the blue-bean bundle into the crook of his mother's arm and smiled approvingly.

"There now. That looks just about right. You two take some time to get to know each other. I'll be back later."

At first, Mary Dell just looked at Howard, studied his face, listened to him breathe, admired his eyelashes. Then, quietly, carefully, she loosened the blue blanket, pulled out his arm, examined his perfect tiny fingers and nails, made a bracelet of her thumb and forefinger, and circled his little wrist while Howard slept peacefully on, eyelids barely fluttering.

After a time, Mary Dell unwrapped the blanket completely, inspected her son's shoulders, torso, the two little legs protruding from the smallest diaper she'd ever seen, his feet and toes, the iodine-stained bandage on his belly that hid the stub of the cord that had connected them one to the other for so many months. She stroked his smooth, impossibly soft skin with her hand, traced the soles of his feet with the tip of her forefinger, eliciting a tiny twitch of response but nothing more.

Removed from the warm cocoon of the blanket, Howard twisted his little body. Mary Dell unbuttoned the top of her nightgown, pulled him closer, keeping him warm in the ample pillow of her breasts. Howard dozed for a few minutes and then yawned. Mary Dell placed the dark nipple of her breast between his pink lips.

At first, Howard did nothing, neither taking it into his mouth or pushing it out. After a minute or so, his lips quivered, clamped down, and Howard sucked at his mother's breast. Not very hard or for very long, just four feeble sucks in succession, but Mary Dell's heart pounded as she counted them off.

When he was finished and lay sleeping again with his cheek against her breast, Mary Dell made a cup of her hand, stroked her son's soft, dark hair, and told him he was a good boy, a smart boy.

Roberta returned a little before one, approaching the bedside with quiet, light steps, and said in a low voice, "Well? What do you think?"

"I think he's perfect," Mary Dell said.

Roberta nodded. "That's what I thought too," she said.

Roberta had been a nurse for longer than Mary Dell had been alive. In that time, she had witnessed a hundred times more joy and sorrow than the average person saw in a lifetime. Sometimes it was hard to watch. Sometimes, driving home to go to bed at the hour most people were just getting up, she cried quiet tears for her patients and their families. In spite of that, Roberta had long ago concluded that every baby was perfect, put on the planet for some good purpose, if only people would give them a chance to prove it. If the mother loved the baby, everything would work out some way or other.

Roberta felt good as she carried Howard back to the NICU. She'd bent a few hospital rules that night, but it didn't matter. This little baby was going to be fine. Thirty-four years on the maternity ward had taught her all about babies and mommas. Indeed it had. Roberta knew the face of love when she saw it.

CHAPTER 18

On the day Lydia Dale and Rob Lee were discharged, Dr. Tibbets decided Howard was doing well enough to be moved from the NICU to the regular newborn nursery. Mary Dell would have been discharged that day as well, but she'd spiked a fever the night before, so Dr. Brownback decided it was best to keep her in the hospital until her temperature returned to normal. Mary Dell was happy to extend her stay. She couldn't imagine going home without Howard.

On the day before mother and baby were to be released, the entire Tudmore-Templeton clan, except Jeb and Cady, who were at their father's house watching reruns of *The Love Boat,* came to the hospital for a visit.

Mary Dell's fever was gone. She sat in a pink vinyl recliner, cradling Howard in one arm and Rob Lee in the other, clenching an unlit cigar between her teeth as Aunt Velvet snapped a picture. When that was done, the babies were handed to Lydia Dale and the photo op was repeated. Then the sisters and babies sat together for several pictures in various poses. The last of the series showed them holding their infants on their laps with arms draped over each other's shoulders, pretending to take exaggerated puffs on their cigars.

The babies were passed among the various relatives, so Velvet could take more pictures. Mary Dell crawled back into bed to watch the proceedings, smiling as she watched her father make faces at his grandsons and thinking about how good it would be to leave the hospital tomorrow with Howard in her arms.

"Honey, did you remember to bring the quilt from the nursery? I want to bring him home in it."

Donny was sitting in a chair on the far side of the room with his head resting against the wall and his hat tilted low over his eyes, dozing.

"It's there in the bag with all the other stuff you wanted." Donny pushed back his hat, revealing dark-circled eyes, and glanced down toward a paper grocery sack at his feet. Besides the baby quilt, the bag was packed with extra diapers, wipes, and the smallest pair of footie baby pajamas he'd been able to find in the baby's dresser, which would still be far too large for Howard, as well as Mary Dell's hair spray, teasing comb, jewelry, stockings, and going-home-from-the-hospital outfit—turquoise spandex leggings, an oversized bright pink jacket with big puffy sleeves, and her favorite pink cowboy boots. Mary Dell would have preferred something a little fancier for the trip home from the hospital, but this was one of the few non-maternity outfits she could fit into, and she hoped the puffed sleeves of the jacket would draw attention away from the pooch of her post-pregnancy waistline.

"Well?" Mary Dell said expectantly. "Could you get it for me?"

Grandma Silky jumped up. "Let the man be, Mary Dell. He looks all tuckered out."

Donny began to protest that he could find the quilt, but Silky was already digging through the grocery sack.

"No, you just sit there and grab forty winks, Donny. Babies being the way they are, this could be the last sleep you get for months. Besides," she said as she pulled Howard's quilt out of the bag, "I want a picture of me holding my great-grandbabies, wrapped up in their quilts. Give me those handsome boys, Dutch."

Dutch walked across the room with Rob Lee, who was already wrapped in the blue-and-yellow Grandmother's Fan quilt Mary Dell had made. Silky laid Howard on the foot of the bed, removed his receiving blanket, and proceeded to bundle him in the orange-pomegranate-lime creation that was so diplomatically refused by Lydia Dale.

Howard hadn't made a peep all morning, but the moment Silky wrapped the quilt over him, he began to howl. His mouth gaped wide in protest, and his little face turned as red as a beet. Mary Dell puckered her lips and made clucking "there there" sounds, but her eyes smiled. Even crying and red-faced, Howard was adorable.

"Will you listen to that? Bawling like a calf! He hasn't made that much noise since the doctor popped him on the bottom. Poor little boy! What's bothering you, baby?"

Grandma Silky laughed. "If I didn't know better, I'd say Howard doesn't care for his new quilt."

"Don't be silly, Granny. I don't even think he can see colors yet."

Mary Dell scooped Howard off the end of the bed, unwrapping the quilt in the process. The moment she did, the baby stopped squalling.

Mary Dell frowned. "It just must be too hot for him. Either that or I forgot to take out a pin. Poor Bubba," she crooned, peering into Howard's beautiful almond eyes, which were open now and gazing placidly at her face. "Did a nasty ol' pin stick the baby? Momma is so sorry. Yes, she is. She'll be more careful next time. Yes, she will."

After posing for pictures with Silky, it was Taffy's turn. Aunt Velvet snapped a photo of her smiling, holding both boys, then beaming as she held Rob Lee alone, and once again, her expression stiff and her beam far dimmer, holding Howard.

After the shutter snapped, Taffy turned him around, looked into his little face, and started to weep. "Oh, you poor little thing! What's going to become of you? Oh, this poor baby!"

Dutch was at her side in an instant. "Hush now, darlin'," he said, patting her shoulder. "Hush."

He looked up at Mary Dell, who was staring at Taffy.

"Don't pay any mind, baby girl. Your momma is just tired. Come on now, Taffy. It's going to be all right. Stop crying."

But Taffy did not stop crying. Instead, she lifted her eyes from Howard's face to her husband's and back again.

"How? How is it going to be all right? Everything has gone wrong. First Lydia Dale gets a divorce, and now my grandson is born a retard!"

Mary Dell had heard that word before, of course, but never in reference to her son. Over the years, she would hear it used the same way again, many times. It would always unleash a flame of fury in her breast, but it never burned quite as high or hot as it did on that day, when that ugly, awful, dehumanizing word came from the lips of her own mother.

Mary Dell swung her legs over the side of the bed and stood up, her face as red as Howard's had been a few minutes before. Donny stood up too, touched his wife on the shoulder, but Mary Dell pushed right past him. She marched across the room and stood in front of her mother.

"Give me my baby."

Taffy sniffled, wiped her eyes on her sleeve, got to her feet, and handed Howard to Mary Dell, who handed him to Donny before turning back to face Taffy.

"Now you listen to me, Momma," she said in a voice that was low and fierce, a tone unlike anything any of them had ever heard her use before, "because I'm only giving you one chance. I'm not going to let you make my baby feel like he's not good enough, or smart enough, or *anything* enough to please you. It's one thing to do it to me, but I won't let you do it to my son. He is beautiful. And smart. And he's going to learn to walk, and run, and read, and go places, and do things you've never even *dreamed* of doing.

"And if you ever, I mean *ever*, call him retarded or use that word in my presence again, that will be the last time you ever see Howard or me."

Taffy's jaw dropped and her eyes, already brimming, spilled over with a fresh wave of weeping. She started to speak, but Mary Dell wouldn't allow it. She lifted her hand and pointed a finger of warning, ramrod straight, at her mother's face.

"I mean it, Momma. Never again."

Taffy's lips twisted. She let out a cry and ran from the room sobbing, the sound of her cries and footsteps echoing down the corridor. For a breath of a moment, the family stood stunned and watched as Mary Dell lowered her hand, walked back to the bed, and got in.

Dutch went to get Taffy. Donny got up and stood next to his wife's bed. Turning his palm backward, Donny laid his fingers on her forehead, feeling for fever. Her skin was warm to his touch, but not overly so.

"You feel all right? You want some water or something?"

She shook her head slightly, then turned and looked at him with a little spark of surprise, as if she'd only just realized he was standing there.

CHAPTER 19

March 1984

Silky tapped on the door of the trailer and waited. When no one answered, she opened the door and yoo-hooed for Mary Dell.

"Come on in, Granny! We're back here!"

Silky followed the sound of her granddaughter's voice, heading toward the nursery. To get there, she had to pick a path through the baby toys, blankets, and picture books that were strewn over the floor of the living room, and then past the kitchen and the sink mounded with dirty dishes, through the dining area, where the table was piled so high with books, magazines, papers, and whatnot that it was impossible to see the wood.

What a mess! Silky understood that when a woman has a newborn, she has to let some things slide just to get by, but this was ridiculous. Mary Dell had always been such a meticulous housekeeper. Even when she was working on a quilt, she insisted on putting the fabric and scraps away every night and covering up her sewing machine instead of leaving it out on the dining room table like most people. Living in such a small place, she said, it was important not to let things get cluttered. What in the world had happened?

She found Mary Dell in the baby's room, toweling off a newly bathed Howard, talking to him in a bright but adult voice as she described the pictures on a homemade mobile that hung over the changing table, bold, black-and-white images of various farm animals.

"And that one is a duck, Howard. Ducks say, 'quack-quack.' Ducks have feathers. Ducks can swim. And that one is a cow. Cows say . . ."

Silky came into the nursery and stood next to the changing table, admiring the pink, wriggling nakedness of her great-grandson. "Well! He's beefing up just fine, isn't he? What's he weigh now?"

"Seven and a half pounds," Mary Dell reported with pride.

"Oh, my! Well, aren't you a good, big boy?" Silky cooed, then grabbed one of Howard's bare feet and pretended to nibble at his toes. "Granny's gonna getchoo! Yes, she is! Granny's gonna get those nekkid jaybird toes!"

"Granny," Mary Dell interrupted, giving Silky an indulgent smile, "it's better if you don't talk baby talk to him."

"Why not? He's a baby, isn't he?"

"I know," Mary Dell agreed, "but I read an article by this doctor that says babies learn to talk better and faster if you speak to them like grown-ups."

"Bah!" Silky retorted. "I used baby talk with your momma and to you and your sister too. All of you turned out just fine. Your momma can talk the hind legs off a horse! Don't know how Dutch puts up with it," she mused.

"Honey, don't go putting too much store in all these baby doctors and experts. I bet not one in five has actually had a baby, so what do they know about it? If you line ten doctors up end to end, they'll all point in different directions. Remember a couple years back, when I had all those chest pains? One doctor told me I had angina. The other told me I had heartburn. I decided to believe the second one, and I've felt fine ever since. Doctors. Is that why you've got all that mess out there on the table? Are you reading all that stuff just so you can figure out how to raise a baby?"

Mary Dell, who by this time had finished diapering and dressing Howard, said in a deliberately patient voice, "No, Granny. I am reading all that stuff to figure out how to raise *Howard*. Every spare second I have, I spend reading up on babies, and Down syndrome, and how to help Howard learn. I bet I've read more books in the last three weeks than I did in all my years in school.

"Of course," she said as she laid the baby in his crib and covered him with a new quilt stitched together from white, black, and red fabrics, "if I had read more books when I was in school, I'd probably be able to get through this stuff faster. Seems I've got to stop and look up every third word. Spent a whole day last week reading up on how babies see. They like black, red, and white best. That's when I decided to redo the nursery."

Mary Dell swept out her arm to draw attention to the room, which Silky realized had been entirely redecorated. In addition to the mural over the crib and the new quilt and new black-and-white-striped bumper pads, the blue walls had been repainted white and a border of red and black ABC blocks circled the room, pasted about three and a half feet up from the floor, the perfect height for the baby to look at as he lay in his crib or on the changing table. The pastel painting of the cow jumping over the moon had been replaced by two smaller pictures in red frames, black-and-white prints of faces, one smiling, one frowning.

This new nursery was stark and modern-looking, like something you saw in one of those magazines about architecture and people who lived in tiny apartments in big cities. It wasn't unattractive, but it wasn't to Silky's taste, especially not in a nursery. It must have taken Mary Dell hours to put away all the old things, repaint the walls, and put up the new, all while trying to plow through that stack of books and take care of her baby and husband. Though, come to think of it, it looked like Mary Dell was only reading books and taking care of the baby, leaving Donny to fend for himself. Maybe that explained why she hadn't seen him in church with the rest of the family for the last three weeks and why she'd twice seen Donny's truck parked outside the Ice House in the middle of the day.

It was natural, she supposed, for a new momma to go a little goofy over her baby at first, sometimes even to the point of neglecting her husband, but they usually calmed down and got back to normal before long. And while Silky thought Mary Dell was right in wanting to learn all she could about Down syndrome and how to help Howard reach his full potential, she thought the way in which she was going about it was . . . well, disproportionate! And if there's one thing Silky believed in, it was proportion.

Making a good life was like making a good cake—you needed a little bit of this, a little bit of that, everything according to its proper measure and not too much of any one ingredient, no matter how delicious it might be. Otherwise, you risked letting one flavor overpower all the others. And if you went way, way overboard? The whole thing might even collapse in the oven or crumble to pieces when you were trying to serve it.

After Howard was tucked in, Silky and Mary Dell tiptoed out of the nursery and into the dining area. Silky stood there looking on as her granddaughter sat down at the table and began poring over books without even offering her a cup of coffee. That's when she decided that Mary Dell's cake was dangerously close to falling. Something needed to be done.

She went into the kitchen and started washing dishes. "Where do you keep your scouring pad?" Mary Dell didn't respond, but Silky found one under the sink. "Never mind. I found it.

"Donny will be home before too long, won't he? What were you thinking of making for supper? Maybe I can get it started for you."

Silky stood there for a minute, waiting. When she got no answer, she became annoyed, put two fingers into her mouth, and whistled.

Mary Dell jumped and hissed, "Hush, Granny! You'll wake the baby!"

The old woman put her hands on her hips. "Mary Dell, I asked you a question. What time will your husband come home, and what were you planning to make for his supper?"

"Oh, I don't know." Mary Dell shrugged. "Late, I guess. There's fish sticks and tater tots in the freezer. He's been heating those up most nights. Either that or picking up some barbecue."

Silky believed in the old adage that the way to a man's heart was through his stomach. The truth of this had been proven to her satisfaction when her late husband, Hooty, caught a whiff of the freshly fried chicken she had stowed in her basket at the church picnic and started following her across the grass, leaving his fiancée sitting alone on a blanket. Naturally, she was horrified by Mary Dell's cavalier attitude regarding her husband's dinner.

"Mary Dell, you can't just let your husband live on fish sticks! I know you're busy taking care of Howard, but your husband needs to be babied a little bit too."

Mary Dell rolled her eyes. "Oh, Granny. Donny understands that Howard is the most important thing right now. Don't worry so much."

Mary Dell lowered her head over the book, squinted, chewed the end of a pencil, then sighed and started flipping the pages of a nearby dictionary, completely ignoring her grandmother.

Silky shook her head and opened the refrigerator. The pickings were slim, but in the vegetable drawer she found a bag of potatoes sprouting a few eyes—but not too soft—and a lemon. In the freezer, behind the fish sticks and tater tots, she discovered a chicken and a bag of peas.

While the chicken was thawing in the microwave (an invention that worked so slick she thought about getting one for herself), Silky finished washing the dishes and wiped down the countertops. Mary Dell was almost out of Crisco, so Silky roasted the chicken instead of frying it, cutting the lemon in half and stuffing it inside the bird, then making a paste of oil, salt, pepper, dried rosemary and thyme and rubbing it over the skin before putting it in the oven. She put the potatoes on to boil, then tidied up the living room, ran the vacuum, and gave the bathroom a quick going-over. When that was done, she mashed the potatoes with butter, salt, and a good grind of pepper, cooked the peas, pouring in a little bacon fat to give them flavor, and pulled the chicken out of the oven.

Mary Dell didn't move during the entire time Silky was working, only stirring when a plaintive wail from the nursery alerted her that Howard had finished his nap.

She lifted her head at his first cry and looked around, seemingly surprised at her home's transformation.

"Granny, you didn't have to do all this."

"No? Well, somebody had to," Silky said as she opened her purse and fished out her car keys. "When Donny gets home, tell him I said hello. But don't tell him I made supper, let him think you did."

Mary Dell gave Silky a peck on the cheek. "Silly old woman. Would you quit worrying? I told you . . ."

"I know what you told me. Now let me tell you something," Silky said with a shake of her finger. "Nobody ever lost money overestimating the fragility of a man's ego. I've got an idea. Why don't I come over on Saturday night and watch the baby while you and Donny go out dancing?"

"Gosh. That's real nice of you, Granny. But . . . Howard's just so little yet. Thanks for cleaning up and making dinner, though. I appreciate it."

The cries coming from the nursery grew louder and more insistent. Mary Dell glanced from her grandmother's face to the hallway and back.

"Oh, go on," Silky said, giving her granddaughter an affectionate nudge toward the nursery. "But mind what I said. Let Donny think you cooked for him. And fix up your hair before he gets home. Put on some lipstick while you're at it."

Silky got into her car, a blue 1964 Buick LeSabre with 18,000 miles on the odometer, and drove to town to pick up groceries and a bottle of blue rinse for her hair. On the way, she passed the Ice House. Donny's truck was parked outside, again.

She thought about parking herself, going inside and giving him a talking-to, but decided against it. This being Too Much, she knew that the story of Donny Bebee's granny-in-law tracking him down at the bar would spread quicker than wildfire in tumbleweed, and she figured Donny didn't need that kind of humiliation right now.

Even so, as Silky drove down the road toward town, pressing down the gas pedal to increase the LeSabre's speed to a zippy thirty-one miles per hour, she couldn't help but glance into the rearview mirror, keeping an eye on Donny's pickup for as long as she could, hoping to see him come out of the Ice House and head for home.

"This ain't good," she mumbled to herself. "No good at all."

CHAPTER 20

When he arrived home, long after Mary Dell had gone to bed, Donny ate the food Silky had prepared for him. He took a spoon out of the drawer and used it to eat potatoes and peas directly from the pot. Then he ripped a leg from the cold chicken carcass and ate it while standing over the sink, staring vacantly out the window into the black night. The next day, he was up early and left the house around four thirty, just as Mary Dell was rising to nurse the baby.

He had not been going to the Ice House every day and drinking himself into a stupor, as Silky feared.

The first time Silky spotted his truck at the Ice House, little more than a week before, was the first time he'd ever gone there without Mary Dell. Since then, he showed up daily, but not until he had finished his work. He arrived every afternoon around three, asked for a pickled egg or some pork rinds and a beer, and nursed it until the bartender started to give him the fish eye, then ordered one more and nursed that until closing time.

He didn't go to the Ice House to get drunk but because he couldn't think of anyplace else to go. And because he was tired. Bone tired. Had been ever since the night of Howard's birth. No matter how hard he tried, he couldn't sleep during the night and couldn't stop himself from working during the day.

He was at the barn or in the pasture by five and drove himself hard all day long, craving the distraction of physical labor, driven to tackle every one of the hard, dirty jobs that he normally had a tendency to put off, leaving the hired men to deal with the cattle and sheep.

He mucked out the horse stalls, tarred the roof of the chicken coop. He replaced the rotten gate posts in the paddock and the loose shingles on the barn. He mended all the fences, dug post holes by hand, vaccinated the calves, and castrated the young bulls. He slaughtered one animal and had the butcher cut up the meat, wrap it, and deliver it back to the ranch to fill the chest freezer. And, even though it was early in the year, he ordered an additional supply of feed and hay and made sure the loft was as full as it possibly could be.

By the time he'd consumed Grandma Silky's roast chicken, he'd finished every chore on his list but one—inspecting the horse stalls for loose or rotting boards. Once that was done, until lambing time, the season of anxious days and long nights when the ewes, simultaneously bred months before, gave birth, the ranch could practically run itself, as much as ranches ever did.

But to say that Donny *planned* to leave wouldn't be true, not at first.

Initially, he had been driven to work because that was Donny's natural reaction to tragedy, the only way he knew to keep himself from thinking too hard or feeling too much. He'd always been that way. That was how the old barn, so old it was about ready to fall down, had been torn down and a new one built in its place. Because when Donny got the telegram saying Graydon had been killed in action, he had to do something to keep himself from falling apart, and the something he'd done was build the barn.

When Howard was born and the doctor told them the child had Down syndrome, Donny reacted the same way. He worked. He worked every day, from dawn to dusk, as hard as he could.

As the days and weeks passed and he saw less and less of his wife and son, he became more and more cognizant that Mary Dell didn't need his help, that he was not only in the way but that his presence distracted and hampered her from caring for Howard. He started thinking about and making a list of what Mary Dell and Howard *would* need, at least in the short term, if something were to happen to him—if he were to die or disappear for some reason.

Not that he expected this to happen, not at any level he could consciously admit to, but just in case.

Arriving at the barn the next morning, he went through his routine. He released the chickens from the coop, fed and watered them, went to the pigpen and fed the sows, then went inside the barn, grabbed a feed bucket, scooped a measure of oats into it, and carried it back to the stalls for Georgeann.

But when he pulled the chain and switched on the bare overhead bulb, he didn't hear the horse's welcoming nicker or see her head sticking out over the top of the stall. Instead, he heard a frantic kicking of hoof on wood, an agonized whinny, the sound of suffering.

Georgeann was down, cast in the stall. Sometime during the night, she had rolled over, gotten one of her forelegs stuck in a loose board and, unable to free herself, had likely panicked and begun to thrash and kick against the boards, finally kicking herself loose, but at a great consequence.

Damn it! Damn it to hell!

It was the last chore on his list, checking those boards. When he'd taken a quick glance a few weeks before, that stall looked perfectly sound, and so he'd left it for last, thinking everything was fine, adding it to the list only from an abundance of caution.

Damn.

Georgeann sputtered and looked up at him with agonized eyes, silently begging him to do something. He opened the stall door and squatted down next to her.

The foreleg was broken; he knew that just by looking. It was dangling at a cruel angle, like a jagged comma.

He was powerless. There was nothing he could do to help or heal her. Breaks like that couldn't be mended. And there's no such thing as a three-legged horse.

Donny stroked Georgeann's neck, sweaty from fear and the effort of freeing herself. "Hey there. I know. I know it hurts. Hush now, girl. Hush. Settle down. Everything's going to be all right," he murmured, even though he knew it wasn't.

When her body became more relaxed and her eyes less panicked, Donny got up, went to his truck, pulled the rifle from the rack, and went back to the stall, killing her clean and quick with one bullet.

The sound of the gunshot, ringing sharp in the half darkness that precedes dawn, startled the sows, set the chickens to clucking, and made up Donny's mind for him, forcing him to admit what he'd feared all along—

that he was powerless. That no matter how hard you work, how hard you try, there are some things that can't be helped or fixed.

He supposed there were men who could live with that, who could stand aside, spread their hands and let it go, but he knew he wasn't one of them.

Donny borrowed a backhoe and buried his horse, did his work, cared for his stock, drove over to the big house, and asked his father-in-law if he could take care of the animals in the morning because he had to do some errands in Waco. Then he drove back to the barn and repaired the loose boards in the vacant stall. When that was done, he went to the Ice House, ordered a bourbon, just one, and tossed it back.

The baby was asleep when he got home, but Mary Dell was still up, sitting at the dining room table, reading an article about the three different kinds of Down syndrome: nondisjunction, translocation, and mosaicism.

Donny showered and changed, put some clean clothes into the paper grocery sack he'd used to bring Mary Dell's things to the hospital, then opened the bedroom window and left the sack outside.

He went into the nursery to see his sleeping child, leaning over the crib to kiss Howard's soft cheek with his chapped lips, laid his heavy hand over the boy's little body and left it there a moment, feeling his chest rise and fall.

"Be a good boy," he whispered.

Mary Dell was still reading, but she looked up when he came into the dining area. "Everything all right?"

"Yes," he said, leaning down to kiss the top of her head, stroking her blond hair with his hand. "Everything's all right."

Donny heated what was left of the chicken, potatoes, and peas in the microwave and brought two plates to the table. They ate dinner together, talking a little but not much, and mostly about Howard. Donny didn't say anything about what happened to Georgeann, but when he got up to clear the dishes, he did tell Mary Dell that he loved her.

Mary Dell looked up at him. "I love you too, darlin'."

"Listen," Donny said as he scraped chicken bones into the trash, "I've got to run into town. I had to borrow Clyde Pickens's backhoe today, and I promised to get it back to him before dark."

"Why didn't you just return it before you came home?"

Donny shrugged. "Wanted to see you first, I guess."

Mary Dell smiled. "You're sweet. Hon, as long as you're out, run by the Tidee-Mart and pick up some Crisco, milk, and a loaf of bread, would you? You want me to write it down?"

"No," Donny said, and kissed her one more time. "No need for that."

CHAPTER 21

Graydon Bebee popped a last bite of cornbread into his mouth and washed it down with a gulp of coffee before getting up from the table.

L. J. "Little Jim" Spreewell, Graydon's boss, who looked to be in no hurry to get back to work, dumped another spoonful of sugar into his cup and flipped through a pile of mail.

"You figure out what's wrong with the tractor yet?" he asked without looking up.

The Spreewells owned a farm outside of Liberal, Kansas, where they grew wheat and corn and raised fifty head of sheep. In exchange for room, board, and one hundred dollars a week, Graydon worked the fields, tended the sheep, and did anything else L. J. said needed doing. Graydon ate his meals with the Spreewells but otherwise kept to himself. He spent nights in his room, a rustically remodeled shed, with no phone, no TV, and no companion except for his old friend, Jack Daniel's. L. J. knew about that, but as long as Graydon didn't let his drinking interfere with his work, he didn't ask questions. They were men of few words, and so the arrangement worked well for both parties.

"Yeah, I took a look. Think it just needs new spark plugs."

L. J. glanced up expectantly. "Well?"

"I'm driving to town to pick some up right now."

L. J. sniffed as if to let Graydon know it was about time and tossed a grocery circular into a wastepaper basket. Graydon settled his battered black Stetson onto his head, the last remnant of his days in Texas, and grabbed the keys to the truck from a hook by the back door.

"Hey, Bebee. You got a letter here." L. J. squinted at the postmark before holding it out to Graydon. "Looks to be from your brother and sister-in-law."

Graydon took the envelope and shoved it in his shirt pocket before heading out the door. He didn't have to look at the return address to know L. J. was right. Donny and Mary Dell were the only people who sent him letters and then only once or twice a year—a card at Christmas and again on his birthday. Graydon never wrote back.

He liked his brother, and he liked Mary Dell too. But he didn't want to talk to them any more than he had to or be reminded of things he'd rather forget. Even though they weren't identical twins and Mary Dell had six inches on her sister, she reminded him too much of Lydia Dale; the facial resemblance was strong. The year Mary Dell started putting pictures of her and Donny on their family Christmas cards was the year Graydon started throwing them away, usually without even opening the envelope.

Graydon hadn't seen his brother since Donny drove

up from Texas about three years back. Things got out of hand. Graydon felt bad about the fight, about blacking his brother's eye and splitting his lip, but he had asked for it, butting into things that were none of his business. It was a shame they'd had to part that way, but Graydon figured it was for the best. Up until then, Donny just hadn't taken the hint. If his brother wasn't married to Mary Dell and living in Too Much, it might have been different, but as it was . . .

After the fight, Donny let him be, sending only those two cards during the year, and Graydon was pretty sure that Mary Dell was the one who actually sent them. But it wasn't Christmas, and his birthday wasn't for another three months. Why were they writing now?

Graydon closed the door of the truck, pulled the envelope out of his pocket, and opened it.

The card was decorated with a drawing of a stork wearing a delivery cap and holding the ties of a blue bundle in its beak and the words "It's A Boy!"

Inside, written in a loopy lady script he figured belonged to Mary Dell, he found a listing of his new nephew's birth statistics and a picture of a baby boy with dark hair and almond-shaped eyes. The card didn't say anything about the baby having Down syndrome, but the people who ran the liquor store in town had a five-year-old daughter, Jenny, with Down's, so Graydon recognized the facial characteristics. She was a sweet little girl. Graydon figured this little guy would be too, but it must have been a shock for Donny, at least at first.

Strange to think that his baby brother was a father. Even stranger to think that Donny hadn't told him the baby was coming. Of course, he'd made it clear that he wanted nothing to do with Donny or his family . . . still. A baby boy. His nephew.

Graydon read the note again and smiled to himself. Howard Hobart Bebee. Huh. So they'd named him after the old man. Graydon wondered if his father knew about that. Probably not. Hell, Graydon didn't even know if his father was still alive—though he supposed he must be. If Howard Bebee had exited this earth, surely there'd have been some sort of cosmic event to announce the news . . . rock faces would have split or meteors fallen from the sky . . . something. His daddy had been a force of nature, as outsized in personality as he'd been in body, a hard-drinking and hard-living grizzly of a man, idolized by his sons and just about everyone who knew him, who had made a small fortune wildcatting oil, then lost even more than that and disappeared. As a boy, Graydon had worshipped his father, but he got over it pretty quick. Donny never did. But then, Donny had been so little when Howard ran out on them. He hadn't lain awake in bed listening to their mother's tears coming from the next room or understood how worried and exhausted she was, working three jobs to support them. Over his mother's protests, Graydon left school as soon as he was able and got a job at the stockyard. It still wasn't easy, but they got by. Grace Bebee had never said a word against Howard in front of the children, not to her dying day. It just wasn't in her nature. Graydon never said anything against his father either, never corrected or amended the stories Grace told about Big Howard's adventures as a wildcatter or tried to offer his little brother a different version of the family history than his mother's. It wasn't his place. But he knew what he knew.

He laid the birth announcement on the seat but held the baby picture carefully between his fingers so he wouldn't leave prints on the photo.

"Isn't he something? Look at all that hair." He shook

his head. "So Donny's a daddy. And I'm an uncle. Damn." He pulled his wallet from the back pocket of his jeans and slipped the photograph carefully inside.

Graydon drove to town and picked up spark plugs. Next he drove to the Rexall, picked out a card that said, "A Baby Boy Is a Gift from Above," slipped a ten-dollar bill inside, signed it, stamped it, mailed it, and drove back to the farm.

CHAPTER 22

Mary Dell's face fell. "Yes, sir. I understand. But if you hear anything, you'll let me know right away, won't you? Thank you, Sheriff. I appreciate it."

Mary Dell hung up the phone and looked at Lydia Dale, who was sitting on a quilt on the living room floor between Rob Lee and Howard, shaking a ring of brightly colored plastic keys above the babies' heads. Rob Lee watched the keys with an alert expression, while Howard's gaze floated around the room, glancing at his aunt only occasionally.

"He says they can't put in a missing persons report yet. He says it's too soon." She smacked her hand against the telephone and let out an exasperated growl. "This is so ridiculous! Of course he's a missing person! Donny wouldn't just up and leave!"

"Well . . . the sheriff might have a point. It's only been one night."

"Two."

"Still. I'm sure he'll turn up soon."

Mary Dell sat down cross-legged on the quilt and stuck her finger into the center of Howard's little hand. The baby gripped hold of it, a skill he'd only recently mastered. Two days ago, Mary Dell would have grinned at his accomplishment and, in spite of what she'd told Silky about talking to him like a grown-up, cooed and burbled and told him what a good bubba-boo he was, yes, he was. Now the most she managed was a distracted half smile.

"I don't know what else to do, sis. I've called every hospital and sheriff's department from Dallas to Houston. Daddy said that Donny came over during the day and asked if he could take care of the stock because he had to drive over to World of Wheels to get new tires for the truck."

"Did you call the tire place?"

Mary Dell nodded. "They didn't sell any tires to Donny Bebee or anybody in a white truck with a gun rack and red stripe on the side. Those tires only had six thousand miles on them. Why would he tell Daddy he was buying new ones? Clyde Pickens was the last person who saw him. Donny returned the backhoe that night, just like he told me he was going to. That's how I heard about Georgeann."

Howard began to fuss, and his little mouth quivered. Before he could work himself up into a full-fledged wail, Mary Dell scooped him into her lap, pulled her blouse up and her brassiere down, and fed him. Howard latched onto her nipple and began sucking, his little hands kneading the globe of her breast.

"Why didn't he tell me about Georgeann? He loved that horse. He was twelve years old when he got her. She was with him all during his rodeo days. It must have about broken his heart to put her down. Why didn't he tell me about that? Do you think that's why he's run off? Because of Georgeann? Think maybe he's just gone off to brood for a couple days?"

Lydia Dale put the plastic keys in Rob Lee's palm. His fingers curled around the red ring and held on for a moment, then dropped the toy on the quilt. Lydia Dale picked it up and repeated the procedure.

"Could be," she said, though her expression was doubtful.

Lydia Dale knew Donny set a great store on Georgeann, but she couldn't see him disappearing over the death of a horse. Lydia Dale's guess was that this had something to do with Howard's birth.

Donny hadn't been himself since learning his son had Down syndrome. Every time she saw him, Lydia Dale thought of a helium balloon that was leaking gas—soft, deflated, bobbing low to the ground and looking a little lost. In the circumstances, it was a normal enough response. The news had to have come as a terrible shock. How could it not? She was sure her sister felt the same way, at least at first, but Mary Dell had worked through the shock quickly, in ways that her husband couldn't.

Donny wasn't good at talking about his feelings. Maybe that was something that ran all through the family; Graydon had been just the same. For as long as she lived, Lydia Dale would never be able to forget the last time she'd seen him.

A tangle of bureaucratic red tape had prevented them from learning that Graydon was not dead and had been released from a Vietnamese POW camp until he was already on his way home. No one had been able to warn him about Lydia Dale's marriage to Jack Benny.

Lydia Dale was coming out of the Tidee-Mart carrying two sacks of groceries when she saw him driving down Main Street in a rented red convertible. Seeing her, he hit the brakes as hard as he could, making them squeal, and jumped out of the car just as Lydia Dale put the grocery sacks into the trunk, revealing her pregnant belly.

Graydon's face froze. His smile shattered into a million pieces, small and sharp, like shards of broken glass. It hurt her heart to see him that way. If she'd known Graydon was alive, she would never have married Jack Benny.

How could she have known? But she felt guilty just the same. The look on Graydon's face made her feel guilty and disloyal and so overwhelmed by the enormity of her mistake that for a moment she thought she might actually be sick. She tried to speak to him, to explain, but he wouldn't even look at her. He got back into the car without saying a word, drove off, and never returned to Too Much.

Maybe it ran in the family. Maybe Donny, likewise faced with a situation he could not change and could not talk about, had done the same thing, retreated. Maybe he'd gone off alone. Maybe not. It was hard to know what a man was thinking or feeling, especially if he wouldn't talk to you. They were more complicated than they appeared at first glance, these Bebee boys.

But Mary Dell was a true Tudmore, cut out of the same cloth as Grandma Silky, sturdy denim or maybe a heavy wool, something plain but strong, hard to cut through, slow to fade, made to last. Yes, that was her sister all over.

When Mary Dell made up her mind to be happy, she was. End of story. She was like one of those inflatable clowns with the weighted bottoms, the kind little boys use to practice boxing. She could roll with the punches, bounce back from any blow and, having righted herself, keep smiling, going on as if nothing had happened. This was Mary Dell's greatest strength, but in this instance, Lydia Dale thought it might also be a weakness.

After the initial shock of the diagnosis, Mary Dell saw Howard as the answer to her prayers, a gift from God. Once she'd made up her mind about that, she couldn't understand that anybody else might not feel the same way or take longer to reach the same conclusion. All she had wanted was a healthy and happy baby, and that's what she'd gotten. She understood the responsibility and challenges that lay before her, but that didn't stop her from being thrilled by this miracle child.

Lydia Dale couldn't help feeling that she was right. Howard was a pretty baby, so sweet. And considering all the problems and complications that could accompany a diagnosis of Down syndrome, he was remarkably, almost miraculously, healthy. Of course Mary Dell was concerned about how to care for Howard and help him learn, but Lydia Dale knew her sister would figure it out. She was completely focused on her child. So much so that she hadn't noticed Donny was suffering and needed comfort.

Lydia Dale knew he'd harbored a secret seed of bitterness about what had happened between her and Graydon, but Donny had always been good to her. How many brothers-in-law would have done what he did? Continued to send checks long after her husband had stopped working at the ranch?

Lydia Dale didn't like to imagine anything but the best about her brother-in-law, but her guess was that Donny, confused, suffering, and in need of comfort, had found it. Lydia Dale picked up Rob Lee, laid him against her shoulder, and pulled back the elastic of his tiny blue jeans, checking his diaper, not because she thought it was dirty but because she didn't want to look her sister in the face just then.

"Did you go up to the Ice House and ask if anybody knew anything? Or if they thought he might be, you know . . . staying with anybody he'd met there?"

Mary Dell frowned, unlatched Howard from the breast, and put him up on her shoulder to burp him. "Donny has not run off with some floozy he met at the Ice House. He's not like that."

Lydia Dale shrugged and laid Rob Lee back on the quilt. She understood the subtext of Mary Dell's comment, the implication that Lydia Dale's husband—ex-husband—*was* "like that," but she took no offense. Jack Benny was a louse, and everybody knew it. Donny wasn't a louse, furthest thing from it, everybody knew that too. Donny Bebee was a good man, but he was still a man, a man under extraordinary pressure. And under the right circumstances . . .

Lydia Dale was trying to think of a gentle way to explain that to her sister, but Mary Dell beat her to the punch.

"Besides," she said as she rubbed her hand in circles over Howard's back, "I already went down to the Ice House and asked. Donny had been going there, every night for about a week. But he never drank much, and he didn't talk to anybody. The bartender said that one night a lady sat down on the stool next to him and asked if he wanted to buy her a drink. Donny didn't say anything, didn't even look at her, just propped his elbow up on the bar so she could see his wedding ring. The gal went off in a huff and Donny sat there nursing his beer until closing time. When he left, he left alone. Every night.

"I don't know where Donny is or why he left, but I know as sure as anything that it wasn't because of another woman. He couldn't do something like that. It's just not in him."

"Well, then, what do you think happened?"

"I don't know. I wish I did," Mary Dell said quietly as she laid Howard back down on the quilt and looked into his beautiful, drowsy eyes. She pushed herself up on her hands and knees and bent down to kiss the baby on his forehead before climbing to her feet.

"Would you keep an eye on him for a minute? I need to call the sheriff's office again. I forgot to tell them the license plate number on the truck."

CHAPTER 23

For a few days, Mary Dell was convinced that Donny's disappearance was the result of an accident or even foul play. By the time his letter arrived, she had begun to suspect otherwise.

If he had been killed in a car accident, or stopped to pay for a fill-up at precisely the moment a hooded gunman had picked to rob the mini-mart and so been shot in the shoulder or taken hostage, or contracted a case of amnesia while on his way to World of Wheels, she'd have heard something by now. Someone would have spotted him somewhere, or seen his truck ditched by the side of a road, or discovered a peacock-blue cowboy shirt with gold stitching on the collar and cuffs and blood-stains on the sleeve stuffed in a trash can in an alley behind a barroom, wouldn't they? There was only one logical explanation: Donny's disappearance was not an accident. The reason no one could find him was because he didn't want to be found.

Mary Dell knew he wasn't coming back. Even so, when the letter arrived, it was hard to open the envelope, hard to read words written by a man whose handwriting she knew as well as her own but whose outlook on the world and response to it was so foreign and confusing that she wondered if she'd ever really known him at all.

Later she would succeed in being grateful for the knowledge that he was safe. She loved him enough for that. But when she opened and read the first lines of the letter he had written and dropped into a mailbox near Midland, Mary Dell was overcome by the thought that it would have been less painful to believe he had perished by accident or violence than to know he had left by choice.

. . . You are so strong, Mary Dell. That's one of the things I've always admired about you. You'll do a better job of raising Howard on your own than with me there, getting in the way. I know you might not believe that right now, but it's true, and in time you'll see I was right. I don't expect you to forgive me for going away or understand why I can't stay, but try to believe me when I tell you I can't. It's not because there's anything wrong with you, honey—there's not a woman on the face of God's green earth who can hold a candle to you—it must be something wrong with me, I guess. Maybe the Tudmores aren't the only family with a Fatal Flaw.

I only took what money was in my wallet, and I left my credit card in the bottom of my sock drawer. You should have enough money in the bank for now. A man paid me $40 to help him stack a load of hay this week, so here's $25 for you and Howard. I know it's not much, but I'll send more when I get myself settled somewhere.

Kiss Howard for me. I love you, Mary Dell. I'm sorry.

Donny

When she finished reading, Mary Dell laid her head on the table and sobbed herself dry. She loved him enough for that too.

CHAPTER 24

For the first time in her life, Mary Dell was depressed. Not just sad, or blue, or wistful, not filled with regret or the fury of a woman scorned, but truly depressed.

When she called her sister in tears and told her about the letter, Lydia Dale came right over. Taffy asked if she could come along too, but Lydia Dale didn't think that would be a good idea. Mary Dell had barely spoken to her mother since coming home from the hospital.

However, Taffy felt this crisis presented the perfect opportunity for her to return to her daughter's good graces. After what Donny had done, surely Mary Dell would realize that her regrettable but innocent utterance of one teeny-weeny offensive word was not so terrible, or at least not spoken with malice. After all, Howard was her grandson and Mary Dell was her daughter and she loved them both, no matter what. And Taffy really did need to talk to Mary Dell about some things.

Dutch was doing his best to keep up with the ranch

work, but considering his age and health, it was too much for him to manage alone, especially since lambing season was just around the corner. Too, there was the question of finances. It wasn't like Donny's departure only affected Mary Dell. This was a blow to the entire family, and Taffy felt this was the ideal time to discuss it. Besides, it was the duty of a mother to come to the aid of her daughter at her moment of anguish and despair. Mary Dell needed her.

It took some doing, but Lydia Dale eventually convinced Taffy that this was *not* the proper moment for a mother-daughter reconciliation or to bring up financial issues, however pressing, and that if she really wanted to help, the best way to do so was to take care of Jeb, Cady, and Rob Lee while Lydia Dale went to help Mary Dell.

In spite of her sister's ministrations, Mary Dell didn't get better. She didn't eat, didn't sleep, and didn't seem interested or capable of caring for Howard. She nursed him, but only when Lydia Dale brought the baby to her and put him to the breast. Other than that, Mary Dell just sat in the rocking chair, alternating between long jags of crying and long stretches of silence spent staring into space. Lydia Dale was afraid to leave her alone. By the third day, she was exhausted and worried because Mary Dell showed no signs of improvement.

On the fourth day, Grandma Silky showed up with a picnic basket over her arm and a face like the business end of an ax.

"I stopped off at the big house before I came down here. Lydia Dale, you need to go home and tend to your children. Cady has been crying herself to sleep at night because she misses you. And Jeb got sent to the principal's office today for passing out Luckies to every boy in the fourth grade and letting them take a peek at a pair of black lace underpants he'd hid in his lunch box."

"What!"

Silky nodded deeply, confirming that Lydia Dale's horror was entirely justified. "He was charging them a nickel each for a peep at Carla Jean's unmentionables. The cigarettes he was giving away for free.

"You need to take that boy in hand, Lydia Dale. He needs a good talking-to. A hairbrush on his behind wouldn't hurt either. Back in my day the principal would have done it for you," she grumbled to herself.

"And when you're done with that, you need to call up your no-account ex-husband and tell him that he needs to keep a better eye on his children. Or at least lock his bedroom door when they come to visit! Get going now," she commanded, pushing Lydia Dale, who had already buckled Rob Lee into his car seat, toward the door. "I'll take care of your sister."

Mary Dell was sitting in the rocking chair next to the window, staring into space with a vacant expression. Her normally buoyant bouffant was flat, and the bags under her eyes were dark from lack of sleep and smudged with a slurry of old mascara and tears. She was dressed in the same clothes she'd been wearing for days, the turquoise spandex pants she'd worn home from the hospital, now too big for her and baggy at the knees, a wrinkled pink paisley blouse, a purple ultrasuede vest with faux-fur trim, and no shoes.

Grandma Silky stood in front of the rocker and clapped her hand over her breast, distressed at the sight of her granddaughter looking so sorry.

"Bless your little cotton socks! Baby girl, you look just awful. But Granny's here now. Everything is going to be all right. Why don't you go get yourself cleaned up while I set the table and put out the supper?"

Silky, used to having her instructions obeyed, turned and went into the kitchen without giving Mary Dell a

backward glance. She put on an apron, made a pitcher of
sweet tea, and unpacked the contents of her picnic basket: homemade biscuits; green beans boiled to a pale
green, then sautéed with plenty of bacon fat; carrots
glazed with a half cup of butter and a whole cup of brown
sugar; potatoes mashed with more butter, salt, pepper,
and pure cream; peppery gravy to go with it; and a whole
chicken, skin-on, cut into quarters, dipped in buttermilk,
dredged in a secret mixture of flour, salt, and spices,
then fried in a cast-iron skillet with Crisco to a crispy
and delicious golden brown. It was the recipe that drove
her late husband Hooty's fiancée straight out of his head
and would, she hoped, do the same for her granddaughter, helping Mary Dell forget Donny and the hurt he'd
done her.

And in case it didn't, just to be sure, Silky had also
brought a bowl of homemade banana pudding topped
with vanilla wafers and whipped cream, a red velvet cake,
and an entire pecan pie, the filling loaded with chopped
nuts and a good tot of bourbon, just to give it some
punch. Silky had great faith in the restorative power of
desserts. Her feeling was that if the Friar had thought to
feed Romeo a nice piece of pie when he discovered the
seemingly deceased Juliet in the family tomb instead of
running off in the night, Romeo would have decided that
life was worth living after all and Mr. Shakespeare would
have had to find himself some other tragedy to write about.

When she finished heating up the food and setting the
table, Silky went back into the living room. She was
shocked to see Mary Dell still sitting in the rocker exactly where she'd left her, looking as disheveled as before.

"Mary Dell, didn't you hear me? I told you to go on
and get yourself cleaned up. Go on, now. Dinner's ready."

But Mary Dell didn't go on. Instead, she turned her head to the side and closed her eyes. Tears seeped out from beneath her closed eyelids, ran down her cheeks to the tip of her chin, and splashed onto the front of the purple vest, leaving a dark, wet blotch on the ultrasuede.

Silky approached the rocker, leaned down to Mary Dell's eye level and, adopting a firmer tone of voice, issued a more specific set of instructions.

"Mary Dell, get up out of that chair, go into the bathroom, take a shower, brush your teeth, put some rollers in your hair, and fix your makeup. Then go put on clean clothes and some shoes and come sit down at the table and eat the nice supper I made you. Mary Dell?"

Mary Dell twisted her neck even farther away, as if she couldn't bear the sound of Silky's voice. "I'm not hungry."

Silky straightened herself up and put her hands on her hips. "Your sister told me you haven't had a bite in three days. Of course you're hungry. And even if that were true, you're nursing a baby. A cow can't make milk on an empty stomach and neither can you. You ought to know that, living on a ranch all your life. What kind of farmer's daughter are you anyway?"

Silky, who had no way of knowing that she had just repeated the very words that Donny had uttered in love before carrying Mary Dell to the hayloft to conceive their long-desired child, was shocked when Mary Dell buried her tearstained face in her hands and began to wail, keening with an intensity generally known only to certain nomadic tribes in the Arab world, all of whom, Silky was sure, were godless infidels. What was going on?

On some level, Silky understood what Mary Dell was going through. She'd lost a husband too. She too was acquainted with grief. But this? This was a grief she could not relate to. It was beyond the bounds of reason and good taste. It was disproportionate! And if there was one thing Silky hated, it was disproportion.

To make the chaos complete, Howard, who had been woken from his nap by the sounds of Mary Dell's howling sobs, added his cries to hers, the two joining together to create what can best be described as a Hallelujah Chorus of misery.

For a moment, Silky was at a complete loss, without the slightest idea of what she should do or say. It was a situation she had very little experience with, and so it confused and frightened her. Silky hated feeling frightened, and so of course this made her angry, and that anger helped her find her tongue.

"Mary Dell Tudmore Templeton Bebee, that will be just about enough of that! Get a hold of yourself right this minute!"

"I can't," Mary Dell wailed. "I just can't! I can't go on without Donny. I want to die, Granny. I just want to lie down and die!"

Silky grabbed her granddaughter by the shoulders and pushed her backward so Mary Dell was forced to look her in the eye.

"Stop that! I am not standing still for any of that talk. Until a few weeks ago, if you had decided to turn into a great big selfish coward, to quit eating and drinking and sleeping, to worry your family half to death and be the guest of honor at your own pity party, then you could have gone right ahead and done it. But you gave up that right on the day Howard was born. You're a momma now, Mary Dell. Mommas *don't* lie down and die! You've got a child to care for, a job to do. So get your butt up out of that chair and start doing it. Because I am too old and ornery to do it for you. And I won't. Neither will your sister. That's your job, baby girl, yours alone. And if *you* don't do it, it won't get done.

"I know your heart's been broke and your dreams have too, and I'm sorry for it. But when your dreams turn to dust, well . . . maybe it's time to vacuum."

Having spoken her mind as plainly as she knew how, Silky marched into the dining room, sat down at the table, and began filling her plate. Howard's cries were growing louder and more insistent by the second. As she ladled gravy into the well of her mashed potatoes, Silky took a moment to be impressed that such a tiny creature could make so much noise.

By the time Silky finished serving herself and saying a silent grace, thanking the Good Lord for making babies so loud and mommas so tender, Howard's cries were beginning to subside a little bit. Her hearing wasn't what it used to be, but beneath the noise of baby tears and muffled sobs, she thought she heard the sound of humming and sung snatches of a lullaby.

A few minutes later, Mary Dell, eyes still rimmed red but cleared clean of black rings by a splash of cold water, entered the dining room with Howard in her arms. She pulled up a chair and took a seat at the table.

"That smells good," she said.

"It is," Silky replied. "Here, baby girl, let me fix you a plate. When you're finished with that, you can have a nice big slice of pie."

CHAPTER 25

The second piece of pie definitely lifted Mary Dell's spirits, but no dessert in the world could mask the fact that she had some very real problems to face.

"I just don't know how I'm going to manage without Donny," she said as she picked up the crimped, golden-brown edge of the piecrust between her fingers and nibbled at it.

"You'll figure it out," Silky assured her. "You're smarter and tougher than you give yourself credit for, honey."

"But I don't know the first thing about running a ranch. Well," she said, reconsidering, "maybe I know the first thing, the basics, but not enough. Not like Donny. I never figured on being a rancher."

"Maybe you don't have to be," Silky reasoned. "Maybe you can find somebody to run it for you and then you can concentrate on what you're really good at and interested in. You hear anything from that lady at the magazine yet?"

Mary Dell popped the last crumb of piecrust into her mouth and moved her head from side to side. "No, and I'm starting to think I never will."

"Don't say that! Take it back, right now. Nobody ever accomplished anything by doubting themselves. Half of success is just showing up, honey, so you just keep on doing what you've been doing. Make your quilts, send in those patterns. You've got a gift, Mary Dell. A very special gift. Sooner or later, somebody is bound to realize how talented you are. Mark my words." Silky pointed the tines of her fork at her granddaughter to underscore her point. "In fact, I wouldn't be surprised if, before it's all said and done, you become a great big fat famous quilting legend."

Mary Dell laughed, the first time she had done so in days, and started gathering up the empty plates.

"Oh, Granny. You're sweet, but I don't think there is such a thing as a quilting legend."

Silky raised her eyebrows. "No? Well, if there isn't, there ought to be. And since it's bound to happen eventually, I can't see any reason why you shouldn't be the one it happens to."

After they cleared the table and washed the dishes, Mary Dell offered to make up the sofa bed for her, but Silky declined. "If I don't sleep in my own bed, I don't sleep at all. Besides, it's probably best to leave you be. You've got some thinking to do."

Mary Dell stood at the door and waved good-bye to her grandmother, taking Howard's little arm and moving it up and down so he could wave too.

"Say bye-bye to Granny, Howard. Say we hope she comes back soon."

Mary Dell took Howard inside and laid him down on

the floor on top of his fruit salad quilt. As soon as she did, he started to cry, so she put him on her lap and read picture books to him, flipping the pages, elaborating on the illustrations, telling him that dinosaurs were extinct, mice gave birth to live babies, and that in lion families, it was the lioness who did all the important work and the daddy lion mostly lay around looking handsome, mating, and roaring real loud.

"Seems to be a lot of that kind of thing going around," Mary Dell said to Howard, whose eyes were beginning to droop.

"Uh-oh. That wasn't nice of me, was it? I'm sorry. I won't say mean things about your daddy again. Being mad never helped anybody anyway, did it? No, sir. Being mad just gives you wrinkles and indigestion. We don't want that, do we? No, we don't. We're going to be fine all on our own, aren't we, Howard? We don't need anybody else; we've got each other."

After bathing and feeding the baby and tucking him into bed, Mary Dell went around the trailer to make sure all the doors and windows were locked. She had never locked the doors before, but she'd never been alone in the house at night before either. It was true that in the weeks since Howard's birth, Donny had rarely been home when she'd gone to bed or when she rose in the morning, but she knew he always *would* be, and that made all the difference. The trailer wasn't large, but suddenly it felt much too big. She opened the doors of the closets to make sure they were empty and drew the living room drapes closed, something else she didn't normally do.

Other than the bank robbery pulled off by Bonnie and Clyde back during the Depression and occasional bouts of gunplay by jealous wives or drunken cowboys, serious crime was all but unknown in Too Much. A part of

Mary Dell felt silly, tiptoeing around locking doors, peeking into closets, and listening for noises. Donny was gone, but other than that, nothing had changed. This was still her house, her town. Why should she be frightened?

Grandma Silky was right; Mary Dell had some thinking to do. In these last four days, she'd hardly moved or spoken. All her attention was turned inward; she'd been feeling but not thinking. Now she had to. She had to figure out a way to survive in a world that no longer included a husband.

She was not helpless without Donny; she'd never been helpless. Nor was she afraid of hard work. But she had relied on Donny for certain things, most of which fell into the broad theme of protection. She'd never worried about noises in the night before, or the possibility of anyone breaking in, because she knew that Donny slept lightly and was a good shot. With Donny around, she'd never worried about money either. Oh, sure, she was the one who kept track of their spending, wrote the checks, filled out the tax forms, and clipped coupons out of the grocery circular every Sunday. And she was the more frugal of the two, more averse to spending than her husband, acquisitions to her fabric stash being the only exception. But Donny was the provider and always had been.

They'd had lean years and fat years. Still, she'd always known that Donny would make sure there was food on the table and gas in the truck. Donny took care of her, of everybody— Granny, Daddy and Momma, Lydia Dale and her family—everybody. And he'd never complained about it. Well, almost never.

She wished she'd told him more often how much she appreciated that. If she had, maybe he wouldn't have left? No. Donny hadn't gone away because he felt unappreciated or because he minded taking care of everybody. He'd gone because he didn't think he could do *enough* to take care of everybody, of Howard and of her. He'd gone because he'd finally run up against a problem he couldn't fix. And that was the difference between them.

Mary Dell didn't see Howard as a problem. Yes, he *had* some problems—what child didn't? But that wasn't the same as *being* a problem. Howard didn't need to be fixed. Howard needed to be loved, guided, taught, provided for, and protected, as any child did. And now it was up to Mary Dell to figure out how to do it, all of it.

She poured herself a cup of cold coffee and put it in the microwave. While it was heating, she dug through the drawer where they kept the checkbooks, ledgers, receipts, and unpaid bills and pulled out anything that looked important. When the timer on the microwave rang, she carried the papers, the coffee, a pen, and a pocket calculator to the kitchen table, pushing aside a stack of books on child care to make room for everything.

For the next hour and a half, she pored over the books and bills, trying to get a handle on what they had, what they owed, and what they could expect to owe in the coming weeks and months. It was very educational—not in a good way.

Even though Mary Dell had always been the one who wrote the checks and balanced the books, she'd never really stood back to take in the big picture, to understand how (and how much) cash flowed in and out of the business in any given year. It was a lot more complicated, expensive, and precarious than she'd ever realized.

At the moment, they had $22,672.96 in the checking account. It sounded like a lot of money, and it was, but with that she had to support the entire family and pay all the bills as well as salaries for their three hired men until some more money came in the door, which wouldn't happen until they sent the cattle to market. And if the drought were to continue, and it probably would, she'd be forced to buy more feed. She shook her head as she added up the feed bills; could they really have spent so much already this year? And how could she afford to buy even more? Especially since it was likely beef prices would drop when ranchers decided to sell off their herds rather than feed them, flooding the market. Of course, that might mean that prices would go up the following year because the supply was low, but Mary Dell's immediate concern was figuring out how to get through *this* year.

Thank heaven for the sheep.

Donny always said ranchers and gamblers were next of kin. That was why he decided to raise sheep as well as cattle, as a means of hedging his bets, hoping that sheep would get them through years when beef profits were down and vice versa. As Mary Dell pored over her papers, she was glad Donny had done so. At the moment, it looked as if their sustenance and salvation lay with the sheep—if the lambing went well. And that was a big if.

A lot of things could go wrong, especially now that Donny wasn't around. A herd as big as theirs required extra hands during lambing season, but the last thing she could afford to do right now was bring on more hired men. They had three already—Pete Samson, his cousin Ikey Truluck, and Moises Rivera. Mary Dell didn't much care for Pete and Ikey; they were raised in Too Much and pretty shiftless, though Donny had always kept them in line. Moises was a hard worker, but he was new and had never been through a lambing season.

And, of course, there was Dutch. With Donny gone, she supposed he'd be the head man now, bless him. Mary Dell loved her father, and he loved her back, but she wasn't blind to his faults. Even in his prime, before age, weight, and diabetes had taken their toll, Dutch was never what you could call a go-getter, and he didn't know sheep, not like Donny did. Bottom line was, even if she were rich as Noodie and Marlena Benton, there was no one she could hire for love or money with Donny's experience and know-how, who would work as hard or care as much about the F-Bar-T and the family as he had.

"Oh, Donny," she whispered aloud. "How could you go off and leave me with all this?"

She felt flushed with the heat that precedes a fall of tears, but she swallowed them back. Weeping wouldn't change anything. She needed solutions, but none came to mind.

Well, none besides tracking Donny down, roping him, hogtying him, and hauling him back to the ranch . . . Maybe that was what she'd have to do. Find him and bring him home. Not forever, not for long, but perhaps for long enough.

Donny was wrong about her being able to raise Howard better without him, wrong about so many, many things, but as wrong as he was, Mary Dell knew he hadn't reached his decisions lightly and that she had little to no chance of getting him to change his mind.

But maybe, just maybe, if she could find him and talk sense to him, make him see that she needed him to come back to Too Much for a year, or six months, or at least through the lambing season, long enough for him to help her get a handle on how to run the ranch herself . . . she would promise that at the end of that time, he could go on his way with no recriminations or guilt . . . that she wouldn't ask for his love or even speak the word. . . . Donny could have the trailer, and she and Howard would move into town or the big house . . . it would be strictly a business relationship . . .

Mary Dell took a last slurp of coffee, which was cold again, and sighed. It was crazy, a long shot even if she could find him. But it was the only shot she had, and she couldn't just sit here and do *nothing*. Granny Silky was right. She was a momma, and mommas didn't have the option of giving up or giving in.

Whether she'd volunteered for the job or not, she was the head of the family now.

CHAPTER 26

The next morning Mary Dell put two suitcases and the stroller into the trunk of her car, then buckled Howard into the car seat.

"We're going to stop up at the big house and see Grandpa. What do you think about that?" she asked, putting her face right next to the baby's and smiling. "And then we're going to run by the Tidee-Mart to buy some car snacks for Momma and a box of Pampers for you. And *then* we're going to go off and have ourselves an adventure! Won't that be fun?"

Howard didn't say anything, just squirmed and yawned, which, like almost everything that precious child did, melted his mother's heart.

"Howard Hobart Bebee, I just love you something terrible. Do you know that? Well, I do!"

When she arrived at the big house, she saw a blue truck parked near the barn. It belonged to Dr. Espinoza, the large-animal vet, who was just about to drive away.

Mary Dell quickly pulled up next to her and jumped out of her car, leaving the door open so Howard would stay cool.

"Hey, Val. What are you doing here? Anything wrong?"

Val put her truck back into park. "I just came out to run the ultrasound on your ewes. The rams did their job. Just about all the girls are bred, and you've got a whole lot of twins coming, some triplets too. You *might* have a real good year."

"Or we might not?"

Val scratched a spot behind her ear and tipped her head to the side, looking a little apologetic. "Well, if Donny was around I wouldn't be so concerned. Getting two or even three lambs from one ewe will double or triple your profits. But multiple births also increase the odds of something going wrong. Dutch marked the ewes as I did the ultrasounds, red for twins, blue for triplets. That way you can put them into separate folds when lambing season comes and keep a closer eye on the ewes carrying multiples."

Mary Dell nodded as Val spoke. She already understood the system; Donny had explained it to her before. "Right. But that's no different than any other year, is it?"

Val propped her elbow up onto the window and rested her chin in her hand. "No, but you've got a *lot* of multiples this year, Mary Dell. Dutch is a good cowman, good enough anyway, but he doesn't know sheep. Cows just stay out on the range and drop their calves on their own. They don't usually need help. But sheep are different. Helps if the man in charge has some experience. Donny had to get a couple of seasons under his belt before he got the hang of it, remember?"

Mary Dell did. They lost one lamb in five that first year, and all their profits too. That was the year they'd had macaroni and cheese for dinner five nights a week.

"Your dad isn't as young as he used to be. I'm just not sure he's up to it."

Mary Dell frowned. "Val, what are you trying to say? Is Daddy sick? Do you think he's . . ."

Val lifted her hand to make it clear she wasn't going there. "No, I mean the diabetes has been an issue for a while, but as far as I can tell, he seems fine. Look, Mary Dell, I'm a vet, not an MD. But if your dad were a border collie, I'd say he's getting on and that his sheep-herding years were behind him. I'd also tell him to take off a few pounds, but," she said with a wry smile, "I imagine his doc has already mentioned that."

"Once or twice," Mary Dell said. "Doesn't seem to have made much difference. Daddy likes his Dr Pepper. Barbecue too."

"Don't we all? Look, Dutch is doing his best but, bottom line, he's not capable of running this ranch long term. Come lambing time, he's going to need a lot of help."

"Yes, I'd already thought about that. I'm working on it."

The vet nodded. "Good. I'm not trying to butt into family business, Mary Dell. I'm just trying to help."

"I know. And I'll take all the advice I can get, believe me. Thanks for coming out. What do I owe you?"

Val smiled and shifted the truck into reverse. "The advice is free. I'll mail you a bill for the ultrasound."

Mary Dell lifted her hand in farewell as Val drove off, a cloud of dust rising up behind her truck.

"I figured."

Dutch was sitting on top of a fence smoking a cigarette. His eyes looked tired, and his shoulders drooped. But when he saw Mary Dell come around the corner holding Howard in her arms, his face lit up. He hopped down from the fence, crushed his cigarette with the toe of his boot, and walked toward them holding out both arms.

"How's my big bubba?" he asked with a grin, taking Howard into his arms, lifting him high over his head and then bringing him down closer so they were practically nose to nose. "Did you come out to see your old grand-daddy? Did you? What do you say, pardner? Wanna saddle up and go for a ride?"

Mary Dell grinned and crossed her arms over her chest, pretending to be offended. "Daddy? In case you hadn't noticed, I'm here too."

Dutch tucked the baby into the crook of one arm, put his other arm over Mary Dell's shoulders, and gave her a kiss on the cheek.

"Hey, baby girl. How're you? I heard you were feeling low, but you can't tell to look at you."

"It was a temporary condition," Mary Dell assured him as they walked toward the pasture fence.

He squeezed her shoulders, then leaned down and planted a kiss on Howard's forehead. "Look at this big old fat boy. Bulking up just good, is he?"

Mary Dell nodded and said in a scolding tone, "Daddy, what are you doing out here smoking? You know it's bad for you. I thought you gave it up."

"I did," Dutch said, ducking his head sheepishly. "Mostly. It's a hard habit to break, baby girl. I only have one a day. Two at the most. You won't go telling your momma, will you? Since they tossed her out of the Women's Club, she's got nothing better to do than nag me from sunup to sundown. I love that woman, but I'll tell you the truth, there's just no living with her when she's in a mood. I've been happy to get out of the house."

"Thanks for helping out, Daddy."

"That's all right, honey. You know I'm glad to do it. But I gotta say, wrangling sheep sure wears a man out," he said with a sigh. "I must be older than I thought."

"Well," Mary Dell said, looking around the yard, "where's your help? We're paying three hands. Why didn't you have them handle the sheep?"

"Moises went to check on the cattle, bring them some feed. We're running low, by the way."

"Again? All right, I'll see about putting in another order. What happened to Pete and Ikey?"

"Called in sick. Said they ate some bad potato salad." Dutch made a sucking sound with his teeth. "More like nursing a hangover, if you ask me. Now that Donny's gone, those two are worthless, not that they were worth much to begin with."

"Well, don't put up with it. Give them what for and tell them to get back to work."

"Easier said than done. They know I can't afford to fire them, not right now. Anyway, don't worry about it. I'll manage. Honey, I didn't get a chance to tell you before, but I'm sorry about Donny." Dutch shook his head. "Never figured he'd run off like that. Always liked that boy. Straight shooter. Hard worker. And a way better rancher than me, that's for sure."

"You're doing fine, Daddy."

They stopped outside at the fence. Mary Dell rested her arms on the top rail and looked out at the sheep pasture. Seemed like more than half of the ewes had red marks on their wool, and she counted at least three who were marked with blue.

"I saw the vet when I drove in. She told me we got a bumper crop of lambs coming on. Looks like she was telling the truth."

"Uh-huh." Dutch stared out at the sheep.

Mary Dell patted his arm. "Don't worry, Daddy. I'm going to get you some help. I'm going to try anyway. That's what I came up here to talk to you about. I'm going to go look for Donny and ask him to come back, just for a while, just through the lambing season."

"You know where he is?"

"No. I mean . . . I got a letter from him. He mailed it from Midland, so I thought I'd try there first, and then maybe Lubbock. It's a little over a hundred miles from one to the other. Maybe he decided to head home?"

Dutch raised his eyebrows doubtfully. "Trying to find one cowboy in all of Texas is like trying to find a needle in a haystack."

"I know, but I've got an advantage; how many cowboys in Texas wear peacock-blue shirts and rhinestone belt buckles? If somebody has seen Donny, they're bound to remember him. He cuts quite a figure, you have to admit."

Dutch chuckled at the truth of this, but Mary Dell could see he wasn't convinced her plan would work. That made two of them.

"I know it's a long shot, Daddy, but I've at least got to *try* to find him. I won't be gone more than five days. If I can't find him by then, I'll come home and . . . well, we'll just figure out something else, that's all. But don't you worry, some way or other, I'm going to get you some help."

Dutch nodded without saying anything. Mary Dell could tell he was a little embarrassed to admit that he needed help, but he was also relieved to hear it was coming. He looked down at Howard, who was beginning to fuss.

"Here, Daddy. I'll take him. We should get going anyway. I just wanted to stop by and let you know what I was up to." She kissed him and took the baby from his arms. "Tell Momma and Lydia Dale where I went, will you?"

Dutch touched her on the shoulder.

"Baby girl, don't you want to run up to the house and tell your momma yourself? She's all torn up to think you're still mad with her. And she's just itching to get her hands on this little baby. She wanted to come see you when you were feeling so low, but Lydia Dale didn't think that would be a good idea."

Mary Dell looked at her father. Silky didn't stop to think if it'd be a good idea to come to her granddaughter's side in her moment of despair. She just baked a pie, got in the car, and came to the rescue. She didn't ask permission; she just did it.

"You know," Dutch went on, "Taffy didn't mean what she said at the hospital that day—not the way it came out. It was a terrible thing to say, but people our age . . . well, it was just ignorance, that's all. And she was upset. Hell, we all were. Took a little getting used to, even for you. Don't try to say it didn't."

"I know," Mary Dell said. "But, Daddy, I got a lot on my plate right now. And Momma . . . every time I see her, there ends up being some kind of drama. I just don't have the energy for it. Or the time. I'll see her when I get back. And I'll bring Howard."

"Thank you, baby girl. I know that'd mean a lot to her. Come on. I'll walk you to the car."

They headed back toward the barn, but after a few steps Dutch stumbled. Mary Dell reached out and grabbed his arm to keep him from falling.

"Daddy! Are you all right?"

"Yes," Dutch said in a disgusted tone as he straightened up and regained his balance. "It's just this fool foot of mine. It wants to drag now and again. It's the diabetes, affects the nerves or some such thing. But I'm fine. Don't worry."

"Daddy," Mary Dell said with a scowl, "you have got to start taking better care of yourself. You've got to start eating right and keeping your blood sugar under control. And you have got to quit smoking. I mean it. Next time I catch you with a cigarette, I *will* tell Momma."

Dutch lifted his eyebrows. "Now, baby girl, you wouldn't do that to me, would you?"

"Just try me and see. I can't have you tripping and breaking your leg or getting sick. I need you! We all do."

Dutch sighed deeply and looked at his grandson, who was staring at him with wide eyes. "Howard, you know what they say about it being a man's world? Well, I'm sorry to be the one to tell you, but it just ain't true."

CHAPTER 27

When she got to the Tidee-Mart, Mary Dell wedged Howard's car seat into the upper rack of her shopping cart and talked to him as they wheeled up and down the aisles, picking up objects and holding them close to his face so he could see that apples were red and peppers were green, brushing his little hand with the feathery tops of orange carrots, opening his curling fingers and rubbing the smooth, firm skin of a half-green banana along his palm.

At the checkout counter, Mary Dell continued her monologue with Howard, repeating the names of items as she piled them on the counter: diapers, baby wipes, Dr Pepper, MoonPies, beef jerky, and bananas.

"Because woman does not live by MoonPies alone, Howard. We just wish we did."

When her basket was nearly empty she heard a familiar voice, a voice like green apples, sweet at the bite but sour to the chew—the voice of Marlena Benton.

"Well, speak of the devil! If it isn't Mary Dell Bebee! Diamond and I were just talking about you, weren't we, Diamond?"

"Yes, we were!" Diamond Pickens giggled and shot Marlena a meaningful glance.

Diamond, Marlena's cousin, was secretary of the Women's Club. She was also Marlena's sycophant-in-chief. This was, of course, an unofficial title, but as does any sycophant worth her salt, Diamond took her duties seriously. It was rare to see Marlena without Diamond dogging her heels and even rarer to hear her express an opinion contrary to her cousin's. Mary Dell felt sorry for Diamond, who was dumb as a watermelon and ugly to boot—not very sorry, but a little. Marlena, she just despised.

"And here you are—Mary Dell Bebee. Or have you gone back to calling yourself Templeton now?" Marlena sighed. "Bless your heart. I heard that your husband walked out on you."

"Yes. There's a lot of that kind of thing going around," Mary Dell said. "Don't know what's wrong with men these days. Irresponsible. Guess their mommas aren't raising 'em right."

Marlena smirked, trying to pretend she didn't understand the insult. Mary Dell smiled sweetly, making it clear that she was not fooled by Marlena's pretended obtuseness.

Marlena craned her neck to look at Howard.

"I heard about your baby." Marlena clucked. "Such a shame. That sort of thing runs in families, doesn't it? I mean, I always thought your daddy was a little . . . well . . . never mind." She sighed. "He does have pretty eyes. That's something, I suppose."

Mary Dell's neck turned red, and she felt the fingers of her right hand clench involuntarily. She wanted with all her heart to plow her fist into Marlena's smug, lip-sticked mouth and follow it up with a left jab directly at the bridge of her thin, pointy nose, but she restrained herself. Howard was too young to be exposed to that kind of violence. Besides, in the unwritten rules of verbal warfare among women, it is well known that the first one to lose her temper also loses the battle. Mary Dell wasn't going to give Marlena the satisfaction.

Mary Dell opened her wallet and looked at the clerk. "What do I owe you?"

"Six dollars and eleven cents, ma'am."

"Shoot. I've only got five-fifty. I'm going to have to run by the bank."

"Maybe you ought to put the MoonPies back," Marlena suggested in a sickly sweet tone. "Might help you take off some of that baby weight."

Mary Dell turned to face her foe.

"Maybe," she said with an icy smile, "but I'm still breast-feeding. It makes you awful hungry. Of course, you'd know all about that, wouldn't you? Seeing as you've had Jack Benny feeding off you for thirty years."

Marlena's eyes blazed and the veins on her neck bulged.

"Well! Maybe if you and that sister of yours could manage to hold on to your men, you'd have enough money to pay for your groceries!"

Mary Dell picked up the beef jerky and handed it back to the clerk, who deducted it from the total.

"True," she said in the sweetest possible tone. "It will be harder to make ends meet now. But I've got an idea how I can make more money than a porcupine has quills. I was thinking that I'd buy Jack Benny for what he'd bring and sell him for what *you* think he's worth." She smiled brightly. "That'd do the trick, don't you think?"

Mary Dell looked at the clerk, who was working so hard to keep from laughing that his face looked like a blister ready to pop.

"That's all right. You can keep the change," she said, then wheeled her groceries and baby right out the door.

"That probably wasn't the smartest thing I ever did," Mary Dell said to Howard as she secured the seat belt around his seat and tugged to make sure it was tight enough. "Marlena holds a grudge longer than anybody I know. But I couldn't help myself. I don't care what people say about me, but anybody who talks mean to you or down to you had better be wearing an asbestos flak jacket, honey! Because I'm going to come at them a hundred miles an hour with my hair on fire and guns blazing! That is the way it is and the way it's going to be!"

Howard blinked at his mother with innocent eyes. Mary Dell laughed and kissed him on the nose.

As they drove out of town, she said a prayer, asking God to look down from heaven, find a spot of peacock blue, and steer her to it. Or, barring that, toward something or someone who would help her family, fill their gaps, and teach her how to shoulder the burden.

"Take the wheel, dear Lord. Show me the way."

She drove north and took highway 84 to Waco, but instead of continuing west when she got there, she felt a sudden urge to take the ramp to 35 North and did so, figuring that having asked for divine direction, it would be rude to resist. She drove north to Fort Worth, then west again through Wichita Falls and Childress, then north across the Oklahoma line, driving as long as she could between Howard's insistent cries, then pulled into the parking lot of the nearest gas station or burger joint to feed him before setting off again. It was slow going with a baby on board.

When she crossed the Kansas border, well after dark, she was exhausted and Howard was howling. The Bluebird Motel promised clean rooms and free local calls, and so Mary Dell pulled into the driveway and checked in for the night.

CHAPTER 28

After Graydon replaced the spark plugs, the tractor ran fine for about a week and then conked out entirely.

Now Graydon lay on his back underneath the old John Deere, flashlight in hand, trying to locate the exact source of the oil leak that was causing the problem. Of course, the real problem, Graydon knew, was that the tractor was about forty years old. It belonged in a museum, not on a working farm. The Spreewell farm was quite a profitable operation, due in no small part to Graydon's hard work. In spite of this, L. J. was too frugal to spring for a new tractor, not until this one finally fell to pieces.

The rich get richer. Maybe that's how. By being so darned cheap.

Graydon heard the popping sound of rubber tires on gravel and wondered who it could be. Being so far from town, they didn't get many visitors. He scooted out from underneath the tractor and walked around the back of the shed, wiping motor oil from his hands with an old bandana.

A car door slammed. He caught a glimpse of a face as he rounded the corner, and for a moment, just until the woman climbing out of the sedan stood up to reveal her full height, his heart pounded.

"Mary Dell?"

She turned toward him with a startled expression, which quickly gave way to a wide grin. "Hey, Graydon. You know, for a second I thought you were Donny. You two sure look alike."

Graydon didn't mention that he'd been thinking the same thing about her, how much she looked like Lydia Dale; taller and with more curves, but just as pretty. Nor did he mention how the sight of her had caused his heart to race.

"Have you seen him?" Mary Dell asked. "Donny?"

Graydon shook his head, surprised by the question. "Well, no. I sure haven't. You don't know where he is?"

The screen door to the farm house slammed, and L. J. walked out onto the stoop. His wife, Grace, followed close behind.

"My sister-in-law," Graydon said by way of explanation and tipped his head in the direction of Mary Dell, who was bent over in the backseat of the car, getting Howard out of his car seat.

"Is the tractor fixed?"

"Working on it. I'm still trying to figure out where that oil is coming from."

L. J. frowned.

Mary Dell, with Howard in her arms, smiled sweetly and said, "Oh, we won't stay long, Mr. Spreewell. Just long enough to say hello and maybe give me a chance to change the baby; do you mind? We were in the neigh-

borhood, so I thought it'd be nice to stop by and introduce Howard to his uncle Graydon."

L. J. wasn't convinced. Nobody stopped by his farm
because they were "just in the neighborhood." She had
to have come out here for a reason. He didn't like people
taking his hired man away from his work, but the
woman had come all the way from Texas, so he couldn't
very well say no.

L. J. looked at Howard, and his frown deepened. "Something wrong with him?"

Mary Dell's bowed lips went flat and the smile left
her eyes. "Not a thing," she said.

Grace poked her husband in the back and stepped out
from behind him.

"He's a sweet little thing, isn't he? Think I see a little
of his uncle in him. Graydon, why don't you take your
sister-in-law out to your room, so she can change the
baby and the two of you can visit. I'll bring some re-
freshments out directly."

"Thank you, ma'am," Mary Dell said, ignoring the
look on Graydon's face. "That's real nice of you."

Graydon walked into the shed that served as his living quarters a step ahead of Mary Dell, nudged an
empty bottle of Jack Daniel's underneath the bed where
she couldn't see it, and quickly pulled the blanket up
over the rumpled sheets.

"It's kind of a mess in here," he mumbled apologeti-
cally. "I don't get much company."

"Do you mind if I lay him down here to change him?"
she said, nodding toward the bed. "He's wet."

Graydon sat down on the only chair, a wooden ladder-
back with wobbly legs and a frayed cane bottom, to

watch. He smiled when Howard, freed from the confines of his diaper, kicked his chubby little legs.

"Cute little fella. He's sure got a lot of hair, doesn't he? Donny did too, when he was born."

Mary Dell slid a clean diaper under Howard's bottom and looked up.

"You haven't seen Donny, have you? He hasn't been here?"

Graydon assured her that he hadn't, reminding her they weren't exactly on speaking terms.

Mary Dell sighed and nodded, as if to say she'd expected as much, then sat down on the bed with Howard in her arms and told him the whole story from the beginning, about how much Donny had wanted a baby, how excited he'd been during the pregnancy, what a blow it had been to him when Howard was born with Down syndrome, how Mary Dell had been so wrapped up in taking care of the baby that she hadn't realized the depth of his distress, and, ultimately, how Donny had disappeared without a trace, leaving no word of his whereabouts until the letter had arrived, how much she needed some help with the ranch and why, though she knew her chances of success were slim at best, Mary Dell had decided to go looking for him.

Halfway through her story, Mrs. Spreewell dropped off a tray with lemon bars and a pitcher of iced tea, assuring Graydon that he could take his time and that she'd square things with L. J.

Mary Dell finished her story at the same time as she finished her tea.

"I planned on going to Midland first and then driving up to Lubbock, but something told me I ought to try here first. Guess I was wrong." She shrugged, tipped her glass up to get the last drops of liquid, then took a bite of a lemon bar.

"Oof!" she said, and made a face. "That'll put some pucker in your lips. Guess Mrs. Spreewell was running low on sugar. Didn't have any in the tea either. I was so thirsty I didn't care but, really, why would anybody drink unsweet tea if they didn't have to?"

Graydon smiled and pulled on his nose. "Grace isn't much of a cook. She's nice enough, though. A whole lot nicer than her husband."

Mary Dell nodded and scanned the sparse barrack of a room with her eyes. "Uh-huh. And you've worked for them all these years?"

"Never planned it out that way. I just figured to be here for a season or two, but . . ." He shifted his shoulders. "I guess it's as good as anyplace. No worse, anyway."

"Suppose not," Mary Dell said. "Well, I guess I should get out of your way and let you get back to work. If you do see Donny, you'll call me right away, won't you?"

"Yes, ma'am. Well, first I'll clean his clock, *then* I'll call you." He gave her a regretful look. "I'm real sorry about this, Mary Dell. For what it's worth, I think Donny's crazy to have run out on you. You and this sweet boy."

He reached out and took hold of Howard's hand. The baby curled his tiny fingers around his uncle's thumb. Graydon grinned.

"Do you want to hold him?"

"Can I?" Graydon responded with a touching mixture of surprise and wonder, like a boy who has just been offered the keys to his daddy's new car.

Mary Dell handed the baby to him, showing him how to support the baby's head in the crook of his elbow.

"Hey, Howard. How are you there, son? I'm your uncle Graydon. What do you think about that?"

Graydon's voice was low and gentle. When he looked up at Mary Dell, there were tears in his eyes.

"He's perfect, Mary Dell. Just perfect. I know things are hard for you now, but on the whole, I think you're a real lucky woman."

"I think so too," she said.

CHAPTER 29

Mary Dell turned the key in the ignition, laid her arm over the back of the seat, looked out the rearview mirror, and shifted the car into reverse.

"Well, Howard, I guess we'll try Lubbock next. Graydon gave me a list of Donny's old friends and hangouts. Maybe we'll get lucky."

She backed the car up to turn it around and was getting ready to pull out when somebody started banging on the trunk.

"Mary Dell! Wait a minute!"

Mary Dell let out a little yelp and clasped her hand to her chest.

"Graydon! You about scared me out of my skin!"

Graydon opened the back passenger-side door and tossed an army-green duffel bag into the backseat, next to Howard.

"Sorry. I was afraid you'd drive off. Hang on a minute, will you? There's something I've got to do. I'll be right back."

Without waiting for her response, Graydon ran toward the back door of the Spreewells' house, letting the screen bang closed behind him. True to his word, he was back about a minute later. He jumped into the front seat and slammed the car door.

"All right. Let's go."

"Go? Go where?"

"To Too Much."

Mary Dell stared at him. "You want to go to Too Much? With us? Why?"

"Because you need some help and I need a job," he replied. "I just quit mine."

It was near noon when they left the farm, so they stopped at a diner in Liberal to eat and discuss the possibility of Graydon's employment at the F-Bar-T in greater detail. The waitress showed them to a booth in the back that was big enough to hold Howard's car seat and then took their order: a bowl of chili with a side of cornbread for Graydon and a chef's salad with extra Thousand Island dressing for Mary Dell.

"Four hundred dollars a month!" Mary Dell exclaimed after hearing his proposal. "I can't pay you four hundred dollars a month."

Graydon took another bite of chili and shrugged. "All right, two hundred. You sure drive a hard bargain."

"That's not what I meant."

"I know what you meant," he said. "But I'm not doing this for the money. Donny left you in a lurch, and I want to help you out. Howard's the only nephew I've got."

"You're sweet, Graydon. You really are. But none of this is your fault. I can't let you leave a perfectly good job and turn your whole life upside down just on my account."

Graydon leaned across the table and looked her in the eye. "First off, that job was a long way from good, and we both know it. Second, maybe it's time my life *was* turned upside down.

"Do you know that you're the first person, aside from the Spreewells, who'd been in my room since I've started working there? When you came through the door, I suddenly saw my life the way it must look to you   bitter bachelor cowboy, living in one dirty room, no friends, no future, nothing to look forward to. Just counting off the days, wasting my life, waiting for it all to be over."

Mary Dell gave him a pitying look and started to say something, but Graydon lifted his hand to stop her.

"Don't, Mary Dell. It's nobody's fault but mine. When things got too hard, I ran off and hid in a hole. Just like Donny's doing now. Just like our daddy did when we were kids. When I was little, I always swore I wouldn't turn out like him, but . . ."

He picked up the cream pitcher, poured a little into his coffee cup, and stirred it thoughtfully.

"Funny that I never saw it until now. Maybe that's what Bebee men do," he mused.

"The Fatal Flaw," Mary Dell said quietly.

"What?"

"Nothing. Listen, Graydon, I can't deny we could use your help, but . . . are you *sure* you want to do this?"

"I've got no love for Too Much, you know that. Once your lambs are born, your cattle go to market, and we can find somebody reliable to take over, then I'll head on down the road. But I'd like to help you get through this rough patch, help you get off to a fresh start now that you're on your own. Who knows? Maybe it'll be a fresh start for me too."

Mary Dell thought about this. She couldn't deny that their meeting seemed to be timed by Providence and that his proposal was an answer to her prayers. And he would doubtless be better off working at the F-Bar-T than he was living in that nasty shed and working for that cranky Mr. Spreewell. But she didn't think it was fair that Graydon should be trying to make up for Donny's mistake. Especially at a price of four hundred a month. That might be reasonable pay, or close to it, for a regular old hired man, but what Graydon was proposing was to really manage the ranch. Mary Dell had no doubt that he was up to the job.

"I've got to pay you more than you're asking for," Mary Dell said as she cut a chunk of tomato into bite-sized pieces. "I won't let you do it for four hundred."

"How about this?" Graydon countered. "You pay me the four hundred. If you have a good year, if the lambing goes good and the beef sells at a decent price, you give me three percent of the profits."

"Eight," Mary Dell countered.

"Five," Graydon said.

"Done."

"Done."

Graydon nodded and resumed eating.

"Just one thing," Mary Dell said. "Where are we going to put you? I'd let you stay with us, but we just have the two bedrooms. You could sleep up at the big house, it's closer to the barns anyway, but since Lydia Dale moved in with the children, they're pretty short on beds too."

"I don't want to stay in the house."

The way he said it made Mary Dell think what he

really meant was he didn't want to stay anywhere Lydia Dale was. She understood his feelings, but they were bound to run into each other. And, anyway, that was all ancient history now. It was time he got over it. Time Lydia Dale got over it too.

Too bad there *weren't* any extra bedrooms at the big house. Now that Lydia Dale was finally free from Jack Benny and with Graydon still single . . . well, she could think of worse ideas than throwing the two of them together. Damn, but he was handsome! But those Bebee brothers always had been.

"You got a tack room?"

Mary Dell jerked a bit, startled by the sound of his voice. "Beg pardon?"

"Do you have a tack room in the barn? If you've got a cot and some blankets, maybe a chair and table, I can bed down there."

"In the barn?" Mary Dell frowned. "That wouldn't be very comfortable. There's no bathroom out there. No kitchen either."

"I've been sleeping in a converted shed with no facilities for years. A tack room won't be much different. And I can't cook anyway. Well, I can scramble an egg and heat up soup, but that's about it. If your folks wouldn't mind me coming in the big house to use the facilities and if your momma would make me a plate of whatever she's cooking, that'd be fine with me. I hope Taffy's a better cook than Grace Spreewell." He winked and scooped up another bite of chili.

"Momma's a very good cook. One of the best in the county," Mary Dell said truthfully. "And Grandma Silky can bake a pie that'll bring tears to your eyes. But you'd better be careful about giving either of them too many compliments on their food. They'll have you fattened up like a Christmas turkey if you're not careful."

Graydon smiled, but barely. "Well, I plan to be on my way before Christmas, so I ought to be safe. That work for you?"

"It does. I feel lucky to have you for as long as you want to stay. Thank you."

Graydon touched his forefinger to his brow in a silent salute and then extended his hand. "So, we've got a deal, then?"

"We do," Mary Dell replied as she shook his hand to seal the bargain. "We sure do."

CHAPTER 30

"Here?"

Taffy's eyebrows lifted as if she wasn't sure she'd heard her daughter correctly. She wiped the blade of the paring knife she'd been using to slice apples on the hem of her apron and frowned.

"Why does he have to stay here? Why can't he stay at your place?"

Mary Dell mentally counted to three.

"Because," she replied in a deliberately even tone, "I've got no extra beds. And it'll be a lot more convenient for him to stay up here, close to the barns and paddocks. He's staying in the barn. Not the house. He won't be in the way."

Taffy put the knife on the counter and folded her arms across her chest. "Won't he? He's going to use our bathroom, which, I'll remind you, is already being shared by six people. *And* you expect me to cook for him. Probably do his laundry too. Like I don't already have enough on my plate. Don't you stand there looking down your nose at me, missy!" Taffy snapped, though Mary Dell hadn't changed her expression at all.

"You've barely spoken to me for weeks, but boy howdy! The second you want something you sure run home to Momma quick enough, don't you?"

Taffy pulled a pastry cutter out of a drawer and started using it to mix cold butter into a mixture of brown sugar, cinnamon, and flour, stabbing at the cobbler topping as if she were trying to inflict bodily harm.

Mary Dell threw up her hands. "This isn't about me *wanting* something! I'm trying to figure out a way to get through the next few months without killing Daddy and losing half our livestock. Don't you see that? I'm trying to keep the farm and this family from falling apart, and I can't do it alone—"

"Your daddy—" Taffy interrupted.

Mary Dell interrupted her right back, determined to make her mother see sense.

"My daddy is about ready to collapse from overwork. He can't go on like he's been doing—but somebody has to! Now, out of the blue, here's Graydon, ready to work, asking for nothing in return but a pittance in pay and a place to lay his head. His coming here is an answer to our prayers, Momma. Don't you see that?"

"All I see is that after all I've already been through, losing my membership in the Women's Club, having to put up with all and sundry gossiping about how my daughters managed to lose two men in one year, you're trying to heap more humiliation on me by asking me to take in *boarders*."

Taffy reached into the mixing bowl and angrily started throwing lumps of sticky dough on top of the sugared apples like she was throwing dirt clods at a stray dog, spilling a good third of it over the side of the cobbler pan in the process.

"Won't Marlena and her henchmen have a time with *that* when they find out?"

"Why do you care what that old peahen thinks?" Mary Dell asked. "It's none of her business. And even if it was, you're not taking in boarders. Graydon is family."

Taffy scraped the spilled dough up off the counter with her hands and dumped it into the pan.

"Not anymore, he's not," she mumbled. "I've had just about enough of those Bebee boys. Thought you would too, by now."

"Don't blame Graydon for what Donny did!" Mary Dell snapped. "It's not fair. He came to help us out of the kindness of his heart, because he *is* family. He's Howard's uncle. We can trust him."

"The way we trusted Donny?" Taffy remarked acidly. She brushed the leftover flour off her hands.

"Stop that," Mary Dell hissed. "And lower your voice. He's out on the porch. He might hear you."

"I don't care if he does. I don't want him staying with us!"

Lydia Dale walked into the kitchen, carrying an empty baby bottle and balancing Rob Lee on her hip. Mary Dell turned toward her, an expression of relief on her face.

"Sis, help me talk some sense into her. I drove up to Kansas, hoping to find Donny. Graydon hadn't seen him, but when he heard what happened, he decided to come with me and—"

Lydia Dale frowned. "Graydon? Graydon Bebee?"

"Of course," Mary Dell said. "How many Graydons do we know? He's here to help with the ranch for a while. Through the lambing season for sure, but longer if I can talk him into it, at least until we can find a qualified manager. He's hardly charging me anything, but he needs a place to stay. I've got no room in the trailer, and all the bedrooms are full here, so he's going to sleep in the tack room."

Lydia Dale's eyes went wide. "Our tack room? But where is he going to eat? And where is he going to—"

"He'll use the bathroom in here," Mary Dell said, "and he can eat whatever it is the rest of the family is eating. All we have to do is make a little more of what we were fixing anyway."

"Are you kidding?" Lydia Dale asked incredulously. "That's just crazy!"

"I know," Mary Dell said. "The tack room isn't very comfortable, but that's the way he wants it. He doesn't want to be a bother to anybody."

Lydia Dale shifted the baby on her hip, set the empty bottle down on the table, and screwed her eyes shut.

"No," she said with a shake of her head, "I don't mean it's crazy that he'd sleep and eat in the barn. I mean it's just crazy! The whole idea is crazy. He can't stay here!"

Taffy, who had been following this exchange closely, crossed her arms over her chest and gave a smug little nod. "That's just what I said. This is our home, not a boardinghouse for stray cowpokes and former in-laws looking for a handout."

"A handout! Graydon is not looking for a handout. He quit his job in Kansas just to come here and help us." Mary Dell threw up her hands. "What is wrong with you two?"

Mary Dell looked at her mother, but Taffy just jerked her chin, picked up her cobbler, and slid it into the oven. Recognizing that immovable expression on her mother's face, Mary Dell turned to her sister.

"What do you have against Graydon? He's never done

anything to you or to any of us. Don't tell me you're blaming him for Donny's mistakes too."

"No." Lydia Dale closed her eyes again, trying to sort out her thoughts. "It's not that. But it's only that I . . . well, I just don't want him staying here. I can't explain why exactly, but I don't! It would be so . . . awkward. And anyway, things aren't that bad. We can hire somebody else."

"Nobody with one-tenth of his experience and who we can be sure has our best interests at heart. Nobody we *know*." Mary Dell spread out her hands to underscore her point.

Taffy closed the door of the oven and went to stand next to Lydia Dale, slipping her arm around her waist. "Well, maybe we'd prefer somebody we don't know quite so well. Lydia Dale understands exactly what I'm talking about. I don't want him staying here. Nobody does, except you."

"And me."

The kitchen door opened, and Dutch came in from the porch. He didn't bother to wipe his boots on the mat like he usually did. Instead, he just strode into the middle of the room and looked at the three women with a stormy expression.

"I saw Graydon hanging out over near the paddock. Seems he heard what you said about him, Taffy, not that you were trying very hard to keep it a secret, and figured he'd take himself off away from the house until things were settled. Which they are," Dutch declared, "as of right now. Graydon is staying."

Taffy started to protest, but Dutch held up his hand to silence her.

"Nope, I'm not hearing any of it. Lydia Dale, I don't know what you've got against that young man, but get over it. Graydon's a good man to help us like this. And we need help. This operation has got beyond me now. I can't manage the hands, and they know it. One of 'em is stealing from us. I count six bags of feed missing. I can't prove who took them, but somebody did. Plus, I'm a cowman. Don't know a darned thing about sheep. Graydon does. We need him."

Taffy made a little clucking sound. "It's not as bad as that."

"Oh, yes, it is," Dutch countered. "Don't you read the papers? We haven't had rain in months. Our pasture is poor and the price of feed is up. Meanwhile, beef prices are low and going lower. We'll be lucky to break even on our cattle. We need a good lambing season just to keep our heads above water, and that means we need Graydon. He's staying."

Lydia Dale's gaze flickered away from her father's. She shifted her shoulders to indicate acquiescence. Taffy scowled and shuffled her feet as though her corns were bothering her. Her mouth opened, but once again, Dutch stayed her protests, this time by pointing his finger directly at the bridge of her nose.

"I mean it, Taffy. Don't test me on this. Graydon is staying and you are going to be nice to him. We're going to wash his shirts, and feed him from our table, and you're going to be hospitable to him. And if you're not," Dutch said, staring at his wife with eyes as focused and bright as two headlights on high beam, "I'll be sleeping on the sofa, and you'll be sleeping alone. Tonight and every night after. Do I make myself clear?"

Taffy, with lips clamped tight, blew a long breath out through her nose, a defeated noise, like air leaking from an inner tube. She turned away, opened a drawer, and started rattling through the silverware, pulling out spoons, knives, and forks—enough for the family and a guest.

Dutch nodded and headed toward the living room, stopping to chuck Rob Lee on the chin.

"Give me this big old boy," he said to Lydia Dale. "He wants to come into the TV room with me, don't you, Bubba? Honey, can you bring us something to drink? Rob Lee and Grandpa are going to see if we can catch the sports report before supper."

"Sure, Daddy," she said, passing the baby over to her father. "One bottle of apple juice and one bottle of beer, coming right up."

Dutch walked out, cooing to his grandson. Lydia Dale filled the baby's bottle, cracked open a Lone Star, and followed. Taffy finished counting out the silverware, slammed the drawer shut, and glared at Mary Dell.

"Well?"

"Well, what?"

"Well, are you just going to stand there with your teeth in your mouth, or are you going to get some bedding out of the linen closet and take it to the tack room? Dinner's almost ready."

"Yes, ma'am." Mary Dell ducked her head to hide her smile.

Taffy called after her, "And you be sure to tell that Graydon Bebee to wipe his boots before he comes into my kitchen!"

CHAPTER 31

Graydon was leaning against the fence, holding a sleeping Howard on his shoulder as he stroked the neck of Dutch's horse, a buckskin bay named Billy Boy. The horse sputtered contentedly as Graydon's hand slid down his coat and stepped closer to the fence, urging him to go on. But when Graydon heard Mary Dell coming with an armload of bedding, he walked toward her.

"Maybe it'd be better if I left."

"Don't do that," Mary Dell said. "Please. I need your help."

"I don't want to cause trouble between you and Taffy."

"Any trouble I have with Momma has been around since long before you showed up. Trust me. I'm sorry you had to hear all that," she said, tilting her head toward the house. "She didn't mean it like it sounded. Momma's had a hard year—mostly because she chooses to take everything so hard. Beats me why she gives a flyin' flip about what Marlena Benton and the rest say about us, but she does."

Graydon nodded and scratched a spot on his neck just below his right ear, the exact same spot Donny had always scratched when he was thinking something through. Mary Dell felt a little catch in her throat, but she swallowed it back.

"Taffy's a proud woman."

"She is," Mary Dell agreed with a little laugh. "Though I can't think why. Look at us. It's not like we've got all that much to be proud of."

Graydon, still holding Howard in his arms, took a long look from left to right, scanning miles of bright blue sky where it met the brown horizon, acres and acres of land, from the flat plain nearest the house where scores of fat, pregnant sheep lolled and dozed in the sun, beyond that to distant, rust-colored hillocks studded with stubborn mesquite trees, and farther still, where the hills sloped downward and met a narrow strip of brownish-green, like a bedraggled hair ribbon, the stingy stream that made the F-Bar-T, small as it was by Texas standards, one of the most desirable ranches in the county.

The stream was just a trickle now, dried up by months of drought. According to family lore that was the state it had been in when Flagadine and George arrived, more than 140 years ago, in the middle of another drought. The other settlers were in too much of a rush to notice such a miserly stream, preferring to stake claims closer to town before somebody else snapped them up. But Flagadine took her time, walked these acres personally, studied the landscape, read the soil, and came to realize that when the drought finally ended and the rains returned, this piddling little stream would swell, overflow its shallow banks, and flood the lowlands, feeding the soil and bringing forth new, tender green grass.

"Well," Graydon said after a long moment, "this may not seem like anything special to people who live in New York, or San Francisco, or any place like that, but to a rancher, to a Texan, this looks an awful lot like heaven. Twelve hundred acres of God's country. The kind of place I used to dream of having myself, back in the days when I used to do that kind of thing. I don't mean to contradict you, Mary Dell, but it seems to me that your family has plenty to be proud of."

Mary Dell moved her eyes across the horizon the way Graydon had, seeing what he had seen the way he had seen it, the stark beauty of the land and the unique heritage that she had only begun to fully appreciate when the responsibility for protecting it fell to her. It was a heritage to be proud of, an inheritance worth fighting for. She knew that. So did Graydon.

She laid her hand lightly on his forearm. "So you'll stay?"

He nodded. "For a while."

"Thank you," she said quietly, locking her eyes with his for just a moment before removing her hand. "I'll just go and make up your bed."

Graydon glanced at the baby. "Why don't we trade loads? I'm used to making my own bed, and I've got to unpack my gear anyway, what there is of it."

He passed Howard over to her, took the pile of blankets and sheets, and loped off toward the barn.

Billy Boy, who had been munching a clump of not-very-green grass he'd discovered growing around a fence post, suddenly jerked his head up, looked around, and sputtered.

Mary Dell approached the paddock and scratched the horse gently between the eyes. "Are you wondering where Graydon ran off to? You like him? Me too."

* * *

Mary Dell was still petting Billy Boy when Graydon returned. The kitchen door opened at the same time, and Jeb stepped out onto the porch.

"Grandma says come in and wash up before supper," he yelled in a singsong voice. "And to wipe your boots when you do."

"Jeb! That's no way to talk to company," Mary Dell scolded. "Somebody'd think you were trying for first prize in a hog-calling contest, hollering like that. Come over here and say hello to your uncle Graydon."

Jeb shuffled toward them, scuffing his boots in the dirt and giving Billy Boy a cautious glance before putting out his hand.

"Nice to meet you, Uncle Graydon."

Graydon shook his hand. "Nice to meet you too, Jeb."

Jeb sniffed and used his hand to swipe at his nose. "Are you my real uncle? Or are you just a boyfriend uncle?"

"Boyfriend uncle?" Mary Dell asked.

Jeb nodded. "Like Carla Jean. Daddy says I'm supposed to call her Aunt Carla Jean. I don't like to. She's not my aunt, she's just Daddy's girlfriend."

Jeb eyed Graydon suspiciously. "Are you Aunt Mary Dell's new boyfriend?"

Mary Dell blushed and started to say something, but Graydon beat her to it.

"I'm not anybody's boyfriend. I'm your uncle Donny's brother. I'm not sure if that makes me your uncle or not," he said evenly, "but it does make me family."

"Well, if you're family, then why haven't I met you before?"

"I've been living up in Kansas for a long time."

"How long?"

"Jeb!" Mary Dell exclaimed. "Uncle Graydon didn't come all the way from Kansas so you could give him the third degree."

"It's all right," Graydon said with a wave of his hand. "He's just curious—means he's thinking." He turned back to Jeb.

"I moved to Kansas before you were born. And before you ask, I'm here now to help out on the ranch for a while, at least through the lambing season."

"Because Uncle Donny left?" Jeb asked. "My daddy left too. He lives in town, but he doesn't work at the ranch anymore."

"Did you help out when he did?"

"No," Jeb said irritably, as if offended by the question.

"There's a lot to do around here," Graydon said. "Sure could use an extra hand if you're interested. I've got to ride out and take a look at the fences tomorrow. Want to come along?"

Jeb looked down and scuffed the toe of his boot in the dirt. "I don't ride. Don't like horses."

Only a slight twitch of his lips told Mary Dell that Graydon was surprised by this information. Why wouldn't he be? Jeb was one of the few boys his age who didn't know how to ride, at least in this part of Texas. Mary Dell knew that Jeb wasn't telling the whole truth about his equestrian experiences. He had ridden, or tried to, once.

When Jeb was about six, Jack Benny had decided to teach him to ride. The boy was tense, frightened of Ranger, a mean-tempered, sixteen-hand-high black horse that Jack Benny rode on the few occasions when he actually showed up to work, and nervous that he would disappoint the father whose approval he so desperately craved. Naturally, that was exactly what happened.

Mary Dell and Lydia Dale were outside the paddock when it did, and Mary Dell could tell by the way her sister gripped the top rail of the fence with both her hands that she was just as nervous as her son.

The first thing that happened was that Jeb approached Ranger from behind, so the horse tried to nip at him. It wasn't Ranger's fault—no horse likes to be snuck up on, though one a little more patient and used to children might have taken it in stride. It wasn't Jeb's fault either; Jack Benny should have told the boy to approach the animal from the side. Actually, he did tell him, but not until Jeb had already made the mistake. Then Jack Benny snapped at his son, asking what the hell was the matter with him? Didn't he even know how to mount a horse?

"Of course not," Lydia Dale mumbled under her breath. "You never took time to teach him."

Mary Dell looked sideways at her sister. Her knuckles were white where they clutched at the rail, and her arm muscles were taut, pushing against it, as if poised to jump the fence and pull Jeb out of the paddock. Mary Dell wished she would.

Jeb's lower lip was trembling as he mounted the horse, and his eyes were wide with fright. Ranger must have seemed like a giant to a child so small. Why hadn't Jack Benny saddled up one of the ponies for him instead?

For a couple of minutes, it seemed like everything would be all right. Ranger, with Jeb astride, clutching the saddle horn for all he was worth, calmly circled the paddock. But when Jack Benny instructed the boy to give the horse a kick in the flanks so he'd pick up some speed and Jeb refused to do so, saying this was fast enough, Jack Benny scowled. He walked quickly to the opposite side of the paddock and slapped Ranger hard on the rump. The horse reared, not a lot but enough. Jeb tumbled off, landed in the dirt, and started to cry. Jack

Benny walked over to the child. Towering over his son with his feet spread and arms crossed, he told Jeb to quit being such a crybaby and demanded that he get up and get back on the horse.

Lydia Dale practically vaulted over the fence and ran across the riding ring to comfort her sobbing son. After ascertaining that Jeb hadn't broken anything in the fall, she picked him up and carried him into the house. Jack Benny sneered as she left, saying it was no wonder Jeb was growing up to be such a momma's boy.

That was the first and last time Jeb had ever tried to mount a horse. Mary Dell wanted to pull Graydon aside and explain the situation but knew she couldn't, not without embarrassing Jeb. But she didn't have to explain; Graydon already seemed to have a pretty good bead on the boy. He'd always been that way, Mary Dell remembered. Not much of a talker but observant, able to understand what any creature, whether it walked on two feet or four, was feeling just by watching it. Donny had that same gift—that was part of what had made him such a good rancher—but Graydon possessed it in even greater measure. Mary Dell felt so lucky that Graydon had come to their aid.

"I used to be a rodeo rider," Graydon said, looking at the top of Jeb's drooping head. "Did you know that? First time I met your aunt was outside a rodeo ring not far from here, at the fair. She tripped and fell and I helped her up. We talked, but just for a second. About the time she got to her feet, they called my name for the bull riding competition."

Jeb lifted his head and looked up at Graydon, clearly impressed. "You were a bull rider?"

"Among other things. That was a good day," Graydon said, smiling just a little. "I took first place in the bull riding. I met your aunt Mary Dell. And later, I met your momma."

"You know my momma?"

"Yep," Graydon answered quickly. "I met the whole family that day. The next day wasn't quite as good, though. I got thrown and broke a rib."

Jeb winced. "Must have been a mean horse."

"Naw." Graydon shrugged. "Horses aren't mean, not naturally. But if they're in pain, or if people mistreat them, or frighten them, sometimes they act mean. If you take time to get to know a horse and let him get to know you, feed him, brush him, let him get familiar with the way you talk and smell, he won't be mean to you or try to throw you. See, that bronc that threw me, he was just scared. He was wild, had never been ridden, and didn't know me from Adam.

"Now that I think of it," Graydon said, almost as if he were talking to himself, letting his gaze drift toward the horizon, "I don't believe I will ride fences tomorrow. Seems to me I should spend the day getting my feet under me. Dutch says y'all are missing some feed. I should introduce myself to the hands, assure them I'm aware of the situation and will be keeping an eye on it."

He paused for a moment, scratched his thinking spot, just below his ear.

"Probably ought to spend some time looking over the stock too, get to know them a little better. Say," he said, looking down at Jeb, "I don't suppose you'd like to help feed and curry the horses in the morning? You're pretty well filled out for your age. I need somebody strong to help me haul hay bales and water buckets, somebody who can show me the ropes and help me get the feel of the place."

Jeb bit his lower lip, turning it from pink to white as

he considered this offer. "I guess so," he said cautiously and then, more stoutly, "Okay."

"Thank you, son," Graydon said, laying his arm on the boy's shoulder. "I sure appreciate the help."

The kitchen door opened. Lydia Dale, carrying the baby and looking irritated, stepped out onto the porch calling, "Jeb! Where are you? Grandma says she sent you out—"

Seeing her eldest standing next to Graydon pulled her up short. She stopped in mid-sentence, closed her mouth, and opened it again.

"Hey."

Graydon touched two fingers to the brim of his hat. "Hey, Lydia Dale."

After an awkward pause she stared straight at Jeb, looking only at him.

"Where have you been? Grandma says she sent you out to round everybody up for supper fifteen minutes ago."

"Sorry, Momma."

She turned her attention to Mary Dell, looking past Graydon as if he were as insubstantial as a breath of wind. "Are you staying for supper?"

Mary Dell shook her head. "Howard still hasn't had his afternoon exercise session."

"Well, the rest of y'all better get in here. The meat is getting cold." She turned on her heel and went quickly back inside, letting the screen door slam behind her.

Jeb trooped obediently across the yard, but stopped when he realized Graydon wasn't following. "You better come on. Granny gets mad when the food gets cold."

"You go on without me. I'm going to head on back to the tack room, get my gear unpacked."

"I thought you already did that," Mary Dell said.

"I'd like to take some time to get settled in. I'm not that hungry."

Mary Dell doubted that, but she didn't blame him for hesitating to sit down at the family dinner table. He hadn't exactly been welcomed with open arms.

"Why don't I go in and fix you a plate?" Mary Dell asked. "I can bring it out to the barn for you."

"Let me!" Jeb exclaimed. "I'll do it. I can bring Uncle Graydon's dinner. And while you're eating, maybe you could tell me about competing on the rodeo circuit? If you don't mind."

"I'd be happy for the company. I'll even pull out the belt buckle I won at the Fort Worth Stock Show," Graydon said with a small smile. "It's silver and big as a saucer. Too heavy to wear, but it looks nice."

Jeb's eyes grew wide. "Real silver?"

"I guess," he said with a shrug. "Never thought to check, but it's got a good shine to it. Anyway, you run in and have your supper. Be sure to help clear the table when you're finished. There's no hurry. Okay?"

"Okay! Yes, sir!" Jeb galloped toward the house, grinning for all he was worth. When he got to the door, he flung it open and rushed inside without bothering to wipe his boots. A moment later, the echo of Taffy's harangue wafted through the air, the words indistinct at such a distance, but the general nature of her complaint was clear enough.

CHAPTER 32

April 1984

Mary Dell was exhausted. Run-ins with her mother always wore her out and in the three weeks since Graydon Bebee had come to the ranch, battles with Taffy were a daily occurrence. Almost always, the thing they fought about was Graydon.

Today, Taffy's tizzy came about because Graydon had fired two of their hired men. Truthfully, Mary Dell wasn't sure of the wisdom of that move, especially so close to the start of lambing season, but Graydon was the ranch manager, and she felt she owed him her support. Too, coming down on the opposite side of any argument Taffy made was habit by now, an itch she just couldn't keep from scratching. But it sure was tiring.

She'd gone to the big house just a little after lunch, summoned to the scene by her mother. Mary Dell didn't want to go, she had so much to do, but knew somebody had to listen to Taffy gripe. If it wasn't her, it would be Dutch or Graydon. Dutch had to put up with enough as it was, and Graydon had his hands full running the ranch, so Mary Dell was on deck.

It should have been a half-hour errand, but by the time they returned home to the trailer, just as the sun was setting, both she and the baby were in bad spirits.

Howard kept tugging at his left ear and fussing during exercises, cried during his bath, and he howled while Mary Dell rocked him for a full hour before finally falling asleep. By the time she tucked him into his crib, it was well after ten.

Mary Dell wasn't feeling very good either. The ranch was at its most beautiful in spring, green leaves were sprouting and little wildflowers were popping up everywhere, so pretty, but the pollen was sure making her miserable. She went into the bathroom and searched through the cabinet for her allergy pills, an over-the-counter medication she'd discovered that seemed to work pretty well. The box of pills was empty, so she went searching through drawers, hoping to find a forgotten supply of medication or at least a reasonable substitute, locating some on Donny's side of the cabinet. It was a prescription, but the bottle said it was for allergies and the pills looked the same, so Mary Dell took two.

She desperately wanted go into her bedroom, flop face-first onto the mattress, and sleep. Howard would be awake in another three hours, maybe less, demanding to be fed. The way he was pulling at his ear made her think he had an ear infection brewing. She'd have to call the pediatrician the next day. But before that and before she could go to bed, she had to eat something, wash the dirty dishes piled in the sink, and go through the week-long backlog of mail that was piled up on the "catchall" counter next to the microwave, the spot where the things she didn't have time to deal with or put away landed until she did have time. By now, it was a big pile and getting bigger, a treacherous clutter glacier, advancing slowly but surely, threatening to engulf the entire countertop. Tired as she was, she had to deal with it now, while the house was quiet.

What had happened to her? She'd always been such a good housekeeper. People had warned her that having a baby changes your life and your priorities, but nothing they'd said prepared her for the reality of parenthood—especially single parenthood of a child with Down syndrome.

And her family wasn't helping either, she thought as she tiptoed out of the nursery, down the hall, and through the living room, gathering up more stray items to add to the catchall pile. Here was Graydon, an absolute godsend in their hour of need, an angel on horseback coming all the way down from Kansas to help them, and Taffy treated him like he was a drifter looking for a handout!

It's not so bad when it's me; I'm used to it. She's been against him from the first second. But she has no call to treat him so mean. I've had it with her! And if she ever says another careless word about Howard—that's it! I'll never speak to her again, and I don't care what Daddy says.

Mary Dell felt a twinge of guilt. She knew she should forgive and forget, but this was easier said than done. She'd never been particularly short-tempered, not until recently. These days, it took just about every ounce of energy she had to keep from exploding, sometimes over the silliest things. She'd always said that there would be less offense given if less offense were taken. But when those offenses were directed toward Howard, it was a whole different ball game. When someone was mean to her baby she became not just offended, but incensed. Marlena Benton didn't know how lucky she was to have escaped their confrontation in the Tidee-Mart with nothing more than a bruised ego. It had taken every ounce of self-control Mary Dell had to keep from planting her fist right into Marlena's smug, overlipsticked mouth.

As she spread pimento cheese on a slice of Wonder Bread and popped the top on a can of Dr Pepper, she wondered if Taffy had ever felt like that about her. She could imagine her mother getting into a catfight to defend Lydia Dale, but it was impossible to conjure a picture of Taffy doing the same for her. No use wondering why; Taffy was Taffy and nothing would change that.

It was her sister's behavior and attitude that really irked her. Hadn't Lydia Dale been the one wringing her hands with worry over how she could help Mary Dell lighten some of the financial burdens and responsibilities that had fallen into her lap? The fact that her twin was now unwilling to do something as simple as display a little hospitality and support when Graydon showed up, offering a real answer to at least some of their immediate problems, made Mary Dell wonder if Lydia Dale was as worried about her as she professed to be.

Mary Dell pulled a stool up to the counter, next to the catchall pile.

She was starting to wonder if Taffy's self-centered ways were rubbing off on Lydia Dale. She didn't like to think that of her own sister, but a lot of women became more and more like their mothers as they aged. Mary Dell had seen it firsthand.

Take Pearl Dingus; when Pearl was a child, she was a

rebel. She took her momma's oft-repeated advice not to "drink, or smoke, or chew, or go around with boys who do," and turned it right on its head. Well, that wasn't quite fair. Pearl didn't ever chew, at least Mary Dell didn't think she did, but she'd done about everything else and had just about driven her parents over the edge. But somehow, as the years passed, Pearl had morphed into her momma's image. She traded in her halter tops and miniskirts for high-button necklines and calf-length hemlines, married a preacher, and started "speaking the truth in love," which, as far as Mary Dell was concerned, was just another word for lecturing, just like her momma did. Mary Dell liked Pearl, even if she was a little self-righteous, and figured it was better that she'd forsaken the road to hell and damnation to follow in her mother's footsteps, but she couldn't say the same thing about her sister turning into a next-generation Taffy. Nothing good could come of that!

How could Lydia Dale have supported Taffy's opinion over hers? She was supposed to be on Mary Dell's side! Other than Dutch, no one was on her side. No one lifted a finger to help! Didn't they see how hard she was working? How trying to care for Howard and figure out a way to keep the ranch together, not to mention stuffing down the grief of being abandoned by her husband just when she needed him most, was wearing her down? How could they be so selfish? She expected that kind of thing from her mother, but she'd never, ever imagined Lydia Dale would abandon her too. The more Mary Dell thought about this, the angrier she became. Washing down a mouthful of pimento cheese sandwich with a long and fortifying swig of Dr Pepper, she started in on the catch-all pile, determined to take control of this mess, if nothing else.

She pulled four quilting magazines out of the pile and shoved them aside, then decided that she'd probably never, ever have five minutes of time to herself to read magazines again and threw them all into the trash. Then, rethinking her action, she pulled her favorite, *Quilt Treasures,* out of the wastebasket performing a quick flip-through to see if maybe, just maybe, the magazine had published one of her quilts but had forgotten to notify her. Next, she started ripping open envelopes one after the other, scanning the contents and dividing them into personal letters, advertisements, and bills.

The stack of personal letters was pathetically small, only one little thank-you note from Mrs. Covey, a lady she knew from church, a recent widow. Mary Dell had shown her how to make her husband's old ties into a memory quilt. The old woman's heartfelt note helped douse Mary Dell's ire, but not enough and not for long. After tossing out the stack of advertisements, Mary Dell started in on the bills. It dwarfed the other two stacks by an exponent of three. All the usual suspects were depressingly present—electricity bills, mortgage bills, insurance bills, tax bills, propane bills, and the car payment, accompanied by the ones that were less regular but also added up—doctor bills, vet bills, feed bills, magazine renewal bills, another from Jimmy's Garage for the oil change and 150,000-mile service on her car, as well as a credit card bill that still carried most of the balance for that ridiculous, over-the-top orgy of Christmas presents that Donny had bought, the toys he'd assured her they could afford and then paid for with a credit card—just months before he left town and left her holding the bag!

The next envelope was the checking account statement, and the news there was no more encouraging. She could pay the bills, but the balance was getting uncomfortably low, and if she wanted to keep a decent safety cushion in their cash reserves, she wouldn't be able to make more than the minimum payment on the credit cards.

Mary Dell knocked back the last swallow of Dr Pepper and smacked the empty can down on the counter in frustration.

How was she supposed to manage all this on her own? With barely a word of encouragement or appreciation from anyone? It was so unfair.

She started to sweep the pile of empty envelopes and paper clutter into the wastepaper basket but saw one more unopened envelope that had escaped her notice. She turned it over. It was from *Quilt Treasures* magazine. There was no window on it and her subscription was paid up, so she knew it wasn't a bill. The return address said C. J. Evard.

Mary Dell had seen and opened many such envelopes in the past, but this time she was sure this wasn't a rejection. It couldn't be. Her quilt was beautiful, perfectly and precisely constructed, not so much as a thread out of place. She had never worked harder on any project. There was no way in the world that C. J. Evard could reject her, not this time. And didn't it say in the Bible that God wouldn't give a person more to deal with than they could bear? If that were true, then the envelope must contain the letter she'd waited so many years to receive. This letter must be *the* letter, because Mary Dell couldn't deal with one more disappointment, not today. She was sure she'd reached her limit.

She clutched the envelope to her pounding chest, took a deep breath, held it, and said a silent prayer before finally ripping the flap open and pulling out a sheet of creamy, white stationery, folded thrice. She opened it.

Dear Quilter,

Thank you very much for your recent submission to *Quilt Treasures* magazine. While your work is interesting, it does not meet our needs at this time.

Cordially . . .

"No!" Mary Dell shouted and then, "Damn it!" And then a whole string of other words that, until that moment, she didn't even know she knew.

But cursing did not make her feel better, nor did kicking the wastepaper basket across the room. That just created more mess that she was going to have to clean up because there was no one else around to do it for her.

She went into the kitchen in search of a MoonPie, thinking the taste of marshmallow and graham covered in chocolate might soothe her, but found the box empty. When she opened the refrigerator she discovered that she'd just drunk the last Dr Pepper. She did spy, far in the back, next to an open box of baking soda, half-hidden behind a jar of pickled peppers and a wilting cabbage, two bottles of Lone Star that Donny had left behind. Mary Dell pulled them out, opened one, and drank it quickly as she paced back and forth, from the refrigerator to the stove and back again, and again, and again. When that bottle was empty she opened the second, took one more turn around the kitchen and then, her mind made up, scrounged through one of the drawers for a pen and sheet of paper, sat down, and began to write a letter, scribbling furiously, pausing only long enough to take generous swigs of beer between sentences.

Later, she would be unable to remember the exact words and phrases she wrote that night. She wasn't a big drinker to start with, and the combination of beer and prescription allergy pills clouded her good sense and her memory.

But Mary Dell recalled that she'd told Miss Evard that she wouldn't know a good quilt if it walked in the door and bit her on the backside, that she lacked the sense that God gave gum trees, and that it cost her, Mary Dell, absolutely nothing to write these things because it was all true and since she was sure that Miss Evard wouldn't read this letter, undoubtedly being too busy riding her high horse to read anybody's letters, it didn't matter anyway.

She did remember the last sentence word for word, and the way the words looked on the page, sloping sloppily down and to the right as it became harder and harder to make her pen behave.

P.S. Though I am paid through the end of the year, please cancel my subscription immediately— I've never thought your magazine, or the quilts in it, were anything all that special. On second thought, rather than cancel my subscription, just let it run to the end. I'll cut the pages up for out- house paper—that way, at least somebody will get some use out of it.

Cordially,

Mary Dell Templeton

When she woke up the next morning, when she *really* woke up, her slumber having been interrupted several times by Howard, who finally fell into a good sleep when dawn was breaking, it was past nine o'clock.

Her head was pounding, and her tongue felt like sandpaper. Whether her hangover was the result of the beer she'd consumed, the pity party she'd thrown herself, Donny's old allergy pills, or some combination of the three, she couldn't say, but she was paying the price for it now.

She stumbled into the kitchen in search of water, aspirin, coffee, and breakfast, hoping to find all four before Howard woke. As she was pouring water into the Mr. Coffee machine, she glanced over to the kitchen counter.

She didn't see the letter.

Forgetting coffee and everything else, she rifled through the papers that were still on the counter and searched the floor, thinking it might have fallen off when she'd gotten up the night before. No luck. She searched the wastepaper basket and the trash can under the sink, digging frantically through eggshells and the heap of sodden black coffee grounds she'd just emptied out, holding out hope that the letter was hidden under the soggy, disgusting mess.

But it wasn't.

She wiped her fingers on a towel, leaving a smear of egg yolk yellow and blackish-brown grit.

"Dear Lord," she said aloud, "I couldn't actually have mailed it. Could I?"

As if in answer, she heard the distant rumbling of an engine and the spinning of tires driving too fast for a gravel road as Wanda Joy Cleary, the crankiest mail carrier in Texas, sped away with Mary Dell's letter stashed inside her mail truck.

Mary Dell put a hand to her pounding forehead.

"Oh, no!"

CHAPTER 33

As soon as Howard woke up, Mary Dell got in the car and drove to the post office, hoping she wasn't too late to intercept the delivery of her foolishly and hastily penned letter.

The Too Much, Texas, post office wasn't an actual building but a small room in the back of the Tidee-Mart, fronted by a single-window counter, partially covered with wire mesh: a one-woman operation. Wanda Joy Cleary, the postmistress, kept short hours that could change without warning, depending on her mood.

Back in the sixties, some enterprising young congressman who was trying to make a name for himself as a cutter of government waste had proposed closing this and a number of other rural postal outlets, but things didn't work out quite like he'd planned. The residents of Too Much, patriots all, were all for cutting wasteful government spending, as long as the waste in question was cut out of somebody else's community, and it didn't take them very long to make this clear to the young lawmaker.

Maida Simpson, Wanda Joy's mother, who had also been postmistress in her day, started a protest campaign that involved mailing boxes of horse dung to that up-and-coming congressman. The population of Too Much didn't even add up to six figures, but the amount of manure required to make a stink isn't as much as you might believe. The congressman got the message. Too Much got to keep its post office. And Maida Simpson got to keep her job, which she passed on to her daughter upon her retirement.

When Mary Dell walked up to the counter and rang the service bell, Wanda Joy was not in a good mood. Of course, no one in town could remember ever seeing Wanda Joy in a good mood, so ringing the bell probably made no difference in the tenor of their exchange. But the second she pressed down on the metal clapper, Mary Dell knew that she'd made a mistake.

Wanda Joy, who was sorting mail with her back to the counter, was clearly visible through the metal mesh window. When Mary Dell tapped on the bell, the post-mistress's shoulders jerked. She turned her head briefly to scowl in Mary Dell's direction, then went back to sorting, ignoring her for a good seven minutes.

Wanda Joy was never seen without a piece of gum in her mouth, not since the day that she'd read an article that said chewing could help relieve feelings of hostility. The speed and pressure with which Wanda Joy chewed her gum was generally a pretty good indication of how hostile she was feeling. As she walked to the counter, she was chomping on a Juicy Fruit at a pace of approximately ninety-seven chews per minute.

"There was no need to go bangin' the bell. I'm not deaf, you know."

Mary Dell hadn't banged the bell. She'd barely tapped it, but figured there was no point in arguing, not if she wanted to get her letter back.

"I'm sorry. You had your back to me, so I thought maybe you didn't know I was standing here."

"I knew," she growled. "But I was busy doing something else. I'm only one person, you know. I've only got two hands."

"Of course you do. I can see that."

"Well, I should hope so. You've got two eyes in your head, don't you? People come in here and bang on that bell like there was some sort of emergency, like the building was on fire or something. Startles the bejeebers out of me. How would you like it if somebody went around ringing bells at you all day long?"

"I see your point, Wanda Joy. It won't happen again."

"Well, I should hope not."

Wanda Joy pulled a metal wastebasket out from under the counter, spat her gum into it, took a fresh piece out of the breast pocket of her blue blouse, unwrapped it, and started chewing again.

"May I help you?"

"Yes," Mary Dell said as she jiggled Howard's umbrella stroller back and forth. He had just begun to fuss; the motion of the stroller sometimes soothed him. "I wrote a letter last night and changed my mind about mailing it. I'd like to get it back."

"Why?"

Mary Dell's personal correspondence was none of the postmistress's business, but Wanda Joy wasn't chewing nearly as quickly now. Perhaps she was warming up to her.

"It's just that . . . well, I never should have written it.

That's all. To tell the truth, I almost don't remember writing it. Not most of it. I *sure* don't remember mailing it." Mary Dell chuckled. "But I guess I must have because I couldn't find it anywhere."

Wanda Joy's chewing slowed to an almost bovine pace. Her forehead creased with curiosity.

"You don't remember writing it? Or mailing it? Did you fall and hit your head or something?"

"No. Nothing like that. It's just that . . . well, I was upset last night. Somebody wrote me a nasty letter. Actually, it wasn't even a nasty letter, it was just a form letter. But this was the fourteenth time and . . .

"Anyway," Mary Dell continued, deciding that Wanda Joy, who was an active member of the strictest Southern Baptist congregation in the county, didn't need to know about the allergy pills or the two bottles of beer, "I've changed my mind. So I'd like my letter back."

Mary Dell held out her hand. Wanda Joy narrowed her eyes and chewed her gum a little faster.

Just then, Howard started to howl. Mary Dell tried jiggling the stroller back and forth more vigorously, but she knew it was no use. When Howard started to cry like that, it would take more than a little stroller jiggling to calm him down again. She'd fed him before leaving the house, so he shouldn't be hungry already. Maybe his ear was still bothering him. Or maybe he didn't like Wanda Joy. She couldn't blame him for that.

Wanda Joy pushed herself up on her tiptoes and peered over the counter to the stroller below and the screaming infant sitting in it. She squinted, peering over the tops of her glasses. "Something wrong with him?"

Mary Dell felt her jaw clench. "Not a thing. He's absolutely perfect."

She unbuckled Howard from his stroller and picked him up. "Wanda Joy," she said, raising her voice so she could be heard over the baby's screams, "are you going to give me my letter or not?"

"No."

"Why? You haven't sent it out yet, have you?"

"No. Matter of fact," she said, turning her head toward the table behind her, "it's sitting in that stack right there. But I can't give it back to you."

"What! Why not?"

Wanda Joy cracked her gum. "Because," she said smugly, clearly enjoying her power, "it doesn't belong to you anymore. The minute that letter went into my mailbag it became property of the United States Postal Service. I can't give it back to you. That would be mail tampering, which is a federal offense."

"Oh, come on, Wanda Joy! You've got to be kidding. It's *my* letter! *I* wrote it, and if I've changed my mind about mailing it, I don't see how that concerns you or the federal government! Besides . . ."

Mary Dell's protests fell on deaf ears, not that it was very easy to make herself heard over Howard's cries, but Wanda Joy wasn't listening anyway. She turned her back on Mary Dell and returned to the task of sorting the mail.

If Mary Dell could have reached through the service window and grabbed her letter, she would have. If not for that metal mesh covering on the window, she might have been able to do just that. Her letter, addressed to C. J. Evard with purple ink in a somewhat wobbly, inebriated version of her own handwriting, was sitting right there in plain sight, mocking her. Mary Dell was convinced that Wanda Joy had placed it on the top of the stack just to frustrate her.

It worked. Mary Dell was frustrated and angry. It was impossible for her to lay her hands on that letter or

Wanda Joy, so she did the only thing she *could* do. She smacked the service bell as hard as she could.

Ding!

Wanda Joy's shoulders jerked, just like before, but she didn't turn around, just kept sorting the mail at a deliberately slow and infuriating pace.

Mary Dell smacked the bell again.

Ding!

Wanda Joy spun around and glared at her.

"Stop that!"

"Give me back my letter, and I will!"

"No! I already told you . . ."

Ding! Ding! DING!

Glaring and with her jaw working as fast as pistons on a Ferrari, Wanda Joy stormed to the counter, reached overhead, and pulled down a grimy-looking white window shade with the word "CLOSED" written on it in red marker and underlined—twice.

Mary Dell didn't care. She smacked the bell again and again, the musical ping of the bell punctuating Howard's cries. It was a pointless gesture, she knew that. No amount of bell banging was going to change Wanda Joy's mind. That letter was as good as delivered. C. J. Evard would read it, and she'd be left looking like a fool, again. Not that she ever had or would meet C. J. Evard, but she didn't like looking foolish, not even to strangers.

On top of that, she'd probably ensured that her own mail would never be properly delivered again. Wanda Joy was not going to forget this anytime soon, but Mary Dell deserved to be heard! It was so unfair! Everything was just so unfair!

Behind the counter, a door slammed. Wanda Joy left the building, exiting through the back. Mary Dell brought her hand down onto the bell one last time, cupping the top of it, causing the tone to turn flat. Her defiance quickly gave way to deflation, and she was left standing at the counter, staring at the shuttered window, and feeling foolish.

Howard was still crying, and Mary Dell shushed him, bouncing him slightly in her arms and patting his back.

"There, there, darlin'."

Mary Dell felt a gentle tap on her shoulder. It was the store clerk, Bob Mayfield, the same man who'd been so amused during her run-in with Marlena Benton. He didn't look amused this time. He looked concerned.

"Miss Mary Dell, are you all right? Is there anything I can do to help you?"

"I'm fine. Sorry to make a scene, but that Wanda Joy . . ." Mary Dell stopped herself. There was no point in getting worked up again. "Anyway, I apologize. Next time I come in, I promise to buy my groceries and leave. No fuss."

"Oh, that's all right," Bob said with a twinkle in his eye. "It's more interesting when you come in, Miss Mary Dell. Sort of livens things up."

CHAPTER 34

Dealing with Wanda Joy would have knocked the wind out of a lesser woman, but Mary Dell was not so easily felled. She decided to regroup and make the most of her day.

After all, she reasoned, the chances of C. J. Evard actually reading that letter were slim to none. Obviously, the editor left that sort of thing to low-level secretaries or mail clerks. If not, Mary Dell wouldn't have gotten all those form letters.

Well, she'd learned her lesson. That was the last time she'd ever waste time submitting patterns to a big magazine. No matter what Grandma Silky said, the world was clearly not in need of a quilting legend at this time, at least not a legend cut from Mary Dell Templeton cloth. Quilting was fun, she told herself, a nice hobby. But she'd been foolish to think it could ever be more than that. Her ranch, this town, this life—this was what she knew and probably all she ever would know. And really, what was so bad about that? There were a lot of people who would have loved to trade places with her. The only thing that mattered now was Howard. She had to care for him and provide for him and, given the limits of her experience and education, making a go of the ranch was the only means she had of doing that.

Howard was still tugging at his ear, so Mary Dell drove over to the pediatrician's office to see about making an appointment. Her timing couldn't have been better. There had been a last-minute cancellation, so Dr. Nystrom, a kind and grandmotherly woman in her early seventies who had been Mary Dell's doctor when she was little, was able to see them right away.

After peering into Howard's ear with a lighted otoscope, Dr. Nystrom said, "Yep. Looks a little red in there. Not too bad, but I'll prescribe an antibiotic. Children with Down syndrome can be especially prone to ear infections because their ear canals are smaller, so this is something we want to stay on top of. You should make sure he sees an audiologist on a regular basis."

"I know," Mary Dell answered. "We've got an appointment at the hospital in Waco next month."

"Good," the doctor said, smiling as she bent over Howard, moving his little arms and legs. "Other than the ear," she said, sounding pleased and just a little surprised, "he looks great. The heart sounded good, weight gain is fine, and for a child with Down syndrome, his muscle tone is pretty good."

"The physical therapist at the hospital taught me some exercises. We go through them at least twice a day, sometimes more."

The doctor nodded approvingly and placed a finger into Howard's palm and smiled when his own tiny fingers wrapped around hers. "No digestion problems?"

"We had a few problems at first, but I read an article

about infant massage and how it can help. Seems to work."

The doctor chucked Howard under the chin and then handed him back to Mary Dell, who cradled him in her arms.

"Well, whatever it is you're doing, keep doing it. You're a good mother. I'm not surprised. Taffy was just the same way with you and your sister."

"She was?"

"Oh, sure," Dr. Nystrom said as she went to the sink and washed her hands. "Did you know that your momma was one of my first patients when I opened my office? She was just a teenager then, and in a lot of ways, she hasn't changed much.

"But Taffy always wanted to fit in, be popular. Well, all girls that age want that, but Taffy didn't figure out that she should have been a little more careful about making sure the girls in town liked her as much as the boys until it was too late. She was just a teenager when she pulled that stunt and stole away Marlena's prom date, and teenagers do dumb things, but"—Dr. Nystrom sighed—"you can't unbake a cake once it's in the oven. Taffy paid the price for her foolishness. And so did Noodie Benton. If you ask me, I think Marlena married him just so she could punish him till death do them part."

The doctor chuckled as she turned off the faucet.

"Anyway, Mary Dell, don't be too hard on Taffy. She loves you and your sister. And she loves this little baby too. Believe me, she does. Did you know she came in to see me last month, all alone? Made a special appointment and asked me to explain Down syndrome to her so she could help you with Howard."

Mary Dell swallowed hard to keep from choking up.

"She did?"

The doctor nodded as she pulled a sheet of paper toweling from the dispenser and dried her hands.

"Uh-huh. Taffy told me all about what happened in the hospital that day. It was cruel, Mary Dell, no doubt about it, but it was cruelty born of ignorance. And it's not the last time you or Howard will face that kind of ignorance."

"I know," Mary Dell said, quietly, "but it makes me so angry."

"You've every right to feel that way. But once you're done being angry, why not take a moment to educate those ignorant people? Help them understand what Down syndrome is, and who Howard is, what he's learning, what he can do now and what he will do someday. You'd be doing them and the world in general a good service.

"And really," the doctor said, smiling as she tapped Howard's little nose with her finger, "could there be a sweeter, more adorable ambassador than this little man? I don't think so."

Mary Dell grinned. "Yes, ma'am. You're right about that."

"I'm right about your momma too. I know she's not the easiest person on earth to deal with, but Taffy loved her children and raised you the best she knew how. That's all any woman can do, Mary Dell. There's no such thing as a perfect mother."

Mary Dell looked down at Howard's sweet face, smoothed his downy hair with her hand.

"But I worry all the time that I won't be a good enough momma to Howard."

"You're doing just fine. And I'm not surprised. When the going gets tough, nobody rises to the occasion like a Tudmore. You come from good stock, Mary Dell, and you *are* a good mother. You're a very good mother."

* * *

"Did you hear that?" Mary Dell asked Howard as they left the pediatrician's office. "Dr. Nystrom says I'm a good momma. What do you think about that?"

Howard looked up at his mother, fixing his beautiful blue eyes on hers, and gave her a big gummy grin. Mary Dell gasped, then she squealed.

"Howard! You smiled! Your very first smile! And it wasn't a gas-bubble smile either; it was a real-to-goodness smile. Yes, it was! And you're only eight weeks old! Wait till I tell Dr. Nystrom. You are a very smart boy, do you know that? Yes, you are. You are Momma's shining star!"

She lifted Howard into the air, high above her head, and spun in a joyous circle, making the baby grin even wider, and then pulled him close and squeezed him to her breast, kissing the top of his downy head.

"You are," she said. "You're my shining star. You know something, now that you're a big boy, able to smile and all, maybe it's time we thought about starting up classes again. Maybe just once a week and only with my special gals. I've missed them. And they will go crazy over you, yes they will. It'll be like having three extra aunties. Won't that be nice?

"Let's go to the dry goods store and see if they've got any new fabric in, something inspiring. What do you think, Bubba? Would that be a good idea?"

He looked up at her and smiled again. Mary Dell bent her head down and kissed his nose and cheeks and forehead and squeezed him yet again.

"Howard Hobart Templeton Bebee, I like the way you think."

CHAPTER 35

Despite its elegant name, Waterson's Dry Goods Emporium was really just a fabric and notions store, and not a very fancy one at that.

The two-story building, dating from 1891, was the first brick structure built in Too Much and one of the few commercial buildings in the downtown area that was not owned by some branch of the Benton family. That they'd made no attempt to do so in this instance was evidence of the fact that Waterson's Dry Goods Emporium was far from a going concern.

Mary Dell's stated purpose in stopping by Waterson's, to look for new and inspiring fabric, was delivered tongue in cheek. Much of the material in the store predated Mary Dell's birth, and the new fabric that did come in was usually far from trend-setting. Mr. Waterson bought much of his stock from liquidation auctions and going-out-of-business sales of stores that couldn't stay afloat, so most of the fabric he sold was out of date and out of style from the minute it arrived.

And the mediocre quality of the goods in Waterson's was not helped by the way it was presented. To start with, there was the lighting. The sparsely spaced collection of fluorescent fixtures gave off light that was dim to begin with and grew dimmer every year.

Mr. Waterson was what Aunt Velvet would have called a typical Too Much male: affable, handsome—or had been in his prime—and utterly lacking in ambition. On top of that he had a bad back, and as he grew older, he found climbing up ladders to change bulbs too strenuous to do very often. He applied the same principle to sweeping, dusting, rearranging stock, or changing the window display. It was all too much work. Mr. Waterson tended to dump fabric bolts wherever he found room for them with no thought of arranging them by color, weight, or purpose. There they sat month after month and year after year, collecting a thin coating of dust that was only disturbed by the occasional movements of the occasional customers who wanted to buy a yard or two of whatever it was that Waterson's was selling.

The only reason Mr. Waterson had managed to eke out a modest living in the dry goods business was that his store was the only place to purchase fabric for thirty miles in any direction, and the women of Too Much had to buy their dress goods somewhere. At least they had, back when most women made their own clothes. The advent of cheap, ready-made clothing meant that it didn't pay to sew your own now, and so most people gave it up.

Only real sewing enthusiasts, people like Mary Dell and Grandma Silky, came to Waterson's anymore. And because Mary Dell hadn't been in since before Howard was born, Mr. Waterson was especially happy to see her.

And Mary Dell, who loved looking at fabric no matter how out of style it might be, was happy to be seen.

"Well, well, well!" Mr. Waterson exclaimed, clapping his hands together when Mary Dell passed over the threshold. "Look who's here! I was beginning to think you'd sold your sewing machine."

"Oh, I'd never do that, Mr. Waterson. But I've been a little busy lately," Mary Dell replied, holding Howard out to the storekeeper.

"Yes, I can see that. Let me see that big boy. Oh, no, honey. Just hold him up for me. My back's been giving me fits this week. I'm too old to tote young 'uns anymore. My! But he's a handsome thing," Mr. Waterson said, smiling and wiggling his fingers in front of Howard's face. "Looks a lot like Donny."

Mary Dell's smile faded a little. "You know Donny walked out on us."

"Yes," the old man said solemnly, "I heard about that. Heard something was wrong with the baby too, but that can't be right. He looks as fine as cream gravy."

Mary Dell blanched a little at the storekeeper's frankness, irritated to know that people in town had been talking about Howard. But, she reminded herself, how could they not? Too Much was a small town that offered few entertainments besides talking about other people's business. She'd been guilty of it herself from time to time. No matter how she felt about it, people *were* going to talk about her and Donny and the baby, at least until some newer and more interesting gossip came along. Best way to deal with it was to meet it head-on.

"Howard has Down syndrome, Mr. Waterson."

"Does he? Well, he's a big, handsome boy. Is he healthy?"

"Very," Mary Dell confirmed. "We just came from Dr. Nystrom's."

"Looks happy too. Is he?"

"Most of the time, except when he's hungry or wet. And he makes me happy."

"Well, then. That's all that matters."

"Yes, sir. You're right about that."

Mary Dell browsed around the store, trying to see if there was anything worth buying.

She picked up a box of silk pins and two spools of ecru thread and put them on the counter. She almost asked Mr. Waterson to cut her a yard of puce-and-olive-green plaid cotton from a bolt she found tucked in a corner with a bunch of corduroys, but Howard started to howl as soon as she pulled it out. When she put it down on the floor so she could pat his back, he stopped.

"That young fella has pretty definite taste in fabric." Mr. Waterson chuckled.

"He must have had a little gas bubble or something," Mary Dell said.

But when she picked up the bolt of plaid a second time, and a third, Howard began to cry again, so Mary Dell put it aside for good. When she pulled a bolt of pickle-green paisley off the shelf, Howard made no sound, so she carried it to the counter and asked Mr. Waterson to cut her a half yard.

"I'm sure glad you came in today," Mr. Waterson said, squinting to find the eighteen-inch mark on the cutting table. "I was worried I might not get to see you before we leave town."

"Leave town? Did somebody leave you a legacy, Mr. Waterson?" she teased. "Are you finally going on that trip to Hawaii you're always talking about?"

"Hawaii? Bah! That was the missus's idea. I don't like the idea of flying over water. Don't like the idea of flying period."

He picked up a pair of heavy, black-handled scissors and cut through the fabric.

"Nope, I don't need to go to Hawaii now or ever. Except for my time in the service, I lived my whole life in Texas, and I intend to die in Texas, but we are leaving town. We're moving to Houston to be closer to the grandchildren just as soon as I can find somebody to buy the store. Of course, things being the way they are, that might not be for some time. People aren't exactly chomping at the bit to go into the dry goods business. Can't blame 'em. It's tougher every year. That's why I want to sell now, while I still can. Don't expect it'll bring much, but hopefully it'll be enough for me and Mabel to retire."

Mary Dell's eyes went wide. "Mr. Waterson, you're really going to sell the store? Who to?"

The old man shrugged as he folded the green paisley into a tidy square and placed it in a brown paper bag. "To whoever's crazy enough to buy it, I guess."

"How about me?"

"You?" He waved her off dismissively. "Mary Dell, you don't want it. You don't."

"How do you know?" she protested.

"Because I do. I'm not asking much, but trust me, it's still too much by half. People have stopped sewing clothes."

"You're not a very good salesman, Mr. Waterson. Maybe that's your problem. Maybe I could do better. Besides, you've got to sell it to somebody."

"I know I do," Waterson said irritably. "But I was hoping to sell it to somebody I don't know. Or at least somebody I don't like. This isn't for you, Mary Dell. This store is a dead end. It'll break your heart and empty your bank account."

"How much do you want for it?"

The old man frowned and scratched his ear. He didn't like talking about money, especially with women. But Mary Dell had this look on her face, a steely expression he recognized, the same expression his missus wore when she'd told him that she didn't care what he thought, that her mother *was* coming to live with them, and if he didn't like it he could just bed down on the sofa for the duration. It was the immovable expression of a stubborn woman with a bee in her bonnet. Oh, yes, he knew it well. There were plenty of stubborn women in Too Much. More per capita, he reckoned, than any town in Texas, and that was saying a lot. Hopefully, Houston would be better.

Mr. Waterson opened the drawer of the practically empty cash register, took out a piece of paper and a pencil, licked the end of it, scribbled a figure, and slid the piece of paper across the counter.

Mary Dell bent her head down so she could read the number. It wasn't as much as she'd feared. Of course, she'd need some extra money to buy new stock and make improvements and . . . well, probably a whole lot of other things she had no way of anticipating. Maybe she could get a loan. How did you go about doing that anyway?

Maybe this wasn't a good idea. After all, she didn't know much about business. No, that wasn't true. She didn't know *anything* about business. She never figured she'd have to. Up until now, Donny had always taken care of everything.

But she could learn, couldn't she? Howard had shown her that. Between her high school graduation and his birth, she'd barely cracked a book, and even when she was in school, she hadn't cracked very many. It just didn't seem that important to her at the time. But Howard was important and since his birth, she'd read a whole shelf of books, many of them very dull and very thick, filled with scientific words and phrases as long as her arm. Sometimes it took her an hour just to read one page because she had to look up every other word, but she'd done it. If she could learn about Down syndrome, she could learn about business.

And she knew all about sewing. No. Quilting. Because Mr. Waterson was right; people had stopped sewing clothes. It wasn't worth the trouble when you could go to the Walmart and buy an outfit for less than you'd have paid for the fabric to make it yourself. These days, people didn't need to sew clothes.

But quilting was more art than necessity, and its popularity was on the upswing. She remembered reading an article about that in *Quilt Treasures* magazine a few years back, talking about how interest in quilting had been steadily gaining momentum since the early sixties, but saying the bicentennial had brought about a big surge of interest in all kinds of home crafts, especially quilting.

That was about the same time Mary Dell had become more interested in quilting than garment construction too, though her transformation had been motivated not by patriotic fervor but by the realization that making a name for herself as a clothing designer and the proprietor of her fantasy boutique, Too Cute Creations, was just as much of a pipe dream as Grandma Silky saying she could turn herself into a quilting legend.

But she did love quilting more than she'd ever loved making clothes. She loved that every quilt she made was different than any quilt she'd ever made before. And she loved the way it worked her brain. She loved looking at an old quilt, mentally deconstructing it and figuring out in her mind how it had gone together. And she loved the thrill of examining a particularly difficult pattern, figuring out a way to do it better, faster, easier, and then passing that knowledge on to her students, seeing their excitement when they finished creating a beautiful quilt that they'd formerly believed was beyond them. For her, that was the real joy of quilting, the satisfaction she gained from offering this piece of herself to others, her knowledge and skill, seeing them make it on their own, sometimes even passing it on to their friends or family, adding another link in the chain. It extended her somehow, made her life larger and more meaningful. Maybe that was it—quilting connected her to people.

And there had been so many advances in the quilting world since she'd taken it up. Now the magazines were filled with advertisements and articles about all kinds of inventions that purported to make quilting easier and give better results. Oh, and all the new fabrics that were coming out! So beautiful, in so many colors and patterns, and made just for quilting—100 percent cotton with not so much as a thread of polyester.

But you couldn't get that gorgeous fabric in Waterson's. You had to drive all the way to Waco to find decent cotton, and even then, the selection was limited. The Suck 'n' Sew Center in Waco, so named because it sold vacuum cleaners as well as sewing machines, had only one small section of quilt fabric. Wouldn't it be wonderful to run a whole shop devoted exclusively to quilts and quilting? And she knew just what she'd call it . . .

"Too Cute Quilts!"

"Pardon?" Mr. Waterson cupped his ear. "What was that?"

Mary Dell blushed, embarrassed by her unintentional outburst.

"Nothing, Mr. Waterson. I was just thinking."

He glanced down at the paper with the purchase price written on it.

"So? You interested? I don't recommend it, and don't say I didn't warn you, but if you're really determined, I guess I might as well sell to you as anybody else."

"I'm interested, Mr. Waterson, but I need a little time. Can you give me a week?"

"Sure." He shrugged. "It's not like people are beating down my door, fighting each other for the opportunity to throw good money down a rat hole. Take a week, if you like. Take two. Don't matter to me."

"One is enough. I just need to talk to some people."

"Like who?"

"Like the bank," she said. "I'll need a loan."

The old man shook his head. "Doubt they'll give it to you. Money's tight. That whole savings-and-loan crisis has bankers scared. Even successful, experienced businessmen can't get loans these days, let alone a woman who's never held a real job."

"Well, I can ask, can't I?"

Offended, and tired of Mr. Waterson's nitpicking and naysaying, Mary Dell picked up the paper sack containing her fabric, pins, and thread and stuffed it into her purse, then bent down to buckle Howard into the stroller.

"Sure you can. It's a free country." Mr. Waterson chuckled.

Mary Dell put her purse on her shoulder and pushed the stroller toward the door.

"And after that? Who you going to talk to next?" Mr. Waterson called out in an eager tone, pressing his palms on the counter and leaning forward as if he couldn't wait to hear what adorable and naïve thing Mary Dell might say next.

"My sister."

"Lydia Dale?" The old man's eyebrows shot up. "What's she know about running a business?"

Mary Dell opened the door and pushed the stroller over the threshold without answering his question.

"Good-bye, Mr. Waterson. I'll get back to you in a week."

He laughed. "Sure thing, Mary Dell. You go right ahead and do that, honey."

Mary Dell closed the door to the emporium a little harder than was necessary, but left without saying anything more to Mr. Waterson. She pushed Howard's stroller down the sidewalk and around the courthouse square to her parking spot, right next to the statue of Flagadine Tudmore.

It was late afternoon and the sun was starting to sink toward the horizon, glinting against the bronze monument. Later she told herself that the sun was playing tricks on her, but just for a moment, when she looked up at that stubborn and steely visage of her celebrated ancestor, she could have sworn that Flagadine winked at her.

CHAPTER 36

Graydon had been up since four, so he decided to lie down on his cot in the tack room and examine the insides of his eyelids until supper. But first, he opened the lid of the old steamer trunk he'd found in a corner under a pile of old horse blankets, pulled out a three-quarters-full bottle of Jack Daniel's from among the empties he had hidden inside.

L. J. Spreewell hadn't cared how much he drank at night as long as he was good to work during the day, but he didn't want the Templetons to know about his liquor habit. Besides, at the Spreewells' he'd just been a hired man. Here he was in charge, he had responsibilities to consider.

Graydon twisted the cap off the bottle and took a slug—just one. He was sorely tempted to take another, but resisted the urge. Jeb would be coming with his supper soon, and he didn't want the boy to smell liquor on his breath.

Graydon counted Jeb among the responsibilities he'd assumed since coming to Too Much. The boy clearly looked up to him, and Graydon wanted to set a good example. He couldn't get through the night without at least one good shot of whiskey, but he was drinking a lot less than he had in Kansas.

After putting the bottle away, Graydon unwrapped a piece of cinnamon chewing gum and popped it into his mouth before kicking off his boots, taking off his shirt, and lying down on the cot.

Three weeks had passed since he'd arrived in Too Much, and not one day of it had been easy. There was a lot to do on a place this size, not that he minded working hard, but working as a hired hand was a whole lot different than being the boss to a bunch of other hired hands—especially the sorry bunch he'd been saddled with.

Moises Rivera was a good hard worker, but Pete Samson and his cousin, Ikey Truluck, were just plain worthless. Ikey was a thief as well, so Graydon had fired him the day before. Pete quit when he heard, which was fine with Graydon. As far as he was concerned, the two of those boys together didn't add up to a pile of dry dung.

But the loss of two hands wasn't fine with Taffy. When she heard the news, Taffy stormed out to the barn and asked him what the Sam Hill he thought he was doing, firing two of their best workers? Especially now, with the ewes about ready to pop?

"I think we've got two or three more days before the lambs come. I hope to find some new hands before then. But even if I can't, we're better off without those two," Graydon answered. "Four more sacks of feed were missing yesterday. I caught Ikey tossing a few handfuls in the bed of Moises's pickup. He was trying to pin the blame on Moises. When I called him on it, he denied everything, asked me who I was going to believe, him or some wetback? Well, I didn't have to think very long about that, especially after I found the missing feed in the trunk of Ikey's Camaro. You can't afford to keep a thief on the payroll, Miss Taffy. A hand who's capable of blaming another hand for his crime is capable of doing a lot worse than just stealing a few sacks of feed."

Taffy made a huffing noise, but she couldn't argue with Graydon's logic.

"But what about Pete?" she barked. "Why did you let him quit? You didn't catch him stealing."

"No, ma'am, but it wouldn't surprise me if he was in on it. He aped everything his cousin did, which wasn't much. Took me longer to get them to do their jobs than to do it myself. We're better off without them," Graydon repeated.

Taffy put her hands on her hips and glared at him. "Well, the next time *you* decide to fire somebody who works on *my* ranch, you'd better just be sure to talk to me before you do it! You hear?"

Graydon lowered his chin just a bit and touched the brim of his Stetson with a single finger. "Pardon me, Miss Taffy, but I thought it was your daughters that owned the ranch now."

A sound that was half growl and half gasp came from Taffy's lips. She stormed back to the house.

Watching her go, Graydon regretted saying that last. There was nothing to be gained from it, but he'd had about enough of Taffy Templeton's high-and-mighty ways. Not to mention the cold shoulder he kept getting from Lydia Dale.

Well, he wasn't here to please Taffy or Lydia Dale. He was here to help Mary Dell and try to do right by his nephew. Little Howard sure was a sweet baby. He was worth whatever grief Taffy and Lydia Dale could dish out. And it felt good getting to know the rest of the family again. Dutch was grateful for his help; so was Mary Dell. They must have told him so ten times a day.

And Jeb was a good boy. Just a little confused, poor kid. Like most boys, Jeb just wanted a little attention and approval. From what Graydon could tell, Jack Benny didn't seem much interested in any of his children. The boy had taken to following him around the ranch like a faithful pup and had perked up considerably since Graydon had started letting him help with the ranch work. He was coming along fine. Last week, he'd even plucked up his courage and taken a ride on Billy Boy. It did Graydon's heart good to see Jeb's grin grow as he walked, then trotted, and finally galloped around the pasture.

Yes, a thing like that made it worth putting up with Taffy's tempers and Lydia Dale's cool demeanor. You had to take the good with the bad. Besides, he enjoyed the work.

This was a fine ranch, best in the county. Once or twice, when he'd been out riding fences or moving the cattle, he'd let himself imagine that it was his name on the deed and that all these beautiful acres belonged to him. It was just a daydream, he knew that, but it didn't hurt anything to dream. That was one of the things he'd loved about ranch work when he was younger—the way it gave him space to breathe and think things through, to imagine what could be. He'd forgotten about that.

On the whole, he figured, his coming to Too Much was a good thing, even if it was only for a few months.

Still lying on his cot, Graydon crossed his feet, tipped his hat forward on his brow to block out the light, and was just about to doze off when he heard the squeak of the big barn door opening and the sound of footsteps treading softly over the dirt floor.

"Come on in," he said, pushing himself into a sitting position when he heard the rap of knuckles on the tack room door. "Door's open."

The door opened slowly, and Lydia Dale's face peeped around the side.

"I brought your supper," she said, glancing down at the tray she held in her hands and the plate piled high with pan-fried steak and gravy, mashed potatoes flecked with black pepper, fried okra, yellow squash casserole baked with cheese and topped with crushed crackers, and a dish of banana pudding with vanilla wafers for dessert.

Graydon leapt to the other side of the room and grabbed his shirt, shoving his arms into the sleeves and buttoning it as fast as he could, rushing so much that he skipped one of the buttons.

Lydia Dale couldn't help but smile when she noticed the gaping spot in the buttons, right in the middle of his abdomen.

"I hope you don't mind it was me that brought your supper," she said. "Jeb and Cady are at Jack Benny's and Daddy's at a lodge meeting in town. It was me or Momma, and I figured you'd rather it was me."

"Uh . . . no. I mean . . . yes, I'd rather it was you." He looked down, noticed the gap in his shirt, and quickly redid the buttons.

"Looks good," he said as Lydia Dale set the tray down on top of an old apple crate that served as Graydon's table. "I love a good steak."

"I remember," Lydia Dale said. "That's why I decided to make that and potatoes with lots of pepper, just the way you like them."

"You made this?"

"I just wanted to thank you for all you've been doing for Jeb. He's a different child since you arrived."

Lydia Dale unwrapped silverware from a paper napkin and laid it out next to the plate. "Here, go ahead and eat while it's hot. Gravy's no good cold."

Graydon pulled a battered wooden chair up to the apple crate, sawed off a piece of meat, put it in his mouth, and closed his eyes, groaning with pleasure.

"Oh, my. Now, that is good," he said, drawing out the last word. "Thank you. But you didn't need to thank me for spending time with Jeb. He's good company."

"Better company than I've been, I bet."

Graydon made no response to this, just started in on his mashed potatoes.

"Do you mind if I sit with you while you eat?"

Graydon shrugged, shook his head, and continued eating. Lydia Dale perched herself on the edge of the cot, there being no chairs available. She sat there quietly, watching him.

Before she'd come out into the barn, she'd had a speech all prepared, an apology, worked out word for word. But now that she was actually in his presence, sitting on his bed, his battered old Stetson sitting right next to her, watching him enjoy the food she'd prepared just for him, she couldn't remember it. She just kept thinking how good he looked, marveling at how little he'd changed over the years.

Of course, appearances were deceiving. Everything *had* changed, at least between them. They were different people than they had been thirteen years ago. Life turned out to be a lot more complicated than they'd figured back then. Remembering that reminded her of what she'd come out here to say.

"Graydon, I . . . I haven't been very friendly since you got here. In fact, I've been downright cold. I guess you noticed."

He shrugged. "I expect you had your reasons."

He took a long swig from the glass of cold sweet tea that accompanied his meal, put down the glass, and turned to face her, his brown eyes boring into hers in a way that made her uncomfortable.

"But now that you've brought it up," he continued, "what were they? As I remember it, you were the one who ran off and got married the second I left the country, not me."

The accusation in his tone caught her by surprise. A wave of guilt washed over her, but it was fleeting and followed by anger.

"That's not fair. They said you'd been killed. Donny came over to the house and showed me the telegram and the letter he'd gotten from your commanding officer, describing how you'd been ambushed by the enemy, but they hadn't been able to identify your remains because the helicopters had flown in and napalmed the whole area and that the bodies of the soldiers who had been killed in the battle were burned beyond recognition. They found your dog tags, and so they knew you'd been killed—that's what the letter said. I didn't want to believe it, but everyone said I had to; they said I had to face facts. What was I supposed to do?"

Graydon didn't look up. "You were supposed to wait."

"I did wait!"

Lydia Dale's shout startled Graydon. He looked into her eyes.

That was what she had wanted for a long time, to look him in the eye to force him to consider things from her perspective, and see that it wasn't her fault, that none of it, the war, the wedding, the misery and mess they'd made of their lives, was her fault.

"Jack Benny started coming around barely a week after we heard you'd been killed in action, saying how sorry he was and that if I needed anyone to talk to, he was available. He tried to keep it low-key at first, but I knew what he had in mind. I told him I wasn't interested in him or anyone, but he just kept coming around, week after week. He brought flowers and when I told him I didn't want them, he showed up with more the next week, this time for Momma.

"Next thing I knew, Momma was inviting him to come over for supper after church, baking him pies, and telling me what a nice boy he was. I still wasn't interested, but he kept coming around week after week, and after a while. . . ."

Lydia Dale spread out her hands and looked up at the unpainted ceiling of the tack room, as if the explanation she was searching for might be hidden there among the cobwebs and rusty nails.

"He made me smile. He can be real sweet when he wants to be, when he's not drinking. He can be funny too, and I hadn't laughed in such a long time. But I didn't love him. When he proposed, I told him that. He got mad, got drunk, and ran his truck into a ditch. But the next week he was back, with a new truck Marlena bought for him and an armful of flowers.

"When he proposed again two months later, I said yes. Momma was thrilled, of course. She called up Marlena first thing and made a lunch date to talk about wedding plans. I think she was more excited about that than the actual wedding. Mary Dell tried to talk me out of it. We argued about it, but I'd made up my mind and basically told her to mind her own business. I should have listened to her. But . . . I didn't."

She looked at him helplessly, hoping he'd say something. When he didn't, she stood up to leave. But as she passed through the door, she grabbed hold of the doorjamb, clutching the rough wood so tightly that her fingertips turned white, standing with her back to him as if trying to make up her mind to go or to stay.

"The thing is . . ." she began and then stopped, leaving the sentence unfinished.

Graydon couldn't see her face, but he could hear the emotion in her voice and see how her fingers released their grip on the doorjamb and moved toward her face, her hand twisting backward to wipe away tears.

She was so lovely, even after three children and so many years, even from behind, with that long blond hair he wanted to stroke and that soft swelling that marked the place where waist became hips, the sweet curve that he remembered so well, that fit his hand so perfectly.

Graydon stood up, took three steps toward her, but stopped himself. He shouldn't touch her. He couldn't. He wasn't the man she thought he was, and maybe he never had been.

And even if things had turned out differently between them, he knew that wasn't what she wanted, not now. And he wasn't sure if it was what he wanted either. He had come here to help Mary Dell and Howard. It wouldn't do to make things any more complicated than they already were. He closed his fingers on empty air and dropped his arm to his side.

After a long silence, she turned around to face him.

"The thing is," she repeated in a steadier tone, "I didn't tell Jack Benny yes when he proposed that second time, not right off. I told him I'd think about it.

"And what I kept thinking was, if we'd gotten married

right away, like you wanted to, instead of waiting until you got back from Vietnam, maybe things would have turned out different. Maybe we'd have been happy, if not forever, at least for a while, even if it had only been for a few months, or a few weeks, or a few days. Or one. It would have been worth it. Even a day with you would have been something to hold on to, something more than the misery I've been left with all because I'd insisted on waiting for the perfect time. And so I said yes.

"Because I figured that something was better than nothing and because I knew that the perfect time had already slipped past me. And because I hoped that Jack Benny might turn out to be better than I thought he was. I hoped he might turn out to be like you, at least a little bit. But that was just . . ."

She sighed and pushed one hand up under her hair, rubbing her scalp and then letting her hand drift down to rest on her neck.

"It was wishful thinking, I guess. But I thought . . . well, it doesn't matter what I thought now, Graydon. It's done, and I did it to myself. And you too, though I didn't know it at the time. For what it's worth, I'm sorry. For both of us."

He looked down at the dirt floor and hooked his thumbs in the pockets of his jeans. It was the only way he could keep himself from touching her.

After a moment, Lydia Dale closed her hand into a fist, tapped on the doorjamb a couple of times, and said, "I'd better leave you to finish your supper."

When she was gone, Graydon sat back down at his makeshift table and began eating but pushed the plate away after a few minutes. His appetite was gone.

He got up, crossed to the corner of the room, and

started pulling the horse blankets off the old trunk. Responsibilities or not, he needed a drink. But before he could open the bottle, he was interrupted by the sound of footsteps running into the barn and Lydia Dale's voice, high-pitched and a little frantic.

"Graydon! Graydon, you'd better come out here!"

CHAPTER 37

Mary Dell started laying on the horn as soon as she drove through the gate and across the cattle guard. She pulled up to the house in a cloud of dust, jammed on the parking brake, and hit the horn again.

Taffy, her hands covered with flour from the piecrust she'd been rolling out, ran out onto the porch. "What in the Sam Hill are you honking like that for? You like to give me a heart attack!"

Mary Dell jumped out of the car and, without bothering to answer her mother's question, shouted, "Where's Lydia Dale?"

"She went to the barn to bring Graydon his supper. Don't know what's taking her so long; she's been gone close to an hour."

Mary Dell unstrapped Howard from his car seat and thrust him into Taffy's arms. "Here, take the baby inside and watch him, will you? I need to talk to Lydia Dale."

Taffy took her grandson into her arms, her expression

a mixture of confusion and fear. "Why? What happened? Is something wrong?"

"Nothing's wrong," she called out. "I'll be right back."

Mary Dell ran toward the barn. Her purse thumped against her hip as she ran. Her big bosoms bounced so vigorously that they threatened to bust the rhinestone buttons on her favorite pink cheetah cowgirl shirt. Her hair, however, which had been teased and sprayed into immobility earlier that day, remained perfectly coiffed. But Mary Dell paid no mind to any of this. The only thing she cared about was finding her sister and telling her what had happened at Waterson's.

Lydia Dale wasn't in the barn or the tack room. Neither was Graydon, though the remains of his half-eaten dinner still sat on the apple crate where he'd left it. Mary Dell went outside again, hooting Lydia Dale's name.

After a second, she heard Graydon's voice echoing back, shouting for her. She ran around the west side of the barn and, coming around the corner, saw that lambing season was definitely upon them. She spotted three ewes lying down, panting and bleating as they labored to bring their offspring into the world.

Mary Dell had seen this before, but it was still kind of amazing to see how, once one ewe went into labor, the others quickly followed suit. Most of the ewes delivered on their own without any need for human intervention or assistance, but a small percentage needed help, and when you had as many sheep as the F-Bar-T did, that small percentage could add up. It was going to be a busy few weeks for Graydon and the hands. And apparently, Mary Dell realized as she jogged toward the far end of the sheepfold, for her sister too.

Because she'd spent so much of her childhood either rehearsing for or competing in pageants, Lydia Dale had never spent much time working on the ranch or with the stock, not like Mary Dell had. And because she had lived in town after her marriage to Jack Benny, she'd never been around during lambing season. But there she was, kneeling on the ground next to a laboring ewe with a huge abdomen that was obviously in trouble. She looked a little frightened but was doing her best to keep the mother still while Graydon, who was kneeling at the business end of the ewe, tried to assess the situation. His right sleeve was rolled past his bicep and his arm up to the elbow was inside the sheep, his eyes screwed shut as he tried to feel for the placement of the unborn lamb inside.

When Mary Dell approached, he opened his eyes. "Have you got a hair ribbon? Shoelaces? Anything I can tie around the legs to help pull it out? We've got triplets in here and they aren't in a good position."

Mary Dell looked down at her feet. "I'm wearing boots. Should I run back to the house and get some twine?"

"Yes," he said, closing his eyes again as he tried to sort out the tangle of legs. "I don't think we have much time."

Mary Dell started to run to the house but stopped short just a few yards away.

"Wait a minute!" she cried and reached into her purse, pulling out the bag from Waterson's and the pickle-green paisley she'd just purchased. "Could this work?"

Without waiting for an answer, Mary Dell put the edge of the fabric between her teeth, bit through the selvage, and began ripping the cotton into strips.

"Give 'em here!" Graydon barked. "Hurry!"

Graydon took his arm out of the sheep but only for as long as it took to tie slipknots into two of the green strips. He looped the fabric rope around the front legs of the lamb he hoped was in the best position for birthing and pulled his arm out again.

"All right," he said, looking at Lydia Dale, "put your hand on her stomach. Tell me when the next contraction starts. When it does, I'm going to try to pull the lamb out. Tell me when it's time. Ready?"

Lydia Dale nodded and laid her hand flat on the ewe's abdomen, her face a mask of concentration. After a few seconds she said, "Hold on. I think . . . I think maybe . . ."

"You think or you know?" Graydon barked. "Which is it?"

"Hang on a second!" Lydia Dale snapped. "Wait. Yes! She's having a contraction! Go!"

Graydon started pulling on the green strips firmly enough to coax the lamb into the birth canal, but gently enough so he wouldn't run the risk of breaking its legs. Three contractions later, the first lamb was out.

Mary Dell and Lydia Dale cheered, but Graydon shushed them and began issuing orders, making it clear there was still work to be done. Another healthy lamb was born a few minutes later, but the third, which had been in a breech position, was stillborn.

Lydia Dale's eyes filled with tears. She laid her hand on the woolly head of the stillborn lamb. "Poor little thing. I wish we could have saved it. I wish I'd called you quicker."

Graydon pushed himself up from the ground, wiped the dirt from his jeans, and settled his hat low on his head.

"You know, not every bad thing that happens is your fault, Lydia Dale. You did fine."

CHAPTER 38

It turned out to be a long night. By morning, the animal population of the F-Bar-T had increased by nine frisky, healthy lambs. The human population was looking decidedly wilted when they gathered in the kitchen for breakfast the next morning. It was the first time Graydon ate with the family. They had business to discuss.

They'd done well, Graydon said, having lost only one more lamb, and that one, he felt, had probably perished in the womb prior to the onset of labor. However, there would be many more nights like this to come, and they were shorthanded.

"Well, we wouldn't *be* shorthanded if you hadn't fired two of our hired men," Taffy snapped as she slid three fried eggs off a cast-iron skillet and onto Graydon's plate.

"The timing wasn't great," Graydon said as he reached for a bottle of Tabasco sauce and decorated his breakfast with several generous red dashes. "But if I had it to do over again, I would."

Dutch poured himself another cup of coffee. "Ikey and Pete always were more trouble than they were worth," he said. "Moises is a good man, and I'll pitch in as best I can, but bottom line, we need more help."

Graydon slurped his coffee. "I know. We need at least a couple of teams of workers, three on a shift, who'll be on call every other night."

Graydon yawned. "First thing after breakfast I'm fixin' to drive into town and see what I can scare up. Figured I'd post a notice on the bulletin board outside the Tidee-Mart, then go and talk to Lester over at the feed store and see if he's heard tell of anybody looking for work."

Dutch made a sucking sound with his teeth and shook his head to convey his doubts. "Gonna be slim pickings."

"Maybe I can find a couple of high school boys. If they're strong and willing to work, I can teach 'em the rest."

Lydia Dale, who had been sitting at the table listening to this exchange while giving Rob Lee a bottle of water, frowned and set the now-empty baby bottle on the table.

"Why hire a couple of kids when Mary Dell and I are sitting right here?"

Graydon glanced up from his coffee and smiled at her, but it was an indulgent smile, the sort of smile a parent gives to an earnest preschooler who has just announced her intention to dig a hole to China using a soup spoon.

"It'd be too much for you."

Mary Dell, who was holding a sleeping Howard in her arms, gazing at his sweet little face and, therefore, not listening all that closely until now, tuned in when she heard the slightly patronizing tone in Graydon's voice. It was the same tone Mr. Waterson had used when he said "good-bye, honey," using an endearment not because he felt endeared to her but because he wanted to let her know how darned cute he thought she was, and how neither he nor anyone else would ever take her seriously. It was the same tone the bank president had used later in the day, when he told her that teaching a few quilting classes for a handful of ladies in her trailer was not adequate training for owning her own business, and that having a good idea wasn't the same as having a business plan and did not qualify her to take out a loan.

Dutch wasn't like that. Her father wasn't ambitious for himself, but he'd always supported her, made her feel important and capable. But he seemed to be an exception to the general inclinations of his sex. What was it about most men? Were they born knowing how to use that tone to make a woman feel foolish and inconsequential even while they professed to have her best interests at heart? Or did they pick it up somehow from their fathers and older brothers?

Donny knew that tone well and had adopted it whenever she'd broached the topic of working outside the home. Back then, especially in the early days of their marriage, she'd thought his insistence on being the sole breadwinner was sort of sweet, a sign of his love and desire to protect her, but now she saw those conversations in a different light.

If Donny hadn't been so dead set against her working, if he had protected her a little less and encouraged her a little more, maybe she would be capable of running her own business, maybe she'd qualify for a bank loan. Maybe a lot of things. But one thing was sure, and it was that Mary Dell was sick and tired of men telling her what she could and couldn't do.

"This is our ranch," Mary Dell said. "Who's going to look out for it better than we will? You didn't think it was too much for us last night. We helped you deliver one set of triplets and two sets of twins. And, I might add, *we* did it with style," she said, pulling her shoulders back. "Whereas you look like fifty miles of bad road."

Graydon lifted his cup in a salutatory gesture.

"Mary Dell, I'm the last man on earth who'd fail to give beauty its due," he said, glancing quickly toward Lydia Dale. "And I was grateful for your help, but that was *one* night. This is going to go on for weeks. It'd be too much for you," he repeated flatly, as though this statement trumped all others.

Mary Dell was ready to continue the argument but was interrupted by the sound of footsteps on the kitchen porch and a chorus of yoo-hooing. The door opened and Silky walked inside, beaming and carrying a big glass bowl covered with plastic wrap, with Velvet right on her heels.

"Hail! Hail! The gang's all here!" Silky chirped as she scanned the circle of faces. She set the bowl down on the table directly in front of Graydon.

"Here you go, young man. I hear you've got a weakness for ambrosia."

"Not especially," Graydon responded, causing the old woman's expression to crease into a frown as she watched him scoop out a big spoonful of the creamy concoction and put it onto his plate. "Not until I tasted yours, Miss Silky."

Silky, charmed by his gallantry, smiled again.

"Aren't you the smooth one? If it gets any deeper in here, we'll need boots and a shovel." She and Velvet pulled up chairs and joined the others around the table.

"We saw some of the new lambs when we drove up. Guess you're going to be pretty busy around here for a while. Better eat all that," Silky said, nodding toward the bowl. "You're going to have to keep your strength up."

"Yes, ma'am," Graydon replied dutifully and began to eat.

Aunt Velvet took the empty cup Taffy offered her and reached for the coffeepot. "What were you all talking about just before we came in? Sounded a little heated." Velvet frowned quizzically. "Something about something being too much for somebody? Too much what? And for whom?"

"For Mary Dell and Lydia Dale," Graydon said. "They helped bring the lambs last night, but they can't keep it up through the rest of the season."

"Why not?" Silky asked.

"Because," Graydon said slowly, not quite able to conceal his impatience with this subject, "ranch work is man's work."

Silky's eyebrows arched and she pulled herself up, ramrod straight, in her chair.

"Man's work? Never heard of it. Unless you're talking about fertilizing eggs or peeing standing up, there isn't anything a man can do that a woman can't do just as well. Man's work indeed," she grumbled. "Give me that!"

Silky grabbed Graydon's spoon right out of his hand and brandished it at him like an admonishing finger, flicking bits of whipped cream off the end as she lectured him.

"After my husband died, I ran this whole place on my own. Did right well too! I had some hired men; you have to on a spread this big. But they didn't do anything I couldn't and didn't do myself. Back when I was in charge of the F-Bar-T, I rode fences, fed stock, dosed sick cattle, rounded up herds, and branded calves.

"When the occasion called for it, I even castrated

bulls. And I still remember how to do it," she said, narrowing her left eye into a laser-sharp glare and poking the spoon menacingly in Graydon's direction. "So don't you go talking to me about 'man's work'!"

"Pardon me, Miss Silky," Graydon said, clearing his throat. "I didn't mean to offend you. I just figured your granddaughters would be too busy, what with the babies and all. I'm going to find some hired men to help out for the rest of the season."

"At this time of year?" She balked. "Everybody in the county needs help now. The only hands left are little boys, sluggards, and drunks. Why don't you use the girls to help on the ranch and hire somebody to take care of the babies?"

Taffy, who was standing at the sink scraping bacon grease from the skillet into a tin can, said, "That's ridiculous. Why should we hire a babysitter? I can take care of the children. Dutch can help me. If he can get Cady and Jeb off to school in the mornings and keep an eye on them after, I can take care of the babies."

"Oh . . . well," Mary Dell said hesitantly, "that's sweet of you, Momma, but it'd be an awful lot to manage. I mean, they're so little. And there are two of them."

Taffy wiped her hands on a dish towel. "Well, it wouldn't be the first time. You are twins, remember? I did all right raising the two of you, didn't I?"

Taffy paused, waiting for some sort of acknowledgment. When none was immediately forthcoming, she put her hands on her hips and turned to face her daughter.

"Now, look here, Mary Dell. If you think I'm not capable of taking care of Howard, you're wrong. I've been watching what you do with him, all that exercise and massage and whatnot. I can do it just as well as you. If

it'd make you feel better, you can write down a list of instructions. Maybe I'm not as bright as you, but I *know*
how to take care of a baby.

"You're always saying how you want everybody to
treat Howard like any other child. Well, why don't you
start doing the same? Lydia Dale leaves Rob Lee with
me all the time, and he's no worse off for it," Taffy said,
gesturing toward the bright-eyed Rob Lee, who gurgled
happily when he caught sight of her face. "Until yesterday, you've hardly even let me hold that child! Howard
is my grandbaby. Who is going to take care of him better
than I can?"

Mary Dell pressed her lips together nervously. Her
own words had come back to haunt her. No hired man
would work as hard or long to care for their ranch as she
and her sister would. And especially after what Dr. Nystrom had told her about Taffy making an appointment so
she could learn about Down syndrome, Mary Dell knew
no babysitter would care for Howard the way his own
grandmother would. Familial love and loyalty was one
of those things that money couldn't buy.

Even so, she didn't want to leave her baby in the care
of anyone else, not even her mother. She didn't want to
be parted from him even for a minute. As badly as she
had longed for a baby of her own for all those many
years, she couldn't have anticipated how much she would
love her Howard.

Somewhere in the Bible, Mary Dell remembered a
verse that spoke of "love that surpasses knowledge."
Until Howard came into her life, such knowledge *had*
been beyond her grasp, but now she thought she understood, at least a little. Motherhood had taught her so
much, including that she was smarter, tougher, and more
resilient than she had believed.

She thought about the day Howard was born, how overwhelmed she'd felt, and remembered what young Dr. Tibbets had told her. . . .

For the rest of his life, Howard is going to run into people who will tell you what he can't do. Don't believe and don't accept it. When people tell him he can't, it's your job to tell him he can, to show him how. You've got to lead by example.

She didn't want to be separated from her baby even for a minute or a day, but she had to lead by example. She had to take care of her family. And she had to show Howard how not to take no for an answer. She had something to prove, to herself, but especially to her son.

Mary Dell had not answered Taffy's question. She'd been lost in her thoughts, but no one else knew that. To the rest of them, it looked like she simply refused to speak to her mother. The silence was uncomfortable.

Graydon wiped his mouth, placed the crumpled paper napkin on his plate, and got up from the table.

"Well, I'm sure you'd do a fine job taking care of the babies, Miss Taffy, but I'm the ranch manager, and I say that working the whole lambing season would just be too much for the ladies. Now, if you'll excuse me, I need to go to town and hire some hands."

"Sit down," Mary Dell said, pointing from Graydon to the chair. "Finish your coffee. I'm not authorizing you to hire anybody. You might be the ranch manager, but I'm the owner, and I say that we're going to get by with the hands we have right here."

Graydon crossed his arms over his chest. "That right? Well, you're not the only owner. Your sister holds half the deed. Maybe she agrees with me."

All eyes were on Lydia Dale. She glanced quickly toward Graydon and then to her sister.

"Are you sure, Mary Dell? I don't want to let anybody down or hold them back. Do you really think we'll be able to keep up with the men?"

"Of course we will," Mary Dell assured her. "You know what they said about Ginger Rogers, don't you? She did everything that Fred Astaire did, only backward and in high heels."

CHAPTER 39

Mary Dell's pronouncement did nothing to change Graydon's opinion, but she was the boss, and he accepted her decision with as much good grace as he could muster.

They decided to break into teams. Starting the next day, everybody would help with the sheep, other stock, and chores during the day, but one team would take the night shift on alternate days, checking on the sheep every two hours, standing by to assist with any difficult births. It was decided that Dutch would be more help wrangling sheep than children, so Silky volunteered to come help Taffy with that and the cooking chores for the duration, and Velvet said she'd be out to help whenever she wasn't needed at the historical society.

Concerned that her speech about being the boss might have bruised Graydon's ego, Mary Dell sat back and let him organize the work schedule and teams. She was surprised that he put her, Moises, and Dutch on one team, which meant Lydia Dale would be working with him. And Lydia Dale seemed completely comfortable with this arrangement. Interesting.

Moises showed up at the ranch about the same time the meeting broke up. He and Graydon got to work. When Lydia Dale said she had to drive to town to pick up Cady and Jeb from their overnight visitation with Jack Benny, Mary Dell asked if she could come along. The babies were both yawning, so Taffy said she'd put them down for their naps and keep an eye on them.

Mary Dell grabbed two Dr Peppers from the refrigerator on her way out the door. She opened both and handed one to her sister as they drove through the gate.

"Thanks," Lydia Dale said, then turned on the radio and hummed along with Kenny Rogers as they bounced over holes and down the dirt road toward town.

"You seem happy," Mary Dell said. "What's up? Did you and Graydon kiss and make up or something?"

Lydia Dale rolled her eyes. "No. I have no interest in or intentions toward Graydon Bebee, not the way you mean it. But I've been too hard on him. He's been real good to the kids."

"He sure has. You know," Mary Dell said brightly, as if the thought had only just occurred to her, "he'd make a wonderful father."

Lydia Dale turned her attention from the road and pointed her finger directly in her sister's face. "Stop it. I'm not looking for a husband. And if I was, I wouldn't need your help. You are the world's worst matchmaker."

"I am not!"

Lydia Dale turned her eyes back toward the road and started reciting a list of names. "Cathy Mae Carradine and Randy Smith, Grace and Gordon Williams, Lila Tyrell and the traveling salesman . . ."

"Ancient history. Doesn't anybody around here ever forget anything?"

"The Lila Tyrell fiasco was only three years ago. The traveling salesman is still in jail on bigamy charges."

Mary Dell shrugged. "So I made a mistake. But that doesn't mean that you and Graydon . . ."

Lydia Dale reached out and gripped a knob on the radio. "Either change the subject, or I'm going to turn the volume up high enough to shatter the windshield. And if you're so darned excited about finding husbands, why not find one for yourself instead of bothering me?"

Mary Dell shook her head and took a drink. "I'm not over Donny. And even if I was, I couldn't imagine loving any man the way I loved him. But," she said in a voice that sounded a little surprised, "I don't think I want a husband anymore. I did that, and it was good while it lasted, but now I want . . . something. Something bigger."

Lydia Dale glanced at her sister, equally surprised by this revelation. Mary Dell had always given every appearance of enjoying marriage. "Like what?"

"I'm not sure. But maybe . . ."

Mary Dell shifted in her seat, angling her body toward her sister. "Howard and I went to the Dry Goods Emporium yesterday."

"And?" Lydia Dale said with a quizzical smile. "Wait. Don't tell me. Mr. Waterson actually got in some new fabric. Something milled in this decade?"

Mary Dell's eyes lit up. "He's decided to retire and sell the business. To me!"

"Really? Where would you get the money?"

"I haven't quite worked that out," Mary Dell said. "It won't be from the bank, that's for sure. The manager said that the timetable for First Reliable Bank to give a loan to someone with no collateral and no real work experience will coincide with hell freezing over and pigs learning to fly."

"He said that?"

"Not quite, but he was so darned smug I wanted to slap him."

Mary Dell put her elbow up near the window and rested her chin in her hand, staring vacantly out as they passed acres and acres of land dotted with scores of grazing cattle, all of it belonging to the F-Bar-T.

"Matter of fact, I've had an urge to slap any number of smug men in the last couple of days. Must be the heat or something." Mary Dell sighed. "You know, Mr. Waterson really isn't asking that much. Business has been bad the last few years. The value lies more in the building than anything else. I've got almost enough to buy the business right this moment, but that wouldn't leave us with any kind of cushion. If lambing season goes bad, or the drought doesn't let up, or if cattle prices take another drop, then we'll need that money. I can't risk it. I told him I'd get back to him within a week to tell him if I want to go ahead with it. Can't see any way of raising that much money in such a short time."

Lydia Dale frowned and a small indentation formed between her eyebrows, the way it did when she was thinking.

"Well, you wouldn't have to have all of it in a week. You'd just need to let him know that you had a way to get it within a reasonable amount of time, right? Say two or three months."

She drummed her fingernails on top of the steering wheel. "What if we put the ranch up as collateral? Not all of it, just part."

"No," Mary Dell said in a definitive voice. "This ranch has been in our family forever. I'm not going to take chances with the F-Bar-T. Besides, buying the Dry Goods Emporium is just the beginning. I've got to make a lot of changes if I hope to make a go of it, and that will take money. I'll need to paint the building, fix the lighting, buy new displays, a new sign, and all new stock.

"See," Mary Dell said, turning back toward her sister and leaning closer, her eyes glittering with enthusiasm, "I want to turn it into a shop just for quilters. We'll carry only one hundred percent cotton made for quilting, the biggest and best selection in this whole part of the state. And we'll have patterns and notions, and all the newest tools and gadgets, all that stuff they advertise in the magazines. And we'll offer classes. Lots of classes! Think about it, sis. If we had eight students a day, five days a week, and all those students were buying their fabric and patterns and such from us . . . well, it just seems to me we'd have to turn a profit! I mean, we'd need more customers than that, but those students would be a pretty good base to begin with. Don't you think?

"And I'm not even figuring in class fees," she mused, talking more to herself than her sister at this point. "That'd help too. But wait . . . no. You know what? I'm not going to charge a class fee, not for beginners anyway. I'll offer a four-week beginner's class, and I won't charge a thing. It'll be kind of a free sample. The supplies they'll buy will make up for any money we're out. *And* once they give quilting a try, see how much fun it is and how cute their quilts turn out, that'll be it!" Mary Dell snapped her fingers to underscore her point. "They'll be hooked like trout! Customers for life!"

Lydia Dale smiled. It had been a long time since she'd seen her sister this happy. "So what do you plan to call this amazing new shop?"

Mary Dell stretched her hands out flat with her thumbs angled into mirrored Ls, then spread them apart, as if she could see it all right in front of her. "Too Cute Quilts," she said with reverence.

Lydia Dale made a face and pretended to gag.

Mary Dell balked. "What? You don't like it? What's wrong with it?"

"It's too *cute,* that's what's wrong with it. Find something a little less precious and a little more elegant."

Mary Dell bit her lip. "I've got it! Mary Dell's Temple of Quilting! Isn't that elegant!"

Lydia Dale rolled her eyes. "No," she said with a laugh, "that's hideous. And possibly blasphemous. Not to mention way, way over-the-top."

"Well, if you're so smart, what would you name it?"

"Oh, I don't know . . . maybe . . . Patchwork Playground?" Lydia Dale frowned. "No. Too cute again. How about Patchwork Palace?"

"I like it!"

"Me too," Lydia Dale said matter-of-factly. "I'd go inside to check it out, and I'm not even a quilter."

"No, but you're going to be. I won't be able to pull this off without your help. Don't!" Mary Dell said, raising her hand to stop Lydia Dale's protest before she even began.

"I know you've never done much quilting, but you already know how to sew, and I can teach you the rest of what you need to know, enough so you can help customers with most of their problems. After all, somebody has to mind the store while I'm doing all that teaching."

"But . . . why would you want me? Why wouldn't you hire somebody who already knows what they're doing? Pearl or Pauline, one of the girls from your class."

"Because I want you. You have something to bring to the party that is a whole lot more important than just knowing how to quilt, something that can't be taught. Certainly not to me." She laughed. "Taste."

Lydia Dale quickly opened her mouth to protest, but

shut it even more quickly and let Mary Dell keep talking, knowing that her sister's self-assessment was right on the money.

"I want your help to run the shop, to cut yardage, stock shelves, and ring up bills on the register because you're my sister and I trust you more than anyone else in this world. And it'd be fun. We'd see each other every day, and our children will grow up together. We can bring Rob Lee and Howard to work with us, there's plenty of room for toys or playpens or whatever else we'd need. It'll be like the old days, Lydia Dale, just like we always dreamed it would be. But beyond that, even beyond the fact that you're my sister, I *need* you.

"Look, no matter how hard I try, I'm always going to be the girl who gets the tacky green ribbon during fair week. Okay, fine. I get it. So what? I love my clothes and my quilts and my style, and I don't intend to change. But I'm not so stupid or so stubborn that I can't recognize the truth; nobody likes my style but me. Well," she said with a shrug, "nobody but Donny, and he's gone.

"But you have taste. You have an eye for color, an appreciation of patterns and textures, and you know how to put them all together in ways that make people stand up and take notice. You should have seen how my gals went on and on over the quilt I made for Rob Lee, the one you picked the fabrics for. They said it was the best quilt I'd ever made. They were right. Even I knew that. We'd make an incredible team, sis. With you choosing the fabrics and me teaching the classes, we'd be unbeatable. We'd have the best quilt shop in Texas."

"Texas, nothing. Probably the best in the world," Lydia Dale said with a smile as she made a left turn and pulled up in front of the little white house she used to share with Jack Benny and her children. "You might just turn out to be a quilting legend after all."

They laughed together, but after a moment, Mary Dell let out another deep sigh.

"It's crazy, I know. There's no way in the world I can pull the money together, not without putting the ranch at risk. I can't do that over some silly dream."

"No," Lydia Dale agreed. "But I don't think you should give up just yet. There's got to be a way we can pull this off."

"We?" Mary Dell looked at her sister and grinned. "Does that mean that you're in? I mean, if we could figure out a way to raise the money?"

"Heck, yes! Of course I am! Do you think I'm going to stand by and let you have all the fun? Besides, once you're a great big fat quilting legend, somebody is going to have to come along to keep you from getting all full of yourself. And somebody," she said with a pointed glance, "is going to have to keep you from making the best-constructed, ugliest quilts in the great state of Texas."

Lydia Dale honked the horn. Jeb ran out, carrying a backpack with his clothes. He didn't look back or wave at Jack Benny, who was standing in the doorway wearing jeans, an undershirt, and a scowl. Carla Jean was there too, wearing too much eye makeup and jeans as tight as a sausage casing.

Cady followed, pausing in the door to give her father a good-bye kiss. Carla Jean bent down as if she expected to be kissed as well, but Cady dodged her puckered lips and raced toward the car after her brother, waving as she ran.

The children jumped into the car and slammed the doors. Carla Jean tossed her hair, whispered something in Jack Benny's ear, and tugged on his arm. He followed her back into the house and closed the front door. Lydia Dale shifted the car into reverse and backed quickly out into the street.

"Hi, Aunt Mary Dell! Hi, Momma!" Cady threw her arms over the front seat and kissed her mother's shoulder.

"Hi yourself, baby girl, and buckle your seat belt right this minute. That's better. Did you have fun?"

Cady shrugged. "Daddy watched football the whole time. Carla Jean made brownies from a box."

"Uh-huh," Lydia Dale said absently, glancing into the rearview mirror to look at her son. "Jeb, what about you? Did you have fun?"

"I don't know why we have to go. Daddy doesn't care if we're there or not."

"Because he's your father, and you're wrong. He does care about you. He's just not very good at showing it, that's all. Guess what Aunt Mary Dell and I did last night?" she asked, making her tone deliberately more cheerful as she changed the subject. "We helped Graydon deliver six baby lambs."

"You did?" Cady's eyes went wide.

"We sure did," Mary Dell confirmed. "And we're going to help deliver a whole lot more. Your momma and I are the newest hands on the F-Bar-T."

"You are?" Jeb asked.

"Yes, indeed. Everybody is going to help. Me, and Momma, and Grandpa are going to work with the stock. Grandma and Granny Silky are going to take care of the house and the cooking and the babies. Aunt Velvet too. The whole family."

"What about me?" Jeb gave his mother a hopeful look. "Do you think Graydon would let me help?"

Lydia Dale looked in the rearview mirror again. "He might, but I won't. I don't want your schoolwork to slide."

"It won't!" Jeb promised eagerly. "I'll keep up with it, I swear I will. I'll do my homework on the bus. And if I don't finish it on the bus, I'll stay in at recess and do it then."

"Yes, I'm sure you would," Lydia Dale said. "Especially since you're already staying in at recess. Mrs. Floyd sent me a note and said you're being punished for shooting spit wads at the girls during a filmstrip. Jeb, I am sick and tired of you always being in trouble at school. I want it to stop, do you hear me?"

"Yes, ma'am. I'm sorry. If you let me help with the lambs, I promise I won't get into any more trouble. I'll do my homework and pay attention in class and be nice to the girls, even Rhonda Jane Reynolds, and . . ."

Lydia Dale cast a doubtful glance into the mirror. "Promise?"

"I do!" Jeb said, eagerly. "I promise!"

"All right," Lydia Dale said slowly. "But if I get one more note from Mrs. Floyd, if she even looks at you sideways, if you miss or rush through even one homework assignment, that'll be the end of it. Understand?"

"Yes, ma'am! Whoo-whee!" Jeb was so excited that if he hadn't been wearing his seat belt, he would have bounced into the roof of the car. Mary Dell smiled. Lydia Dale winked at her.

"What about me?" Cady pouted. "I want to help."

"You can help take care of the babies," Mary Dell replied. "Howard eats kind of slow from the bottle and Grandma is going to be awful busy. Would you like to be in charge of sitting in the rocker and feeding him?"

"Yes, ma'am! I can do that!"

"All right, then. Every day, after school, that will be your job."

"Okay!"

Mary Dell looked over at her sister and smiled. "Now, you see what I'm saying? We'll be great together. It's all about teamwork."

"That's right," Lydia Dale said in a teasing tone. "If enough Templeton-Tudmores put their heads together, there's nothing they can't do. Birth a lamb, open a quilt shop, conquer a medium-sized country . . . Did you ever think about running for Congress?"

Mary Dell laughed and Lydia Dale joined in. They laughed as they passed through the outskirts of town, where the spaces between the houses grew longer and longer until, finally, there were no houses at all, to the end of the pavement and the beginning of the dirt, bouncing over potholes and gravel and bumps in the road, past flat plains and rolling hills of grassland, driving to the northwest as the sun rose high and hotter in the sky, until they passed under the arch of the wrought-iron gate, to the land and life they shared with each other and those who had come before.

CHAPTER 40

Three nights later, during a particularly difficult delivery, Lydia Dale reached in and repositioned an unborn lamb that was in trouble and delivered it all on her own. Graydon was impressed.

"I wasn't too excited about letting you and Mary Dell help with the lambing . . ."

"Really?" Lydia Dale teased. "Gee, I'd never have guessed. You being so reluctant to give your opinions and all."

Graydon scratched his left ear and smiled a little. "I deserved that. Anyway, I wanted to tell you I was wrong . . ."

"Beg pardon?" Lydia Dale cupped her hand to her ear.

"I was wrong."

Lydia Dale laughed. "I just wanted you to say it again. That's the first time in my life I've ever heard a man come right out and say so."

"Well, savor the experience. Could be a long time before it happens again."

It was close to morning. Lydia Dale smiled to herself as they walked through the half-light of the coming dawn, past a pen where newborn lambs slept peacefully next to their dozing mothers, toward another that held ewes with blue marks on their coats, indicating the presence of twins in utero. It was quiet. For the first time in days, none of the sheep seemed to be in labor, not one of them was bleating or bawling in distress. It was nice to have this moment of rest, to feel tired but peaceful, knowing she had done a good night's work. And it was good too to have shared that night's work with Graydon. She liked him. That shouldn't have been a surprise to her considering that so many years ago she had loved him, but this was different. She *liked* him now.

She appreciated his quiet humor and solid good sense, his character, the way he talked to the men who worked for him, with authority but not a hint of arrogance. She liked the way he treated her kids too, the way he listened to them, the way Jack Benny never had, not to his children or to her. And she liked that he could admit when he'd been wrong. She felt comfortable with him, in some ways more comfortable than she'd ever felt when they were engaged. That had been wonderful, that experience of being so breathlessly, hopelessly in love, exhilarating and intoxicating, like tippling champagne, but it had also made her feel a bit out of control. Even at the time, she'd found love a little frightening.

But now they were friends, and friendship was what she needed. She felt like she could be satisfied like this, just walking silently, matching her steps to his, for a long, long time, but when Graydon's voice broke the silence, that was all right with her too.

"I don't know how you manage it, Lydia Dale. Not

you or your sister. I swear I don't. All day long you take care of the kids, or help on the ranch, or both. Then you take turns staying up all night to help with the sheep. And come breakfast, you still look fresh as a daisy while the rest of us sit staring into the bottom of our coffee cups, using toothpicks to keep our eyelids open. How do you do it? Mary Dell says it's due to clean living and Aqua Net hair spray, but I have to think there's more to it."

"Well"—Lydia Dale laughed—"you can't under-estimate the power of good beauty aids, but I suspect it's just practice. I've been a mother for ten years, which means I haven't had a full night's sleep for a decade. I'm on call every night, sometimes all night, to deal with every-thing from croup and teething to nightmares and bed-wetting. Getting up to make the rounds of sheep every couple of hours isn't all that different."

"Well, you're a wonder," he said, in a voice that sounded as if he really meant it. "The way you handle yourself, and your kids, and everything that comes your way . . . I respect you, Lydia Dale. I really do."

She ducked her head, glad for the semidarkness that hid the blush of pleasure she felt rising on her cheeks.

"Another first," she whispered.

"Excuse me?" Graydon said, tipping his head to one side.

"Nothing," she replied, not knowing how to explain how much the word meant to her. She had been valued and pursued for beauty, and discounted because of the same. Never before had she earned a man's respect. Until this moment, she had not realized how much she had de-sired this.

"Thank you, Graydon."

He nodded and shoved his hands in his pockets. They stood together next to the fence, listening to the silence.

"Well," he finally said, "seems like everything is under control for the moment. Guess we should try to catch a few winks while we can."

"I was wondering if it'd be all right for me to take a day off tomorrow?"

"Sure. You've earned it. We'll be all right for one day." Graydon started toward the barn. "See you at breakfast."

"Graydon," she called after him, "I won't be at breakfast. I'm going to sleep for a little while and then go run an errand. Will you tell everybody I'll be home later? Probably in time for supper, but if I'm late, tell Momma not to wait."

"You're running an errand before breakfast and won't be back before supper? What are you up to?"

Lydia Dale squirmed under his questioning. "It's a surprise. But I don't want anybody to know about it because I'm not sure how it'll turn out. Promise you won't tell."

"Not if you don't want me to."

CHAPTER 41

By the time Graydon showed up in the morning, everybody already knew that Lydia Dale wouldn't be there for breakfast.

A little after six, Taffy went into Lydia Dale's bedroom, the same room she had shared with Mary Dell when they were children. She decided to sneak Rob Lee out of his crib, dress him, and feed him so Lydia Dale could sleep a little longer. But when she quietly opened the door to the bedroom, neither Lydia Dale nor the baby was there. Puzzled, Taffy went back to her room to look for Dutch, but he was missing as well.

Taffy was Methodist, born and bred, and had been raised to take a practical, measured and, well . . . methodical approach to religion. But Too Much was full of folks who took every word of the Bible absolutely literally, chapter and verse. She'd gone to school with plenty of children from those families and, as a child, had been fascinated, and sometimes frightened, by their interpretation of the scriptures. She remembered, in particular, what they'd told her about the Rapture and how, in the Last Days, the righteous would be miraculously spirited to heaven while the unrighteous would be left on earth to endure floods, famines, and other horrors.

Her pastor had never preached about the Rapture, not once in all the years she'd been going to church, but as her schoolmates had pointed out to her, it was right there in black and white, in the book of Matthew *and* in Luke: "Two men shall be in the field; the one will be taken and the other left behind."

It had been a long time since Taffy had thought about this, but when she couldn't find her daughter, grand-baby, and husband, it all came flooding back and a terrible thought occurred to Taffy—what if she'd been left behind?

She hadn't always been the sort of woman she ought to be; she knew that. She was vain and covetous and often short-tempered with her husband. Dutch was a good man. She was lucky to have him. But . . . where was he? Where was everybody?

She scurried down the hall, her heart pounding in her ears as loudly as the kitten heels of her silver lamé bedroom slippers pounded against the Mexican tile floor. She opened the door of the catchall room-turned-bedroom that the children shared and was relieved to see two tousled heads resting on the pillows. She sighed and rested her hand over her palpitating heart.

Thank heaven! They were still there, both of them.

She suddenly felt very foolish. Of course they were still there. Where else would they be? How could she have let herself get so worked up? And Dutch must be around as well, Lydia Dale and the baby too. They couldn't just have disappeared into thin air. Of course not.

* * *

Dutch, too impatient to wait for the coffeemaker to finish brewing, was standing in the kitchen with his cup positioned directly under the drip mechanism when he heard Taffy scream.

Leaving his cup behind, he ran toward the direction of her howls as quickly as was possible for a man missing half his left foot. Upon arriving in the living room he saw his wife, pink foam curlers still in her hair, sobbing as she stood in front of the display cabinet that held all of Lydia Dale's old tiaras and pageant memorabilia. Or rather, that had previously held those items. The cabinet was empty.

His first thought was that they'd been robbed, but the television, the stereo, his autographed picture of Tom Landry, legendary head coach of the Dallas Cowboys, and everything else of value was still there.

Why would anybody steal all of the girls' old pageant memorabilia? Or almost all of it? There were two tiaras left in the case, both of which belonged to Mary Dell, the only two crowns she'd ever brought home during her brief career as a beauty queen.

Dutch was about to return to the kitchen to phone the sheriff but was interrupted in his errand when Taffy emitted an even louder wave of sobbing and ran off toward Lydia Dale's bedroom. He hobbled along behind as quick as he could, nearly stumbling when his ears were pierced by another shriek from Taffy.

"They're gone! All gone!"

Taffy stood at the door of the cedar closet, the one she'd had him build specifically to hold the girls' old pageant dresses. The gowns were missing—all except those few that had belonged to Mary Dell.

Taffy spun around to face him, tears in her eyes. "I don't understand," she said weakly. "Who would do such a thing? Lydia Dale is gone, the baby too. Where could they be?"

Dutch scratched the stubble on his still-unshaved chin, just as baffled as his bride. Taffy's eyes grew wide with fright as a new possibility occurred to her.

"Oh, Dutch! Oh, my gosh . . . what if they've been kidnapped! What if someone snuck in here in the middle of the night and kidnapped them?"

Dutch looked at the window, closed tight to keep the air-conditioning in. No one had tampered with it. And when he'd let out the cat a few minutes before, the door was still locked.

"Honey," he said. "Calm down. Our room is right next door. If somebody had broken in, we'd have heard it. There has to be some explanation."

"Then what is it?" Taffy's voice was high and shrill, verging on hysterical. "Where could they be? And why would their pageant treasures be missing?"

"I don't know," Dutch said helplessly, "but there must be—"

The sound of Graydon's voice, coming from the kitchen and sounding somewhat urgent, cut Dutch off in mid-sentence. He headed for the kitchen with Taffy on his heels and found Graydon on his knees, using an enormous wad of paper towels to mop a pool of hot coffee from the linoleum.

"Shoot!" Dutch exclaimed, then pulled another bunch of towels from the roll and joined Graydon on the floor. "I ran off and left the cup under there when Taffy started hollering. Forgot all about it."

"Hollering about what?"

"Lydia Dale and Rob Lee," Taffy said in a panicked voice. "Somebody kidnapped them! And the dresses, the tiaras . . . all Lydia Dale's pageant treasures. They're all missing. Will you two forget about the coffee? We've got to call the sheriff right now!"

Graydon smiled and sat up on his haunches, the wet brown paper towels still in hand.

"You don't need to do that, Miss Taffy. Lydia Dale got up early to run some errands. She hopes to be back by supper but wants you to go ahead and eat without her if she's not. She asked me to tell you when I saw you at breakfast."

"Errands?" Taffy sniffled and put her hands on her hips, her fright replaced by irritation. "She got up to run errands in the middle of the night and won't be back until supper? And she took all her pageant treasures with her? Why?"

"She didn't say, just that she'd be back tonight and to tell you not to worry."

Taffy threw her hands up in the air. "Oh, she did, did she?"

Taffy delayed serving until eight, then she fed the children and sent them to bed. But in spite of what Graydon said, Taffy was worried. Everyone was. They assembled in the kitchen so they could worry together and speculate as to what could explain this very strange behavior on the part of Lydia Dale.

"It's just not like her," Taffy said, passing a platter of barbecued ribs down the table. "The last time she did something like this was when she ran off and got married. You don't think . . ."

"Of course not," Mary Dell said, dismissing the suggestion with a wave of her hand. "That's the last thing on her mind. She's not interested in finding another husband, now or ever. She told me so."

Graydon choked on the lemonade he'd been drinking. Dutch gave him a look, then started pounding him on the back.

"You all right?"

Graydon nodded, then coughed. "Fine, thanks. Swallowed wrong."

CHAPTER 42

Lydia Dale was relieved when Rob Lee finally quit crying and fell asleep a few miles outside of Waco. The closer she came to home, the more nervous she got about how the family would react to what she'd done.

No, that wasn't quite true. Only Taffy's response caused her concern; everyone else would be fine. Dutch would be supportive, as he always was. Mary Dell might be hesitant at first, perhaps even feel a little guilty, but she would get past that. Taffy would . . . Well, who knew what Taffy would do?

Lydia Dale took the last two miles of her journey at very slow speed, partly to avoid hitting potholes, but mostly to give herself time to mentally rehearse the possible menu of her mother's reactions and think up responses to each. The thing to do, she concluded, was to keep things light and cheerful, to act as if she was shocked that Taffy would be upset. And why should Taffy be upset? After all, she hadn't done anything wrong.

By the time she drove through the gate, she felt ready to face her mother. But her confidence waned when she pulled up to the house and saw Taffy already standing on the porch, frowning with her arms crossed over her chest, looking exactly like she used to when Lydia Dale was a teenager and had stayed out past her curfew. Lydia Dale turned off the ignition, jammed on the parking brake, and opened the car door.

"Hey, Momma. Kids asleep? Thanks for keeping an eye on them."

Taffy ignored her greeting. "Where in the world have you been? You had us worried half to death."

Dutch, Mary Dell, and Graydon joined Taffy on the porch. Lydia Dale opened the back door to retrieve Rob Lee from his car seat.

"I had some errands to run. Didn't Graydon tell you?"

"What kind of errands take sixteen hours to run? Where have you been?"

"Fort Worth."

"Fort Worth! Why in the world did you go there? And why did you take your old pageant treasures?"

Lydia Dale, who had only slept seven hours out of the previous forty-eight, decided she was too tired to keep up the pretense of cheerfulness. It obviously wasn't going to work anyway.

"Before we go through the third degree," she sighed, "could somebody help me bring in my stuff? Sis?"

Graydon beat Mary Dell to it. He strode quickly toward the car and grabbed Rob Lee's car seat.

"Let me take him. I'll put him to bed."

Lydia Dale smiled gratefully and handed the sleeping baby off to Graydon, who took him inside; then she retrieved her purse and the diaper bag from the front seat.

"What about the rest of it?" Taffy asked. "Don't tell

me you stuffed them all in the trunk. They'll be all crushed!"

"You mean the gowns?" Lydia Dale held her breath a moment before deciding to get it out and over with. "They aren't there. I drove up to Fort Worth today to meet with two pageant coaches, a lady who sells quinceañera dresses, and a junk man . . ."

"A junk man!"

Lydia Dale plowed ahead, ignoring her mother's outburst: ". . . and sold them—the gowns, the tiaras, the scepters, everything. It's all gone."

She had expected Taffy to sob, or shout, possibly even to faint, but instead she just stood there, staring at her with an expression of disbelief tinged by something deeper and harder to pinpoint—betrayal and profound disappointment, the look of a child who has just been told that there is not and never was a Santa Claus. It was harder to take than a harangue. Lydia Dale had known that selling her pageant memorabilia would anger Taffy. She hadn't realized it would hurt her.

"Momma . . ."

She stepped toward her mother, arms open, but Taffy wouldn't submit to the embrace. Instead, she held up one hand and turned her face toward the wall, two tears slipping silently from beneath her closed eyelids. Dutch came over to comfort his wife, placing one hand between her shoulder blades and moving it in small circles.

Mary Dell looked almost as shocked as Taffy. "Sis, if you needed money, you should have talked to me. All you had to do was ask."

"I know that," Lydia Dale said quietly. "You've always been there for me. When Jack Benny didn't carry his weight or show up for work, you wrote out his paychecks just as if he had. And when he left us, you still kept sending them, even after Donny left you to carry on alone and take care of all of us. I know you'd do anything to help me, sis. Just like I would for you. All you have to do is ask. But the thing is, you never *do* ask.

"The other day, in the car, when you told me about maybe being able to buy the dry goods store . . . you were all lit up," Lydia Dale said, her own face brightening as she remembered. "I hadn't seen you that happy in a long time, and I decided that I wanted to help you stay that way. A couple of days ago, I realized that I could."

Lydia Dale took the diaper bag off her shoulder and set it down in the dirt. Taffy, tears still in her eyes, turned and watched along with the others as Lydia Dale opened her purse and took out a white envelope with a blue rubber band around the middle, so fat that the flap wouldn't close over the contents.

"Yesterday, I talked to Mr. Waterson. He wouldn't budge on the price, but I got him to agree that if we could put five thousand dollars down now and another five before you open, and then seven hundred a month until the loan is paid off, the store is yours. He's going to carry the loan for you. We'll have to get some papers drawn up so it'll be legal and all, but he's agreed to everything and he's not even going to charge you any interest."

"What?" Mary Dell blinked in disbelief. "Why would he do that?"

"Because he's not stupid," Lydia Dale said. "You're the only real prospective buyer he has, or likely will have. He's not doing you any favors letting you buy it, trust me. I took a look at his books; his sales have been down every year for the last five. Mr. Waterson doesn't have the energy or vision to reverse that trend, but you do," Lydia Dale said, holding the envelope out to her sister. "There's six thousand two hundred and fifty-two dollars in here. Go ahead. Take it."

Mary Dell pressed her hand over her mouth. After a moment she pulled it away and said, "I can't take it, sis. It's too much."

"No, it's not," Lydia Dale protested. "Mary Dell, do you remember when we were thirteen and that revival came to town? The one with the big, tall preacher who had a voice like a foghorn?"

Mary Dell nodded. "They set the tent up in that vacant lot where the kids like to play football. I remember."

"Remember how we only went to the revival because a bunch of the boys from school bragged how they were going to let a snake loose in the tent?" Lydia Dale went on, knowing that her sister recalled it all perfectly well. "We thought it would be funny to see all the ladies scream and we wanted to show off to the boys.

"But then that preacher started preaching, starting out low and slow, then going a little faster and a little louder, then a little faster and a little louder still, steady and sure, like a freight train pulling a load uphill, until he got to the top and hurtled down the other side, bellowing that there were people sitting in that tent who were going to hell for having impure thoughts . . ."

Mary Dell smiled. "He came to stand in front of us, looking right at us, and you thought he knew what we were up to and that wanting to see the women scream at the sight of a snake was what he meant by 'impure thoughts.' "

"Uh-huh," Lydia Dale confirmed. "I started to cry. And all the people around us started moaning and praying, thinking that I was laboring under a burden of sin, which I suppose I was, just not the way they thought.

"When they started the music for the altar call, I wanted to go up front. You hissed at me and grabbed my sleeve, told me that we'd already gotten ourselves saved at Vacation Bible School three years before, and that once you'd been saved you couldn't get *more* saved, and to sit down and quit trying to make a fool of myself."

Mary Dell was grinning now, and her shoulders shook with laughter as she remembered that day.

"But you wouldn't listen," she said, picking up the story where Lydia Dale left off. "You were terrified of going to hell. I was so mad at you because most every boy in our class was there, and I knew if you went down the aisle, they'd be making fun of you from then until doomsday."

"That's right," Lydia Dale said, "and they did too. Not quite until doomsday, but nearly. But I did it anyway.

"And at the last minute, you grabbed my hand and came with me, right up to that big old preacher, who laid his hands on our heads and prayed while the band played 'Don't You Hear Jerusalem Moan.' Do you remember what you said to me, right before we went up?"

Mary Dell shook her head.

"You said that I was your sister and that wherever I was going, heaven or hell or on a fool's errand, I wasn't going without you. I've never forgotten that."

Lydia Dale swiped at her eyes with the back of her hand, leaving a blackish smear. "I don't know if this idea of opening a quilt shop will turn out to be a little piece of heaven, or hell, or a fool's errand. But whatever it is, I'm going to be with you every step of the way. So you're going to take this money, and you're not going to feel guilty about it. Not for one minute. Why should you? Those gowns are as much yours as mine anyway. You sewed most of them."

"From fabric I bought!" Taffy shouted.

Having recovered from her momentary shock, Taffy launched into the sort of tirade Lydia Dale had been expecting. Eyes blazing, she pushed Dutch aside and marched down the porch steps to do battle with her daughter.

"Do you know how hard I worked so you could go to those pageants and win those tiaras? How many miles I drove, how much money I spent, how many hours I spent helping you rehearse? Do you have any idea of all I went through for that? Do you?"

Taffy threw up her hands in disgust. "And now, without so much as a by-your-leave and after all *I've* done for you," she snapped, clearly slighted that Lydia Dale had mentioned only Mary Dell's sacrifice, "you run off and sell off our best memories to a junk man. A *junk* man!"

Taffy stood in front of her daughter with her chin jutting forward and her hands on her hips, demanding an answer.

"Momma, do you ever stop and listen to yourself? I wish you would. Whose 'best memories' are you talking about? Look around," she said, spreading her hands, "and you'll see *my* best memories. This place, this house, our family—those are the prizes I carry with me. I don't need a display case filled with rhinestone tiaras and titles to imaginary kingdoms to hold on to because they're all right here," she said, pressing her hand to her heart.

"But if I can sell off a few dusty old relics that you *say* belong to me so that someone I love, someone that you love too, can have a chance to make *new* memories, then I say call up the junk man. And tell him to bring cash."

Lydia Dale reached down, picked up the diaper bag, and looped it over her shoulder once again.

"I'm going to bed now. I've got to get up early and help with the sheep."

She kissed her mother and father good night, hugged her sister and pressed the money-filled envelope in her hand, then straightened her shoulders and, with head held high, walked through the door looking more like a queen than she ever had.

When she glided past the darkened corner of the kitchen where Graydon, who had been hesitant to walk onto the porch in the middle of such a personal family exchange, was hidden, it was everything he could do to keep himself from reaching out from the shadows to pull her into his arms.

CHAPTER 43

Mary Dell and Moises were on call that night and would make their first round of the night in another hour, but Graydon took a stroll to the sheep pens before turning in just the same. The four ewes currently in labor appeared to be doing fine on their own, so he headed to the tack room, lit the kerosene lantern, and pulled off his boots.

He hadn't had more than four hours of sleep at a stretch in the last three weeks. And yet he knew that if he lay down, he wouldn't be able to sleep. His mind was too filled with thoughts of Lydia Dale to grant him rest.

She was as beautiful to him as she'd ever been, in some ways more beautiful than she'd been at eighteen, when he first laid eyes on her. Motherhood and maturity had made her body more womanly and even more desirable, at least to him. How was it that every man in town was not in hot pursuit of her? How could they fail to see what he saw in Lydia Dale—a lovely, kindhearted, strong-willed woman who had more strength and courage than he'd given her credit for? Perhaps this too was something that had come as a by-product of motherhood and maturity, a filling out and filling in that endowed her with a depth and complexity that made him realize he'd only just begun to appreciate all there was to her. He figured a man could spend a lifetime trying to really understand everything she was, and that he'd like to do exactly that.

How was it possible that Jack Benny had pushed her away and abandoned those three beautiful children? Graydon couldn't understand it, but one thing he knew for sure: Jack Benny didn't deserve a woman as fine as Lydia Dale. Then again, neither did he.

Graydon unbuttoned his shirt and sat down to eat the cold chicken Taffy had wrapped for him. It was good, but Graydon wasn't enjoying it the way he usually did.

He felt anxious and unsettled, not exactly angry, but filled with the kind of nervous energy and generalized discontent that sometimes sends normally peaceful men into barrooms in search of a fistfight.

He pushed the plate aside and paced back and forth across the room in his stocking feet for a few minutes, finally stopping in front of the steamer trunk in the corner, craving relief. He pulled the horse blankets off the trunk, opened the lid, and bent down to reach for one of the black-labeled bottles. But his fingers froze only inches from the object of his desire, the liquid comfort that had numbed his emotions, dulled his painful memories, and clouded his judgment for so many years—for too many years.

Graydon closed his empty fingers into a fist, dropped his head down, and closed his eyes, thinking. He tapped his fist against the inside wall of the trunk in a steady drumbeat for more than a minute until, having made up his mind, he opened his eyes and lowered his torso into the trunk. Moving quickly, he filled his arms with liquor bottles, then toted his burden out to the old shed where the trash barrels and garden tools were stored.

One by one, he opened the bottles and poured the contents onto the ground, leaving a dark, wet circle on the thirsty soil, then tossed the empties into one of the barrels before pulling a couple of cast-off newspapers out of another barrel and laying them on top.

When the job was done, he went back to the tack room, sat on the edge of the bed, and pulled off his socks. The soles were stained brownish red with dirt picked up on his journey to the tool shed, so he tossed them aside, took off his jeans, turned out the lamp, got into bed, and immediately fell asleep.

CHAPTER 44

May 1984

"Hey, Mr. Waterson!" Mary Dell tootled cheerily, waving as she walked in the door of the Dry Goods Emporium.

The old man looked up from the stack of mail he was sorting.

"Hey, yourself," he grunted. "You're looking happy this morning."

"I am. A decent night's sleep will do that for a person. The lambs are all delivered."

She didn't mention that she'd been in a good mood ever since she'd put the first payment down on the store. She hadn't been this excited about life in general since she was a teenager sitting on the floor of her bedroom, surrounded by fabric swatches and sketches of the beautiful dresses she planned to make and sell in the someday boutique she would own in downtown Too Much.

And now, after all these years, her dream was about to come true.

Oh, yes, she was happy. She was happier than words could express, so she didn't try to, not to Mr. Waterson. He seemed a little glum today, preoccupied. Perhaps he was having regrets about selling. Or perhaps he was offended about the way she'd gone on and on about her big plans for improvements once she and Lydia Dale took over the shop, taking it as a criticism of the way he'd run the place.

Of course, she didn't think he'd done anything like what he could have with the store, but she would never have come right out and said it. That wouldn't have been polite, and anyway, she didn't want to hurt his feelings. She liked Mr. Waterson.

"That must be a relief to have it over and done with," he said. "Had a good season, did you?"

Mary Dell nodded and strolled over to a rack that held a mishmash of fabric, gingham, seersucker, polyester, flannel, corduroy, sateen, and more, in all sorts of colors and textures, all sitting on the same shelf in a big disorganized jumble.

"Yes, sir," she confirmed as she rubbed the corner of a blue-and-white plaid between her fingers before rejecting it as a little too thick for her purposes. "Almost as good as when Donny was running things. And Graydon says he'll stay on for a while, so that's good news too. I thought I'd celebrate by buying some fabric for a new quilt. I need to make up a sample for the first class I'm going to offer when we open the shop."

Mr. Waterson stepped out from behind the counter. "Alone? Isn't your sister supposed to be helping you pick out all the fabric from here on out?"

"She is, but she's home keeping an eye on the babies. Howard has a cold. And the colors for this quilt will be simple—red, white, and blue—so she figured she could trust me with that. But she did tell me to tell you that if I start to stray, you're supposed to throw a lasso over me and rein me in."

Mary Dell winked, and the old man snorted out half a laugh. Mary Dell smiled, pleased that she'd cheered him up a little.

"Well, you can't go far wrong with red, white, and blue," Mr. Waterson said as he started hunting through piles of dusty fabric bolts and pulling out likely candidates. "The colors of the great state of Texas."

"Not to mention the rest of the country."

"Them too, I guess," he said with a begrudging shrug. "Anyway, red, white, and blue is a crowd pleaser. What pattern are you going to use?"

"One of my own," Mary Dell said, grunting as she struggled to yank out a bolt of red-and-white ticking stripe that was wedged tightly between one of black denim and another of purplish-puce polyester. "A medallion quilt. I'm using a Lone Star for the center."

"A Lone Star? That's pretty complicated, isn't it?"

"Not if you use the all-new, can't-fail Mary Dell Method to make it," she said, batting her eyelashes playfully and sweeping her hands into a graceful position on her left, like a spokesmodel displaying a fabulous new appliance on sale today for just four low payments of nine ninety-nine. She giggled and dropped her pose.

"If you don't make the star too big, it's not as hard as it looks. And I have worked out some new piecing techniques that make things much easier."

"Well," Mr. Waterson replied philosophically, "it's a good choice if you can pull it off. Texans love a Lone Star."

"That's what I thought too. Just seems like the right way to start."

Mr. Waterson picked up two bolts of six he'd selected and carried them to the counter. Mary Dell followed behind, carrying the fabric he'd left along with several more selections of her own, piling them in a stack that reached to the top of her head. After looking over the options, Mary Dell decided she might as well take a half yard of each plus two full yards of a dark blue studded with white stars for the background.

Mr. Waterson began cutting the fabric, but instead of squinting like he usually did, straining to find the correct marks on the cutting table, he frowned, pressing his lips into a line as he sliced through a length of red-and-blue-striped cotton. Mary Dell asked him if he was feeling all right.

"I'm fine," he said, waving her off. "Actually, I'm relieved. I was kind of worried that something would go wrong at the ranch and you'd change your mind about buying the store."

"Oh, I'm still going to buy it. I need a little time to pull everything together, but I'll have the second payment for you at the end of June, just like we agreed."

"Good," he said with a tired little smile and unrolled the bolt of stars on blue. "I know you've got plans for big changes, Mary Dell, but I'm glad people will still be able to buy fabric here. My family has been selling dry goods in Too Much since 1919. Isn't that something?"

He stopped in mid-cut and cast his eyes around the shop as if he'd never seen it before, or might never see it again.

"You know, I'm going to miss this old place. I didn't think I would somehow. Must be getting sentimental in my old age." He sighed. "But it's time to go, and the sooner the better. Mabel's been feeling poorly lately, no energy. I think the heat is too much for her. The sooner I get her out of here and down to Houston, the better."

"Well, it's not going to be any cooler in Houston," she said. "It's still Texas."

"I know that," he said as he rang up her purchase on the register, sounding a little irritated. "But I'm going to rent us one of those condominiums, the kind with swimming pools and central air. No more fans or window units for us. That ought to perk Mabel right up, don't you think? She's not as young as she used to be."

"None of us are," Mary Dell said, handing over her money. "And a swimming pool sounds good to me. You know, I've never gone swimming in a pool, just Puny Pond. Think they'll have less frogs in a pool than a pond?" she asked in a deliberately innocent tone.

Mr. Waterson smiled, picking up on the joke. "Dunno. They sure couldn't have more. Here you go," he said, handing the bag with her fabric inside over the counter.

"Thanks, Mr. Waterson," she replied and turned to leave.

He waved good-bye and returned to the task of sorting the mail. Just as she reached the door, Mr. Waterson called out, "Hold on a minute! There's something here for you."

"For me?"

"Well, technically it's for me, at least until the end of June. But I don't have any need for it and you do. Here you go," he said, holding out a thick manila envelope. "A catalog from a fabric wholesaler."

CHAPTER 45

"Oh, look at this," Mary Dell said, picking up a swatch of fabric with big purple cabbage roses and pink ribbons on a background of seafoam green. "We have *got* to order a bolt of this."

Lydia Dale rolled her eyes. "That's what you say about all of them. Remember the plan. We can only afford to order five hundred bolts to start, so we need to focus on simple patterns that most anyone will like in basic colors that most everyone needs. Later, once we start making some money, we'll bring in more specialty prints."

She took the swatch from her sister and made a face. "But we will never, under any circumstances, order *this*. Looks like wallpaper from a two-dollar bordello."

"Here," she said, handing Mary Dell a stack of white-on-white fabric swatches, "you work with these. Pick any five you want."

Mary Dell frowned and began flipping morosely

through the fabrics. "You sure know how to take the fun out of shopping."

"We're not shopping, we're buying—for the shop, not for us. What about this?" Lydia Dale held up a white-and-bright-yellow windowpane check. "It comes in six different colors."

"Better," Mary Dell said.

Mary Dell took one of the windowpane swatches, a bright blue one, and placed it on the floor directly between Howard and Rob Lee, who were lying stomach-down on the carpet, which was strewn with toys, rattles, and stuffed animals.

"What do you think, boys? Should we order some of this?"

Howard pushed up on his little arms, his face turning pink with effort, and smiled. Mary Dell laughed.

"I'll take that as a yes. Seems you inherited your aunt's good taste."

"He's sure holding his head up good now," Lydia Dale commented, smiling at Howard as she pushed a blue rattle with a teddy bear on it a little closer to Rob Lee, who was struggling to reach it.

"Yep," Mary Dell said with pride. "He can keep it up for fifteen seconds. I timed him."

Mary Dell put the fabric aside and got down on her stomach, almost nose to nose with Howard, who pushed his head up again so he could see his mother's face. "Now we're going to work on rolling over. When did Rob Lee start rolling?"

"Last week. It's not a competition, sis."

"I know," Mary Dell said, reaching out a finger for the baby to grasp. "Howard is doing great. But it helps me to know what Rob Lee can do and when he started doing it so I can see what's on the horizon for Howard. Hey, speaking of children, how are Cady and Jeb? I haven't seen them as much since the end of lambing."

"Cady is fine. Nagging me about wanting to go to cheerleading camp this summer," Lydia Dale said, examining a stack of small-scale floral prints in muted shades of blue, red, and brown. "Even if we could afford it, she's still too young. But I guess one of the Benton girls from her class is going. She keeps rubbing it in Cady's face."

Mary Dell shook her head. "Meanness just runs through that whole family."

"Seems to," Lydia Dale agreed. "But don't forget my babies are half Benton, too."

"Tudmore genes trump Benton meanness any day of the week," Mary Dell declared. "Your children are proof of that."

"I hope so," Lydia Dale said, "but some days I have my doubts."

"Jeb giving you trouble again?" Mary Dell placed a ring of plastic keys in Howard's hand, waiting until he had a good grip before sitting up to face her sister.

"A little. Jack Benny's the real problem. As usual," Lydia Dale muttered. "Jeb hates going to see his daddy on Fridays. He keeps begging me to let him stay home."

"Why don't you? Sounds like Jack Benny isn't all that interested in seeing him anyway."

"He's not. But if I tried to change the visitation, Jack Benny would take me to court just to make life miserable for me." She sighed. "I shouldn't complain. Jeb's actually doing better. He's passing his classes. Not by much, but it's an improvement. Graydon said that if he failed any of his subjects, he wouldn't let him help with the horses after school."

Mary Dell laid out eight swatches of white fabric on

the carpet, considered the choices, took away two, and considered some more.

"And that did the trick?"

"Uh-huh. Jeb loves to ride now. Graydon is teaching him how to rope too. They've been making some noise about Jeb entering the breakaway roping event at the fair this year." Lydia Dale smiled to herself. "We'll see."

"Graydon is good people," Mary Dell said, noting the wistful look in her sister's eyes. Lydia Dale nodded.

"I saw the two of you walking to the west hills the other day."

"Graydon wanted to see the bluebonnets."

"Well, that sounds awfully romantic," Mary Dell said knowingly.

"Stop it." Lydia Dale tossed a swatch at her sister.

"I mean it," Mary Dell said. "It does sound romantic. Is something going on between you two?" She leaned forward, eager for an answer. "Are you falling in love?"

Lydia Dale made an exasperated noise, picked up another stack of swatches, and started flipping through them.

"Don't be silly. I've got three children, one of them an infant, and I'm trying to help you open a quilt shop. I don't have time to fall in love. I don't *want* to fall in love."

Mary Dell reached out, grabbed her sister by the wrist, and looked her in the eye.

"Love isn't always about what you want. Sometimes it just *is*. That's why they call it falling in love, because sometimes you just can't help yourself."

"Like the Fatal Flaw?" Lydia Dale asked in a mocking tone. "You've been spending too much time with Aunt Velvet."

"No, not like that," Mary Dell said urgently. "Falling

in love is different. You know it is because you fell in love once before, with Graydon. Is it happening again?"

Lydia Dale's cheeks flushed pink. She pulled her hand away and started sorting fabric swatches again, deliberately avoiding her twin's penetrating gaze.

"I don't know. Maybe," she said softly. "He wants to take me out."

Mary Dell's eyes went wide. "Out? Like on a date? A real date? What did you say?"

A mischievous little smile bowed Lydia Dale's lips.

"I said I'd love to. If the kids can come too."

By the end of the afternoon, the sisters had put aside 716 swatches to consider as possible candidates for their initial order. It had been 715, but Mary Dell quietly slipped the purple-rose print back into the stack while Lydia Dale's back was turned.

They would have happily continued with their task, narrowing their options to the final five hundred, but Lydia Dale wanted to be home in time to meet the school bus.

Lydia Dale was changing Rob Lee's diaper, and Mary Dell was picking up toys when she heard the familiar sound of tires speeding too fast over gravel and an engine backfiring.

"There's the mail," Mary Dell said.

Lydia Dale looked up from her task. "Why is Wanda Joy so late with the delivery?"

"This is her usual time," Mary Dell said. "At least it is now. I'm the last one on the route."

Lydia Dale looked perplexed. "She delivers to the big house before nine every morning, and we're just a quarter mile up the road. Why would she deliver to everybody else in town and then come all the way back out here?"

"Because I'm being punished," Mary Dell said, then tossed a musical teddy bear into the toy basket. "Don't worry about it. Would you mind keeping an eye on Howard while I run out to the mailbox? I'll be right back."

"Sure."

Mary Dell kissed Howard on the nose, telling him to be a good boy for Auntie Lydia Dale, then hopped to her feet and jogged out the front door.

Lydia Dale finished putting on Rob Lee's diaper, grabbed one of his chubby feet, and pretended to nibble on his toes, making the baby giggle with delight.

"Oh, you are delicious, Rob Lee Benton! And so are you!" she exclaimed, scooping Howard up from the floor and giving him a squeeze. He smiled at her, drooling his delight. Lydia Dale squeezed him again, lifted him up high and, after a quick sniff, decided that her nephew could also use a clean diaper.

She'd just finished changing Howard when she heard her sister shouting her name. Lydia Dale stood up with a baby in each arm and looked out the front window. Mary Dell was running at top speed down the driveway, waving a piece of paper over her head, her big bosoms bouncing so hard they almost hit her in the chin.

"What in the world?" Lydia Dale muttered to herself. She walked quickly to the front door, opening it just as Mary Dell came bounding in and collapsed with her back against the door.

"What is it?" she asked, looking down at the letter Mary Dell held in her hand. "Is it from Donny?"

Still too winded to speak, Mary Dell just shook her head. She closed her eyes and took in several deliberately big breaths.

"C. J. Evard."

Lydia Dale's jaw dropped. "The magazine editor? The one you're always going on and on about? The one who rejected all your quilt designs?" Mary Dell bobbed her head. "What does she want?"

"Me!" Mary Dell exclaimed. "She wants me! She wants me to come to Dallas and bring my quilts. Ahhh!!!"

Mary Dell squealed with excitement and Lydia Dale joined in, her delight matching Mary Dell's and her squeals even louder. The sisters danced a celebratory circle in the middle of the living room, their babies held between them, Rob Lee giggling at this impromptu ring-around-the-rosy and Howard expressing his pleasure with a wide and toothless grin.

This went on for some time. Each time Mary Dell would quit squealing and get hold of herself, Lydia Dale would shout, "Dallas! You're going to Dallas to meet C. J. Evard!" and the party would start all over again.

When they finally calmed down, Lydia Dale said, "I can't believe it! This is fabulous, Mary Dell. I'm so proud of you! You never gave up. Just think, after all this time and all those submissions, she finally sent for you. What do you think changed her mind?"

Mary Dell's eyes got very wide and her complexion turned suddenly pale.

"The letter . . ." She clapped her hand over her mouth. "Oh, no. That stupid, stupid letter."

"What letter?"

"The letter I wrote one night when I was mad, after Donny left. I'd had about all I could take and then I got another of those form-letter rejections from the magazine and I . . . well, I kind of went off the deep end. I wrote this terrible, terrible letter to C. J. Evard, calling her all kinds of names. It was crazy, but I was mad, and I'd accidentally taken one of Donny's old prescriptions, thinking it was an allergy pill. Then I had a couple of beers and . . ."

"Beers?" Lydia Dale laid Howard back down on the floor, then settled Rob Lee into his car seat. "You hardly ever drink beer. And I've never seen you drink two."

"Yes," Mary Dell replied grimly, "and there's a reason for that. Because it makes me do stupid, stupid things!" She smacked herself on the forehead and groaned.

"This is a nightmare. I've waited years to meet C. J. Evard and now, when I finally get the chance, it's only because she wants to holler at me in person. Well, I'm just not going to go," Mary Dell said, setting her jaw. "I've humiliated myself enough for one lifetime."

"Are you crazy? Give me that!"

Lydia Dale snatched the letter from her sister's hand, pulled the sheet of thick, creamy stationery from the envelope, and read a portion of it aloud.

" 'Upon reviewing the body of your submissions during the past seven years, we are intrigued by your technique and would like to see more. . . .' Mary Dell, this woman isn't mad at you. Look here," Lydia Dale said, pointing to a paragraph, "it says they booked you a hotel room. Nobody pays for a hotel room just so they can holler at somebody else."

Mary Dell bit her lip, considering this. "Do you think so?"

"She's interested in your quilts and wants to see more. Here," Lydia Dale continued, moving her eyes to the final paragraph. "She says she is greatly looking forward to meeting you in their offices at two o'clock on the twenty—"

Lydia Dale stopped in mid-sentence. She flipped the envelope over and examined the postmark.

"This was mailed almost two weeks ago. The mailman could have walked it from Dallas to Too Much in that time."

"Two weeks?" Mary Dell took the envelope from her sister, looked at it, and scowled. "Not the mail*man*. The mail*woman*. I bet Wanda Joy has been holding on to this for days. You know, I've had just about enough of this." Mary Dell's fingers curled into a fist. "Next time I go into the post office, I'm going to . . ."

"You don't have time for that!" Lydia Dale said, throwing up her hands. "Aren't you listening? Your appointment with C. J. Evard is at two o'clock on the twenty-fourth. You've got to be in Dallas the day after tomorrow!"

"The day after tomorrow?" Mary Dell grabbed the letter back from her sister and scanned the final paragraph.

"Well, I can't do it," she said weakly. "I just can't. There's no way I can be ready by then. I . . . I've got to pull my quilts together, and I'd have to pack. I don't have a thing to wear. And I'm supposed to see the lawyer about drawing up the papers for the quilt shop. And they made a hotel reservation?" She looked at the letter again. "What am I supposed to do about Howard? I can't take him to some hotel in Dallas."

"Don't be silly," Lydia Dale said. "I'll go see the lawyer. And you can leave Howard with me and Momma. It's just for one night. And you have plenty of pretty clothes. I'll help you pack your suitcase and the quilts. We'll do it first thing tomorrow."

Mary Dell shook her head. "There's not enough time. And I hate big cities."

"How would you know? You've never been to one."

"That's not true," Mary Dell said with a jerk of her chin. "I went to Dallas on my honeymoon. Didn't like it."

Lydia Dale sighed impatiently. "As I recall, the only things you saw on your honeymoon were the emergency room at Parkland Memorial Hospital and the inside of your hotel room. I'm guessing that Dallas has a little more to offer than that."

"No," Mary Dell said. "It's too much. It's too soon. It's a waste of time. And who cares about C. J. Evard anyway? Who does she think she is? Sending me rejections for seven years and then thinking she can just snap her fingers and I'll come running up to Dallas on a minute's notice. As if I don't have more important things to do."

"But you *don't* have more important things to do! Not the day after tomorrow, you don't." Lydia Dale grabbed her sister by the shoulders. "Mary Dell, you've waited seven years for this moment. Don't let it slip through your fingers just because you're scared."

Mary Dell swallowed hard, knowing that her sister had read her right. She was scared, scared that after so many years spent dreaming of exactly this, the dream might be too wonderful to come true. It would be terrible to come so close . . .

"What if she doesn't like me? Or my quilts? What if it's just another rejection, but this time she's planning to deliver it in person?"

Lydia Dale shrugged. "Well . . . then at least you'd know the truth. And at least you'd be able to look in the mirror and know you tried. That's got to be better than spending the rest of your life wondering what might have been, isn't it?"

"Maybe. I suppose," Mary Dell said hesitantly. "But what if . . ."

"No," Lydia Dale said stalwartly. "I'm not going to listen to any more of this. I was born three and a half minutes before you; that gives me seniority. So you listen to me, Mary Dell. I don't care if I have to beat your butt with a mesquite switch, or hogtie you and put you on the next bus to Dallas, you are going to that meeting. You can do this, Mary Dell. You hear me? You can!"

CHAPTER 46

"Stop it, Jeb," Cady said in a voice that was halfway between a giggle and whine. "Mom! Make Jeb stop!"

Lydia Dale turned around to face the backseat. "Jeb, stop throwing popcorn at your sister. And, Cady, you quit egging him on. Settle down and watch the movie."

"She started it!"

"I did not!"

"I don't care who started it," Lydia Dale said in that particular tone of voice the children knew signaled imminent punishment. "Both of you, stop it. You hear me?"

"Yes, ma'am," they chorused glumly.

Lydia Dale turned back to the movie. Mr. Miyagi was showing Daniel how to "wax on" and "wax off" his car, and Daniel was questioning what this had to do with learning karate. Keeping her eyes glued to the screen, Lydia Dale's fingers crept across the front seat until they met Graydon's, and he took hold of her hand.

Graydon glanced in the rearview mirror and saw

Cady stick her tongue out at her brother. Jeb quickly returned the sentiment.

"You know what would taste good right now? A cherry slushie." Graydon reached into the back pocket of his jeans. "Hey, kids. Would you run to the concession stand and buy me a slushie? Get yourselves one too."

The children broke into cheers.

"You already bought them popcorn," Lydia Dale reminded him.

"Popcorn makes you thirsty," Graydon said as he handed a bill over the backseat to Jeb. "Besides, it's the first day of summer vacation. We're celebrating."

"Could be a long summer," Lydia Dale mumbled. Graydon scratched his nose and grinned.

"Get your momma a drink too. Lime, right?"

Lydia Dale nodded, wondering how he'd remembered.

"Okay, lime slushie for your momma. Cherry for me. While you're at it, get some red licorice and Milk Duds, too. Got that, partner?"

"Yes, sir," Jeb said. "Does Cady have to come?"

"Somebody's got to help you carry it."

Jeb sighed and opened the back door of the sedan. "Come on, runt."

"Don't call me runt. Mom!"

Lydia Dale turned around again. "Go!" she commanded.

The children got out of the car and scampered toward the concession stand at the back of the drive-in, weaving their way between the rows of parked cars, ducking their heads to avoid hitting the cables of the window speakers.

After they were gone, Graydon lifted his arm and rested it on the back of the seat. Lydia Dale slid a little closer.

"You know, when I told you I'd only go out with you if the kids could come too, I didn't figure you'd actually take me up on it." She looked up at him with a little smile. "Guess I have to give you points for bravery."

"Not really. I always go to the drive-in on first dates," Graydon said and reached into the popcorn bucket that sat on Lydia Dale's lap.

"Oh, you do, do you?"

He tossed a few kernels of popcorn into his mouth. "Uh-huh. Of course, this is the first date I've been on in . . . let me think now . . . thirteen years."

Graydon laughed. Lydia Dale slapped him playfully before taking a handful of popcorn for herself and settling back into the crook of his arm. He smelled good, like leather and new rope and shaving cream.

Jack Benny had smelled of shaving cream too, but also of cigarettes and beer. Or worse, of cigarettes and whiskey. Whenever she'd gotten that whiff of whiskey on his breath, she knew they were in for a bumpy night. And back in their dating days, whenever Jack Benny had got her alone, his arms coiled immediately around her, groping and searching, and he whispered in her ear, pleading with her to "be sweet" to him. It was like trying to fight off an octopus. Sometimes, she'd lost the fight. Not that he'd ever forced himself on her, but sometimes, just to keep him from crossing the line, she'd ended up doing things she'd rather not have done. It always made her feel so cheap. Why had she allowed it? Because she was young, she guessed, and because she didn't know how to stand up for herself or to say no.

Thank heaven she'd outgrown that.

A lot had happened to her in the last year: She'd been betrayed, humiliated, abandoned, divorced, and left to fend for herself and her children. None of it had been easy or fun. But she'd learned from it, by gosh she had.

And she was never going to let somebody mistreat her or her children again. She knew how to say no now.

But she didn't have to say no to Graydon. He didn't push. She didn't feel manipulated or out of control when she was with him. She liked the way his arm felt around her shoulder, strong and solid and safe. She knew that he would like to kiss her if she'd let him, that all she had to do was lift her chin, look up at him with invitation in her eyes, and he would lower his lips to meet hers. She knew that he wanted to do just that. But that wasn't all he wanted. He liked to talk to her too.

Jack Benny had never been much of a talker. Well, no, that wasn't quite right. He talked plenty, and he was always joking around. At first, she'd liked that. He seemed so energetic, and it was flattering, the way he pursued her. But before long, she realized that he never talked about things that mattered, never discussed his thoughts, or feelings, or plans with her. And he never listened to her. It was a one-way conversation. No, not even that. It was a monologue.

Now that she thought about it, if you measured on word count alone, Graydon talked considerably less than Jack Benny ever had. But he managed to say a whole lot more.

"You know," Graydon said, looking out the windshield toward the bottom of the movie screen where a gang of kids were playing on a swing set, "we used to go to the drive-in when I was little.

"We didn't have much money. But every now and again, the drive-in would have carload night, your whole car could get in for the price of one ticket."

Graydon scratched his neck and smiled, remembering.

"We'd throw a bunch of blankets and pillows in the back of the pickup. Mom would mix up a pitcher of red

Kool-Aid and pour it into mason jars, pop some corn, and put it into brown paper sacks. Best popcorn in the world," he said wistfully. "She poured on so much butter it left grease stains on the paper. Donny and I, and sometimes some of the neighbor kids, would pile in the back and off we'd go. We'd swing on the swings, just like this bunch," he said, nodding toward the playground beneath the big screen, "and we'd run back and forth to the bathrooms, and have fights with the pillows, just about everything but watch the movie. Sometimes Mom would get so mad she'd get out and spank whichever one of us she could catch hold of, not hard, just hard enough to get our attention. In the end, we'd all fall asleep in the back, curled up like a pack of pups."

"Your mom sounds nice."

"She was," Graydon said slowly. "But those nights at the drive-in were some of the best memories I have of her. She was sweet but tired. Life just beat down on her. We were so poor, so busy working to survive that we barely had a chance to live.

"That's why I started working the rodeo circuit. I entered a breakaway roping competition when I was eleven and won. The prize was ten dollars. More money than I'd ever seen in my life, so I got the crazy idea that rodeo work was the way to make money fast."

"Why didn't you go back to it when you got back from Vietnam?"

Graydon shook his head. "Partly because I was too old and out of shape by then. But mostly because I was too busy feeling sorry for myself. I gave up."

"You still feel sorry for yourself?" she asked

He reached up his hand and stroked her hair. "Not very. Not now."

She twisted toward him, lifted her eyes to his. His lips were soft and his kisses were sweet, just like she remembered. Better than she remembered. She pulled away. The kids might come back any moment, and if she didn't stop now . . .

Lydia Dale scooted back across the seat a few inches, to a safe distance. "Mary Dell said that you're staying until Christmas."

He nodded and took another handful of popcorn from the bucket. "Maybe longer. If you want me to."

"Graydon, I . . . I was married to Jack Benny for a long time. And I'm still trying to figure out . . ."

"It's okay," he said casually. "I'm in no hurry. I can wait till you're ready."

She looked down at her lap. She didn't want to hurt his feelings, but she didn't want to give him false hope either. For his sake and her own, she had to be honest.

"I might never be ready. You should know that. I don't want to waste your time."

He munched his popcorn. "I was living in a shed in Kansas. You're not wasting my time."

"And now you're living in a tack room in Texas. What's the difference?"

He took her hand. "Everything. Before, I had nobody. Now I've got friends. I've got family. People who need me," he said. "Mary Dell, Howard . . ."

And me, she thought but didn't say so.

"And Jeb. He's a different boy now," she said.

"He's a good boy."

"You're good with him."

"Well, I like kids. Always did. In fact," he said, "next time we go on a date, let's bring the babies too."

Lydia Dale laughed. "I think they're better off at home with Momma and Daddy. Besides, you don't think Mary Dell is going to let Howard go to the movies without her, do you? It's only for one night, but we practically had to pry him out of her arms when she left."

Outside, they heard the sound of two childish voices approaching, hissing and arguing about who was going to get the first crack at the Milk Duds. Graydon removed his arm from the back of the seat.

"Do you think she's having fun in Dallas?"

Lydia Dale scooted all the way back to the passenger side of the seat as the kids clambered inside, handing off drink cups and candy boxes to Graydon.

"I don't know. She hasn't called yet. But I doubt it," she said. "Mary Dell doesn't like big cities."

CHAPTER 47

Mary Dell thought the Dallas traffic was bad enough during her honeymoon trip, but Big D had added a number of newer, wider, faster freeways in the thirteen years since then, and a whole lot more residents. One second, cars and trucks and semis would fly past her at twenty or thirty miles above the speed limit, and in the next everything would come to a screeching halt and she'd find herself sitting in the middle of a vast sea of gridlocked vehicles.

The air-conditioning on Dutch's pickup was broken, but after a couple of minutes of sucking in the exhaust of idling cars, she decided that death from heat exhaustion was preferable to death by asphyxiation, and she rolled up the window.

"I don't care how bad the tread was on my tires," she muttered to herself, "I shouldn't have let Daddy talk me into taking the truck. As long as I'm stuck here, I might as well figure out where I'm going."

She had thought she knew exactly where she was headed, but everything looked so different than she remembered. Keeping one hand on the wheel and one eye on the traffic, she pulled a road map out of the glove compartment and spread it out across the steering wheel. She'd almost figured out where she was when the truck driver stopped behind her let out a blast that made her lose her place. She jumped in fright and then glared into her rearview mirror. The angry trucker pointed at her, then to the road ahead, signaling that the traffic was moving again and Mary Dell was blocking it.

Feeling like a bumpkin, she blushed and tried to put the pickup in gear, but she was so nervous that she let the clutch out too quick and stalled. She fired up the engine again and shifted into gear as fast as she could, but by the time she did, a half dozen other drivers were honking at her. By the time she finally got moving, her nerves were so jangled that she missed her exit but didn't realize it for a good three miles. She took the first exit she could find and stuck to regular surface streets from then on. Eventually, she found her way downtown.

Commerce was a long street, but Mary Dell figured that if she just stayed on it she'd find the address eventually, so she drove slowly along the curbside, searching for address numbers, so pleased when she finally found the 1300 block that she didn't notice the grandeur of her surroundings until she pulled in front of the hotel, got out of the pickup, and looked up.

She had to hinge her neck back as far as it would go to see the place where building gave way to skyline.

"Holy cow! If you stacked every building in downtown Too Much one on top of the other, I bet you could fit them all inside with space to spare."

She stood there, open-mouthed, mentally trying to count the stories, when a fresh-faced young man in a blue suit came up to her and said, "May I take your car, ma'am?"

Mary Dell scowled at him. "Now, why would I let you do that?"

"Are you checking into the hotel? If so, I can park your car for you."

"Oh . . . yes. Of course," she stammered, feeling like an idiot.

She'd seen parking valets in movies and television programs, but she'd never actually been in a hotel that had one. Her previous experiences with overnight accommodations were limited to the cheap motels and tourist cabins she had shared with Taffy and Lydia Dale during her brief career on the pageant circuit and those few nights in the Belmont during her honeymoon.

At the time, the Belmont had seemed very elegant, but as she fell in step behind the uniformed bellman who carried the battered, borrowed suitcases that held her clothes, cosmetics, and quilts, following him across carpets so thick her feet sank into them as if she were walking barefoot on a sandy beach through a two-storied lobby paneled in gleaming wood, she realized it was possible she hadn't truly understood what the word "elegant" meant, not until now.

The bellman took her to the check-in desk, where a row of clerks with matching uniforms and matching smiles awaited her. She picked the clerk in the middle, a young blond woman with a name tag that said "Stacy." Stacy handed her a key to room 1708 and said that Bobby, the bellman, would show her the way and bring up the luggage, then wished her a pleasant stay.

The room was elegant too. The honey-colored carpet wasn't quite as thick as the carpet in the lobby, but almost, and the dark cherrywood furniture was polished to a shine. Gold brocade curtains hung from the ceiling to the floor, framing the big picture window. The bed-spread and shams matched the curtains. Mary Dell had never seen a bed with so many pillows.

Bobby brought in her suitcases, placing them on a stand he pulled out of the closet, showed her the minibar filled with candy bars, jars of nuts, cans of soda and beer, and teeny-tiny bottles of liquor, then asked her if she wanted anything else.

"What else *could* I want?"

Bobby smiled, hesitated a moment, then said, "Well, if anything comes to mind, just dial zero and ask the operator."

He started toward the door when Mary Dell realized that his hesitation had been in anticipation of a tip. She'd seen that on television too, just like the parking valets. Wait . . . was she supposed to have tipped the parking man too? Maybe the desk clerk? Well, it was too late.

"Hold on. Just give me a second," she said, scrounging through her purse in search of a dollar bill. "Here you go."

Bobby smiled. "Thank you, ma'am."

When he left she investigated the rest of the room. The closet held a collection of hangers made from the same color of wood as the furniture, as well as a half dozen padded lingerie hangers covered with cream-colored satin. There was a black metal box on the upper shelf, a safe, with a sign reminding guests to lock up their jewelry and valuables.

"Well, la-di-da!" She shook her head in amazement and muttered, "If I'd known there was a safe, I'd have brought my diamond bracelet and emerald tiara."

The bathroom had tiny bottles of shampoo, conditioner, body lotion, shower gel, bubble bath, mouthwash, and a box containing an emery board, shower cap, and sewing kit, plus two bars of gardenia-scented soap wrapped in cream-colored paper with gold lettering that said "The Adolphus."

There was marble on the floor, a heat lamp in the ceiling, a towel warmer on the wall, which Mary Dell mistakenly believed was for drying laundry, and a bathtub big enough to take a swim in. There was a toilet, of course, with a gold handle that matched the faucets on the tub and sink. Standing next to it was something she'd never seen before, not even on television, not quite a toilet and not quite a sink. Later, she would learn it was a bidet and would blush as she recalled thinking it might be a place to wash out stockings.

When she closed the door to the bathroom, she discovered a plush, white terry-cloth robe hanging on the back of the bathroom door. A little tag on the hanger said the robe was for the use of guests during their stay. It looked new. She wondered if they put out a brand-new robe for every guest. If so, it seemed like an awfully extravagant arrangement, but she was starting to think that anything might be possible in such surroundings.

She would have dearly loved to fill up the tub and have a good soak, but there wasn't time for that. She had to get ready for her meeting with C. J. Evard.

The sudden reminder of the purpose of her visit made her pulse rush and her stomach lurch. For a moment, she thought she was going to be sick, but she closed her eyes and pushed past the urge.

After she'd changed her clothes, brushed her teeth, freshened her makeup, then curled, teased, and sprayed her hair, Mary Dell stood in front of the mirror to give herself a final once-over. The hot-pink satin blouse matched her lipstick perfectly, but the white jacket and slacks Lydia Dale had picked out for her were a little boring. Surely an important meeting in a big city demanded something more elegant.

She went back to the suitcase and pulled out a ballerina skirt she'd sewn from layers and layers of black and pink tulle, fixed to a waistband of pink satin ribbon and trimmed with rhinestones along the hem. When they were packing, Lydia Dale had rejected the skirt, but Mary Dell snuck it into the suitcase when she wasn't looking. Mary Dell kept the jacket and blouse, but exchanged the slacks for the skirt and changed her shoes as well, opting for a pair of black-and-white spectator pumps with a peekaboo toe and three-inch heels that she'd bought at the Methodist yard sale, and replacing the pearl studs Lydia Dale had chosen in favor of her favorite drop earrings, featuring a pair of pink mother-of-pearl half-moons hung with strings of pink glass and finished with smaller pink stars, also in mother-of-pearl.

Mary Dell stood in front of the mirror and smiled at her reflection, feeling beautiful. She shook her head, admiring the way the pink stars barely brushed her shoulders, then spun around in a circle to see how the rhinestones on the hem of the ballet skirt caught the light.

"Elegant," she declared. "Very elegant."

CHAPTER 48

Mary Dell arrived at the offices of *Quilt Treasures* at exactly two o'clock. After informing the receptionist that she was there to see C. J. Evard, she sat down on a white leather sofa to wait, admiring the striking display of quilts hung on the walls. They were all red and white, and they all appeared to be antiques. Mary Dell very much wanted to get up and take a closer look, to inspect the backs and examine the stitching, but she didn't think that would be quite polite, so she stayed where she was, picked up a magazine from the table, and flipped through the most recent issue of *Quilt Treasures*.

The receptionist's phone buzzed. After a brief conversation, she hung up and smiled at Mary Dell.

"Ms. Templeton? Mr. Evard will see you now."

Mary Dell gathered her things, her purse and the two huge shopping bags that contained her quilts, and got to her feet.

"Thank you . . . Wait a minute . . . Did you say *Mr.* Evard?"

Aside from his gender, C. J. Evard was all the things Mary Dell had imagined: intelligent, well read, well spoken, well dressed, a passionate collector and maker of quilts.

"Really? You do? *You* do?" Mary Dell asked with amazement. "I never met a man who stitched quilts."

"There are a few of us out there. I started my career as a thread salesman," he said, in the gentle twang of a Texas native who hadn't let success and wealth permit him to forget his roots. "My territory was the entire Southwest, so I traveled a lot of miles, visited a lot of customers, some of whom were quilters. I was fascinated by quilts from the get-go. I'm not sure why; maybe because every quilt comes with a history, tells a story of real people living real life.

"I really saw quilts as true objects of art, but better than conventional art because people actually used them— kept warm in them, had picnics on them, wrapped babies in them, sometimes made babies under them," he said with a gentle smile. "What other kind of art is so intimately involved with the daily lives of ordinary people?

"Money was tight, but I started buying quilts," he continued. "I couldn't afford some of the quilts I really wanted, the truly spectacular ones, so I figured I'd better learn to make them myself. Of course, I'm still not good enough to make quilts as spectacular as the ones I coveted as a young salesman, but," he said with a wink, "I'm still learning."

Mary Dell laughed nervously. "Well, it was my mistake, Mr. Evard. When I saw your name in the magazine,

I assumed you were a woman. I figured C. J. stood for Claudia Jean."

Mr. Evard crooked his index finger, ran it along one side of his neatly trimmed beard, and shook his head, looking as if he was sorry to disappoint her.

"No. My real name is unpronounceable to most people and impossible to spell, so—long before Larry Hagman and the *Dallas* TV show made it fashionable—I started using my initials."

He shifted slightly forward in his leather desk chair, reached into the interior breast pocket of his suit, and withdrew a long, thin cigar.

"Lanceros," he said by way of explanation. "Davidoff Number Ones. Do you mind?"

"Of course not," Mary Dell said. "Go right ahead."

She wasn't crazy about cigar smoke or tobacco in general, but it was his office; he could do as he liked. And when he lit up, she found the smell of this particular cigar somewhat pleasant and manly, not at all like the cheap stogies some of the men who frequented the Ice House liked to puff. And she had to admit, C. J. Evard certainly looked good with a cigar.

How handsome he was! She supposed he was a decade older than Dutch, but he was in much better shape. He was lean; not even a hint of paunch hung over his silver belt buckle. His skin was tanned but not bronze, leathery but in a good way, the complexion of a man who loves the outdoors or at least plays a lot of golf. His hair, like his beard, was a distinguished silver-gray, a color that made his bright blue eyes look even brighter. And Mary Dell had never seen a better-dressed man. His black Western suit with the arrowhead yoke and subtle tan stitching fit so perfectly that Mary Dell correctly guessed it had been made just for him. His bolo tie had a sterling silver slide inset with turquoise, and he wore sterling silver collar tips with his starched white shirt. His boots were black too, custom made from alligator hide, and if Mary Dell had realized how much he paid for them, she probably would have choked on the Dr Pepper that Mr. Evard himself had poured her when she sat down in a leather chair on the opposite side of his big walnut desk. C. J. Evard was a real Texas gentleman and looked the part.

But that big desk of his, specifically what she spotted lying upon it, concerned Mary Dell—the letter she had written in a moment of despair and mailed in an episode of amnesia. There it sat, accusing her, filling her with dread that increased with every second that passed without Mr. Evard asking her who she thought she was to have sent him such a foolish and insulting letter.

Finally, unable to stand it anymore, she blurted out, "Mr. Evard, about the letter I sent to you. I'm so sorry about that. I wasn't myself when I wrote it and . . ."

C. J. sucked on his cigar and held the smoke in his mouth for a moment before tipping back his head and blowing it out toward the ceiling.

He dismissed her apology with a wave of his cigar. "I've gotten worse, believe me. And your complaint wasn't unfounded. I never did see your submissions, not a single one of the fifteen you made over the years.

"We get hundreds of submissions every month. Some junior assistant editor weeds them out, generates a form letter like those you received, and sends it out under my signature. The first time I ever heard of you was when this came across my desk," he said, picking up the letter and looking at it again.

"Very expressive. You're a good writer, Ms. Templeton."

"Please, call me Mary Dell."

"Only if you call me C. J." He took another puff on his cigar. "After reading your letter, I asked my secretary to dig up your earlier submissions. She did, and I was impressed with what I saw."

He put down his cigar, resting it in the groove of a lead crystal ashtray, and picked up a file folder that was sitting on the other side of the desk.

"I can see why the lower-level staffers rejected your work," he said, flipping through papers and photographs. "I don't mean to be harsh, Mary Dell, but your color choices leave a lot to be desired."

"You're not the first to mention it."

He glanced up from the papers, looked her over from head to toe, and muttered, "No. I suppose not.

"But," he said, going on in a louder voice, "what I saw that those assistant editors missed is that your construction is impeccable, your designs innovative, and that you seem to have a real knack for coming up with techniques to make potentially complicated patterns easy enough so that intermediate or even beginning quilters can get good results. At least, that's how it appears on paper. I can't really make a judgment until I see your work."

He put down the file folder and nodded eagerly at the two large shopping bags sitting next to Mary Dell's chair.

"Are the quilts in there?"

Mary Dell opened the bags, started pulling out quilts and stacking them in a pile on the white carpeting. Leaving his cigar, C. J. came out from behind his desk and stood over her as she flipped back quilt after quilt, murmuring admiration over each one, his eyes shining like blue beacons as he leaned down to examine their workmanship.

"They look just as good on the back as the front," he said approvingly. "As they should but so seldom do. Who taught you to quilt?"

"My grandma Silky taught me how to sew clothes; our family has bred expert needlewomen since Daniel Boone was a boy. But quilting was something I learned on my own, mostly through trial and error. I've been teaching in my home for a few years now, so I had plenty of opportunities to practice on my students—poor things."

"Your hand quilting is lovely, but this . . ."

To Mary Dell's astonishment, he actually got down on his hands and knees to get a better look at one of her lap quilts, with pieced tulip blocks placed on the diagonal, each flower made from a different color fabric, alternated with plain blocks that she'd quilted with her own tulip design, using a different color of thread for each block.

"*This* is amazing. I think you would have been better off with just one color of tulip, or even three, but . . ." His eyes scanned the surface of the quilt, as if he couldn't quite believe his eyes. "You quilted this on a sewing machine? I've rarely seen anyone use any technique besides stitch in the ditch for a machine-quilted project."

Mary Dell smiled, pleased that he'd noticed. "A lot of people are embarrassed to be caught using a machine for quilting instead of stitching it by hand, so they sew along the seams of the block to hide it. But that seemed silly to me. You're not fooling anyone anyway, so why not go for broke? Show off what you can really do with a machine. It took a little trial and error, but once I got the hang of it . . ."

She got down next to him on the floor, careful of the tulle skirt, and traced her finger over a section of the border that she was particularly pleased with, a quilted vine festooned with leaves and tiny tulip shapes.

"Pretty, isn't it? I love the look of hand quilting, but it takes time that I don't always have. I was able to quilt this in three days."

"Really?" He sat back on his haunches, clearly impressed. "That fast?"

"Yes, sir," Mary Dell replied proudly. "Now, some people say that a quilt made by machine isn't a real quilt. But do you know what I call a machine-sewn quilt? Done."

Mary Dell laughed at her own joke, and C. J. grinned.

"I like you, Mary Dell. You've got spunk. And you're one heckuva quilter. I'd like to publish some of your designs in the magazine. That is, if we can find someone to help you regulate your enthusiasm for color—"

He pulled aside the tulip quilt to reveal the last quilt in the stack, Rob Lee's baby quilt. He stopped in midsentence.

"Well . . . will you look at this," he said in a hushed voice. "Grandmother's Flower Garden is one of my favorite blocks. How did you ever come up with the idea of using half and three-quarter rounds to create this serpentine effect? So unusual. And your color selections . . . Blue and yellow is an obvious combination, but adding sapphire and violet to the mix gives it a whole different dimension. Beautiful." He looked up at her with a respectful but somewhat perplexed expression.

"Thank you," she said. "But I can't take credit for the colors. My sister, Lydia Dale, picked those out. She can't quilt, and I can't pick fabric, but together, we're the complete package—two sides of the same coin, you might say. Without Lydia Dale to help me, I'd never have worked up the courage to open up the quilt shop."

C. J. got up from the floor, then reached out to offer Mary Dell a hand.

"You own a quilt shop?" He went back to his desk and picked up his still-smoldering cigar.

"Not yet. We're going to take possession of the building at the end of the month, but we'll have a lot of work to do before we can open. Everything always costs more than you think it will, what with inventory and renovations and such. I can't afford to do too much at once. I've got to think about the family and the ranch, of course . . ."

"The ranch?"

"My sister and I own a ranch too—cattle and sheep. It's been in our family for generations."

C. J. took a deep draw on his cigar, making the tip glow orange, a thoughtful expression on his face.

"So you're a lady rancher, a quilt teacher and designer, and you're about to buy your own shop? That's amazing."

He glanced at a clock on the edge of his desk.

"I've got an editorial meeting starting in a few minutes. But would you like to join my wife and me for dinner this evening? I'd like to hear more about your quilts and your shop and your family, and I'm sure Libby would too."

"Thank you. That sounds wonderful. I was kind of wondering what I was going to do with myself tonight."

C. J. picked up his telephone. "Oh, there's no end of things to do in Dallas. Start off with a visit to Neiman Marcus. It's just around the corner from your hotel. Libby can spend hours there."

He smiled wryly and pressed a button on the phone. "Miss Whatley, would you please call the Mansion and make a reservation for three people at seven o'clock? And arrange for a car to pick Ms. Templeton up at the hotel at six forty-five."

CHAPTER 49

Before it became the first five-diamond, five-star hotel in the state of Texas, the Mansion on Turtle Creek really was a mansion, built by a cotton mogul in 1908. President and Mrs. Franklin Delano Roosevelt once stayed there as guests of the owners, and Tennessee Williams wrote the play *Summer and Smoke* during a visit in the 1940s.

Though it changed hands many times before being purchased in 1979 by Caroline Rose Hunt and undergoing a twenty-one-million-dollar transformation to turn it into a world-class restaurant, and later expanded to include a 143-room hotel, the sixteenth-century Renaissance Italian–style structure continued to retain the intimate feel of a private home, albeit a private home owned by a very wealthy family. Those who crossed its threshold were treated like visiting celebrities as, indeed, many were.

It was probably just as well that Mary Dell knew

nothing of the illustrious history of the establishment, or that the governor, two state senators, and a TV star were among the other guests seated in the dining room that night. She was awed enough by her surroundings as it was and by the elegance of the other patrons, including Mrs. Evard, or Libby, who was wearing a black knit cocktail dress with modestly sized shoulder pads and a black silk ruffle and bow on the hem. The dress was a little sedate for Mary Dell, who was relieved she'd thought to bring her gold lamé wrap dress with the extra-big shoulder pads with her to Dallas, but Libby's emerald and gold pendant and matching earrings were stunning, and Mary Dell told her so.

"I got them at Neiman's." Libby leaned closer and whispered conspiratorially, "Thirty percent off."

Mary Dell smiled, feeling more at ease. Libby Evard was elegant and wealthy, but under all her finery she was still just a woman who got into her girdle one leg at a time and liked a bargain, just like everybody else.

"Yes," C. J. said in a dry tone, "Libby saves me hundreds of dollars at Neiman's every week."

"Aren't you lucky?" Libby said in a flirtatious tone.

C. J. took his wife's hand and lifted it to his lips. "I certainly am," he said, then looked up to address a waiter. "Good evening, Gene. We'll have the usual."

"Bombay Sapphire and tonic for you, Mr. Evard, and a Dubonnet on the rocks for Mrs. Evard. Very good, sir. And for the lady?"

"Mary Dell, what would you like?" C. J. asked. "A martini? A glass of white wine?"

"Oh, no," Mary Dell said quickly. "Alcohol does bad things to me. I'd better stick with Dr Pepper."

They chatted easily over their drinks, though Mary Dell did most of the talking, answering C. J.'s questions about Too Much, her family, the ranch, and her hopes for the future. She didn't mean to go on so, but the Evards were so easy to talk to. And they seemed genuinely interested in what she had to say. C. J. waved the waiter off twice before finally saying they should order.

The menu listed all kinds of dishes that Mary Dell had never heard of, and some of it was in French, and to make matters more confusing, there were no prices listed. Mary Dell didn't want to embarrass her hosts or the waiter by pointing out the mistake, nor did she wish to be rude and accidentally order the most expensive thing on the menu, so, after a moment, she asked C. J. to choose for her.

The tortilla soup, a specialty of the house, was delicious, made from a rich tomato-and-chicken broth with just a bit of spicy heat and topped with a sprinkling of avocados, white cotija cheese, and strips of fried tortillas. While C. J. and Mary Dell enjoyed their soup, Libby nibbled a green salad.

"I hope I get to see your quilts someday," Libby said. "C. J. says some of your techniques are revolutionary."

"Oh, I don't think so," Mary Dell said. "I'm just doing what comes naturally."

"Naturally to you," C. J. said, pointing his soup spoon in her direction, "but not to everyone. You have a gift. I was thinking about your Lone Star quilt, the one you're going to use for the first class in your new shop. I'd like to publish it in the magazine. That issue wouldn't be out until spring, so your students would still get first crack at it. Would that be all right with you?"

Mary Dell nearly choked on her soup. "Would it? Does a cactus have spines?"

"Good, good. The pay isn't much, but we'll include a sidebar about your shop, maybe with a photo of you and your sister under the sign. It'll be good publicity."

"Really?" Mary Dell put her hand over her mouth to

cover her shock. "Thank you, C. J. A thing like that could put the Patchwork Palace on the map!"

"Patchwork Palace," Libby repeated with a smile. "What a darling name. I told C. J. that he should have chosen a more interesting name for his business. White Star Fabrics doesn't have any magic."

C. J. lifted his hands in an exasperated gesture. "Yes, it does. How many times have I told you? This is a Texas company, and I wanted the name to reflect that—a white star, like on the flag."

"If you wanted it to evoke Texas, you should have called it Lone Star Fabrics. Or Alamo Fabrics. White Star could be anything from anywhere," Libby said with a shrug, then speared a cherry tomato with her fork.

Mary Dell frowned, not sure she was following the conversation correctly. "White Star . . . that's the company we're planning on getting most of our fabric from. Mr. Evard—I mean, C. J., what's your connection to White Star?"

"I own it," he said simply. "I own a couple of different businesses. The magazine is just one of them and by far the least profitable. That's something I do to indulge my love of quilts. Remember I told you about how I started off selling thread?"

Mary Dell put down her spoon and listened, fascinated by his story, barely noticing when a waiter removed her soup plate and replaced it with a tiny dish of grapefruit sorbet.

"That's what started it all," C. J. continued. "I'm a good salesman, but I wanted more. One of my customers was a small textile mill. They made cotton prints to sell in dry goods stores, you know."

"Yes, I know."

"Well, I had an idea of improving the quality of the material and implementing new designs, creating high-quality fabric specifically for quilts. Now, the owner of this particular textile mill had a daughter. She was very beautiful but very spoiled."

C. J. glanced at his wife, who was primly dabbing vinaigrette from her lips with the edge of her linen napkin, and his eyes twinkled.

"Her father was so anxious to get her off his hands that he let me have the mill, but only on condition that I marry her."

Libby pretended to slap his hand. "C. J. Evard, that's a lie, and you know it. My father didn't want you to have me or the mill. He only let me marry you because I threatened to run away from home, and he only let you buy the mill because his doctor said if he didn't quit working so hard he was going to drop dead of a stroke. Which he did, but not for another twelve years.

"But," Libby said, leaning toward Mary Dell, "Daddy wouldn't give C. J. even a penny's break on the price. He had to sell his quilt collection and our car to come up with the money. My C. J. is a self-made man," she said proudly.

Mary Dell took a tentative bite of the sorbet. It was cold and icy, like eating a snow cone with a spoon, a little bitter, but good.

"Just like Mary Dell," C. J. said.

"Now you're just teasing me," Mary Dell said. "I haven't made anything of myself."

"Not yet, but you will. You and I are cut out of the same cloth. If not, you wouldn't have submitted all those quilt patterns over the years—fifteen! That's got to be a record. But even in the face of all those rejections, you didn't give up."

"But sometimes I wanted to."

"But you didn't," C. J. said. "That's what matters. You know, before Libby civilized me, I used to be a bit of a gambler. That's all behind me, but I still know a winner when I see one. And I think you're a winner, Miss Mary Dell. The quilt shop could be just the beginning.

"Too Much sounds like a wonderful place with a proud history. You must never abandon your roots, Mary Dell, or forget where you came from. But don't forget that there's a great big world out there too, with all kinds of new people, experiences, ideas—all sorts of discoveries and adventures. I'll bet your ancestor Flagadine would agree with me. After all, it was that spirit of adventure, the desire for something more, that brought her to Texas in the first place, wasn't it? I bet there's a lot of her in you."

"I hope so," Mary Dell said with a smile.

"If you're open to the possibilities, there's no telling what might happen."

Mary Dell swallowed another bite of sorbet. "You mean I might become a quilting legend?" She laughed and waved her hand. "That's just something silly my grandma Silky says."

C. J.'s expression remained serious. "Your grandma Silky might be right. This is an exciting time in the quilting world. This is a new generation of quilters with a new kind of passion and energy, a willingness to innovate and take risks. They're looking for someone to show them how. Why shouldn't it be you?"

"I can see why you were such a good salesman."

"I'm serious, Mary Dell. I think you're on the verge of finding your best self, and I believe you'll use it to bring out the best in a lot of other people."

Mary Dell stared vacantly into her sorbet dish, considering this. It was one thing to dismiss that kind of talk when it came from Grandma Silky, but when Mr. C. J. Evard, founder and president of White Star Fabrics, publisher of *Quilt Treasures* magazine, offered you advice, you'd have to be a fool not to pay attention. She was going to have to spend more time thinking about this, but there was something she wanted to get to the bottom of first.

She looked up. "Can I ask you a question?"

"Of course," he declared. "Anything."

Mary Dell looked to the right and then the left, to make sure no one was listening.

"Why are we eating ice cream before dinner?"

While enjoying their dinner Mary Dell and C. J. had the filet mignon with béarnaise sauce; Libby had sautéed Dover sole—the Evards explained the tradition of serving a sorbet as a means of cleansing the palate between courses, the purpose of various types of forks, the difference between red and white wineglasses, and that a lady who is the guest of a gentleman in a fine dining establishment is often presented a menu without prices.

During a trip to the restroom, Libby explained the concept of leaving a little something for the attendant, which led to a discussion of gratuities in general—who to tip, who not to tip, and how much to leave. It was a very informative dinner, and the Evards imparted their wisdom without making Mary Dell feel the least bit awkward.

"After all," Libby said, "people aren't born knowing these things. C. J. and I certainly weren't. Honey," she said, addressing her husband, "remember that time we went to the country club, and you drank the finger bowl?"

C. J. laughed. "How could I forget? Learn from our mistakes, Mary Dell, and feel free to ask us anything. This might be your first time dining at the Mansion, but it won't be your last."

$\mathscr{C}$HAPTER 50

C. J. was right. Mary Dell would dine at the Mansion again in later years, eventually becoming such a regular patron that waiters would bring her Dr Pepper without even bothering to ask for her order. But she would never forget that first visit, the exquisitely beautiful room, the starched tablecloths and sparkling cutlery, the delicious food, the kindness of her hosts, or what happened at dessert.

Mary Dell had just sampled the chocolate mousse and made a joke about being relieved not to find any antlers when Libby asked if she had any pictures of her family.

"As a matter of fact . . ." she said, quickly pulling out her wallet and passing around snapshots of Taffy and Dutch, Silky and Velvet, Lydia Dale and the children, and, finally, Howard.

Libby took the picture, and her hand flew to her

mouth. "Oh, my Lord," she murmured through the lattice of her fingers. "C. J., have you seen this?"

Up until then, C. J. had perused the photos politely but briefly, as most men would, but when Libby handed him the snapshot of Howard, he stared at it for a long while. His eyes filled with tears. Libby reached over and squeezed his arm.

"Your son has Down syndrome?" he asked. "So did my little brother. He was eight when he died. Heart."

Mary Dell wasn't sure what to say. She wanted to ask him about his brother, to know if they'd been close, if he'd lived at home or in an institution, if C. J. had been with him when he died, but she didn't think it was her place to pry into a subject that was obviously still so painful.

"I'm so sorry," she said quietly.

"And your son . . . Howard? Is he . . . ?"

"Doing real well," she assured him. "Very healthy, and his heart is perfect. He can smile and lift his head on his own. When I get home, I'm going to teach him to roll over."

"That's good. Very good."

C. J. crooked his index finger and touched his knuckle to the corner of his eye. He cleared his throat, regaining his composure.

"Mary Dell, there's something I want to propose to you. I'd like you to carry White Star fabric in your shop."

"Of course," she replied. "I was going to do that anyway."

"I'd like you to carry twenty-five hundred bolts."

Mary Dell's stomach lurched.

"But . . . I can't. Not that I don't want to, but . . . where would I get the money?"

"Yes, yes. I know," C. J. said in a distracted voice and started patting the front of his jacket, trying to feel if there was another cigar inside. "But you've only got one chance to make a first impression. In a town as small as Too Much, you're going to have to attract people from out of town to survive. The Patchwork Palace needs to become a destination. But people won't drive out of their way to visit your shop if you don't have an inventory that's worth the trip.

"Here's what I propose: You make White Star your exclusive wholesaler. In exchange, I will send you twenty-five hundred bolts of our best quilting fabric . . . ah, ah, ah!" He held up a cautioning finger as he saw Mary Dell's mouth open to protest. "Let me finish.

"I will send you the fabric, but you don't have to pay me for it—not up front. I'm going to supply it to you on commission. What you sell, you pay for. What you don't sell, you can send back."

"Without paying for it?" Mary Dell held up her hand. "No, C. J. Absolutely not. I can't let you do me special favors just because I have a son with Down syndrome. It's not fair to you. And it's not good business."

"How would you know?" he countered. "I've been at this for forty years. You haven't even opened your doors yet. And since I own the company, I can do whatever I want."

He frowned and pulled a cigar out of his pocket. Libby clutched at her husband's sleeve and gave him a look. C. J. made a little growling sound. "I know, I know," he said and clenched the unlit cigar between his teeth.

"Yes, Mary Dell. I lost a brother to Down syndrome. I couldn't help him, so I'd like to help Howard, and you. Would that be bad business? No. Absolutely not.

"If your shop starts off on the right foot, I've gained a customer for life. I'll make money, you'll make money, and everyone will be happy. *But*," he said, taking the unlit cigar from between his teeth and pointing it at her, "if your shop fails because your inventory is so small that people don't come or don't come back, I'll have lost a customer and an opportunity."

He picked up his cigar, wedged it back between his teeth, crossed his arms over his chest, and gave her a triumphant look, daring her to dispute his logic.

Mary Dell smiled. "You *are* a good salesman, C. J., but I'm not buying. I'm not going to take advantage of you just because of Howard. Nothing you can say will change my mind."

In the end, in spite of her protestations, he wore her down. White Star Fabrics would be the exclusive supplier of the Patchwork Palace, and the Patchwork Palace would sell that fabric on commission, but only for the initial order of 2,500 bolts. After that, they'd have to pay up front, just like everybody else. On this point, Mary Dell was immovable. She and C. J. shook on it and that was that; the deal was sealed.

It was after eleven when the driver dropped her off at the hotel. She knew she should go to sleep, but she couldn't. She felt like going dancing, or sliding down the big brass banister in the hotel lobby, or opening up the windows and hollering for pure joy. She wanted to call home and tell Lydia Dale about everything that had happened, but she didn't know how to make a long-distance call on the hotel telephone, and anyway, it was too late to call.

Instead, she opened the minibar, pulled out a Dr Pepper, and poured it into a cut-crystal glass and carried it with her into the bathroom, then filled up the tub, using the entire bottle of bubble bath.

After abandoning her dress in a gold lamé heap on the marble floor, she slipped into the hot, sweet-smelling water, took a long drink from the crystal goblet of cherry-and-cola nectar, then settled back in the bathtub, wreathed by mounds of bubbles, an angel floating on a gardenia-scented cloud.

"I could get so used to this."

CHAPTER 51

Lydia Dale was feeling frazzled. It was only the second day of summer vacation, and already she felt ready to take a switch to the kids. They'd been bickering since breakfast.

Jeb knew just how to push his baby sister's buttons, and Cady, not old enough to realize that she was doing exactly what he wanted, came right back at him. Lydia Dale was so frustrated that she punished them both. She cut off their television privileges, took away Cady's Barbies, and forbade Jeb from going out to help Graydon. Of course, this left them with nothing to do besides pick on each other even more. Taking away Jeb's barn privileges seemed to be the only threat that got his attention, except today it hadn't. After warning them both three times, she had no choice but to follow through.

She knew that Jeb was acting up because it was Friday and he was anxious and angry about having to go to

Jack Benny's that afternoon, but what could she do? Ignore the judge's orders?

Taffy and Dutch went to Waco just before lunch. Dutch had a doctor's appointment in the afternoon, and they were going to get some new tires on Mary Dell's car beforehand. The doctor was running late, so Taffy didn't get back to watch the babies when she'd said she would. Lydia Dale would have brought them with her, but there wasn't room for all five of them in the truck. So between all of that and the kids' fighting and Jeb's dawdling when they finally *were* able to leave, she was more than an hour late dropping the kids off at Jack Benny's.

Cady kissed her good-bye before running to the house, but Jeb wouldn't speak to her. He slammed the door when he got out of the truck, didn't wave to her, and didn't say anything to his daddy when Jack Benny strode past, heading toward the truck, holding a Lone Star and looking angry. But then, Jack Benny didn't say anything to him either.

Jack Benny spat a brown stream of tobacco onto the ground as he approached the truck.

Wonderful, Lydia Dale thought as she rolled down the window. *Because cigarettes weren't disgusting enough.*

Jack Benny stood right next to her door, spread his boot-shod feet, hooked his thumb into his belt, took a slug from his beer, and stood there, posing, not saying anything, just staring daggers at her.

He was trying to intimidate her, to get her to apologize, but Lydia Dale was done apologizing to Jack Benny, and she wasn't going to let him or anyone intimidate her ever again.

"Where the hell have you been?" he finally asked. "I've got better things to do than sit around waiting for you to show up."

"I doubt that. You haven't worked in months."

She couldn't believe she'd actually said that. She knew from experience that there was no point in arguing with him, especially after he'd had a couple of beers, but the words just slipped out. Judging from the look on his face, Jack Benny couldn't believe she'd said it either.

He started cussing, going through the entire long list of expletives that Lydia Dale figured made up a good 20 percent of his vocabulary, words she mostly hadn't even known the meaning of until after they'd gotten married and had their first fight.

Lydia Dale turned the key in the ignition. "If you want to talk to me, then you need to clean up your language. Because I am not in the mood for this today, Jack Benny. I'm really not."

"That's nothing new," he sneered. "When were you ever in the mood for anything?"

"With you? Never. But I managed to give you three children anyway. Why don't you go back inside and play with them instead of standing out here trying to pick a fight with me?"

"Three?" He worked up another mouthful of spit, took aim, and let fly right on her front tire. "Don't you mean two?"

Lydia Dale turned off the engine.

"What are you talking about?" she said in a flat voice. "Don't tell me that you've heard Marlena tell that lie so many times you've actually started to believe it. Rob Lee is yours, and you know it."

His eyes narrowed to slits, like he was taking aim down a gun barrel. "What I know is that we weren't together but that one time in four months . . ."

"Because you were too busy drinking and bedding every sorry piece of trash in a fifty-mile radius to come home nights!"

". . . and you turn up pregnant." He held up his index finger. "One time. In four months. It took us a year to have Cady, and that was when we were trying. And you expect me to believe I knocked you up after one time?

"That kid's not mine, and you know it. You got pregnant and then slept with me, lured me into bed so nobody would know what you'd done. You," he said in a voice dripping with disgust. "Always so high and mighty, so pure, pushing me away, acting like you're better than everybody else. Your family too. You're nothing. Nothing."

"Lured you? I lured *you?*" Lydia Dale laughed aloud. "You begged me to go to bed with you that night, Jack Benny. You fed me liquor and told me lies about how it was all over between you and Carla Jean. And then you cried. You bawled like a baby and begged me to take you back. And I believed you. I actually believed you!"

She laughed again, partly from disbelief at the extent of her previous gullibility and partly from the irony of it all. Was it really possible that her ex-husband, the biggest serial adulterer in Central Texas, was standing there accusing her of getting pregnant by another man and then seducing him to cover up her indiscretion? He couldn't be serious. He knew what had happened the night Rob Lee had been conceived.

But as he always had when confronted with inconvenient truths or his own failings, Jack Benny simply disregarded the facts and shifted the blame.

"It's not my kid," he hissed. "You tried to trick me. You tried to pass that Bebee bastard off as mine."

"That Bebee . . ." she stammered, incredulous. "Jack Benny, even *you* can't be that stupid. Graydon Bebee didn't even come to Too Much until after Rob Lee was born. He's not the father of my child, you are. Believe me, I wish he was Graydon's baby. I wish he was anyone's but yours—"

Seething with jealousy for a woman he no longer wanted, Jack Benny piled his words on top of hers, listening to no one, acknowledging no facts, hearing nothing except that she wished that someone else had fathered her child.

"Momma warned me about you. And those Bebees . . . That damned Donny, always trying to boss me around, lording it over me. And his brother, coming after my wife, then trying to take my son, turning my children against me . . ."

Lydia Dale rolled her eyes, dismissing his drunken tirade. "Go inside, Jack Benny. Sleep it off."

Infuriated, he shouted and threw his beer bottle down as hard as he could. It shattered, spraying beer and foam and bits of glass on the gravel. Jack Benny lunged toward the open truck window as if to strike her, but Lydia Dale pulled back, dodging him easily.

There was a squeak and a bang, the sound of the screen door opening and closing. Lydia Dale looked up and saw Jeb standing on the stoop with Carla Jean right behind him.

"Momma? You okay?"

Jack Benny spun around. "Go back inside!"

Lydia Dale shot Jack Benny a hateful look, then called out to her boy. "It's all right, honey. I'm leaving in a second. Go on back inside now, okay?"

Jeb hesitated a moment. Carla Jean leaned down, put her hand gently on Jeb's shoulder, and whispered something in his ear. Jeb frowned and went inside. Carla Jean followed him, but not before looking to the truck and letting her eyes meet Lydia Dale's, silently letting her know that, whatever issues stood between the two of them, she'd keep an eye on the children. Lydia Dale lifted her chin, acknowledging the message.

Lydia Dale saw Jeb shadowed on the other side of the screen door, standing by, listening in, making sure she was all right.

Poor Jeb. Poor, confused child. He was a good boy. She shouldn't have been so harsh with him that morning. She didn't want to leave him here with Jack Benny in this condition, but she knew what kind of explosion would result if she told the kids to get back in the car. Even so, if Carla Jean hadn't been on the scene, she'd have done exactly that. Strange to think that she was actually grateful for the presence of her husband's mistress.

She turned on the ignition again and shifted into reverse.

"Jack Benny Benton, if you ever try to strike me again, I'll call the sheriff so fast you won't know what hit you. And the next time you're drunk when I drop the kids off, I'll take you back to court and get the judge to cancel your visitation rights."

"I'm not drunk," he snarled. "I had two beers."

Her temples were starting to throb. She was worn out from arguing with him, and there was no point to it anyway. She glanced into the rearview mirror, looking for broken glass.

"I don't have time for this. I've got to get to the dry goods store before it closes. I'll pick the kids up at the usual time tomorrow. But I meant what I said about the judge. You hear me?"

He walked alongside the truck as she backed up, keeping close to the open window.

"The dry goods store? What do you need there?"

This being Too Much, he already knew that she and Mary Dell were buying the store. Everybody did. She answered, not because it was any of his business, but because she was tired.

"I have to drop off some paperwork from the lawyer. We're closing the deal at the end of the month."

He worked his mouth and spat.

"That right? I wouldn't be too sure of that if I was you."

He thumped the hood twice with his fist and swaggered toward the house with a smirk on his face.

"But we had a deal!"

Mr. Waterson walked away from her, toting a bolt of fabric across the shop, his eyes on the floor. The old man, usually so direct, hadn't looked at her straight since she'd come in the door. He seemed embarrassed and ashamed, and he ought to be, Lydia Dale thought to herself. They'd had a deal.

"I never signed anything," he said, grunting as he shoved the bolt of blue gingham into an already overcrowded shelf. "Marlena is offering me a lot more money. Four thousand more. And she's willing to pay cash."

"Because she's willing to do anything to get her hands on this building!"

Lydia Dale closed her eyes and told herself to calm down. Shouting wasn't going to get her anywhere, but she had to get through to him.

"Mr. Waterson, Marlena isn't interested in running a dry goods business. She just wants to keep my sister and me from going into business, any kind of business. She hates me, and she's willing to spend any amount of money to hurt me and my family. Don't you see that?"

He pushed past her and walked to the ribbon rack.

"Whatever feud you have going with Marlena Benton is none of my business."

He turned his back to her, pulled out some yellow grosgrain ribbon, wound it tight on the spool, and secured the loose end with a straight pin.

"But don't you see? If you sell to Marlena, not only will the Bentons have control of one of the last commercial buildings not already in their hands, but there will never be another yard of fabric or inch of ribbon sold in this store. The whole history of your family will disappear, like there'd never been any Watersons in Too Much. Are you really willing to let that happen?"

He stopped what he was doing, clutching a spool of green rickrack in his aged hands, thinking. Lydia Dale held her breath.

"I can't help that," he said after a few seconds. "Marlena is offering more. She's paying cash. I'll give you back the money you paid me."

"We don't want the money. We want the store."

Lydia Dale walked to the ribbon rack, blocking his path. He stared at the scuffed wooden floor, refusing to meet her gaze, but Lydia Dale would not be refused.

"We had a deal," she said quietly. "You and Mary Dell shook on it. And in Texas, so my daddy says, a man's handshake is better than a contract. A man's handshake is his word."

Mr. Waterson lifted his head, looked at her. His eyes were red.

"Your daddy is right. But I have to sell to Marlena. I don't have a choice. The doctor called a few days ago, wanted us to come into his office. Mabel has the cancer."

Lydia Dale clutched at her throat. "Oh, Mr. Waterson. I'm so sorry. Is there anything they can do?"

Mr. Waterson pulled a dingy handkerchief from his pocket, blew his nose, and shook his head.

"The doc doesn't think so. He says she's got six months, maybe a year." Mr. Waterson turned his head, looking out the front window of the shop to the empty street.

"I'm sorry about backing out, Lydia Dale. I know how much your sister wants to open her quilt shop, and believe me, I'd much rather sell it to her than Marlena Benton. But I need money, and I need it now.

"I'm taking Mabel to Hawaii. And Paris. And anyplace else she wants to go. I'm going to be good to her, the way I should have been all along. And then, when she's seen all she wants to see or can see, I'm going to bring her home to Texas, to our son's house in Houston, so she can be with the children. And then . . . well, I'll figure that out later. The only thing that matters right now is Mabel."

He turned around, walked to the ribbon display, and began to rewind a spool of green rickrack, plunging the pin deep into the end so it would hold fast.

"I'm sorry, Lydia Dale, but I need that money now."

Lydia Dale reached out and laid her hand on the old man's arm.

"I know."

She turned to go, her eyes brimming with tears for an old man filled with regrets, and an old woman coming to the end of her life, and for her sister who was somewhere on the road between Too Much and Dallas, whose dream was slipping away, though she didn't even know it yet, stolen by a vindictive, blackhearted woman who liked to hurt people just because she could.

It wasn't fair. It wasn't right. And it was her fault.

Marlena didn't have anything against Mary Dell, other than she was Lydia Dale's sister. She was only trying to hurt Mary Dell because she knew that nothing on earth would hurt Lydia Dale more. Lydia Dale reached out for the doorknob, clutching it so tight her knuckles went white.

"I can't let her do this," she whispered. "I've got to stop her. I've got to try."

She turned around.

"What if we paid you cash?"

Mr. Waterson looked up from his ribbons. "What?"

She walked toward him, moving quickly, talking fast. "What if we paid you cash? We can't match Marlena's price, but if we paid you cash up front, very soon, ten days from now, would you sell it to us instead of her?"

"But," he said, "where would you get that kind of money so fast?"

"That's our worry," she said, though she'd been asking herself the very same thing. "I just need to know if you'll let us have the store if we pay cash. Will you?"

The old man looked vacantly across the room, took in a deep breath, let it out slowly.

"Well, I'd a darned sight rather see it in your hands than Marlena's," he mused. "There'd be enough, I think, without the extra four thousand. And we did have a deal."

He sniffed, scratched his nose, and looked her in the eye.

"Yes. If you can pay me cash within ten days," he said, emphasizing the last phrase, "I'll sell to you and your sister."

"And if Marlena comes back and offers you more?"

"I'll tell her to go to hell," the old man said.

Lydia Dale smiled. "Would you like to shake on that?"

"Yes, ma'am," he said, and stuck out his hand. "I surely would."

CHAPTER 52

It had been an exhausting few days. Mary Dell's body was almost as tired as her brain, but sleep eluded her.

She lay in the dark, wondering how it was possible to go from the pinnacles of triumph to the depths of despair in the course of twenty-four hours and trying to figure out what, if anything, she could do about it. Lydia Dale had bought them some time, but Mary Dell couldn't think of a way to come up with the entire payment they would need to take ownership of the shop, not within ten days—soon to be nine days, she noted, glancing at the glowing face of her clock radio.

She planned to make another visit to the bank manager first thing on Monday, but doubted he would be willing to loan them the money. Lydia Dale was more optimistic about their chances for obtaining a loan, especially given C. J. Evard's generous offer to give them fabric on commission, but her sister was optimistic by nature. Normally, Mary Dell was too, but Lydia Dale hadn't seen the way the bank manager had talked to her the first time. He'd dismissed her out of hand, making her feel as dumb as a doll, basically telling her to go home and tend to her washing and cooking and ironing and leave business to the menfolk.

She'd briefly considered asking Mr. Evard for a loan, but rejected the idea almost as quickly as it came to her. He was a kind man, a generous one, but Mary Dell couldn't ask him for the money. Generosity has its limits, and besides, she barely knew him.

And it wasn't like she *had* to open a quilt shop. Now that Graydon was in the picture, she was convinced that the ranch could support the family. She hoped he'd stay on with them forever, but even if he didn't, he'd shown her what to do. She could hire a new manager and run things herself, if need be. No, she didn't have to open the quilt shop.

But she wanted to, so very much, much more than she'd realized. Her trip to Dallas had only fanned that desire. Too Much was her home, her history, the taproot of her strength, and it always would be. But Mr. Evard was right—there was a whole big world out there. She wanted to be part of it, to taste and see all that life had to offer, to open doors for herself, her son, her family, and her town.

Only twenty-four hours ago it all seemed possible; every avenue was open to her. Now all she could see were dead ends. And all because Marlena Benton was so hateful.

She supposed she should hate her back, and she sure didn't feel like tucking her into bed with a cookie and a kiss, but mostly, and much to her surprise, she felt sorry for Marlena. What kind of misery must it be to live life so eaten up by jealousy and the desire for revenge?

Mary Dell didn't have time or mental energy to waste

on hatred or on revenge. All she could think of was that money and time were running out for her and her dreams. Try as she might, she couldn't come up with any earthly way to get her hands on so much cash in such a short time.

In moments of darkness and despair, Silky was often known to quote one of her favorite verses from the Bible: "For I know the plans I have for you, declares the Lord, plans to prosper you and not to harm you, plans to give you hope and a future." When Mary Dell got into bed at the hotel the night before, smelling of gardenias, slipping into the cool luxury of freshly ironed sheets, and closing her eyes, that verse had floated unbidden into her thoughts, and she'd been filled with gratitude that God had given her such incontrovertible confirmation of His plan, plans that meshed so perfectly with her own desires.

Now she didn't know what to think. Was God paving the way for a divine plan for her life? Or putting up roadblocks to keep her from heading down a dangerous path? Was she wrong to want this so much? Every thought that came to mind seemed to circle round on itself. Sleep was obviously not going to come anytime soon, so she decided she might as well get up. She put on her red Chinese silk robe with the dragons embroidered in gold.

"If you do want me to buy Waterson's," she said, casting her eyes toward the ceiling as she cinched her belt around her waist, "you're going to have to do the heavy lifting, because I've got nothing."

She slid her feet into a pair of pink marabou bedroom slippers and tiptoed down the hall as quietly as possible, stopping to check on Howard before going to the kitchen.

She took the milk carton out of the refrigerator and searched for a glass. She didn't bother turning on the light switch; the moon was giving off plenty of light. More than enough light. Was there a full moon?

She walked to the sink and peered out the window. Instead of seeing a yellow orb in a clear sky, she saw an angry orange glow on the ground, about a quarter mile off. Mary Dell gasped and dropped her glass. It stayed intact, but the milk splashed onto the counter, dripping onto the floor and down the drain.

She picked up the phone and punched in a number.

"Pick up the phone!" she begged. "Pick up, pick up!"

On the fifth ring, Dutch answered, mumbling and irritated, stupid with sleep.

"Daddy! It's Mary Dell. Daddy, wake up. Listen to me. You've got to wake everybody up. The barn is on fire!"

ℭHAPTER 53

It was like the end of the world.

Heat like hellfire, a sound of rushing wind, hungry orange walls of flames, the bawl of terrified beasts, acrid smoke that choked lungs and made eyes tear and burn, voices hollering and hawing, panicked animals herded away from flames and into the fields, arms that ached from the weight of buckets, the howl of sirens, flashes of red light, and sprays of water, the dousing of flames but not soon enough, the coming of dawn, charred beams still standing, black and smoldering, like skeletons of martyred saints, the drop of adrenaline, the weariness and hopelessness that comes so suddenly, wrapping tight as a shroud, the truth that is sometimes too much to bear, that feels like the end of the world.

* * *

Corney Tate took off his helmet and wiped his brow with the back of his hand, leaving a streak of soot and sweat. "I'm sorry we couldn't save the barn, Dutch."

"You saved the house. That's the most important thing."

Corney shook Dutch's hand, accepting his thanks.

"Well, it could have been worse, Dutch. A lot worse. You saved your stock, most of it anyway, thanks to this young man. Graydon, if we would have gotten here sooner, I'd have sat on you myself to keep you from going back into the barn for the animals. But you're one brave son of a gun, I'll say that for you. Brave or crazy. You'd make a darned good fireman. If you're ever looking for work . . ."

"Thanks, Chief, but I think I'll stick with ranching," Graydon said with a weary half smile that quickly faded. "I don't understand how it happened. I checked the stock before turning in and when I woke up, I was choking on smoke, and the loft was in flames. It doesn't make sense."

"We'll be out again tomorrow to do an investigation, but it's been so dry that most anything could have started it. A cigarette butt, a spark from a lantern . . ."

Graydon shook his head. "I don't smoke, and I doused the lantern before I went to sleep. And it started in the loft, not the tack room."

"Well, it could have been a spark from something, even static electricity. Wouldn't take much in this weather." Corney put a big arm on Graydon's shoulder. "Without you, these folks might have lost everything. It's a miracle they didn't."

Chief Tate climbed into the cab of his truck and drove away, sticking his beefy arm out the window to bid them farewell.

When the truck was gone and the dust settled, Dutch

turned to his daughters and said, "I guess we'd better start cleaning up."

Mary Dell shook her head. "You're tired, Daddy. Go inside and get some sleep. Moises will be here soon. Me and Lydia Dale can help Graydon until he gets here. We'll wake you up when it's time to eat."

"You sure?" Dutch said uncertainly. "I don't think I could sleep, but my leg is bothering me. Maybe I'll go and spell your momma, keep an eye on the babies so she can make breakfast."

"You do that," Lydia Dale urged.

Considering what could have happened, they had been lucky, incredibly so. Graydon had managed to get all the horses out, throwing his jacket and an old towel over their eyes and leading them out two at a time. Then he'd gone back for the sheep, opening the pens and herding them into the pasture. He'd gotten them all out, but they'd lost four of the lambs to smoke inhalation. The chickens were all dead, but the hogs were fine. It could have been so much worse.

The barn was a total loss, and of course, all the hay and feed was gone. They'd have to get some more right away. They'd need a backhoe to take down the scorched frame of the barn, but in the meantime, there was shattered glass to sweep up and piles of debris to clear away.

"Thank heaven we've got insurance," Mary Dell said.

"You should call them right away," Graydon said. "The sooner you do, the sooner we'll get a check and be able to start rebuilding. Then call the feed store and ask Lester if they can bring us out a load of hay and some feed today."

"All right," she said and started jogging toward the house. "I'll come back out to help as soon as I'm done."

Graydon turned in a slow circle, cataloging the devastation. "You know, until the insurance adjuster gets here and we've got a backhoe, there's not all that much we can do." He rubbed his neck, thinking. "Well, I've got to bury those lambs and chickens. And we better get the broken glass up before somebody steps on it or drives over it."

Lydia Dale bobbed her head, agreeing with his assessment. "I'll get the shovel and broom."

The shed windows were dirty to begin with, but the added layer of soot from the fire obscured most of the light from the glass, making it hard to find anything. She laid her hands on the shovel almost immediately and quite by accident, just by reaching her hand out to find the wall and bumping against the handle. The broom was harder to locate; prolonged searching left her empty-handed.

She groped around the boxes and barrels, shoving aside newspapers and a couple of old tarps, hoping to stumble upon a flashlight. Her efforts were rewarded when she reached into a box and laid her hand on a grooved metal cylinder. She flipped the switch, hoping the batteries were still good. They were.

She moved the beam slowly around the walls of the shed, but paused when the light moved over the top of one of the barrels and glinted against some glass. She moved to the barrel, looked inside, and found empty liquor bottles—one, two, three . . . eight empty bottles of Jack Daniel's whiskey.

Lydia Dale pressed a fist against her lips. Her pulse raced. She felt disoriented, almost dizzy, not quite certain of what her discovery meant. But then, when she heard Graydon calling her name, coming toward her, her uncertainty was replaced by fury and loathing, fury at him for turning out to be exactly what she'd feared he would be, loathing for herself for being so gullible, for being made a fool of yet again.

"Don't worry about the broom," Graydon said. "I found it leaning against the side of the house."

He opened the door wider, standing in silhouette between the darkness inside and the early light of day. "Lydia Dale? Are you all right?"

She turned to face him, an empty bottle clutched in her fist. "Is this yours? Are all these yours?"

He hesitated barely a breath before answering. "Yes. But I didn't empty them, if that's what you're thinking. I mean, I didn't drink them. Not all of them. I poured out more than half of them about a month ago."

"And you expect me to believe that?"

He shifted his weight, spread his feet, and tilted his hat farther back on his brow. "I don't care if you believe it or not. It's true. I stopped drinking a month ago. Not that it's any of your business if I did or didn't. I never drank during the day, and I never let it get in the way of my work."

"I see," she said and crossed her arms over her chest. "You only drank at night, so you think that makes it all right. You think that it doesn't matter as long as nobody sees you. But when you get drunk and fall asleep with a lit cigarette in your hand . . ."

"I don't smoke. I've never smoked."

". . . or stumble around in a stupor and knock over lantern, then it is my business!"

"That's not what happened," he said, his voi and precise, the voice of a man who coul pushed so far.

"Then what did happen? Fires don't st and you were the only one out there."

"I don't know. But I wasn't drink any fire."

"Somebody had to!"

"Maybe, but it wasn't me."

"Oh, no. Of course not! You're just the big hero, the cowboy who rides in and saves the day, the guy who braves the flames to rescue the stock, who births all the lambs and fires the thieving hands, who waltzes back after disappearing for years and wins back everyone's trust, who makes little boys look up to him, the man who makes everybody fall in love with him," she sobbed, "and then turns around and breaks their hearts!"

Tears coursed down her face. She pressed the heels of her palms to her eyes and took in a gasping breath, trying to regain control. Graydon took a step toward her, moving into the dim light, a shadow reaching out to her. She pulled away.

"I want you to leave."

"Don't," he warned her. "Don't accuse me of things I didn't do. And don't tell me to leave unless you mean it."

"I do mean it. Mary Dell hired you, but half this ranch is mine. I want you off my land. Right now."

Arm at his side, he clenched and unclenched his fist, then reached up, settled his Stetson square on his head, and walked away.

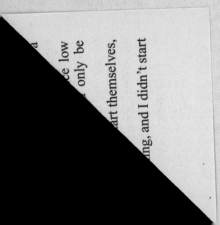

CHAPTER 54

When Mary Dell got home to the trailer and leaned down to unbuckle Howard from his car seat later that morning, she noticed the side mirror of her car was broken.

"Maybe that explains it," she said to Howard, who was trying, unsuccessfully, to grab hold of her necklace. "Something must have brought on all this bad luck. Mr. Waterson backs out on our deal, the barn burns, and we lose our ranch manager all in the same weekend. And it's not even Sunday yet."

She was grimy and her hair and clothing smelled like smoke, but Howard's needs came first, so she carried the baby inside, changed his diaper, and nursed him, thinking about Graydon all the while. She'd lost her ranch manager, it was true, but more than that, she'd lost a friend. And Howard had lost an uncle, the man she was hoping would be his role model as he grew up, someone who would show him how to ride and rope and whittle and be a man, someone who would be a father figure to her boy, the way he'd been to Jeb. Poor Jeb. He was such a troubled child. He was going to take the news of Graydon's departure so hard.

In a day or two, Mary Dell figured she'd call those people up in Kansas, the Spreewells, to see if he'd gone back to work for them, but she held out little hope of finding him. Graydon knew how to disappear when he felt like it, as he'd proven before. Those Bebee boys were good at that. It was their fatal flaw, Graydon had said so himself. And he knew how to hold a grudge too. Though, in this instance, she couldn't blame him.

She couldn't believe he'd started the fire, not even accidentally. If he had, he'd have owned up to it. And she didn't care how many empty liquor bottles he'd left behind—if Graydon Bebee said he'd stopped drinking, then he had. He wasn't a perfect man, no man was, but he was honest. Mary Dell understood why her sister had flown off the handle when she discovered those empty bottles in the shed; Jack Benny's drinking had been the cause of so much of her misery. But she wished Lydia Dale had stopped to think before she'd acted, to remember that Graydon Bebee was not Jack Benny Benton.

Well, there was no help for it now. Graydon was long gone, surely never to return. And Lydia Dale was on her way to pick up the kids from their father's, and she'd have to tell them what had happened.

Mary Dell sighed to herself as she tucked Howard into his crib. Graydon's disappearance was going to break Jeb's heart. It had already broken Lydia Dale's. Anybody with eyes in their head could see that Lydia Dale was in love with Graydon.

* * *

Mary Dell crept out of the nursery and down the hallway toward her room, unbuttoning her blouse on the way, thinking how good it would be to get that smoke smell out of her hair. She pushed open the bedroom door and gasped, finding it was already occupied.

"Jeb!" she exclaimed, clutching at her blouse and buttoning it up as quickly as she could.

"What are you doing here? Oh, honey! What happened to you?"

Jeb's face was streaked with soot and dirt and snot. His clothes were disheveled and his hair was a mess, his cowlick standing up like someone had called it to attention. Upon closer inspection, Mary Dell saw that there were red marks on his face and hands and that one of his eyebrows was singed.

"Oh, Jeb. Were you in the barn? What in the world were you doing there?"

Without waiting for his answer, Mary Dell steered the child into the bathroom and made him sit on the lid of the toilet while she got out her first-aid kit and filled the sink with cold water.

She squatted down in front of him and carefully wiped his face with a cold, wet washcloth. "Does that hurt?"

Jeb winced but shook his head anyway.

Mary Dell pressed her lips together, wondering if she should just take him directly to the doctor. The burns didn't seem too bad, there was no blistering, but still . . .

Mary Dell opened a tube of first-aid cream and dabbed it on his left cheek and eyebrow. "Baby, what were you doing in the barn?"

"Hiding. Daddy got mad and sent me to bed with no supper. I didn't do anything, Aunt Mary Dell," he said earnestly. "I swear I didn't. Daddy asked me what I'd been doing all week, and when I told him that Uncle

Graydon was teaching me how to rope so I could enter
the breakaway competition at the fair, Daddy got mad.
He called me names, and slapped me, and sent me to
bed. I didn't do anything!"

Mary Dell reached up and tenderly tried to smooth
his hair. "I know, baby. I believe you."

"When it got dark," Jeb went on, "I climbed out the
window and came home."

"But . . . that's six miles. You walked six miles in the
dark all by yourself?" She closed her eyes for a moment.
Anything could have happened to him; he could have
been hit by a car or attacked by a coyote. Clearly, the
child had a guardian angel.

"I knew Momma would be mad at me for running
away," Jeb said quietly. "So I snuck into the barn and
climbed into the hayloft. I thought I'd sleep there. But . . ."

He hung his head.

"But what, Jeb?"

"I stole a pack of Daddy's cigarettes. When I went to
light one up, I accidentally dropped the match. The hay
caught fire. I tried to put it out. I stomped on it and used
my jacket to cover it, but it got so big, so fast. My hands
got burned and I got scared, so I ran off into the field.
And then I remembered Uncle Graydon and the stock. I
was running back to warn him when I saw him run out
of the barn, leading the horses.

"I hid out for a while, watching, to make sure everybody was all right. And then . . . then I didn't know what
to do, so I came over here."

He looked up at her with a miserable, guilt-ridden expression, his eyes swimming with tears and his nose
running.

"I'm so sorry," he gasped, giving way to sobs. "I . . . I
didn't mean to do it. I didn't mean to . . ."

Mary Dell wrapped her arms around the boy and pulled him to her big bosom, rocking him like a baby, her own eyes filling with tears. "I know you didn't, honey. I know."

He buried his head on her shoulder, blubbering, saying he was sorry over and over again.

"It's all my fault. Daddy hates me and now Momma will too."

"You're wrong," Mary Dell murmured. "Your momma could never hate you. She loves you. You're her baby. Don't you know that?"

Face still pressed against her shoulder, he shook his head and mumbled, "She's got Rob Lee."

He sniffled again and looked up at her with pleading eyes. "Graydon is going to be so mad. He said if he ever caught me smoking, he wouldn't let me ride for a month. What am I going to tell him, Aunt Mary Dell? Do you think he's going to hate me too?"

Mary Dell swallowed hard and squeezed him as tight as she could. "Oh, my sweet boy."

CHAPTER 55

When she got to Jack Benny's house and discovered that Jeb was missing, Lydia Dale was frantic and furious by turns. Where could he have run off to? And how was it possible that Jack Benny hadn't noticed his son was missing until this morning?

"Didn't you even bother to check on him before you went to bed?" she yelled. "Or were you too drunk for that?" It seemed a distinct possibility; he was wearing the same clothes he'd been in the day before.

A shouting match ensued, so loud that one of the neighbors called the sheriff. Vida Smollet, a capable and calm woman of about thirty-five, was the sheriff on duty. She got Lydia Dale and Jack Benny to settle down and explain what was going on, then quickly inter-viewed Cady to get her take on what had happened and what might have made her brother run away. Next she radioed in a missing child report and made a phone call to the F-Bar-T. When Dutch told her that Jeb hadn't showed up there, she asked him to go search around the place and said she'd be there in a few minutes to help.

"Jack Benny, you stay here in case Jeb comes back," she instructed. "If he does, call the sheriff's department and wait for me or another officer to arrive. You're not to yell at him or touch him in any way."

When Jack Benny started to answer back, Vida pointed right at him.

"Sir, I'd advise you to think before you speak. I'm going to file a report with the children's and family services department about all this, and your attitude will be taken into account. At the moment, I'd say you can count on supervised visitation with your children for a good while to come. If you'd like to lose your visitation rights entirely, then just keep it up. Am I making myself clear?"

Jack Benny glared at her and kicked the dirt with the toe of his boot. Vida turned toward Lydia Dale.

"You and Cady follow me out to the ranch. If Jeb's not there already, chances are he's headed that way." She placed her hand on Lydia Dale's shoulder. "Don't worry, hon. We'll find him."

Mary Dell and Jeb arrived on the scene literally seconds after Lydia Dale and Vida. Vida climbed out of the patrol car, saw Jeb, and immediately made a call on her radio to say the missing child had been found.

While Jeb, clinging to Mary Dell's hand, tearfully explained why he'd run away, how the fire had started, and all that came after, an emotional tornado churned inside Lydia Dale. She was by turns filled with fury, terror, relief, anguish, gratitude, and confusion, but more than all that, she was filled with self-recrimination.

After she'd given Jeb a stern talking-to and a hug, then sent him off to help Dutch with the cleanup, she let her head flop back onto the headrest of her father's blue velvet recliner.

"I'm a terrible mother," she said to the ceiling.

"Oh, stop that," Mary Dell said. "You are not."

"Yes, I am. If I wasn't, Jeb wouldn't be such a mess. You know, he was such a happy baby. Always smiling, so precious. And now, ten years later, he's angry, he's sad, and he's an arsonist. How did I manage to ruin a perfect child in just ten short years?"

Mary Dell moved from the sofa to the recliner and perched herself on the arm.

"First off, no child is perfect. Second, Jeb isn't an arsonist. The fire was an accident. Jeb *is* sad and angry, but he's not malicious. What with Jack Benny being . . . you know, Jack Benny," she said, rolling her eyes, "and the new baby, and the divorce, can you blame him? He's been through a lot."

Lydia Dale nodded. "The divorce . . . it all started with the divorce."

"No, ma'am," Mary Dell said firmly. "It all started when you married that good-for-nothing varmint. Jack Benny is lazy, he's a drunk, he chases women, and he's so low he'd have to look up to see hell. I know it's been rough, but divorcing him was the smartest thing you've done in a decade."

"It wasn't like he left me with a lot of other options," Lydia Dale said.

"Then why are you blaming yourself?" Mary Dell punched her gently in the shoulder and then followed up with a quick hug. "It's going to be all right in the end. Jeb's a good boy. He's just a little confused."

"And I ran off the one person who was helping him get unconfused. What's wrong with me? How could I have talked to Graydon like that? Accused him of being a drunk and a liar and kicked him off the place. How?"

"Because," Mary Dell said, "you've been lied to before. And because the sight of all those liquor bottles scared you something awful—almost as much as the thought of being in love."

Lydia Dale tipped her head back and looked up at Mary Dell. "How come you know so much?"

"Well, I'm smarter than I look. Also, I'm your sister; I know you pretty well by now. We were wombmates, remember?"

"Guess that explains it," she said with a little smile, then began chewing at her thumbnail, staring vacantly across the room.

"How am I going to tell Jeb that Graydon is gone and won't be coming back? He's either going to blame himself or blame me."

She sighed. "I hope it's me."

CHAPTER 56

The next few days were more than usually busy. Mary Dell went to talk to the manager at First Reliable Bank on Monday and was, as she'd predicted, turned down for a loan. She made her pitch to three other banks in the following days and was encouraged when a loan officer in Waco, a woman and a quilter herself, said she thought Mary Dell's proposal had merit, but was ultimately turned down by the manager. The clock was ticking. By Thursday Mary Dell knew she wasn't going to be able to raise the money to buy Waterson's Dry Goods Emporium.

"It's time to face facts," she said when the family, including Silky and Velvet, gathered at the big house later that day.

Dutch was outside playing hide-and-seek with the big kids. It was the first time in days that anyone had been able to coax Jeb into doing anything besides moping.

Silky stood at the stove, frying chicken, and Velvet at the sink, peeling peaches. Lydia Dale sat in a chair with a receiving blanket over her shoulder, nursing Rob Lee. Mary Dell was setting the table while Taffy sat at the head of it with Howard on her knee, making silly faces at him, trying to get him to smile, which he did readily, to her delight.

"None of the bank managers will give me the time of day," Mary Dell said despondently as she circled the kitchen table, laying out silverware. "Well, maybe they were right. Maybe it wasn't a good idea."

Taffy made a buzzing sound with her lips. Howard beamed in response, his blue eyes laughing.

"It *was* a good idea," she said, looking up at Mary Dell. "If anybody could have made that old dry goods store into a going concern, you and your sister could. Those bank managers just don't have any vision. The odds were against you and so was Marlena Benton, the old she-devil."

Silky raised her eyebrows and turned over a chicken breast, revealing a crispy, golden-brown skin. "She-devil? I thought you and Marlena were bosom buddies. I thought you wanted to be just like her."

Taffy stared at her mother as if she'd never heard anything so preposterous. "Where'd you get such an idea? I can't stand Marlena. Never could."

"Huh. You don't say." Silky gave Velvet a little wink and turned another piece of chicken. Velvet smiled.

"There's no profit trying to figure out who to blame," Mary Dell said. "It's over and done with. Best thing to do now is forget about it and get back to work. I need to rebuild the barn and see about hiring a ranch manager. The insurance adjuster said the claim ought to be approved next week."

Aunt Velvet rinsed the peach juice off her hands and wiped them on her apron. "Mary Dell, just how badly do you want to open this quilt shop?"

Mary Dell stood near the head of the table with a spoon clutched in her hand, considering the question.

The idea of owning a quilt shop had excited her from the first, but initially, it had been the kind of excitement she experienced when creating a new quilt design or discovering a method for making an old design easier to stitch, the thrill that comes from imagining a new adventure, facing a new challenge. Later, when she began to consider the example she might be setting for Howard by overcoming the obstacles in her path and opening the shop, the thrill of adventure took on a deeper purpose.

But it was her journey to Dallas that really sealed the deal. C. J. Evard had helped her see what it might be like to soar beyond the narrow boundaries she'd set for herself, to push herself cognitively and creatively. Suddenly, she felt like a new car out for a test drive; she longed to be out on the highway with the gas pedal pushed to the floor, to use all her gears and leave the pack behind, to show everybody, her family, her child, herself, and the world what she had under the hood.

And now . . . now that the door was shut and the boundaries were closing in . . .

Mary Dell blinked a few times. "Pretty bad, Aunt Velvet. There's only one thing I've ever wanted more, and that was Howard."

She bent down over Taffy's shoulder to kiss Howard on the head, burying her face in his downy hair, and chided herself. If she could only have had one answered prayer in her life and that prayer was Howard, she'd never have right or reason to complain. And she wasn't complaining, but having stood on the threshold of a new world, it was hard to close the door without feeling a pang of regret for what might have been.

Velvet looked at Silky and raised her brows, as if to say she'd thought as much. Silky lowered the flame under the skillet and turned her back to the stove so she could see her granddaughter.

"If you want it so much, why are you giving up?"

Mary Dell frowned, wondering if her grandmother was starting to lose her hearing. "I told you, Granny," she said, speaking loudly and distinctly, "I just can't raise the money. I've tried everything."

"There's no need to holler at me," Silky replied with a scowl. "I heard you. I just don't believe you. You've tried some things, the easy things, but you haven't tried everything."

"Like what?"

Silky glanced at Velvet, a question in her eyes. Velvet gave a brief nod, as if granting her permission to speak.

"Velvet and I were talking it over. Mary Dell, when it comes to quilting, you've got a gift, a special and remarkable gift. We always thought so, but on the other hand, what do we know? We're just a couple of old ladies from Too Much, and of course, we're not exactly impartial judges. But when a man like C. J. Evard sees what we see within five minutes of meeting you, then that is something you need to pay attention to, that and your heart. And since it means so much to you . . ." She paused a moment, took in a deep breath, and let it out quickly.

"We think you ought to sell off some land."

Mary Dell stared at her grandmother, wondering if her own hearing was going bad.

"Excuse me? Are you telling me to sell land so I can raise the money to buy a quilt shop? Flagadine's land? Our land?"

She looked at her mother and sister, then back to her grandmother and aunt.

"Are you crazy?"

"Well, I think that's a question that was settled a long time ago," Silky replied, "but yes. We're telling you to sell off some land. Not a lot, just as much as you'd need to buy and stock the shop and then fix up the building proper. If you're going to do it, honey, you should do it right. Selling a hundred acres ought to cover it, a hundred and fifty at the most."

Mary Dell turned her face to the wall. "I am not listening to this," she said. "And even if I was, who'd be willing to buy just a hundred acres of our land? For cash and by Monday morning? Nobody in Too Much has that kind of money on hand."

Velvet stepped forward. "The Bentons do," she said. "Marlena would buy a piece of our land in a heartbeat, any piece we'd offer, just so she could say she'd done it."

Mary Dell threw up her hands. "You are crazy! The both of you! No, Aunt Velvet. Absolutely not. I am not going to sell even one acre of the F-Bar-T. Especially not to Marlena Benton!" she shouted.

Silky, who didn't appreciate being called crazy, shouted back. Velvet stepped between the two to try and calm them down, but had to raise her voice to be heard. Lydia Dale took Rob Lee off her breast, set him on her shoulder, and got up to put in her two cents, arguing that they weren't going to miss one little piece of ground. Taffy weighed in too, but felt conflicted by the proposition and argued both sides of the question at once—she loved the idea of Mary Dell and Lydia Dale owning a quilt shop, but hated to think of how Marlena would gloat if she got hold of even a little of their land. The sound of five female voices raised in conflict upset Howard, and he began to howl in protest. Then Rob Lee, distressed at being taken from his mother's breast before his stomach was full, added his cries to his cousin's.

The din of women arguing and infants crying was so great that nobody heard the sound of a truck pulling up outside, and the childish shouts of joy that greeted the driver, or noticed when the door from the porch to the kitchen opened and someone stepped inside, carrying a shopping bag.

In fact, the commotion was so deafening that not one of the women stopped for so much as a breath until Graydon Bebee, who tried once or twice to announce his presence using a more modulated tone, finally waded into the middle of the fracas, stuck his pinkie fingers into each side of his mouth, blasted out an earsplitting whistle, and hollered louder than all of them.

"What in the hubs of hell is going on here!"

CHAPTER 57

The second he finished speaking, the raised voices and cacophony of discord was replaced by cheers of greeting and, in the case of Lydia Dale, by tears.

With Rob Lee still in her arms, she ran to Graydon and collapsed on his chest in sobs, saying she was sorry over and over and over again. Graydon embraced them, mother and child, and kissed the top of Lydia Dale's head.

"It's all right," he whispered. "Jeb and Dutch told me everything. You don't have to apologize; you were trying to protect the family. I understand. Shh. It's all over."

Tears still streaming, Lydia Dale looked into his handsome face, as if afraid to believe him.

"Don't cry now, sweet girl. I'm back."

He kissed her on the mouth, and she kissed him back. The sideline observers, who now included Dutch, Jeb, and Cady, exchanged sighs of relief and smiles of approval. Aunt Velvet smiled too, but blushed as she did, averting her maiden eyes from the clinging couple.

When they finally loosened their grip on one another, Graydon grinned. "I brought you a present."

He took three big strides across the kitchen and picked up the bag he'd left next to the door. Opening it, he pulled out a satin evening gown of starlight white with a full skirt, tiny waist, and a scoop neckline, with 150 turquoise bugle beads hand-stitched to the smooth satin bodice.

"My pageant gown!" Lydia Dale squealed.

Graydon beamed, pleased that she was so pleased. "The one you were wearing the first time I laid eyes on you. I drove up to Fort Worth and bought it back. Figured something this pretty has to stay in the family."

"Oh, Graydon!" she cried and rushed back into his arms.

Velvet looked at Silky and nodded approvingly. "It's gratifying to see that some young people still retain a sense of history and an appreciation for family relics."

"Miss Taffy," Graydon said, "this is for you." He reached deep into the bag and emerged holding a tiny two-and-a-half-inch-tall tiara decorated with curves of rhinestones arranged around a crystal teardrop centerpiece. "Something to put in your display cabinet."

"Lydia Dale's first crown! Little Miss Goody Gumdrop!" Taffy sniffled and her eyes went wet. "You're a good man, Graydon Bebee. I said so from the first."

As usual, no one bothered to question the accuracy of Taffy's statement. They were too happy to worry about that.

When supper was served, they all took their seats around the table and bowed their heads as Dutch prayed over the meal, thanking God for the food and the safe return of their good friend, Graydon. The amens were said with more than usual gusto.

Graydon bit into a piece of fried chicken and groaned with pleasure. "Miss Silky, your chicken is worth the drive."

Silky smiled. "Glad you like it. And, as it happens, we're having your other favorite for dessert, ambrosia salad."

"You must have had a premonition that I'd be back." He took another bite and said, "Hey, nobody answered my question. What were you all arguing about when I came in?"

Mary Dell started to explain, but was quickly interrupted by Silky, then by Velvet, then Taffy, and Lydia Dale in turn. In less than a minute, the battle was back on and continued until Mary Dell slammed her hand so hard against the table that the silverware rattled.

"Enough!" she shouted, shocking them into silence.

"Now, listen to me, all of you! Yes, I want to buy that quilt shop so bad it makes my bones hurt. But this isn't just about me. It's about our legacy as Tudmores. It's a trust, a sacred trust. Trying to convince me to violate that trust by letting even one acre of land pass out of family hands is a waste of breath. So let's just drop the subject right now."

The immovable expression on Mary Dell's face silenced any thought of protest, though Silky mumbled something under her breath about pigheadedness being another Tudmore legacy. Everyone picked up their forks and resumed eating.

After an awkward moment, Graydon cleared his throat, breaking the silence.

"For what it's worth, Mary Dell, I think you're right. And I sure admire you for sticking to your convictions. But I was wondering . . . if you could sell land to somebody *inside* the family, would you?"

Mary Dell's mouth was too full to answer him immediately, or to point out the obvious, that nobody in the family had any money to spare and that was why the subject of selling had come up in the first place. But she didn't have to answer. Without waiting for her response, Graydon made his intentions perfectly clear.

"I went to Fort Worth to buy back Lydia Dale's gown and tiara, but before that, I drove back up to Kansas. Emptied out my bank account. I was kind of surprised at how much there was in there, but I hadn't spent my wages on anything but new blue jeans and liquor for the past ten years or so. And now that I'm giving up liquor for good, I've got to find someplace to put my money, so I was thinking . . ."

He pulled a tiny blue box from his pocket and opened it, revealing a platinum ring with a single marquis-cut diamond in the center. Lydia Dale gasped.

"Mary Dell, if your sister would agree to make me the happiest man in Texas by saying she'd marry me and if I promised to honor her, love her, cherish her, and pass the ranch on to Cady and any daughters we might have when death parts us, do you think you might be willing to sell to me then? Because, if Lydia Dale says yes, that hundred acres would still be in the family, wouldn't it?"

Mary Dell had swallowed her food some time before, but now she had to swallow again, to choke back tears.

"It sure would, Graydon."

Graydon got up from his chair and knelt down. "What do you say, sweet girl? Is it a deal?"

CHAPTER 58

September 1984

Remodeling the old dry goods store took a full four weeks longer than planned, but the results were worth the wait.

They tore out the ugly drop ceiling and fluorescent lights, and then, in keeping with the old-timey Western feel they were going for, installed ceiling tiles with a Lone Star pattern in pressed tin and a score of schoolhouse pendant fixtures, unfortunately delivered two weeks later than promised, that gave off plenty of bright, clear light.

It hadn't been in their original plan, but when they ripped up the scarred linoleum prior to the installation of new vinyl, they discovered beautiful old wooden boards underneath and decided to refinish them in a warm cherry color topped with three coats of varnish so that they gleamed when sunlight beamed through the new, bigger display window. That added an extra week to the schedule but made a world of difference in the look and feel of the shop.

They salvaged the old display cabinets that Mr. Waterson left behind, sanding and refinishing them to match the floor. Graydon and Dutch, with Jeb assisting, built extra cabinets so there would be room for twice as much fabric as before.

They knocked out the wall between the front of the shop and the windowless room that Mr. Waterson had used to store his extra stock. This gave them room for more fabric, a corner to display notions, and a gated, half-walled toy room where the children of customers, and someday Howard and Rob Lee, could play while their parents shopped.

They took the upper floor of the building, which housed the one-bedroom apartment where Mr. and Mrs. Waterson had begun their married life, right down to the studs, leaving only one wall with a mural of Hawaiian palm trees on a white-sand beach, painted and signed by Mabel Waterson in 1940, untouched. The space was turned into an office with a kitchenette and a nursery where Howard and Rob Lee could nap, plus two medium-sized classrooms outfitted with tables, built-in ironing stations, and loaner sewing machines. The rooms were separated by a folding wall that could be opened to accommodate bigger classes, if needed.

"We can only hope," Mary Dell said when she tested the folding wall for the first time.

When it came to paint, Mary Dell had her heart set on a color called Playboy Pink. Lydia Dale explained that a more neutral shade would be a better background to display class samples. Mary Dell eventually acquiesced, allowing the walls to be painted with three coats of Natural Muslin, but not until Lydia Dale agreed they could use Playboy Pink in the bathroom.

The bathroom had to be redone entirely, and when they pulled out the old toilet, they discovered a leak that cost them another week and an extra five hundred dollars to repair. The bathroom was finally finished in early September, the day before the first of three delivery trucks pulled up in front of the shop.

The first two trucks contained 2,500 bolts of gorgeous, fine-loomed, 100 percent cotton White Star quilting fabric. The third delivery truck carried four white rocking chairs and a custom carved sign with a picture of a red, white, and blue quilt in the lower left corner and shiny gold, Western-style lettering that read . . .

THE PATCHWORK PALACE

ESTABLISHED 1984 — TEMPLETON SISTERS, PROPRIETORS

Mary Dell and Lydia Dale placed the rockers on the walkway in front of the shop as soon as they came off the truck, but they had to wait until the next day for Graydon, Dutch, and Moises to hang the sign.

Even with help from the family, it took three days to get all the fabric, notions, patterns, pattern books, and whatnot unpacked, arranged, and rearranged on the shelves. But at 3:12 in the morning, just six hours and forty-eight minutes before they were scheduled to open, Mary Dell slid the last bolt of fabric into place.

"Well? What do you think?"

Lydia Dale turned in a circle and clasped her hands under her chin.

"Perfect!"

*   *   *

Though the delay of their grand opening was unintentional, it turned out to be for the best. The town of Too Much hadn't had a new addition to the commercial area in years, and people were naturally interested in the transformation of the old Dry Goods Emporium.

Everyone commented on how good the building looked with a fresh coat of paint and flower boxes out front, and how nice it was that the Templeton girls had put up that black sign with gold letters saying WATERSON BUILDING at the top of the second floor. But it was speculation about what was going on inside that really got people talking.

Trucks were parked in front of the shop all summer long, and men wearing tool belts and painter's coveralls passed through the door every day, and there was a great noise of buzz saws and hammers coming from within, but no one could see inside because Mary Dell, whose inborn streak of showmanship was just beginning to blossom, had covered the windows and beveled glass door with brown butcher paper. By August, the curiosity about what was going on behind that brown paper was pretty intense. But when word got out that the grand opening was to be delayed another month, anticipation reached a fever pitch.

A crowd began to gather outside more than an hour before opening. It was a good thing Mary Dell stood back a bit when she unlocked and opened the door at precisely ten o'clock; if not, she might have been trampled.

It was also a good thing that Taffy, as well as Mary Dell's old students, Pearl, Pauline and Sweetums, volunteered to help out that day, otherwise they'd never have been able to keep up. Silky and Velvet arrived just after the opening and stayed until four, circulating among the customers with trays, offering cups of cold lemonade and Silky's special peach crumble bars.

Ten minutes after they arrived, a man came through the door carrying an enormous spray of two dozen yellow roses and a note of congratulations from C. J. Evard. Mr. Evard, the man informed them, had called the shop personally and paid him extra to bring those flowers all the way from Waco, there being no florist in Too Much. Mary Dell buried her nose in the bouquet to breathe in the scent before placing them on a stand in the center of the front window, where everyone could see them.

Not long after, a package arrived, delivered by Wanda Joy herself, who avoided making eye contact with Mary Dell but loitered around the shop for a good ten minutes and had two cups of lemonade before returning to her route.

The postmark said Amarillo, but the handwriting was familiar. Donny had sent one hundred dollars and a present, an electronic calculator. The card that came with it said . . .

> I thought this might come in handy. Congratulations. I'm so proud of you.
> Love always,
>
> Donny

How had he known? Who had told him about the shop? Mary Dell read the card twice, found a tissue so she could blow her nose, and went back to work. She had no time for tears today.

Howard was there too. Knowing how busy the day would be, Graydon and Dutch offered to watch all the kids, but Mary Dell wanted Howard with her, deciding it was high time her boy met the people of Too Much.

Dr. Nystrom came in first thing and insisted on carrying him around on her hip, cooing about how handsome he was and asking him what he thought of this fabric or that, while she chose material for the log cabin quilt she'd always intended to make but had never found time for. Before long, a couple of the Methodist Church ladies, who already knew Howard from the nursery during services, came along and decided they needed a pretty baby to help them pick out their fabric as well, and on and on it went for most of the day, with Howard being passed from customer to customer, friends and strangers alike, some who had questions about Down syndrome that Mary Dell was perfectly happy to answer, and all of whom agreed they'd never seen a baby with prettier eyes or a sweeter disposition. By three o'clock, Howard Hobart Bebee had met and charmed half the women in Too Much, gaining so many admirers that Mary Dell practically had to pry him away so she could put him down for a nap in the second-floor nursery.

Except for a few glitches with the cash register, which Mary Dell and Lydia Dale were still trying to get the hang of, things went remarkably smoothly. Customers were patient even when the line for the cutting table stretched all the way to the door and had nothing but praise for the shop, the quality of the goods offered, and the owners. One woman did grumble a little about the cost of the yardage compared to the prices Mr. Waterson charged, but Lydia Dale noted that this didn't deter her from purchasing three four-yard cuts of fabric, sixteen fat quarters, three spools of thread, and one of the new rotary cutters Mary Dell was demonstrating at a table in the notions section. As Mary Dell had predicted, people went crazy over those cutters. By day's end, they'd completely sold out of cutters and mats.

The class sign-ups went well too. The Lone Star class

filled up so quickly that Mary Dell added a second session, and by the end of the day the beginners' class was filled too. Most of the sign-ups came from people who'd come into the shop only out of curiosity and never planned on taking up quilting. But the sight of all those beautiful class sample quilts displayed on the walls, along with reassurances from Pearl, Pauline, and Sweetums that Mary Dell was a wonderful instructor and really would be able to teach them to quilt, changed many minds that day.

Traffic was busiest in the first two hours of the day, ebbing a little at lunchtime, but it picked up at around one fifteen and stayed steady for most of the day, not slowing until four forty, which was when Mary Dell gave Pauline, Pearl, and Sweetums her thanks, as well as bags filled with fabric that Lydia Dale had chosen just for them, and sent them on their way.

"We couldn't have done it without you," she said, hugging each of them in turn.

At four forty-five, Marlena Benton showed up, flanked by Lena Brooks, the new treasurer of the Women's Club, who was also relatively new to Too Much, having married a local man and moved to town from Tulsa only three months previously, and Diamond Pickens, Marlena's ever-present sycophant, secretary, and kin.

Lena was first through the door. Mary Dell gave her a friendly wave and greeted her by name. Lena waved back and started cooing about how sweet the shop was, but stopped when she noticed that Marlena was staring at her with the intensity and heat of a laser.

Lydia Dale blanched at the sight of her ex-mother-in-law and went to the back of the shop and busied herself reshelving pattern books. Taffy took over Lydia Dale's spot at the register, saying nothing but keeping her eyes glued to Marlena. Mary Dell, however, walked right up to the trio and, in the pleasantest possible tone, asked if she could help them.

Lena started to answer but was interrupted by Marlena, who sighed deeply, glancing around the shop with a disdainful expression.

"I doubt it. I was hoping to find some fabric that might do to make my gown for the Christmas Ball, but . . ." She rubbed a corner of a fabric from a nearby bolt between her thumb and forefinger, then released it with a look of disgust, as if she were tossing aside a used tissue. "It's obvious that nothing you carry is even remotely appropriate."

"Probably not. We can sell you fabric to make a quilt or, if you don't know how already, we can teach you to make a quilt, but we don't sell dress goods. For that you'll need to go to Waco."

Mary Dell's lips bowed into a smile, and in a voice that sounded like saccharin tastes, sweet but bitter and just as artificial, said, "Would you like me to draw you a map, Marlena?"

Diamond stepped back nervously. Lena frowned, a little crease of confusion appearing between her brows, as if she wasn't entirely sure what was going on.

The corner of Marlena's lips twitched almost imperceptibly, as if she'd just received a pinch, but she recovered quickly.

"That's all right. I'll probably make a run up to Dallas and get something at Neiman's anyway. Homemade fashions are always so . . . quaint, aren't they?"

She covered her mouth with her hand, feigning surprise. "Bless your heart. I'm so sorry, Mary Dell. I forgot. You make all your own clothes, don't you?"

Marlena's eyes moved slowly over Mary Dell's frame,

taking in every inch of the zebra-print wrap dress she'd made especially for the grand opening and paired with a red alligator belt and purple suede platform shoes.

"Yes, I can see you do. Well, considering how you spend your time, you know, shoveling sheep pens and such, I suppose homemade is fine. Of course, if you were going to the Christmas Ball," she said, launching a pointed and gleeful glance in Taffy's direction, "it'd be different. But since you're not . . ."

"Oh, I'm going to the Christmas Ball," Mary Dell said casually. "The whole family is going: me, Lydia Dale, Momma, Granny, Aunt Velvet, and the menfolk too. The Patchwork Palace is a sponsor. Didn't you know?"

Taffy let out a little gasp of delight. Mary Dell looked back at her and winked before turning back to Marlena, whose eyes were so wide with shock that it looked like somebody had goosed her with a cattle prod.

"What!" she shouted to Mary Dell, then spun around to face Lena. "What!"

The crease that had formed between Lena's brows deepened to a crevasse, her confusion complete.

"That's right. Patchwork Palace is a gold-level sponsor. They'll get a table by the bandstand and a full-page ad in the program."

"You can't be serious! You sold them a sponsorship to the Christmas Ball? Why didn't you check with me first?"

"You didn't tell me to check with you," Lena said, sounding a little annoyed. "You said to go out and sell a bronze sponsorship and a gold sponsorship or we wouldn't have enough money to pay the printer or the deposit for the caterer, so I did. Hazel Dawn over at the Primp 'n' Perm bought the bronze, and Mary Dell took the gold."

"Well, you can just turn around and un-sell that gold sponsorship right now!" Marlena barked.

"I can't do that," Lena said. "It wouldn't be right, and I'm not even sure it would be legal. The ball is open to the public; anybody can buy a ticket. On top of that, the program proofs are already at the printer. Patchwork Palace is all over it."

Marlena's nostrils flared.

"I don't care," she hissed. "The Christmas Ball is Too Much's most important and exclusive event. We are not going to lower our standards just because some low-class climber thinks she can buy her way up the social ladder."

Lydia Dale's voice rang out from the back of the shop. "Take that back!"

She threw a pattern book down on the table and advanced quickly toward Marlena.

"Don't you dare speak to my sister like that! Take it back right now, Marlena, or so help me . . ." Lydia Dale's fingers curled into a fist.

Taffy ran out from behind the register, putting herself between Marlena and Lydia Dale.

"Now, honey. Calm down. I won't let my girl sink to catfighting."

"Momma's right," Mary Dell said, yawning to indicate her complete disregard and walking back toward the register. "She's not worth it. Calm down."

"I will," Lydia Dale said in a low and dangerous tone, "when she takes it back."

"I'm not taking back anything," Marlena snipped. "You're low class and always have been, the whole pack of you. Your aunt is a crazy old spinster who dresses like she's going to a funeral. Your mother was a circus freak . . ."

"Momma was the star of a Wild West show," Taffy said evenly.

"Your daughters are loose women with no morals

who couldn't hold on to their men. Ha! And you're no
better, Taffeta Templeton. The only reason you've kept
hold of your husband is because Dutch is dumb as a watermelon. No wonder your grandchild was born a retard.
Blood will tell, I always say . . ."

There is a noise that a wooden bat makes when it
smacks a leather baseball right in the sweet spot, a
whoosh-crack that some athletes have described as the
most satisfying sound in the world. The sound of Taffy
Templeton's right fist making contact with the lower left
portion of Marlena Benton's jaw was very similar to that
sweet smack of wood against leather, and more satisfying to witness than a home run.

"Momma!" Mary Dell and Lydia Dale cried in uni-
son, their voices a mixture of shock and delight, as Marlena toppled backward, landing in a pile on the wooden
floor and losing a shoe in the process.

"Marlena!" Diamond cried at the same moment, scut-
tling to her president's side.

Diamond crouched on the floor with the thought of
helping Marlena to her feet, but changed her mind when
she saw Taffy plowing toward them. Abandoning Marlena to her fate, Diamond leapt to her feet, ran out the
door and into the street, quaking with fear and wringing
her hands. Lena, not knowing what else to do, followed
her and stood in the street, not sure if she should go
home or wait for Marlena.

She didn't have to wait long.

Before her daughters could restrain her, though, in
truth, they didn't try all that hard to do so, Taffy grabbed
Marlena by her dress collar, yanked her to her feet,
dragged her out the front door of the shop, and gave her
such a shove that she flew backward once again and
landed on her behind in the street.

Taffy stood with her hands on her hips, the look on her face so murderous that Marlena was afraid to rise and sat on the ground with only one shoe, propped up on her elbows with her legs askew.

"Now, you listen to me, Marlena Benton, because I'm only going to say this once. I don't care what you say about me, and I don't give a rattlesnake's rear end if you have me blackballed from polite society for the rest of my days, but I'm warning you, if I hear you ever, I mean *ever,* use that word to refer to my grandson, or anyone, ever again . . . I will kick your skinny behind so hard you'll land on the Mexico side of the Rio Grande. Am I making myself clear?"

Marlena was too stunned to do more than give her head a quick bob, and Taffy was too consumed by anger to hear the sound of her daughters' convulsive laughter. Taffy turned on her heel and stomped back into the quilt shop, only to return a moment later with Marlena's pink pump, which she flung onto the street next to its owner before going back inside and slamming the door.

The immediate danger having passed, Diamond came running, helped Marlena to her feet, and tried frantically to brush the dirt from the back of her dress, whacking at her backside like she was beating a rug.

"Stop that!" Marlena spat. "Hand me my shoe."

Marlena grabbed Diamond's shoulder to steady herself while she replaced her pink pump, the heel of which had come loose during the fracas, then pushed her cousin away. She straightened her shoulders and limped off with Diamond in her wake, fussing and fretting. Lena followed her too, but turned around and walked backward for a few steps, giving the Templeton twins an apologetic shrug before going on her way.

Lydia Dale was laughing so hard she could hardly

breathe, let alone speak, but Mary Dell recovered herself enough to walk into the middle of the street, holding
her hands to her mouth like a megaphone.

"Marlena, are you *sure* you don't want to learn to
quilt? We've still got a few spots in the beginners' class!"

CHAPTER 59

Mary Dell chewed nervously on her thumbnail as Lydia Dale shuffled through the last stack of bills quick as a gambler dealing a hand of poker, counting under her breath, an expression of complete concentration on her face. When she finished, she licked the end of the pencil, wrote a number at the end of a column, and added them up twice on their new electronic calculator and then again with her pencil.

"Well? How'd we do?"

Lydia Dale put down the pencil.

"Great," she said, sounding almost dazed. "Actually . . . it's better than great. We made as much today as I'd projected we'd make in a week and a half. It's unbelievable!" She paused to chew on the pencil eraser. "Maybe I better add it up again."

Mary Dell reached out and snatched the pencil away. "You don't need to check the math. Look around you! There's not a rotary cutter or mat in sight, ten percent of the pattern racks are empty, and there are so many fabric bolts stacked behind the cutting counter that we're going to have to come in an hour early tomorrow to reshelve them. We did it, sis. Eight days of business in one. Believe it!"

She let loose a whoop of joy and threw out her arms. The sisters hugged, dancing in a lumbering circle. When they were finished, Taffy came and put one arm around each of her daughters, her face beaming.

"I am so proud of you!" she said, planting a kiss on each of their cheeks. "So proud! You know, I was thinking . . . after the barn is done, maybe we ought to think about putting in a pool."

Mary Dell smiled. Taffy was still Taffy. But after today, Mary Dell had a feeling she'd find her mother's character quirks a lot less irritating.

"One good day doesn't make a good month or a good year, Momma. Things will drop off now that people have had their curiosity satisfied, and we spent a lot more than we figured on the remodeling, but we're off to a good start. Not a put-in-a-pool-and-fly-first-class-to-Europe start, but a good one."

"I suppose you're right," Taffy said philosophically. "And if we're going to make any improvements to the ranch, I guess we'd better start by building on an extra bedroom. I don't guess Graydon will want to keep sleeping in the tack room after the wedding."

"Good thinking, Momma."

A faint cry came from upstairs, quickly increasing in volume and intensity.

Mary Dell cast her eyes toward the ceiling. "Howard's up. Sounds like he's hungry too. Why don't you two head home? I'll feed the baby and lock up."

"Are you sure?" Lydia Dale asked. "I can stay for a while."

Mary Dell shook her head. "No, you go on home. The kids are waiting for you. Rob Lee's probably hungry too. I won't be long."

Taffy and Lydia Dale gathered up their things. Taffy paused at the door and looked back at her daughter. "Do you want to come for supper?"

"Thanks, Momma, but I'm so tired I just want to go home and go to bed. Maybe tomorrow."

Taffy nodded, got halfway through the door, and changed her mind. She walked back to Mary Dell and gave her a squeeze. "I want you to know that I meant what I said; I'm proud of you. Always have been. And I love you. Always did."

Mary Dell squeezed her back. "I love you too, Momma."

Mary Dell fed and changed Howard, then carried him downstairs and laid him down on a quilt with some toys while she took a quick inventory of the notions and made notes about what to reorder. She thought about reshelving the fabric, but it was a big job and she just didn't have the energy to tackle it right then. Now that the grand opening adrenaline rush was subsiding, she realized that her feet were killing her and she felt about as tired as she could ever remember feeling. Still, she didn't want to go home. Not just yet.

It felt so good to be alone in the shop, her shop, hers and Lydia Dale's, this special spot suspended somewhere between heaven and Texas, to look around and see so many of the display shelves missing fabric, and that many of the bolts that were on display were decidedly thinner than they'd been that morning, to walk to the checkout counter and see a stack of completely empty bolts lying on the floor, to open a three-ring binder and see so many names of future students, pages where every line was filled with names, with an asterisk at the bottom of one page and two more names beside it, the start of a waiting list.

They were making money, at least for the moment, and that felt good. She had a son to provide for, a family to support. But there was more to what she was feeling than that, though it took her a moment to put her finger on it. It was the names. All those names, names of people she knew, names of strangers, names that weren't even written in the book yet, names of people who had not yet come through the door, but they would . . .

Oh, yes, they would.

And they would fall in love with this sweet little shop, even if they'd never sewn a stitch, especially if they'd never sewn a stitch, and look up to the wall at a beautiful quilt she had made from beautiful fabrics her sister had chosen, with a mixture of longing and anxiety, wondering if they could make one themselves, afraid the answer was no. But she would come alongside them as they stood there, tell them a joke or a story, put an arm around their shoulder, put them at their ease, convince them to write their name in the book, and then she would help them, encourage them, teach them, and when their quilt was finished they would be amazed at what they'd learned, amazed at what they could accomplish. Amazed. Just like she felt right at that moment.

She'd found it, just like Mr. Evard said she would—her best self.

She was not rich and likely never would be. She was not wise or as good as she wanted to be. But she had something special to offer, a gift that she was born to share. She knew it, and the knowing amazed her.

She thought about everything that had happened in

the last year, remembering that it was almost a year ago to the day that she'd learned she was pregnant with Howard. She'd had a baby, lost her husband, been in the pit of despair, grabbed on to a rope and climbed out, found hope, and lost it, and found it again. All that in a year, while the Earth made a single circuit 'round the sun.

She could never have imagined how exciting it would be, or how hard. It was just as well. If she had known, she would probably have been too scared to make the trip. But she knew something now that she hadn't known before: that no matter how rocky the road ahead might be, no matter how hard the journey or steep the climb, she would make it to the finish line. She was a survivor.

Mary Dell picked Howard up from the floor. He snuggled close, cooing contentedly, as she locked the back door and began switching off the lights. They walked to the front of the shop and paused at the little table in the center of the window. Mary Dell lowered her face into the mass of yellow roses and breathed deeply.

"Here, honey," she said, holding Howard nearer to the bouquet. "Smell the flowers. Aren't they pretty?"

She picked out the most perfect of the blossoms, pulled it from the vase, and stroked his cheek with the petals.

"So soft. Let's take this one home and press it in a book, so we'll always remember today. All right?"

She shifted him to a more comfortable position on her hip and walked toward the door. Lena Brooks was standing on the other side, but with her back turned slightly away, an indecisive posture. Mary Dell opened the door.

"Have you made up your mind about coming in?"

"Oh. Hi, Mary Dell." Lena turned around, looking a

little sheepish, but her awkwardness disappeared when she noticed the baby. "Is this Howard? What a cutie!"

"This is Howard," Mary Dell confirmed with a smile, then opened the door as wide as it would go. "Do you want to come in?"

"No . . . I mean, I know you're closed and probably headed home, but . . . well, I just wanted to come by and tell you I'm sorry about everything that happened today. About the Christmas Ball and all that stuff Marlena said . . . you know."

Lena held a finger out to Howard. He grabbed it and pulled it to his mouth.

"He's so precious. And Marlena . . . well, she's just hateful. I told her so later."

"Uh-oh. You'd better watch yourself. Go shooting off your mouth like that to Marlena and you'll get yourself kicked out of the club."

"Too late," Lena said with a smile. "I resigned. I only joined because I was new in town and wanted to meet some people. See, my husband has to travel a lot, so I'm on my own and, well . . . Too Much is a lot different than Tulsa."

"Oh, yes. I can believe that."

"Well, when I heard about the Women's Club, how they do a lot of charity work and all, it seemed like a good thing to get involved with. And it would be, if not for Marlena. I never met anybody so mean," she said, sounding genuinely surprised. "And yet, they all suck up to her. Why is that?"

"Darned if I know." Mary Dell laughed. "If you figure it out, be sure to tell me. But don't worry. There's plenty of nice people in Too Much."

Lena smiled. "I'm beginning to see that. Anyway, I don't want to keep you, but I saw the lights were still on and just wanted to stop in and apologize."

"Well, that's sweet of you, but there was no need. You didn't say those nasty things, Marlena did. But"—Mary Dell winked—"I bet she'll think twice about saying them again after what Momma gave her."

"I know! I couldn't believe it. Neither could Marlena." She giggled, but her expression turned serious after a moment. "But you know, she was talking about calling the sheriff, having your mother arrested for assault and battery."

Mary Dell waved off the young woman's concern. "Don't worry about it. It'll never happen. If she called in the law she'd have to tell her story to the sheriff, a lawyer, a judge, and next thing you know, it'd be all over town. Trust me, the last thing Marlena wants is for everybody in Too Much to be talking about the day Taffy Tudmore Templeton kicked her keister."

"I hope so. Well, I should let you go. Good night, Mary Dell."

"Good night."

Lena got as far as the door. "Mary Dell? I was wondering . . . and with everything that happened today, I'd understand if you'd rather not . . . but could you teach me how to quilt?"

"I'd love to."

Mary Dell beamed, and the weariness of a moment before was banished. With Howard still on her hip, she walked to a basket near the checkout counter and pulled out a nine-patch kit from the pile.

"Do you like blue and yellow?"

"Sure," Lena said, looking at the picture on the front of the package. "This is so pretty. You really think I could make this?"

"Well, you won't know until you try. Let's get started."

Lena's eyes went wide. "You mean now? But weren't you headed home for supper? I mean . . . you must have things you'd rather do with your evening than teach me how to quilt."

"Things I'd rather do?" Mary Dell switched on the overhead lights and then paused to consider the question. "No, ma'am. Not a one."

New York Times *bestselling author Marie Bostwick welcomes readers back to the quirky, unforgettable town of Too Much, Texas, in a heartwarming, richly satisfying story of friendship and moving forward . . .*

FROM HERE TO HOME

Mary Dell Templeton prefers the quiet charms of Too Much to the bright lights of Dallas any day. She's relieved to be moving back to her hometown—and bringing her cable TV show, *Quintessential Quilting,* with her. There are just a couple of wrinkles in her plan. Her son, Howard, who is her talented co-host and color consultant, and happens to have Down syndrome, wants to stay in Dallas and become more independent. Meanwhile, Mary Dell's new boss hopes to attract a different demographic—by bringing in a younger co-host.

What Holly Whittaker knows about quilting wouldn't fill a thimble, but she's smart and ambitious. Her career hinges on outshining the formidable Mary Dell in order to earn her own show. Yet as Holly adapts to small-town living and begins a new romance, and Mary Dell considers rekindling an old one, the two find unlikely kinship. For as Mary Dell knows, the women of Too Much have a knack for untangling the knottiest problems when they work together. And sometimes the pattern for happiness is as simple and surprising as it is beautiful . . .

A Kensington trade paperback and e-book
on sale April 2016.

Read on for a special preview!

Mary Dell Templeton voluntarily ended her short-lived career as a beauty queen at the age of thirteen but, like so many true daughters of the Lone Star state, she was still a devoted fan of pageants.

She loved the sparkle of them, the hot lights and rhinestones, the Lipizzaner-like dance numbers with scores of grinning girls prancing and wheeling around the stage surrounded by plenty of flags and flash and shot at multiple camera angles to disguise the fact at least half of the contestants had never taken a dance class. But more than all that, Mary Dell loved the possibilities of pageants, the fact that on any given day any one of those girls—even those from tiniest, most no-account, underdog towns that nobody had ever heard of—might suddenly have the best day of her life and, illuminated by an unprecedented and unexpected spark, shine as she had never before and, at the end of the night, be crowned the Queen of Everything.

That was what made pageants so exciting. Because

you never knew what might happen or who might come out on top.

Of course, the downside was that the reign of a Queen of Everything was so short, limited to a single, flashbulb-fast year. Once it was over, the queen had to yield her crown and scepter to a new monarch, and get off the stage. That part was sad, and the sort of thing that had been on Mary Dell's mind lately, especially after spending the afternoon reading figures on the slipping viewership for Quintessential Quilting, the HHNTV show she co-hosted with her son, Howard. Those ratings would definitely be a topic of discussion during her meeting with Gary Beatty, the head of programming, who was flying to Dallas from Los Angeles on Monday.

It was time to renew her contract—or not. Gary forwarded the ratings to her late on Friday afternoon deliberately, Mary Dell was sure, so she'd spend the whole weekend stewing over them, softening her up so he could get more favorable terms. Gary always had been a tough negotiator. Usually, Mary Dell enjoyed the battle but this year she wondered if she was up to the task. Was it was time to get herself an agent? Maybe. But she couldn't hire one before Monday. She'd have to go it alone.

A swell of applause came from the television as Miss Nebraska, who had given a flawless performance of a Brahms piano sonata, rose from the keyboard and sank into a graceful curtsy. Next, the camera turned to Rachel McEnroe, a singer/actress whose star had burned brilliantly in the nineties but who was now rarely seen aside from appearances doing color commentary for pageants and parades, as well as the occasional mouthwash commercial.

Miss McEnroe flashed a smile, informed the viewers

that, after a few messages from the sponsors and a musical interlude by herself, it would be nearly time to announce the top ten finalists. "So stay tuned, America! We'll be right back!"

Mary Dell lowered the sound, slid her feet into a pair of black marabou slippers, the heels adding another three inches to her nearly six-foot frame.

"Where are you going?" Howard asked, turning toward his mother. "Rachel McEnroe is next. She's your favorite."

"I'm going to get a Dr Pepper. You want one?"

Howard shook his head. "You okay, Momma?"

Mary Dell hadn't said a word about her worries or emitted so much as a sigh but Howard, always so empathetic, had picked up on her mood. Worry gave way to pleasure, as it always did when she looked at her son's face.

Nearly thirty years before, when the doctor informed her that her baby had Down syndrome, Mary Dell had fallen into a deep but temporary despair. If only she could have known then that Howard would grow up to be such a capable young man, unfailingly honest and kind, possessing not an atom of guile or meanness but more than a usual share of artistic inclination, color sensitivity, and showmanship.

But who could have predicted that? When Howard was a baby, who could have seen what a bright light he would grow up to be? How he would change the world's perceptions about people with Down syndrome? And who could have foreseen how the gift of being Howard's mother would define and enrich her, bringing her unspeakable joy, boundless love, and completion, filling the empty places in her heart? She wouldn't be who she was without Howard.

It was like she always said: you never knew what

might happen or who might come out on top. The sun rose anew every morning and when it did, you might be about to have the best day of your life. Even on days when it was too dark to see clearly, there was a plan and if you just kept going, you were bound to find it.

Those few words pretty much summed up Mary Dell's approach to life. It wasn't complicated or particularly profound philosophy but it had gotten her through some very dark times including years of infertility, the shock of being told that her baby had Down syndrome, the heartbreak of being abandoned by her husband, career derailments, financial woes, and more.

In short, like Hamlet, Mary Dell had suffered the heartaches and "thousand natural shocks that flesh is heir to," but unlike him, she had survived—perhaps because she was less philosophical and prone to introspection than the melancholy Dane. Through it all, Mary Dell endured, even when tragedies came on so relentlessly, one after another, as they had during that time she had named, "the worst, bad year."

In comparison to the worst, bad year, her current career concerns were practically inconsequential. Things would work out in the end.

"I'm fine," she assured Howard. "I *am* a little worried about Miss Texas sliding off-key during her song," she said, "but I bet she made up points in the swimsuit competition. That girl has more curves than a Coke bottle."

Mary Dell tottered on feathered heels toward the door but was stopped by the sound of Howard's voice.

"Momma?" His question was strangely sharp, as though he had suddenly remembered something he'd been meaning to bring up for some time.

"Yes, baby? What is it?"

"Do I hafta . . ." Howard's voice became an indecipherable mumble, which was unusual. Years of speech therapy had ensured that Howard could speak with clarity. The only times he lapsed into mumbling was when he was ill, over tired, or upset.

Mary Dell frowned, examining his face to see if he looked pale or flushed, ultimately concluding that he must be tired. It was getting late.

"I'm sorry, baby. Could you say that again?"

Howard shook his head. "Not important."

"What?"

Howard licked his lips, hesitated, spoke again. "I wanted to talk about . . ." He stopped in mid-sentence. "Never mind. Do you need me at the meeting on Monday?"

"Not if you've got something else to do."

"Jenna invited me for a sleepover so I could see her new painting and go out for barbeque. Mrs. Morris said she'll pick me up and bring me back Tuesday. Can I go?"

Mary Dell nodded. "Of course, baby. Sounds like fun."

Howard sighed and rolled his eyes. "Momma, when are you going to stop calling me baby? I'm almost thirty. Too old for that."

"Never." She walked toward him. "I'll always be your momma and you'll always be my baby. And don't you forget it."

She kissed him on top of the head.

"Call me when the commercials are done. I don't want to miss Rachel McEnroe. That lady can sing the paint off the walls. Don't you think, baby?"

Howard turned up the volume. "Yes, ma'am. She sure can."

Mary Dell was looking through the cupboard for a bag of tortilla chips when the phone rang. Jeb, her eldest nephew, was calling from North Dakota. He sounded upset.

"I can't stand for it anymore, Aunt Mary Dell. He shows up late, drunk, or not at all. He picks fights with the other members of the crew. So I fired him."

"Oh, Jeb, no! Think of all he's been through. Jeb, please. He's your brother."

"That's the reason I stuck out my neck, getting him this job," Jeb said. "Seeing as he's a veteran, my bosses were willing to give him a chance. But I won't tolerate that kind of crap from anybody else and I sure can't put up with it from my little brother. Keeping him on is undermining my leadership. I waited five years to get promoted to crew chief. I can't afford to lose my job on account of Rob Lee.

"Aunt Mary Dell, you can't help somebody who doesn't want to be helped. If Rob Lee wants to ruin his life, there's nothing we can do to stop him."

"Maybe not," Mary Dell said, "but I have to try. I promised your mother . . ."

She was interrupted by the sound of Howard's voice, shouting from the TV room, "Momma! Commercial's over!"

Mary Dell pressed the phone to her big bosom and called out, "I'll be there in a minute, baby. I'm talking to your cousin Jeb. "

She put the receiver back to her ear, her voice stern. "Put Rob Lee on the line. I want to talk to him."

"He's not here."

"Where is he?"

"Don't know. Don't care," Jeb said testily. "He walked in the door, picked a fight, and threw the first punch. *That's* when I fired him. Right before I threw him out of the house."

Mary Dell gave an exasperated growl, befuddled as ever by men's preference for bashing out each other's brains over sitting down to talk. She wondered why God, having surely having understood in advance the effects of testosterone, invented it in the first place. But that was a question for another day.

"I'm done," Jeb declared. "I've got my own family to consider. Cindy was real sweet about letting Rob Lee move in with us, crowded as it was. You can't find a decent room to rent for less than a thousand a week since the oil boom. But she's had it. So have I. My kids were watching when Rob Lee blacked my eye. Flannery is so upset, she's still crying. He can't stay here, Aunt Mary Dell. He flat can't. I'm only calling because I thought you ought to know what happened."

For a moment, Mary Dell was tempted to remind him of the tough times he'd been through, of the confused, angry, wounded little boy who had run away from home in the wake of his father's alcoholism and the ugly divorce that followed, how he hid out in the barn and accidentally set it afire while smoking contraband cigarettes, and how she stood by him in all his terrors and troubles. But that wouldn't be fair.

Jeb had taken Rob Lee in at her request. He'd tried his best to help his brother but he couldn't. Rob Lee was her problem. Twelve years before, she promised Lydia Dale she'd watch out for her children, including Rob Lee. Mary Dell never backed down from a promise, especially not a promise made to her sister.

"All right," she said, her voice weary. "But do one thing for me. Find your brother, sober him up, and put him on a bus back home."

"Home to Dallas?"

Mary Dell sucked her lower lip, thinking. "No. Home to Too Much."

"Is that a good idea? Having Cady and Rob Lee living in the same house?"

"You know your sister better than that," Mary Dell countered. "Cady doesn't blame Rob Lee."

"She doesn't have to. He's doing a real good job of blaming himself. Seeing Cady and Linne will only remind him . . ."

Jeb's words were interrupted by an electronic beep signaling an incoming call. Mary Dell glanced quickly at the telephone screen and noted the familiar area code. Who would be calling her from Too Much at this hour on a Saturday night?

"Jeb," she said, cutting him off, her sense of being overwhelmed registering as irritation, "find your brother and put him on that bus. You hear me?"

"Yes, ma'am," he said, his quick acquiescence signaling he understood the discussion was over. Jeb, too, had spent some years in the Marines. He knew how to take orders. "I'll start looking for him."

"Thank you," she said, quickly but in a gentler tone. "Call me when you find him, all right? I've got to take this call."

Clicking over to the incoming line, Mary Dell was surprised to hear Pearl Dingus answer her greeting. Pearl, one of her very first quilting students, now worked part-time in Mary Dell's quilt shop, The Patchwork Palace, back in her hometown of Too Much, Texas. She wasn't the sort of friend to call up just to shoot the breeze after ten o' clock, not unless she had news, probably bad, to relay.

"What's wrong? Was there an accident? A fire? Has the shop burned down?"

"Everything at the shop is fine. I'm calling about your momma," Pearl said.

Mary Dell took in a sharp breath and held it, imagining the worst, not stopping to consider that had Taffy suddenly died, Cady, her niece, would likely be the one calling to tell her, not Pearl.

"Mary Dell, have you talked to Taffy lately?"

"Yes," she said slowly, wondering where this was leading. "Last week. I call out to the ranch every Sunday. Pearl, what's this about?"

"Then you know Taffy's acting loopy."

"I don't know if I'd call her loopy," Mary Dell replied, her heartbeat slowing now that she knew her mother was still among the living. "She's forgetful, maybe. Scattered. Who isn't at eighty-five?"

"Mary Dell, this is more than being scattered. It's one thing for an old lady to forget her wedding anniversary or her coat. It's another thing to forget she ever was married. Or to put on clothes."

"*Clothes*! Pearl, what are you talking about?"

"I'm talking about Taffy losing what was left of her marbles. Your momma is under the impression that she is twenty-five, single, and the cutest little trick in shoe leather. She's been batting her eyelashes at every man in Too Much, eligible or otherwise. And this afternoon, I found her walking down the sidewalk, bold as you please, wearing nothing but pearls, high heels, and a slip!"

"Oh, good Lord." Mary Dell covered her face with one hand, trying to block out the mental image of her mother sashaying around town in her underwear. "Why didn't Cady call me?"

"Because Cady doesn't know about it. She called from the hospital early this morning and asked if I could open the shop for her. Moises had a stroke—"

"No! Is he all right?"

"Think so," Pearl reported. "But he won't be able to work for a while. You're going to need to find a new ranch manager until he recovers. Maybe permanently.

Anyway, I was unlocking the store when I saw Taffy strolling down the block, half-naked and whistling. I brought her inside, wrapped her in three yards of calico and drove her home to the F-Bar-T."

Mary Dell groaned. "Oh, Pearl. I'm so sorry. How did she even get to town? We sold her car after she ran it into the gate last year."

"She got hold of the keys to Moises' pickup. I found it parked on the square with the front wheels up on the curb. My Jimmy drove it back to the ranch. Taffy was very grateful," Pearl said wryly. "She kissed him on the lips and said they should go out and watch the sun set over Puny Pond sometime, then she sat down in your dad's old recliner and fell asleep. Guess all the excitement wore her out, thank heaven. I told the hands to keep an eye on her until Cady got home but not to say anything about Taffy's field trip. That poor girl has enough to worry about."

"What do you mean?" Mary Dell's brow pleated into lines of concern and she pressed the phone closer to her ear, as if increasing the volume of Pearl's words might help her make sense of them. "I talked to Cady the day before yesterday. She said everything was fine."

"Well, it's not," Pearl countered. "While you're up there in Dallas, being famous fulltime, your niece is all alone in Too Much trying to hold everything together with baling wire and hope. She has a daughter to raise, a quilt shop to run, a ranch to oversee, and a loopy grandmother to ride herd on!"

"Momma isn't loopy," Mary Dell insisted. "She's just confused. And Moises runs the ranch, not Cady. Well, he did. We'll find somebody to fill in for him until he's better. I'll try to get down there for a few days next week and . . ."

"Next week? Mary Dell Templeton, wake up and smell

the coffee! Your momma is overdrawn at the memory
bank and your niece is sick with grief. I know it's been
three years but the pain is still fresh. I can see it in her
eyes."

Mary Dell was silent for a moment. She knew exactly
what Pearl was talking about. She had seen that same
look in her niece's eyes.

Cady's husband, Nick, had been a Marine stationed in
Afghanistan, serving in the same unit as Rob Lee. In
fact, it was Rob Lee who had introduced Cady and Nick.
While on patrol with Rob Lee and two other Marines,
Nick was killed in a roadside explosion. Rob Lee was
the only one of the four who survived.

They say time heals all wounds but, in Mary Dell's
opinion, whoever said that must not have been hurt that
bad. Some things you never get over, not really, as Mary
Dell knew from experience. Absent husbands were one
of them.

It wasn't like Cady was just lying around in a dark
room. She took care of her daughter, six-year old Linne,
managed the shop, and tended to all the family business
that Mary Dell, in her absence, could not. She kept busy.
Maybe too busy? Busy enough so she wouldn't have to
feel?

Mary Dell knew what that was like too.

"Mary Dell Templeton, do you hear what I'm saying
to you? Your family needs you. And not just for a few
days. You've got to come home. For good."

"You don't think I want to?" Mary Dell barked in response, offended and angry that Pearl so misunderstood
her motives. "I only moved up here *because* of the family. Don't you get it? My show shoots in Dallas. And the
show is the only reason that the quilt shop has survived
all these years . . ."

"That may be but I'm telling you . . ."

"No," Mary Dell said firmly, interrupting Pearl's interruption. "That isn't what *may* be. That's what *is*."

The call didn't end well. Pearl was long on "should" but short on "how." And Mary Dell was tired.

It was easy for Pearl. She had a husband to lean on whereas Mary Dell had to go it alone. She'd done so for a long, long time.

When Donny left, weeks after Howard was born, she'd had to figure out how to transform quilting from a hobby to a business, opening The Patchwork Palace with her sister, getting her patterns published in magazines, sometimes teaching at guilds, anything she could think of to keep the wolf from the door. And it worked.

Later, during the worst, bad year, when her dear Grandma Silky and Aunt Velvet had died within weeks of each other, followed three months later by the car accident that had instantly taken the lives of her father, Dutch, and her brother-in-law, Graydon, and then her beloved twin sister, Lydia Dale, three days later, Mary Dell had to reinvent herself yet again.

Economic downturns have no respect for private grief. With the quilt shop struggling and the responsibility of keeping the entire family together resting on her shoulders, Mary Dell moved to Dallas where she could get more and bigger teaching jobs. She thought her banishment would last a year, two at most, until things turned around. Except they didn't. The quilt shop continued to struggle and so did the ranch.

Hoping it might bring a little money and bring a little notoriety to The Patchwork Palace, Mary Dell brushed the dust off a book she'd written years before, based on her experiences teaching Howard to quilt and, later, using him as her "chief fabric consultant" and submitted it to a small publishing house. *Family Ties* didn't sell many copies but it brought her to the attention Gary Beatty, who offered her and Howard their own television show. The rest was history.

These days, Mary Dell spoke at a lot of trade shows and quilt conferences. During the Q&A someone would invariably asked her what the secret was to running a successful quilt shop. Mary Dell's answer never varied.

"Get yourself a show on a national cable network," she'd say.

After the laughter died down, she would go on to give a more serious answer but, in a sense, she wasn't joking. It was the show that saved them, the shop, the ranch, and, in some ways, even Mary Dell herself. And all because of something nobody could have predicted, a lucky break.

Someone once said, "You can't get hit by lighting if you ain't standing in the rain."

Nobody could stand in the rain longer than Mary Dell Templeton.

BETWEEN HEAVEN AND TEXAS

Marie Bostwick

ABOUT THIS GUIDE

The following questions are intended to
enhance your group's reading of
Between Heaven and Texas.

DISCUSSION QUESTIONS

1. As the story opens, Mary Dell is only minutes away from walking down the aisle, but she is having second thoughts. Why was she so hesitant to go through with the wedding? Were her concerns legitimate, or was this just a normal case of wedding jitters? Have you been or known a bride who had second thoughts in the days or hours before a wedding ceremony? Did they or you go through with it? Or not? Whatever decision was made, did it turn out for the best? If not, why not?

2. As the years pass and Mary Dell is unable to carry a pregnancy to term, she considers adopting a child. However, her husband, Donny, isn't enthusiastic about the idea. Why do you think he feels that way? Why is Mary Dell more open to the idea of adoption than her husband?

3. If you've adopted a child, known a family who has adopted, or have grown up as an adopted child, what advice would you offer to a couple who is considering taking this step? Does it vary from the advice you'd offer to a couple considering having a biological child? How or how not?

4. Mary Dell and her fraternal twin, Lydia Dale, were close as children. Though the sisters love each other and live in the same town, they have grown apart as they've grown older. What circumstances or attitudes brought that about? Have you experienced a similar situation with a sibling, fam-

ily member, or friend? Were you able to resolve the problem? If so, how? Or, if you're still feeling distant or estranged from someone with whom you were close in former days, what steps do you think you could take to heal this situation?

5. When Howard is born with Down syndrome, Mary Dell and Donny are understandably stunned. Within a few weeks of Howard's birth, Donny leaves Too Much and deserts his family. While it would be easy to dismiss Donny as selfish or weak, his reasons for abandoning his family are more complex than that. What factors in Donny's character and/or history do you think brought him to this? Why do you think Mary Dell was more able than her husband to cope with the reality of Howard's disability? Is there such a thing as the "weaker sex"? Or do you think each sex has its own set of weaknesses or strengths, depending on the situation?

6. After Howard's birth, Mary Dell's mother, Taffy, thoughtlessly uses the "R-word" in reference to her grandson and elicits a furious response from Mary Dell. Do you think Mary Dell was right to speak to her mother so harshly? If not, how do you think she should have responded? How do you respond when someone uses cruel or cutting language to belittle or marginalize a person or group because of a disability, race, sex, or characteristics beyond their control? Do you ignore or confront? Why? If you choose to confront or have decided that you're going to in the future, what do you think is the most effective means of doing so?

7. Mary Dell works hard to become better informed
    about Down syndrome so she can be a better
    mother, teacher, and advocate for Howard. At some
    level, most mothers become an advocate for their
    children. Do you think that is a good thing or a
    bad thing? Is advocacy a role that can get out of
    hand for parents? Why or why not?

8. After Donny leaves, Mary Dell sinks into depres-
    sion. Her grandma Silky arrives on the scene,
    bearing desserts and advice, the latter delivered
    in fairly stark tones. Silky informs her grand-
    daughter that upon becoming a mother, Mary Dell
    gave up her right to fall apart, that she has to stay
    strong for her child no matter what. Do you think
    that is true? Do you think it is fair? If you're a
    mother, have you ever gone through a time when
    you felt you had to maintain a façade of strength
    for the sake of your family? If you're a daughter,
    have you ever witnessed your mother doing the
    same?

9. Mary Dell is a technically skilled quilter. But she
    doesn't hit her true stride in quilting until she
    joins forces with Lydia Dale, who has the gift for
    choosing fabrics that her sibling lacks. Working
    together, the sisters are greater than the sum of
    their parts. Do you have a skill or talent that was
    magnified when you teamed up with a friend or
    family member? Did working together enhance
    your relationship as much as your talents? Tell the
    group about it.

10. Lydia Dale and Graydon were in love once and
    planned to marry. However, circumstances and

miscommunication got in the way of their plans. Now that circumstances have thrown them back together again, Lydia Dale and Graydon are very different people than they were previously. What has changed about them? Are those changes for the better? For the worse? What about you? Have you ever crossed paths with an old boyfriend or girlfriend after a space of years? What kinds of feelings did that bring forth? Were you regretful? Wistful? Relieved? Unable to imagine what you'd ever seen in that person? Unable to imagine how you'd let them get away?

11. Aunt Velvet makes much of the Tudmore family's "Fatal Flaw," a tendency for the women of the line to lose their normally solid good sense in the presence of a certain sort of man. For good or bad, Mary Dell and Lydia Dale fell hard for handsome cowboys. Just for fun: What kind of man makes you go weak in the knees? A cowboy? A fireman? A man in uniform? A man who knows how to fix your car? Your computer? Your dinner?

12. As a little girl, Mary Dell dreamed of owning her own dress shop in downtown Too Much. Her dream faded with the passage of time, almost forgotten until she stumbles upon an unexpected opportunity to resurrect it, albeit in a different form, by buying a quilt shop. How about you? Do you have a youthful dream that you've let fade? Or one that has never faded but that you've been afraid to speak of or pursue? If you feel comfortable, tell the group about it. Discuss the fears and obstacles that have impeded you; brainstorm about

ways to overcome them. If you're ready, you might even want to consider making this your day of declaration, telling the group that you're ready to brush the dust off that deferred dream, begin working to make it come true, and asking for their support in the process.